Edited b

Legends

Terry Pratchett

Anne McCaffrey

George R.R. Martin

Tad Williams

Robert Jordan

Legends

New works by the
Masters of Modern Fantasy

Discworld
Pern
A Song of Ice And Fire
Memory, Sorrow and Thorn
The Wheel of Time

Voyager

LEGENDS

edited by Robert Silverberg

◆

TERRY PRATCHETT
ANNE MCCAFFREY
GEORGE R. R. MARTIN
TAD WILLIAMS
ROBERT JORDAN

HarperCollins*Publishers*

Voyager
An Imprint of HarperCollins*Publishers*
77–85 Fulham Palace Road,
Hammersmith, London W6 8JB

The *Voyager* website address is:
www.voyager-books.com

Special overseas edition 1999
1 3 5 7 9 8 6 4 2

First published in Great Britain in one volume with LEGENDS:
Dark Tower, Sword of Truth, Tales of Alvin Maker, Majipoor,
Earthsea, Riftwar Saga, by *Voyager* 1998

A catalogue record for this book
is available from the British Library

ISBN 0 00 648394 1

Typeset in Stone Serif
by Palimpsest Book Production Limited, Polmont, Stirlingshire
Printed and bound in Great Britain

For Marty and Ralph
Who certainly know why

Contents

INTRODUCTION

Here is a book of visions and miracles – eleven rich, robust new stories by the best known and most accomplished modern creators of fantasy fiction, each one set in the special universe of the imagination that made that writer famous throughout the world.

Fantasy is the oldest branch of imaginative literature – as old as the human imagination itself. It is not difficult to believe that the same artistic impulse that produced the extraordinary cave paintings of Altamira and the Chauvet Cave, fifteen and twenty and even thirty thousand years ago, also probably produced astounding tales of gods and demons, of talismans and spells, of dragons and werewolves, of wondrous lands beyond the horizon – tales that fur-clad shamans recited to fascinated audiences around the campfires of Ice-Age Europe. So, too, in torrid Africa, in the China of prehistory, in ancient India, in the Americas: everywhere, in fact, on and on back through time for thousands or even hundreds of thousands of years. I like to think that the storytelling impulse is universal – that there have been storytellers as long as there have been beings in this world that could be spoken of as 'human' – and that those storytellers have in particular devoted their skills and energies and talents, throughout our long evolutionary path, to the creation of extraordinary marvels and wonders.

We will never know, of course, what tales the Cro-Magnon storytellers told their spellbound audiences on those frosty nights in ancient France. But surely there were strong components of the fantastic in them. The evidence of the oldest stories that *have* survived argues in favour of that. If fantasy can be defined as literature that depicts the world beyond that of mundane reality, and mankind's struggle to assert dominance over that world, then the most ancient story that *has* come down to us – the Sumerian tale of the hero Gilgamesh, which dates from about 2500 BC – is fantasy, for its theme is Gilgamesh's quest for eternal life.

Homer's *Odyssey*, abounding as it does in shapeshifters and wizards and sorceresses, in Cyclopses and many-headed man-eating creatures, is rich with fantastic elements too, as are any number of other Greek and Roman tales. As we come closer to our own times we meet the dread monster Grendel of the Anglo-Saxon *Beowulf*, the Midgard serpent and the dragon Fafnir and the apocalyptic Fenris-wolf of the Norse sagas, the hapless immortality-craving Dr Faustus of German legend, the myriad enchanters of *The Thousand and One Nights*, the far-larger-than-life heroes of the Welsh *Mabinogion* and the Persian *Shah-Nameh*, and an infinity of other strange and wonderful creations.

Nor did the impulse towards the creation of the fantastic disappear as the modern era, the era of microscopes and telescopes, of steam engines and railway systems, of telegraphs and phonographs and electric light, came into being. Our fascination with the unseen and the unseeable did not end simply because so many things previously thought impossible now had become realities. What is more fantastic, after all, than having the sound of an entire symphony orchestra rise up out of a flat disc of plastic? Or to speak into a device that one holds in one's hand, and be heard and understood ten thousand miles away? But the same century that gave us the inventions of Thomas Alva Edison and Alexander Graham Bell gave us Lewis Carroll's two incomparable tales of Alice's adventures in other realities, H. Rider Haggard's innumerable novels of lost civilizations, and Mary Wollstonecraft Shelley's *Frankenstein*.

Nor did the twentieth century – the century of air travel and atomic energy, of television and computers, of open-heart surgery and sex-change operations – see us losing our taste for tales of the extraordinary. A host of machine-age fantasists –

James Branch Cabell and A. Merritt and Lord Dunsany, E. R. Eddison and Mervyn Peake and L. Frank Baum, H. P. Lovecraft and Robert E. Howard and J. R. R. Tolkien, to name a few of the best-known ones – kept the world well supplied with wondrous tales of the fantastic.

One change of tone did occur in the twentieth century, though, with the rise to popularity of science fiction – the branch of fantasy that applies immense ingenuity to the task of making the impossible, or at least the implausible, seem altogether probable. As science fiction – which was given its essential nature well over a hundred years ago by Jules Verne and H. G. Wells, and developed in modern times by such writers as Robert A. Heinlein, Isaac Asimov and Aldous Huxley – came to exert its immense appeal on the atomic-age reading public – 'pure' fantasy fiction, that is, fantasy that makes no attempt at empirical explanation of its wonders – came to be thought of as something largely reserved for children, like myths and fairy tales.

The older kind of fantasy never disappeared, of course. But in the United States, at least, it went into eclipse for nearly fifty years. Science fiction, meanwhile, manifested itself to the reading public in the form of magazines with names like *Amazing Stories* and *Astounding Science Fiction* and readerships composed largely of boys and earnest young men with an interest in gadgets and scientific disputation. The only American magazine dealing in the material we define as fantasy fiction was *Weird Tales*, founded in 1923, but that magazine published not only fantasy but a great many other kinds of genre fiction that might not be thought of as fantasy today – tales of pure terror, for example, with no speculative content.

The separation between fantasy and science fiction is not always easy to locate, but some distinctions are fairly clear-cut, if not entirely rigid. Stories that deal with androids and robots, spaceships, alien beings, time machines, viruses from outer space, galactic empires, and the like, usually can be described as science fiction. These are all matters that are *conceptually possible* within the framework of scientific law as we currently understand it. (Although such things as time machines and faster-than-light vehicles certainly stretch that framework to its limits, and perhaps beyond them.) Fantasy, meanwhile, uses as its material that which is *generally believed to be impossible or nonexistent* in our culture: wizards and warlocks, elves and goblins, werewolves and vampires, unicorns and enchanted princesses, efficacious incantations and spells.

Fantasy fiction *per se* did not have a real magazine of its own until 1939, when John W. Campbell, Jr, the foremost science-fiction editor of his time, brought *Unknown* (later called *Unknown Worlds*) into being in order to allow his writers greater imaginative latitude than his definitions of science fiction would permit. Many of the same writers who had turned Campbell's *Astounding Science Fiction* into the most notable magazine of its type yet published – Robert A. Heinlein, L. Sprague de Camp, Theodore Sturgeon, Lester del Rey, Jack Williamson – also became mainstays of *Unknown*, and the general structural approach was similar: postulate a far-out idea and develop all its consequences to a logical conclusion. The stories about being nasty to water gnomes or selling your soul to the devil wound up in *Unknown*; those about travelling in time or voyaging to distant planets were published in *Astounding*.

But *Unknown*, though it was cherished with great fondness by its readers and writers, never attained much of a public following, and when wartime paper shortages forced Campbell to choose between his two magazines in 1943, *Unknown* was swiftly killed, never to reappear. Postwar attempts by nostalgic ex-contributors to *Unknown* to recapture its special flavour were largely unsuccessful; H. L. Gold's *Beyond* lasted ten issues, Lester del Rey's *Fantasy Fiction* managed only four. Only *The Magazine of Fantasy*, edited by Anthony Boucher and J. Francis McComas, succeeded in establishing itself as a permanent entity, and even that magazine found it wisest to change its name to *Fantasy and Science Fiction* with its second issue. When science fiction became a fixture of paperback publishing in the 1950s, fantasy once again lagged behind: few fantasy novels were paperbacked, and most of them – Jack Vance's *The Dying Earth* and the early reprints of H. P. Lovecraft and Robert E. Howard are good examples – quickly vanished from view and became collector's items.

It all began to change in the late 1960s, when the sudden availability of paperback editions of J. R. R. Tolkien's *Lord of the Rings* trilogy (previously kept from paperback by an unwilling hardcover publisher) aroused a hunger for fantasy fiction in millions of readers that has, so far, been insatiable. Tolkien's books were such an emphatic commercial success that publishers rushed to find writers who could produce imitative trilogies, and the world was flooded with huge Hobbitesque novels, many of which sold in extraordinary quantities themselves. Robert Howard's *Conan* novels, once admired only by a small band of ardent cultists, began to win vast numbers of new readers about the same time. And a few years later Ballantine Books, Tolkien's paperback publishers, brought out an extraordinary series of books in its Adult Fantasy series, edited by Lin Carter, which made all the elegant classic masterpieces of such fantasists as E. R. Eddison, James Branch Cabell, Lord Dunsany and Mervyn Peake available to modern readers. And, ever since, fantasy has been a dominant factor in modern publishing. What had been a neglected step-sibling of science fiction fifty years ago is, today, an immensely popular genre.

In the wake of the great success of the Tolkien trilogy, newer writers have come along with their own deeply imagined worlds of fantasy, and have captured large and enthusiastic audiences themselves. In the late 1960s, Ursula Le Guin began her searching and sensitive Earthsea series, and Anne McCaffrey co-opted the ancient fantastic theme of the dragon for her Pern novels, which live on the borderline between fantasy and science fiction. Stephen King, some years later, won a readership of astounding magnitude by plumbing the archetypical fears of humanity and transforming them into powerful novels that occupied fantasy's darker terrain. Terry Pratchett, on the other hand, has magnificently demonstrated the comic power of satiric fantasy. Such writers as Orson Scott Card and Raymond E. Feist have won huge followings for their Alvin Maker and Riftwar books. More recently Robert Jordan's mammoth Wheel of Time series, George R. R. Martin's Song of Ice and Fire books, and Terry Goodkind's Sword of Truth tales have taken their place in the pantheon of modern fantasy, as has Tad Williams' Memory, Sorrow and Thorn series.

And here is the whole bunch of them, brought together in one huge anthology in which fantasy enthusiasts can revel for weeks. A new Earthsea story, a new tale of Pern, a new Dark Tower adventure, a new segment in Pratchett's playful Discworld series, and all the rest that you'll find herein – there has never been a book like this before. Gathering such an elite collection of first-magnitude stars into a single volume has not been an easy task. My gratitude herewith for the special assistance of Martin H. Greenberg, Ralph Vicinanza, Stephen King, John Helfers and Virginia Kidd, who in one way or another made my editorial task immensely less difficult than it otherwise would have been. And, too, although it goes without saying that I'm grateful to my wife, Karen, for her inestimable help in every phase of this intricate project, I think I'll say it anyway – not just because she's a terrific person, but because she came up with what unquestionably was the smartest idea of the whole enterprise.

Robert Silverberg
December 1997

Discworld

TERRY PRATCHETT

Discworld

TERRY PRATCHETT

The Colour of Magic (1983)
The Light Fantastic (1988)
Equal Rites (1988)
Mort (1989)
Sourcery (1989)
Wyrd Sisters (1990)
Pyramids (1990)
Guards! Guards! (1991)
Eric (1991)
Moving Pictures (1992)
Reaper Man (1992)
Witches Abroad (1994)
Small Gods (1994)
Lords and Ladies (1994)
Interesting Times (1995)
Soul Music (1995)
Maskerade (1995)
Men at Arms (1996)
Feet of Clay (1996)
Hogfather (1996)
Jingo (1997)
The Last Continent (1998)

Discworld is a flat world supported by four elephants standing on top of a huge turtle swimming endlessly through space. Using this classic mythological concept as his starting point, Pratchett cheerfully lampoons a vast range of targets – Shakespeare, Creationism theory, heroic fantasy, etc., etc. – and ventures into such far-flung realms as ancient Egypt, the Aztec Empire, and Renaissance Italy for further raw material. When he is not satirizing historical periods or cultures, Pratchett allows much of the action to centre around Ankh-Morpork, a melting-pot of a fantasy city that's a mix of Renaissance Florence, Victorian London, and present-day New York.

The series uses fantasy as a fairground mirror, reflecting back at us a distorted but recognizable image of twentieth-century concerns (for example, equal-opportunity and affirmative-action laws take on new dimensions when you've got vampires, werewolves, and zombies among your citizens . . .).

The books can be roughly divided into four groups:

In the Rincewind series (*The Colour of Magic, The Light Fantastic, Sourcery, Eric, Interesting Times*) the protagonist is an incompetent, cowardly (or very clear-thinking) magician who is constantly trying to escape some danger only to run into something ten times worse. However unfortunate his misadventures become, in the end he manages to triumph and to restore Discworld to a semblance of order, as order is understood there. The primary satiric object of these books is a lampoon of heroic fantasy, complete with all the genre staples – trolls, wizards, and similar fauna. *Sourcery*, for example, is a parody of the Lovecraftian netherworlds; *Eric* is a spoof of the Faustian deal-with-the-devil theme.

The Granny Weatherwax series (*Equal Rites, Wyrd Systers, Witches Abroad, Lords and Ladies, Maskerade*) introduces one of the most popular characters in the series, a witch of iron constitution, steel morals, and reinforced-concrete pride who takes charge in any situation; like a Western hero, she's technically a bad witch who does good. A rewriting of *The Phantom of the Opera* forms the basis for *Maskerade*, and *A Midsummer Night's Dream* is lampooned in *Lords and Ladies*, with Shakespeare's more genteel fairies replaced by haughty, vicious elves from Celtic folklore.

The four books comprising the Death series (*Mort, Reaper Man, Soul Music, Hogfather*) follow the trials of Death, a humourless entity who secretly harbours a soft spot for humanity, and whose inability to understand these same humans creates real pathos. In *Mort*, Death takes a vacation, leaving his even more soft-hearted apprentices to carry on while he's gone. *Reaper Man* follows Death when he becomes – temporarily – mortal, and learns what humanity *really* means.

The City Watch books (*Guards! Guards!, Men at Arms, Feet of Clay*) combine fantasy with elements of the police-procedural mystery novel, with appropriately lively results. *Guards! Guards!* finds the grubby but honest Ankh-Morpork Night Watch battling a dragon who wants to assassinate the city's Patrician and install a new puppet ruler. *Men at Arms* tracks a serial killer running amok with Discworld's only gun (designed by Discworld's equivalent of Leonardo da Vinci).

The stand-alone novel *Pyramids* injects some modern thinking into a version of Egypt of the Pharaohs. *Moving Pictures* uses the Discworld toolbox to examine the real magic of the movies. *Small Gods* provides a darkly humorous look at the rise of a religion whose one 'truth' is that the Discworld is actually spherical instead of flat.

In 'The Sea and Little Fishes' Pratchett offers a new adventure of Granny Weatherwax, a highly competitive spirit who believes that coming in second is another term for losing.

◆

The Sea and Little Fishes

BY TERRY PRATCHETT

Trouble began, and not for the first time, with an apple.

There was a bag of them on Granny Weatherwax's bleached and spotless table. Red and round, shiny and fruity, if they'd known the future they should have ticked like bombs.

'Keep the lot, old Hopcroft said I could have as many as I wanted,' said Nanny Ogg. She gave her sister witch a sidelong glance. 'Tasty, a bit wrinkled, but a damn good keeper.'

'He *named* an *apple* after *you*?' said Granny. Each word was an acid drop on the air.

''Cos of my rosy cheeks,' said Nanny Ogg. 'An' I cured his leg for him after he fell off that ladder last year. An' I made him up some jollop for his bald head.'

'It didn't work, though,' said Granny. 'That wig he wears, that's a terrible thing to see on a man still alive.'

'But he was pleased I took an interest.'

Granny Weatherwax didn't take her eyes off the bag. Fruit and vegetables grew famously in the mountains' hot summers and cold winters. Percy Hopcroft was the premier grower and definitely a keen man when it came to sexual antics among the horticulture with a camel-hair brush.

'He sells his apple trees all over the place,' Nanny Ogg went on. 'Funny, eh, to think that pretty soon thousands of people will be having a bite of Nanny Ogg.'

'Thousands more,' said Granny, tartly. Nanny's wild youth was an open book, although only available in plain covers.

'Thank you, Esme.' Nanny Ogg looked wistful for a moment,

and then opened her mouth in mock concern. 'Oh, you ain't *jealous*, are you, Esme? You ain't begrudging me my little moment in the sun?'

'Me? Jealous? Why should I be jealous? It's only an *apple*. It's not as if it's anything important.'

'That's what I thought. It's just a little frippery to humour an old lady,' said Nanny. 'So how are things with you, then?'

'Fine. Fine.'

'Got your winter wood in, have you?'

'Mostly.'

'Good,' said Nanny. 'Good.'

They sat in silence. On the windowpane a butterfly, awoken by the unseasonable warmth, beat a little tattoo in an effort to reach the September sun.

'Your potatoes . . . got them dug, then?' said Nanny.

'Yes.'

'We got a good crop off ours this year.'

'Good.'

'Salted your beans, have you?'

'Yes.'

'I expect you're looking forward to the Trials next week?'

'Yes.'

'I expect you've been practising?'

'No.'

It seemed to Nanny that, despite the sunlight, the shadows were deepening in the corners of the room. The very air itself was growing dark. A witch's cottage gets sensitive to the moods of its occupant. But she plunged on. Fools rush in, but they are laggards compared to little old ladies with nothing left to fear.

'You coming over to dinner on Sunday?'

'What're you havin'?'

'Pork.'

'With apple sauce?'

'Ye –'

'No,' said Granny.

There was a creaking behind Nanny. The door had swung open. Someone who wasn't a witch would have rationalized this, would have said that of course it was only the wind. And Nanny Ogg was quite prepared to go along with this, but would have added: *why* was it only the wind, and how come the wind had managed to lift the latch?

'Oh, well, can't sit here chatting all day,' she said, standing up quickly. 'Always busy at this time of year, ain't it?'

'Yes.'

'So I'll be off, then.'

'Goodbye.'

The wind blew the door shut again as Nanny hurried off down the path.

It occurred to her that, just possibly, she may have gone a bit too far. But only a bit.

The trouble with being a witch – at least, the trouble with being a witch as far as some people were concerned – was that you got stuck out here in the country. But that was fine by Nanny. Everything she wanted was out here. Everything she'd *ever* wanted was here, although in her youth she'd run out of men a few times. Foreign parts were all right to visit but they weren't really serious. They had interestin' new drinks and the grub was fun, but foreign parts was where you went to do what might need to be done and then you came back here, a place that was real. Nanny Ogg was happy in small places.

Of course, she reflected as she crossed the lawn, she didn't have this view out of her window. Nanny lived down in the town, but Granny could look out across the forest and over the plains and all the way to the great round horizon of the Discworld.

A view like that, Nanny reasoned, could probably suck your mind right out of your head.

They'd told her the world was round and flat, which was common sense, and went through space on the back of four elephants standing on the shell of a turtle, which didn't have to make sense. It was all happening Out There somewhere, and it could continue to do so with Nanny's blessing and disinterest so long as she could live in a personal world about ten miles across, which she carried around with her.

But Esme Weatherwax needed more than this little kingdom could contain. She was the *other* kind of witch.

And Nanny saw it as her job to stop Granny Weatherwax getting bored. The business with the apples was petty enough, a spiteful little triumph when you got down to it, but Esme needed something to make every day worthwhile and if it had to be anger and jealousy then so be it. Granny would now scheme for some little victory, some tiny humiliation that only the two of them would ever know about, and that'd be that. Nanny was confident that she could deal with her friend in a bad mood, but not when she was bored. A witch who is bored might do *anything*.

People said things like 'we had to make our own amusements in those days' as if this signalled some kind of moral worth, and perhaps it did, but the last thing you wanted a witch to do was get bored and start making her own amusements, because witches sometimes had famously erratic ideas about what was amusing. And Esme was undoubtedly the most powerful witch the mountains had seen for generations.

Still, the Trials were coming up, and they always set Esme Weatherwax all right for a few weeks. She rose to competition like a trout to a fly.

Nanny Ogg always looked forward to the Witch Trials. You got a good day out and of course there was a big bonfire. Whoever heard of a Witch Trial without a good bonfire afterwards?

And afterwards you could roast potatoes in the ashes.

The afternoon melted into the evening, and the shadows in corners and under stools and tables crept out and ran together.

Granny rocked gently in her chair as the darkness wrapped itself around her. She had a look of deep concentration.

The logs in the fireplace collapsed into the embers, which winked out one by one.

The night thickened.

The old clock ticked on the mantelpiece and, for some length of time, there was no other sound.

There came a faint rustling. The paper bag on the table moved and then began to crinkle like a deflating balloon. Slowly, the still air filled with a heavy smell of decay.

After a while the first maggot crawled out.

Nanny Ogg was back home and just pouring a pint of beer when there was a knock. She put down the jug with a sigh, and went and opened the door.

'Oh, hello, ladies. What're you doing in these parts? And on such a chilly evening, too?'

Nanny backed into the room, ahead of three more witches. They wore the black cloaks and pointy hats traditionally associated with their craft, although this served to make each one look different. There is nothing like a uniform for allowing one to express one's individuality. A tweak here and a tuck there are little details that scream all the louder in the apparent, well, uniformity.

Gammer Beavis's hat, for example, had a very flat brim and a point you could clean your ear with. Nanny liked Gammer Beavis. She might be a bit too educated, so that sometimes it overflowed out of her mouth, but she did her own shoe repairs and took snuff and, in Nanny Ogg's small world view, things like this meant that someone was All Right.

Old Mother Dismass's clothes had that disarray of someone who, because of a detached retina in her second sight, was living in a variety of times all at once. Mental confusion is bad enough in normal people, but much worse when the mind has an occult twist. You just had to hope it was only her underwear she was wearing on the outside.

It was getting worse, Nanny knew. Sometimes her knock would be heard on the door a few hours before she arrived. Her footprints would turn up several days later.

Nanny's heart sank at the sight of the third witch, and it wasn't because Letice Earwig was a bad woman. Quite the reverse, in fact. She was considered to be decent, well-meaning and kind, at least to less-aggressive animals and the cleaner sort of children. And she would always do you a good turn. The trouble was, though, that she would do you a good turn for your own good even if a good turn wasn't what was good for you. You ended up mentally turned the other way, and that wasn't good.

And she was married. Nanny had nothing against witches being married. It wasn't as if there were *rules*. She herself had had many husbands, and had even been married to three of them. But Mr Earwig was a retired wizard with a suspiciously large amount of gold, and Nanny suspected that Letice did witchcraft as something to keep herself occupied, in much the same way that other women of a certain class might embroider kneelers for the church or visit the poor.

And she had money. Nanny did not have money and therefore was predisposed to dislike those who did. Letice had a black velvet cloak so fine that if looked as if a hole had been cut out of the world. Nanny did not. Nanny did not *want* a fine velvet cloak and did not aspire to such things. So she didn't see why other people should have them.

''Evening, Gytha. How are you keeping, in yourself?' said Gammer Beavis.

Nanny took her pipe out of her mouth. 'Fit as a fiddle. Come on in.'

'Ain't this rain dreadful?' said Mother Dismass. Nanny looked at the sky. It was frosty purple. But it was probably raining wherever Mother's mind was at.

'Come along in and dry off, then,' she said kindly.

'May fortunate stars shine on this our meeting,' said Letice. Nanny nodded understandingly. Letice always sounded as though she'd learned her witchcraft out of a not very imaginative book.

'Yeah, right,' she said.

There was some polite conversation while Nanny prepared tea and scones. Then Gammer Beavis, in a tone that clearly indicated that the official part of the visit was beginning, said,

'We're here as the Trials committee, Nanny.'

'Oh? Yes?'

'I expect you'll be entering?'

'Oh, yes. I'll do my little turn.' Nanny glanced at Letice. There was a smile on that face that she wasn't entirely happy with.

'There's a lot of interest this year,' Gammer went on. 'More girls are taking it up lately.'

'To get boys, one feels,' said Letice, and sniffed. Nanny didn't comment. Using witchcraft to get boys seemed a damn good use for it as far as she was concerned. It was, in a way, one of the fundamental uses.

'That's nice,' she said. 'Always looks good, a big turnout. But.'

'I beg your pardon?' said Letice.

'I said "but",' said Nanny, ''cos someone's going to say "but", right? This little chat has got a big "but" coming up. I can tell.'

She knew this was flying in the face of protocol. There should be at least seven more minutes of small talk before anyone got around to the point, but Letice's presence was getting on her nerves.

'It's about Esme Weatherwax,' said Gammer Beavis.

'Yes?' said Nanny, without surprise.

'I suppose she's entering?'

'Never known her stay away.'

Letice sighed.

'I suppose you . . . couldn't persuade her to . . . not to enter this year?'

Nanny looked shocked.

'With an axe, you mean?'

In unison, the three witches sat back.

'You see –' Gammer began, a bit shamefaced.

'Frankly, Mrs Ogg,' said Letice, 'it is very hard to get other people to enter when they know that Miss Weatherwax is entering. She always wins.'

'Yes,' said Nanny. 'It's a competition.'

'But she *always* wins!'

'So?'

'In *other* types of competition,' said Letice, 'one is normally only allowed to win for three years in a row and then one takes a back seat for a while.'

'Yeah, but this is witching,' said Nanny. 'The rules is different.'

'How so?'

'There ain't none.'

Letice twitched her skirt. 'Perhaps it is time there were,' she said.

'Ah,' said Nanny. 'And you just going to go up and tell Esme that? You up for this, Gammer?'

Gammer Beavis didn't meet her gaze. Old Mother Dismass was gazing at last week.

'I understand Miss Weatherwax is a very proud woman,' said Letice.

Nanny Ogg puffed at her pipe again.

'You might as well say the sea is full of water,' she said.

The other witches were silent for a moment.

'I daresay that was a valuable comment,' said Letice, 'but I didn't understand it.'

'If there ain't no water in the sea, it ain't the sea,' said Nanny Ogg. 'It's just a damn great hole in the ground. Thing about Esme is . . .' Nanny took another noisy pull at the pipe, 'she's *all* pride, see? She ain't just a proud *person*.'

'Then perhaps she should learn to be a bit more humble . . .'

'What's she got to be humble about?' said Nanny sharply.

But Letice, like a lot of people with marshmallow on the outside, had a hard core that was not easily compressed.

'The woman clearly has a natural talent and, really, she should be grateful for . . .'

Nanny Ogg stopped listening at this point. *The woman*, she thought. So that was how it was going.

It was the same in just about every trade. Sooner or later someone decided it needed organizing, and the one thing you could be sure of was that the organizers weren't going to be the people who, by general acknowledgement, were at the top of their craft. *They* were working too hard. To be fair, it generally wasn't done by the worst, neither. They were working hard, too. They had to.

No, it was done by the ones who had just enough time and inclination to scurry and bustle. And, to be fair again, the world *needed* people who scurried and bustled. You just didn't have to like them very much.

The lull told her that Letice had finished.

'Really? Now, me,' said Nanny, 'I'm the one who's *nat'rally* talented. Us Oggs've got witchcraft in our blood. I never really had to sweat at it. Esme, now . . . she's got a bit, true enough, but it ain't a lot. She just makes it work harder'n hell. And you're going to tell her she's not to?'

'We were rather hoping you would,' said Letice.

Nanny opened her mouth to deliver one or two swearwords, and then stopped.

'Tell you what,' she said, '*you* can tell her tomorrow, and I'll come with you to hold her back.'

Granny Weatherwax was gathering Herbs when they came up the track.

Everyday herbs of sickroom and kitchen are known as simples. Granny's Herbs weren't simples. They were complicateds or they were nothing. And there was none of the airy-fairy business with a pretty basket and a pair of dainty snippers. Granny used a knife. And a chair held in front of her. And a leather hat, gloves and apron as secondary lines of defence.

Even she didn't know where some of the Herbs came from. Roots and seeds were traded all over the world, and maybe further. Some had flowers that turned as you passed by, some fired their thorns at passing birds and several were staked, not so that they wouldn't fall over, but so they'd still be there next day.

Nanny Ogg, who never bothered to grow any herb you couldn't smoke or stuff a chicken with, heard her mutter, 'Right, you buggers –'

'Good morning, Miss Weatherwax,' said Letice Earwig loudly.

Granny Weatherwax stiffened, and then lowered the chair very carefully and turned around.

'It's Mistress,' she said.

'Whatever,' said Letice brightly. 'I trust you are keeping well?'

'Up till now,' said Granny. She nodded almost imperceptibly at the other three witches.

There was a thrumming silence, which appalled Nanny Ogg.

They should have been invited in for a cup of something. That was how the ritual went. It was gross bad manners to keep people standing around. Nearly, but not quite, as bad as calling an elderly unmarried witch 'Miss'.

'You've come about the Trials,' said Granny. Letice almost fainted.

'Er, how did –'

''Cos you look like a committee. It don't take much reasoning,' said Granny, pulling off her gloves. 'We didn't used to need a committee. The news just got around and we all turned up. Now suddenly there's folk *arrangin'* things.' For a moment Granny looked as though she was fighting some serious internal battle, and then she added in throwaway tones: 'Kettle's on. You'd better come in.'

Nanny relaxed. Maybe there were some customs even Granny Weatherwax wouldn't defy, after all. Even if someone was your worst enemy, you invited them in and gave them tea and biscuits. In fact, the worser your enemy, the better the crockery you got out and the higher the quality of the biscuits. You might wish black hell on 'em later, but while they were under your roof you'd feed 'em till they choked.

Her dark little eyes noted that the kitchen table gleamed and was still damp from scrubbing.

After cups had been poured and pleasantries exchanged, or at least offered by Letice and received in silence by Granny, the self-elected chairwoman wriggled in her seat and said:

'There's such a lot of interest in the Trials this year, Miss . . . Mistress Weatherwax.'

'Good.'

'It does look as though witchcraft in the Ramtops is going through something of a renaissance, in fact.'

'A renaissance, eh? There's a thing.'

'It's such a good route to empowerment for young women, don't you think?'

Many people could say things in a cutting way, Nanny knew. But Granny Weatherwax could *listen* in a cutting way. She could make something sound stupid just by hearing it.

'That's a good hat you've got there,' said Granny. 'Velvet, is it? Not made local, I expect.'

Letice touched the brim and gave a little laugh.

'It's from Boggi's in Ankh-Morpork,' she said.

'Oh? Shop-bought?'

Nanny Ogg glanced at the corner of the room, where a battered wooden cone stood on a stand. Pinned to it were lengths of black calico and strips of willow wood, the foundations for Granny's spring hat.

'*Tailor-made,*' said Letice.

'And those hatpins you've got,' Granny went on. 'All them crescent moons and cat shapes –'

'You've got a brooch that's crescent-shaped, too, ain't that so, Esme?' said Nanny Ogg, deciding it was time for a warning shot. Granny occasionally had a lot to say about jewellery on witches when she was feeling in an acid mood.

'This is true, Gytha. I have a brooch what is shaped like a crescent. That's just the truth of the shape it happens to be. Very practical shape for holding a cloak, is a crescent. But I don't *mean* nothing by it. Anyway, you interrupted just as I was about to remark to Mrs Earwig how fetchin' her hatpins are. Very *witchy*.'

Nanny, swivelling like a spectator at a tennis match, glanced at Letice to see if this deadly bolt had gone home. But the woman was actually *smiling*. Some people just couldn't spot the obvious on the end of a ten-pound hammer.

'On the subject of witchcraft,' said Letice, with the born chairwoman's touch for the enforced segue, 'I thought I might raise with you the question of your *participation* in the Trials.'

'Yes?'

'Do you . . . ah . . . don't you think it is unfair to other people that you win every year?'

Granny Weatherwax looked down at the floor and then up at the ceiling.

'No,' she said, eventually. 'I'm better'n them.'

'You don't think it is a little dispiriting for the other contestants?'

Once again, the floor to ceiling search.

'No,' said Granny.

'But they start off knowing they're not going to win.'

'So do I.'

'Oh, no, you surely –'

'I *meant* that I start off knowing they're not goin' to win, too,' said Granny witheringly. 'And they ought to start off knowing *I'm* not going to win. No wonder they lose, if they ain't getting their minds right.'

'It does rather dash their enthusiasm.'

Granny looked genuinely puzzled. 'What's wrong with 'em striving to come second?' she said.

Letice plunged on.

'What we were hoping to persuade you to do, Esme, is to accept an emeritus position. You would perhaps make a nice little speech of encouragement, present the award, and . . . and possibly even be, er, one of the judges . . .'

'There's going to be judges?' said Granny. 'We've never had *judges*. Everyone just used to know who'd won.'

'That's true,' said Nanny. She remembered the scenes at the end of one or two trials. When Granny Weatherwax won, everyone knew. 'Oh, that's very true.'

'It would be a very nice gesture,' Letice went on.

'Who decided there would be judges?' said Granny.

'Er . . . the committee . . . which is . . . that is . . . a few of us got together. Only to steer things . . .'

'Oh. I see,' said Granny. 'Flags?'

'Pardon?'

'Are you going to have them lines of little flags? And maybe someone selling apples on a stick, that kind of thing?'

'Some bunting would certainly be –'

'Right. Don't forget the bonfire.'

'So long as it's nice and safe.'

'Oh. Right. Things should be nice. And safe,' said Granny.

Mrs Earwig perceptibly sighed with relief. 'Well, that's sorted out nicely,' she said.

'Is it?' said Granny.

'I thought we'd agreed that –'

'Had we? Really?' She picked up the poker from the hearth and prodded fiercely at the fire. 'I'll give matters my consideration.'

'I wonder if I may be frank for a moment, Mistress Weatherwax?' said Letice. The poker paused in mid-prod.

'Yes?'

'Times are changing, you know. Now, I think I know why you feel it necessary to be so overbearing and unpleasant to everyone, but believe me when I tell you, as a friend, that you'd find it so much easier if you just relaxed a little bit and tried being nicer, like our sister Gytha here.'

Nanny Ogg's smile had fossilized into a mask. Letice didn't seem to notice.

'You seem to have all the witches in awe of you for fifty miles around,' she went on. 'Now, I daresay you have some valuable skills, but witchcraft isn't about being an old grump and frightening people any more. I'm telling you this as a friend –'

'Call again whenever you're passing,' said Granny.

This was a signal. Nanny Ogg stood up hurriedly.

'I thought we could discuss –' Letice protested.

'I'll walk with you all down to the main track,' said Nanny, hauling the other witches out of their seats.

'Gytha!' said Granny sharply, as the group reached the door.

'Yes, Esme?'

'You'll come back here afterwards, I expect.'

'Yes, Esme.'

Nanny ran to catch up with the trio on the path.

Letice had what Nanny thought of as a deliberate walk. It had been wrong to judge her by the floppy jowls and the over-fussy hair and the silly way she waggled her hands as she talked. She was a witch, after all. Scratch any witch and . . . well, you'd be facing a witch you'd just scratched.

'She is not a nice person,' Letice trilled. But it was the trill of some large hunting bird.

'You're right there,' said Nanny. 'But –'

'It's high time she was taken down a peg or two!'

'We-ell . . .'

'She bullies you most terribly, Mrs Ogg. A married lady of *your* mature years, too!'

Just for a moment, Nanny's eyes narrowed.

'It's her way,' she said.

'A very petty and nasty way, to my mind!'

'Oh, yes,' said Nanny simply. 'Ways often are. But look, you –'

'Will you be bringing anything to the produce stall, Gytha?' said Gammer Beavis quickly.

'Oh, a couple of bottles, I expect,' said Nanny, deflating.

'Oh, homemade wine?' said Letice. 'How nice.'

'Sort of like wine, yes. Well, here's the path,' said Nanny. 'I'll just . . . I'll just nip back and say goodnight –'

'It's belittling, you know, the way you run around after her,' said Letice.

'Yes. Well. You get used to people. Goodnight to you.'

When she got back to the cottage Granny Weatherwax was standing in the middle of the kitchen floor with a face like an unmade bed and her arms folded. One foot tapped on the floor.

'She married a wizard,' said Granny, as soon as her friend had entered. 'You can't tell me that's right.'

'Well, wizards *can* marry, you know. They just have to hand in the staff and pointy hat. There's no actual law says they can't, so long as they gives up wizarding. They're supposed to be married to the job.'

'I should reckon it's a job being married to *her*,' said Granny. Her face screwed up in a sour smile.

'Been pickling much this year?' said Nanny, employing a fresh association of ideas around the word 'vinegar' which had just popped into her head.

'My onions all got the screwfly.'

'That's a pity. You like onions.'

'Even screwflies've got to eat,' said Granny. She glared at the door. '*Nice*,' she said.

'She's got a knitted cover on the lid in her privy,' said Nanny.

'Pink?'

'Yes.'

'Nice.'

'She's not *bad*,' said Nanny. 'She does good work over in Fiddler's Elbow. People speak highly of her.'

Granny sniffed. 'Do they speak highly of me?' she said.

'No, they speaks *quietly* of you, Esme.'

'Good. Did you see her hatpins?'

'I thought they were rather . . . nice, Esme.'

'That's witchcraft today. All jewellery and no drawers.'

Nanny, who considered both to be optional, tried to build an embankment against the rising tide of ire.

'You could think of it as an honour, really, them not wanting you to take part.'

'That's nice.'

Nanny sighed.

'Sometimes nice is worth tryin', Esme,' she said.

'I never does anyone a bad turn if I can't do 'em a good one, Gytha, you know that. I don't have to do no frills or fancy labels.'

Nanny sighed. Of course, it was true. Granny was an old-fashioned witch. She didn't do good for people, she did right by them. But Nanny knew that people don't always appreciate right. Like old Pollitt the other day, when he fell off his horse. What he wanted was a painkiller. What he *needed* was the few seconds of agony as Granny popped the joint back into place. The trouble was, people remembered the pain.

You got on a lot better with people when you remembered to put frills round it, and took an interest and said things like 'How are you?'. Esme didn't bother with that kind of stuff because she knew already. Nanny Ogg knew too, but also knew that letting on you knew gave people the serious willies.

She put her head on one side. Granny's foot was still tapping.

'You planning anything, Esme? I know you. You've got that look.'

'What look, pray?'

'That look you had when that bandit was found naked up a tree and cryin' all the time and goin' on about the horrible thing that was after him. Funny thing, we never found any pawprints. *That* look.'

'He deserved more'n that for what he done.'

'Yeah . . . well, you had that look just before ole Hoggett was found beaten black and blue in his own pigsty and wouldn't talk about it.'

'You mean old Hoggett the wife-beater? Or old Hoggett who won't never lift his hand to a woman no more?' said Granny. The thing her lips had pursed into may have been called a smile.

'And it's the look you had the time all the snow slid down on ole Millson's house just after he called you an interfering old baggage,' said Nanny.

Granny hesitated. Nanny was pretty sure that had been natural causes, and also that Granny knew she suspected this, and that pride was fighting a battle with honesty –

'That's as may be,' said Granny, noncommittally.

'Like someone who might go along to the Trials and . . . do something,' said Nanny.

Her friend's glare should have made the air sizzle.

'Oh? So that's what you think of me? That's what we've come to, have we?'

'Letice thinks we should move with the times –'

'Well? I moves with the times. We ought to move with the times. No one said we ought to give them a *push*. I expect you'll be wanting to be going, Gytha. I want to be alone with my thoughts!'

Nanny's own thoughts, as she scurried home in relief, were that Granny Weatherwax was not an advertisement for witchcraft. Oh, she was one of the *best* at it, no doubt about that. At a certain kind, certainly. But a girl starting out in life might well say to herself, is this it? You worked hard and denied yourself things and what you got at the end of it was hard work and self-denial?

Granny wasn't exactly friendless, but what she commanded mostly was respect. People learned to respect stormclouds, too.

They refreshed the ground. You needed them. But they weren't nice.

Nanny Ogg went to bed in three flannelette nightdresses, because sharp frosts were already pricking the autumn air. She was also in a troubled frame of mind.

Some sort of war had been declared, she knew. Granny could do some terrible things when roused, and the fact that they'd been done to those who richly deserved them didn't make them any the less terrible. She'd be planning something pretty dreadful, Nanny Ogg knew.

She herself didn't like winning things. Winning was a habit that was hard to break and brought you a dangerous status that was hard to defend. You'd walk uneasily through life, always on the lookout for the next girl with a better broomstick and a quicker hand on the frog.

She turned over under the mountain of eiderdowns.

In Granny Weatherwax's world-view was no room for second place. You won, or you were a loser. There was nothing *wrong* with being a loser except for the fact that, of course, you weren't the winner. Nanny had always pursued the policy of being a good loser. People *liked* you when you *almost* won, and bought you drinks. 'She only just lost' was a much better compliment than 'she only just won'.

Runners-up had more fun, she reckoned. But it wasn't a word Granny had much time for.

In her own darkened cottage, Granny Weatherwax sat and watched the fire die.

It was a grey-walled room, the colour that old plaster gets not so much from dirt as from age. There was not a thing in it that wasn't useful, utilitarian, earned its keep. Every flat surface in Nanny Ogg's cottage had been pressed into service as a holder for ornaments and potted plants. People gave Nanny Ogg things. Cheap fairground tat, Granny always called it. At least, in public. What she thought of it in the privacy of her own head, she never said.

She rocked gently as the last ember winked out.

It's hard to contemplate, in the grey hours of the night, that probably the only reason people would come to your funeral would be to make sure you're dead.

Next day, Percy Hopcroft opened his back door and looked straight up into the blue stare of Granny Weatherwax.

'Oh my,' he said, under his breath.

Granny gave an awkward little cough.

'Mr Hopcroft, I've come about them apples you named after Mrs Ogg,' she said.

Percy's knees began to tremble, and his wig started to slide off the back of his head to the hoped-for security of the floor.

'I should like to thank you for doing it because it has made her very happy,' Granny went on, in a tone of voice which would have struck one who knew her as curiously monotonous. 'She has done a lot of fine work and it's about time she got her little reward. It was a very nice thought. And so I have brung you this little token –' Hopcroft jumped backwards as Granny's hand dipped swiftly into her apron and produced a small black bottle '– which is very rare because of the rare herbs in it. What are rare. Extremely rare herbs.'

Eventually it crept over Hopcroft that he was supposed to take the bottle. He gripped the top of it very carefully, as if it might whistle or develop legs.

'Uh . . . thank you ver' much,' he mumbled.

Granny nodded stiffly.

'Blessings be upon this house,' she said, and turned and walked away down the path.

Hopcroft shut the door carefully, and then flung himself against it.

'You start packing right now!' he shouted to his wife, who'd been watching from the kitchen door.

'What? Our whole life's here! We can't just run away from it!'

'Better to run than hop, woman! What's *she* want from me? What's she *want*? She's never *nice*!'

Mrs Hopcroft stood firm. She'd just got the cottage looking right and they'd bought a new pump. Some things were hard to leave.

'Let's just stop and think, then,' she said. 'What's in that bottle?'

Hopcroft held it at arm's length. 'Do *you* want to find out?'

'Stop shaking, man! She didn't actually threaten, did she?'

'She said "blessings be upon this house"! Sounds pretty damn threatening to *me*! That was Granny Weatherwax, that was!'

He put the bottle on the table. They stared at it, standing in the cautious leaning position of people who were ready to run if anything began to happen.

'Says "Haire Reſtorer" on the label,' said Mrs Hopcroft.

'I ain't using it!'

'She'll ask us about it later. That's her way.'

'If you think for one moment I'm –'

'We can try it out on the dog.'

'That's a good cow.'

William Poorchick awoke from his reverie on the milking stool and looked around the meadow, his hands still working the beast's teats.

There was a black pointy hat rising over the hedge. He gave such a start that he started to milk into his left boot.

'Gives plenty of milk, does she?'

'Yes, Mistress Weatherwax!' William quavered.

'That's good. Long may she continue to do so, that's what I say. Good-day to you.'

And the pointy hat continued up the lane.

Poorchick stared after it. Then he grabbed the bucket and, squelching at every other step, hurried into the barn and yelled for his son.

'Rummage! You get down here right now!'

His son appeared at the hayloft, pitchfork still in his hand.

'What's up, Dad?'

'You take Daphne down to the market right now, understand?'

'What? But she's our best milker, Dad!'

'*Was*, son, was! Granny Weatherwax just put a curse on her! Sell her now before her horns drop off!'

'What'd she say, Dad?'

'She said . . . she said . . . "Long may she continue to give milk" . . .' Poorchick hesitated.

'Doesn't sound *awfully* like a curse, Dad,' said Rummage. 'I mean . . . not like your gen'ral curse. Sounds a bit hopeful, really,' said his son.

'Well . . . it was the way . . . she . . . said . . . it . . .'

'What sort of way, Dad?'

'Well . . . like . . . cheerfully.'

'You all right, Dad?'

'It was . . . the way . . .' Poorchick paused. 'Well, it's not right,' he continued. 'It's not right! She's got no right to go around being cheerful at people! She's never cheerful! And my *boot* is *full* of *milk*!'

Today Nanny Ogg was taking some time out to tend her secret still in the woods. As a still it was the best-kept secret there could be, since everyone in the kingdom knew exactly where it was, and a secret kept by so many people must be very secret indeed. Even the king knew, and knew enough to pretend he didn't know, and that meant he didn't have to ask her for any taxes and she didn't have to refuse. And every year at Hogswatch he got a barrel of what honey might be if only bees weren't teetotal. And everyone understood the situation, no one had to pay any money and so, in a small way, the world was a happier place. And no one was cursed until their teeth fell out.

Nanny was dozing. Keeping an eye on a still was a day and night job. But finally the sound of people repeatedly calling her name got too much for her.

No one would come into the clearing, of course. That would mean admitting that they knew where it was. So they were blundering around in the surrounding bushes. She pushed her way through, and was greeted with some looks of feigned surprise that would have done credit to any amateur dramatic company.

'Well, what do you lot want?' she demanded.

'Oh, Mrs Ogg, we thought you might be . . . taking a walk in the woods,' said Poorchick, while a scent that could clean glass wafted on the breeze. 'You got to do something! It's Mistress Weatherwax!'

'What's she done?'

'You tell 'er, Mister Hampicker!'

The man next to Poorchick took off his hat quickly and held it respectfully in front of him in the ai-señor-the-bandidos-have-raided-our-villages position.

'Well, ma'am, my lad and I were digging for a well and then she come past –'

'Granny Weatherwax?'

'Yes'm, and she said –' Hampicker gulped, '"You won't find any water there, my good man. You'd be better off looking in the hollow by the chestnut tree." An' we dug on down anyway and *we never found no water!*'

Nanny lit her pipe. She didn't smoke around the still since that time when a careless spark had sent the barrel she was sitting on a hundred yards into the air. She'd been lucky that a fir tree had broken her fall.

'So . . . *then* you dug in the hollow by the chestnut tree?' she said mildly.

Hampicker looked shocked. '*No*'m! There's no telling *what* she wanted us to find there!'

'And she cursed my cow!' said Poorchick.

'Really? What did she say?'

'She said, may she give a lot of milk!' Poorchick stopped. Once again, now that he came to say it . . .

'Well, it was the way she said it,' he added, weakly.

'And what kind of way was that?'

'Nicely!'

'Nicely?'

'Smilin' and everything! I don't dare drink the stuff now!'

Nanny was mystified.

'Can't quite see the problem –'

'You tell that to Mr Hopcroft's dog,' said Poorchick. 'Hopcroft daren't leave the poor thing on account of her! The whole family's going mad! There's him shearing, his wife sharpening the scissors, and the two lads out all the time looking for fresh places to dump the hair!'

Patient questioning on Nanny's part elucidated the role the Haire Reſtorer had played in this.

'And he gave it . . . ?'

'Half the bottle, Mrs Ogg.'

'Even though Esme writes "A right small spoonful once a week" on the label? And even then you need to wear roomy trousers.'

'He said he was so nervous, Mrs Ogg! I mean, what's she playing at? Our wives are keepin' the kids indoors. I mean, s'posin' she smiled at them?'

'Well?'

'She's a witch!'

'So'm I, an' I smiles at 'em,' said Nanny Ogg. 'They're always runnin' after me for sweets.'

'Yes, but . . . you're . . . I mean . . . she . . . I mean . . . you don't . . . I mean. Well –'

'And she's a good woman,' said Nanny. Common sense prompted her to add, 'In her own way. I expect there *is* water down in the hollow, and Poorchick's cow'll give good milk, and if Hopcroft won't read the labels on bottles then he deserves a head you can see your face in, and if you think Esme Weatherwax'd curse kids you've got the sense of a earthworm. She'd cuss 'em, yes, all day long. But not curse 'em. She don't aim that low.'

'Yes, yes,' Poorchick almost moaned, 'but it don't *feel* right, that's what we're saying. Her going round being *nice*, a man don't know if he's got a leg to stand on.'

'Or hop on,' said Hampicker darkly.

'All right, all right, I'll see about it,' said Nanny.

'People shouldn't go around not doin' what you expect,' said Poorchick weakly. 'It gets people on edge.'

'And we'll keep an eye on your sti –' Hampicker said, and then staggered backwards grasping his stomach and wheezing.

'Don't mind him, it's the stress,' said Poorchick, rubbing his elbow. 'Been picking herbs, Mrs Ogg?'

'That's right,' said Nanny, hurrying away across the leaves.

'So shall I put the fire out for you, then?' Poorchick shouted.

Granny was sitting outside her house when Nanny Ogg hurried up the path. She was sorting through a sack of old clothes. Elderly garments were scattered around her.

And she was humming. Nanny Ogg started to worry. The Granny Weatherwax she knew didn't approve of music.

And she smiled when she saw Nanny, or at least the corners of her mouth turned up. That was *really* worrying. Granny normally only smiled if something bad was happening to someone deserving.

'Why, Gytha, how nice to see you!'

'You all right, Esme?'

'Never felt better, dear.' The humming continued.

'Er . . . sorting out rags, are you?' said Nanny. 'Going to make that quilt?'

It was one of Granny Weatherwax's firm beliefs that one day she'd make a patchwork quilt. However, it is a task that requires patience, and hence in fifteen years she'd got as far as three patches. But she collected old clothes anyway. A lot of witches did. It was a witch thing. Old clothes had personality, like old houses. When it came to clothes with a bit of wear left in them, a witch had no pride at all.

'It's in here somewhere . . .' Granny mumbled. 'Aha, here we are . . .'

She flourished a garment. It was basically pink.

'Knew it was here,' she went on. 'Hardly worn, either. And about my size, too.'

'You're going to *wear* it?' said Nanny.

Granny's piercing blue cut-you-off-at-the-knees gaze was turned upon her. Nanny would have been relieved at a reply like 'No, I'm going to eat it, you daft old fool'. Instead her friend relaxed and said, a little concerned:

'You don't think it'd suit me?'

There was lace around the collar. Nanny swallowed.

'You usually wear black. Well, a bit more than usually. More like always.'

'And a very sad sight I look too,' said Granny robustly. 'It's about time I brightened myself up a bit, don't you think?'

'And it's so very . . . pink.'

Granny put it aside and to Nanny's horror took her by the hand and said earnestly, 'And, you know, I reckon I've been far too dog-in-the-manger about this Trials business, Gytha –'

'Bitch-in-the-manger,' said Nanny Ogg, absent-mindedly.

For a moment Granny's eyes became two sapphires again.

'What?'

'Er . . . you'd be a bitch-in-the-manger,' Nanny mumbled. 'Not a dog.'

'Ah? Oh, yes. Thank you for pointing that out. Well, I thought, it *is* time I stepped back a bit, and went along and cheered on the younger folks. I mean, I have to say, I . . . really haven't been very nice to people, have I . . .'

'Er . . .'

'I've tried *being* nice,' Granny went on. 'It didn't turn out like I expected, I'm sorry to say.'

'You've never been really . . . *good* at nice,' said Nanny.

Granny smiled. Hard though she stared, Nanny was unable to spot anything other than earnest concern.

'Perhaps I'll get better with practice,' she said.

She patted Nanny's hand. And Nanny stared at her hand as though something horrible had happened to it.

'It's just that everyone's more used to you being . . . firm,' she said.

'I thought I might make some jam and cakes for the produce stall,' said Granny.

'Oh . . . good.'

'Are there any sick people want visitin'?'

Nanny stared at the trees. It was getting worse and worse. She rummaged in her memory for anyone in the locality sick enough to warrant a ministering visit but still well enough to survive the shock of a ministering visit by Granny Weatherwax.

When it came to practical psychology and the more robust type of folk physiotherapy Granny was without equal; in fact, she could even do the latter at a distance, for many a pain-racked soul had left their beds and walked, nay, run at the news that she was coming.

'Everyone's pretty well at the moment,' said Nanny diplomatically.

'Any old folk want cheerin' up?'

It was taken for granted by both women that *old people* did not include them. A witch aged ninety-seven would not have included herself. Old people happened to other people.

'All fairly cheerful right now,' said Nanny.

'Maybe I could tell stories to the kiddies?'

Nanny nodded. Granny had done that once before, when the mood had briefly taken her. It had worked pretty well, as far as the children were concerned. They'd listened with open-mouthed attention and apparent enjoyment to a traditional old folk legend. The problem had come when they'd gone home afterwards and asked the meaning of words like 'disembowelled'.

'I could sit in a rocking chair while I tell 'em,' Granny added. 'That's how it's done, I recall. And I could make them some of my special treacle-toffee apples. Wouldn't that be nice?'

Nanny nodded again, in a sort of horrified reverie. She realized that only she stood in the way of a wholesale rampage of niceness.

'Toffee,' she said. 'Would that be the sort you did that shatters like glass, or that sort where our boy Pewsey had to have his mouth levered open with a spoon?'

'I reckon I know what I did wrong last time.'

'You know you and sugar don't get along, Esme. Remember them all-day suckers you made?'

'They *did* last all day, Gytha.'

'Only 'cos our Pewsey couldn't get it out of his little mouth until we pulled two of his teeth, Esme. You ought to stick to pickles. You and pickles goes well.'

'I've got to do *something*, Gytha. I can't be an old grump all the time. I know! I'll help at the Trials. Bound to be a lot that needs doing, eh?'

Nanny grinned inwardly. So *that* was it.

'Why, yes. I'm sure Mrs Earwig will be happy to tell you what to do.' And more fool her if she does, she thought, because I can tell you're planning something.

'I shall talk to her,' said Granny. 'I'm sure there's a million things I could do to help, if I set my mind to it.'

'And I'm sure you will,' said Nanny heartily. 'I've a feelin' you're going to make a big difference.'

Granny started to rummage in the bag again.

'You are going to be along as well, aren't you, Gytha?'

'Me?' said Nanny. 'I wouldn't miss it for worlds.'

Nanny got up especially early. If there was going to be any unpleasantness she wanted a ringside seat.

What there was, was bunting. It was hanging from tree to tree in terrible brightly-coloured loops as she walked towards the Trials.

There was something oddly familiar about it, too. It should not technically be possible for anyone with a pair of scissors to be unable to cut out a triangle, but someone had managed it. And it was also obvious that the flags had been made from old clothes, painstakingly cut up. Nanny knew this because not many real flags have collars.

In the trials field, people were setting up stalls and falling over children. The committee were standing uncertainly under a tree, occasionally glancing up at a pink figure at the top of a very long ladder.

'She was here before it was light,' said Letice, as Nanny approached. 'She said she'd been up all night making the flags.'

'Tell her about the cakes,' said Gammer Beavis darkly.

'She made *cakes*?' said Nanny. 'But she can't cook!'

The committee shuffled aside. A lot of the ladies contributed to the food for the Trials. It was a tradition and an informal competition in its own right. At the centre of the spread of covered plates was a large platter piled high with . . . things, of indefinite colour and shape. It looked as though a herd of small cows had eaten a lot of raisins and then been ill. They were Ur-cakes, prehistoric cakes, cakes of great weight and presence that had no place among the iced dainties.

'She's never had the knack of it,' said Nanny weakly. 'Has anyone tried one?'

'Hahaha,' said Gammer solemnly.

'Tough, are they?'

'You could beat a troll to death.'

'But she was so . . . sort of . . . *proud* of them,' said Letice. 'And then there's . . . the jam.'

It was a large pot. It seemed to be filled with solidified purple lava.

'Nice . . . colour,' said Nanny. 'Anyone tasted it?'

'We couldn't get the spoon out,' said Gammer.

'Oh, I'm sure –'

'We only got it in with a hammer.'

'What's she planning, Mrs Ogg? She's got a weak and vengeful nature,' said Letice. 'You're her friend,' she added, her tone suggesting that this was as much an accusation as a statement.

'I don't know what she's thinking, Mrs Earwig.'

'I thought she was staying away.'

'She said she was going to take an interest and encourage the young 'uns.'

'She is planning something,' said Letice, darkly. 'Those cakes are a plot to undermine my authority.'

'No, that's how she always cooks,' said Nanny. 'She just hasn't got the knack.' Your authority, eh?

'She's nearly finished the flags,' Gammer reported. 'Now she's going to try to make herself useful again.'

'Well . . . I suppose we could ask her to do the Lucky Dip.'

Nanny looked blank. 'You mean where kids fish around in a big tub full of bran to see what they can pull out?'

'Yes.'

'You're going to let *Granny Weatherwax* do that?'

'Yes.'

'Only she's got a funny sense of humour, if you know what I mean.'

'Good morning to you all!'

It was Granny Weatherwax's voice. Nanny Ogg had known it for most of her life. But it had that strange edge to it again. It sounded nice.

'We was wondering if you could supervise the bran tub, Miss Weatherwax.'

Nanny flinched. But Granny merely said: 'Happy to, Mrs Earwig. I can't wait to see the expressions on their little faces as they pull out the goodies.'

Nor can I, Nanny thought.

When the others had scurried off she sidled up to her friend.

'Why're you doing this?' she said.

'I really don't know what you mean, Gytha.'

'I seen you face down terrible creatures, Esme. I once seen you catch a unicorn, for goodness' sake. What're you plannin'?'

'I still don't know what you mean, Gytha.'

'Are you angry 'cos they won't let you enter, and now you're plannin' horrible revenge?'

For a moment they both looked at the field. It was beginning to fill up. People were bowling for pigs and fighting on the greasy pole. The Lancre Volunteer Band was trying to play a medley of popular tunes, and it was only a pity that each musician was playing a different one. Small children were fighting. It was going to be a scorcher of a day, probably the last one of the year.

Their eyes were drawn to the roped-off square in the centre of the field.

'Are you going to enter the Trials, Gytha?' said Granny.

'You never answered my question!'

'What question was that?'

Nanny decided not to hammer on a locked door. 'Yes, I am going to have a go, as it happens,' she said.

'I certainly hope you win, then. I'd cheer you on, only that wouldn't be fair to the others. I shall merge into the background and be as quiet as a little mouse.'

Nanny tried guile. Her face spread into a wide pink grin, and she nudged her friend.

'Right, right,' she said. 'Only . . . you can tell me, right? I wouldn't like to miss it when it happens. So if you could just give me a little signal when you're going to do *it*, eh?'

'What's it you're referring to, Gytha?'

'Esme Weatherwax, sometimes I could really give you a bloody good slap!'

'Oh dear.'

Nanny Ogg didn't often swear, or at least use words beyond the boundaries of what the Lancrastrians thought of as 'colourful language'. She *looked* as if she habitually used bad words, and had just thought up a good one, but mostly witches are quite careful about what they say. You can never be sure what the words are going to do when they're out of earshot. But now she swore under her breath and caused small brief fires to start in the dry grass.

This put her in just about the right frame of mind for the Cursing.

It was said that once upon a time this had been done on a living, breathing subject, at least at the start of the event, but that wasn't right for a family day out and for several hundred years the Curses had been directed at Unlucky Charlie who was, however you looked at it, nothing more than a scarecrow. And since curses are generally directed at the mind of the cursed, this presented a major problem, because even 'May your straw go mouldy and your carrot fall off' didn't make much impression on a pumpkin. But points were given for general style and inventiveness.

There wasn't much pressure for those in any case. Everyone knew what event counted, and it wasn't Unlucky Charlie.

One year Granny Weatherwax had made the pumpkin explode. No one had ever worked out how she'd done it.

Someone would walk away at the end of today and everyone would know they were the winner, whatever the points said. You could win the Witch With The Pointiest Hat prize and the broomstick dressage, but that was just for the audience. What counted was the Trick you'd been working on all summer.

Nanny had drawn last place, at number nineteen. A lot of witches had turned up this year. News of Granny Weatherwax's withdrawal had got around, and nothing moves faster than news in the occult community since it doesn't just have to travel at ground level. Many pointy hats moved and nodded among the crowds.

Witches are among themselves generally as sociable as cats but, as also with cats, there are locations and times and neutral grounds where they meet at something like peace. And what was going on was a sort of slow, complicated dance . . .

The witches walked around saying hello to one another, and rushing to meet newcomers, and innocent bystanders might have believed that here was a meeting of old friends. Which, at one level, it probably was. But Nanny watched through a witch's eyes, and saw the subtle positioning, the careful weighing-up, the little changes of stance, the eye-contact finely tuned by intensity and length.

And when a witch was in the arena, especially if she was comparatively unknown, all the others found some excuse to keep an eye on her, preferably without appearing to do so.

It *was* like watching cats. Cats spend a lot of time carefully eyeing one another. When they have to fight, that's merely to rubber-stamp something that's already been decided in their heads.

Nanny knew all this. And she also knew most of the witches to be kind (on the whole), gentle (to the meek), generous (to the deserving; the undeserving got more than they bargained for), and by and large quite dedicated to a life that really offered more kicks than kisses. Not one of them lived in a house made of confectionery, although some of the conscientious younger ones had experimented with various crispbreads. Even children who deserved it were not slammed into their ovens. Generally they did what they'd always done – smooth the passage of their neighbours into and out of the world, and help them over some of the nastier hurdles in between.

You needed to be a special kind of person to do that. You

needed a special kind of ear, because you saw people in circumstances where they were inclined to tell you things, like where the money is buried or who the father was or how come they'd got a black eye again. And you needed a special kind of mouth, the sort that stayed shut. Keeping secrets made you powerful. Being powerful earned you respect. Respect was hard currency.

And within this sisterhood – except that it wasn't a sisterhood, it was a loose assortment of chronic non-joiners; a group of witches wasn't a coven, it was a small war – there was always this awareness of position. It had nothing to do with anything the other world thought of as status. Nothing was ever said. But if an elderly witch died the local witches would attend her funeral for a few last words, and then go solemnly home alone, with the little insistent thought at the back of their minds: 'I've moved up one.'

And newcomers were watched very, very carefully.

''Morning, Mrs Ogg,' said a voice behind her. 'I trust I find you well?'

'How'd'yer do, Mistress Shimmy,' said Nanny, turning. Her mental filing system threw up a card: Clarity Shimmy, lives over towards Cutshade with her old mum, takes snuff, good with animals. 'How's your mother keepin'?'

'We buried her last month, Mrs Ogg.'

Nanny Ogg quite liked Clarity, because she didn't see her very often.

'Oh dear . . .' she said.

'But I shall tell her you asked after her, anyway,' said Clarity. She glanced briefly towards the ring. 'Who's the fat girl on now? Got a backside on her like a bowling ball on a short seesaw.'

'That's Agnes Nitt.'

'That's a good cursin' voice she's got there. You know you've been cursed with a voice like that.'

'Oh yes, she's been blessed with a good voice for cursin',' said Nanny politely. 'Esme Weatherwax an' me gave her a few tips,' she added.

Clarity's head turned.

At the far edge of the field, a small pink shape sat alone

behind the Lucky Dip. It did not seem to be drawing a big crowd.

Clarity leaned closer.

'What's she . . . er . . . doing?'

'I don't know,' said Nanny. 'I think she's decided to be nice about it.'

'Esme? *Nice* about it?'

'Er . . . yes,' said Nanny. It didn't sound any better now she was telling someone.

Clarity stared at her. Nanny saw her make a little sign with her left hand, and then hurry off.

The pointy hats were bunching up now. There were little groups of three or four. You could see the points come together, cluster in animated conversation, and then open out again like a flower, and turn towards the distant blob of pinkness. Then a hat would leave that group and head off purposefully to another one, where the process would start all over again. It was a bit like watching very slow nuclear fission. There was a lot of excitement, and soon there would be an explosion.

Every so often someone would turn and look at Nanny, so she hurried away among the sideshows until she fetched up beside the stall of the dwarf Zakzak Stronginthearm, maker and purveyor of occult knicknackery to the more impressionable. He nodded at her cheerfully over the top of a display saying 'Lucky Horseshoes $2 Each'.

'Hello, Mrs Ogg,' he said.

Nanny realized she was flustered.

'What's lucky about 'em?' she said, picking up a horseshoe.

'Well, I get two dollars each for them,' said Stronginthearm.

'And that makes them lucky?'

'Lucky for me,' said Stronginthearm. 'I expect you'll be wanting one too, Mrs Ogg? I'd have fetched along another box if I'd known they'd be so popular. Some of the ladies've bought two.'

There was an inflection to the word 'ladies'.

'*Witches* have been buying lucky horseshoes?' said Nanny.

'Like there's no tomorrow,' said Zakzak. He frowned for a

moment. They *had* been witches, after all. 'Er . . . there will be . . . won't there?' he added.

'I'm very nearly certain of it,' said Nanny, which didn't seem to comfort him.

'Suddenly been doing a roaring trade in protective herbs, too,' said Zakzak. And, being a dwarf, which meant that he'd see the Flood as a marvellous opportunity to sell towels, he added, 'Can I interest you, Mrs Ogg?'

Nanny shook her head. If trouble was going to come from the direction everyone had been looking, then a sprig of rue wasn't going to be much help. A large oak tree'd be better, but only maybe.

The atmosphere was changing. The sky was a wide pale blue, but there was thunder on the horizons of the mind. The witches were uneasy and with so many in one place the nervousness was bouncing from one to another and, amplified, rebroadcasting itself to everyone. It meant that even ordinary people who thought that a rune was a dried plum were beginning to feel a deep, existential worry, the kind that causes you to snap at your kids and want a drink.

Nanny peered through a gap between a couple of stalls. The pink figure was still sitting patiently, and a little crestfallen, behind the barrel. There was, as it were, a huge queue of no one at all.

Then Nanny scuttled from the cover of one tent to another until she could see the produce stand. It had already been doing a busy trade but there, forlorn in the middle of the cloth, was the pile of terrible cakes. And the jar of jam. Some wag had chalked up a sign beside it: 'Get Thee ſpoon out of thee Jar, 3 tries for A Penney!!!'

She thought she'd been careful to stay concealed, but she heard the straw rustle behind her. The committee had tracked her down.

'That's your handwriting, isn't it, Mrs Earwig?' she said. 'That's cruel. That ain't . . . nice.'

'We've decided you're to go and talk to Miss Weatherwax,' said Letice. 'She's got to stop it.'

'Stop what?'

'She's doing something to people's heads! She's come here to put the 'fluence on us, right? Everyone knows she does head magic. We can all feel it! She's spoiling it for everyone!'

'She's only sitting there,' said Nanny.

'Ah, *yes*, but *how* is she sitting there, may we ask?'

Nanny peered around the stall again.

'Well . . . like normal. You know . . . bent in the middle and the knees . . .'

Letice waved a finger sternly.

'Now you listen to me, Gytha Ogg –'

'If you want her to go away, you go and tell her!' snapped Nanny. 'I'm fed up with –'

There was the piercing scream of a child.

The witches stared at one another, and then ran across the field to the Lucky Dip.

A small boy was writhing on the ground, sobbing.

It was Pewsey, Nanny's youngest grandchild.

Her stomach turned to ice. She snatched him up, and glared into Granny's face.

'What have you done to him, you –' she began.

'Don't*wanna*dolly! Don't*wanna*dolly! Wanna*soljer*! Wanna-wannawanna*SOLJER*!'

Now Nanny looked down at the rag doll in Pewsey's sticky hand, and the expression of affronted tearful rage on such of his face as could be seen around his screaming mouth –

'Oi*wannawannaSOLJER!*'

– and then at the other witches, and at Granny Weatherwax's face, and felt the horrible cold shame welling up from her boots.

'I said he could put it back and have another go,' said Granny meekly. 'But he just wouldn't listen.'

'– *wannawannaSOL* –'

'Pewsey Ogg, if you don't shut up right this minute Nanny will –' Nanny Ogg began, and dredged up the nastiest punishment she could think of, 'Nanny won't give you a sweetie ever again!'

Pewsey closed his mouth, stunned into silence by this unimaginable threat. Then, to Nanny's horror, Letice Earwig drew herself up and said, 'Miss Weatherwax, we would prefer it if you left.'

'Am I being a bother?' said Granny. 'I hope I'm not being a bother. I don't *want* to be a bother. He just took a lucky dip and –'

'You're . . . upsetting people.'

Any minute now, Nanny thought. Any minute now she's going to raise her head and narrow her eyes and if Letice doesn't take two steps backwards she'll be a lot tougher than me.

'I can't stay and watch?' Granny said quietly.

'I know your game,' said Letice. 'You're planning to spoil it, aren't you? You can't stand the thought of being beaten, so you're intending something nasty.'

Three steps back, Nanny thought. Else there won't be anything left but bones. Any minute now . . .

'Oh, I wouldn't like anyone to think I was spoiling anything,' said Granny. She sighed, and stood up. 'I'll be off home . . .'

'No you won't!' snapped Nanny Ogg, pushing her back down on to the chair. 'What do *you* think of this, Beryl Dismass? And you, Letty Parkin?'

'They're all –' Letice began.

'I weren't talking to you!'

The witches behind Mrs Earwig avoided Nanny's gaze.

'Well, it's not that . . . I mean, we don't think . . .' began Beryl awkwardly. 'That is . . . I've always had a lot of respect for . . . but . . . well, it *is* for everyone . . .'

Her voice trailed off. Letice looked triumphant.

'Really? I think we *had* better be going after all, then,' said Nanny sourly. 'I don't like the comp'ny in these parts.' She looked around. 'Agnes? You give me a hand to get Granny home . . .'

'I really don't need . . .' Granny began, but the other two each took an arm and gently propelled her through the crowd, which parted to let them through and turned to watch them go.

'Probably the best for all concerned, in the circumstances,' said Letice. Several of the witches tried not to look at her face.

There were scraps of material all over the floor in Granny's kitchen, and gouts of congealed jam had dripped off the edge of the table and formed an immovable mound on the floor. The jam saucepan had been left in the stone sink to soak, although it was clear that the iron would rust away before the jam ever softened.

There was a row of empty pickle jars as well.

Granny sat down and folded her hands in her lap.

'Want a cup of tea, Esme?' said Nanny Ogg.

'No, dear, thank you. You get on back to the Trials. Don't you worry about me.'

'You sure?'

'I'll just sit here quiet. Don't you worry.'

'I'm not going back!' Agnes hissed, as they left. 'I don't like the way Letice smiles . . .'

'You once told me you didn't like the way Esme *frowns*,' said Nanny.

'Yes, but you can trust a frown. Er . . . you don't think she's losing it, do you?'

'No one'll be able to find it if she has,' said Nanny. 'No, you come on back with me. I'm *sure* she's planning . . . something.' I wish the hell I knew what it is, she thought. I'm not sure I can take any more waiting.

She could feel the mounting tension before they reached the field. Of course, there was *always* tension, that was part of the Trials, but this kind had a sour, unpleasant taste. The sideshows were still going on but ordinary folk were leaving, spooked by sensations they couldn't put their finger on which nevertheless had them under their thumb. As for the witches themselves, they had that look worn by actors about two minutes from the end of a horror movie, when they know the monster is about to make its final leap and now it's only a matter of which door.

Letice was surrounded by witches. Nanny could hear raised

voices. She nudged another witch, who was watching gloomily.

'What's happening, Winnie?'

'Oh, Reena Trump made a pig's ear of her piece and her friends say she ought to have another go because she was so nervous.'

'That's a shame.'

'And Virago Johnson ran off 'cos her weather spell went wrong.'

'Left under a bit of a cloud, did she?'

'And I was all thumbs when I had a go. You could be in with a chance, Gytha.'

'Oh, I've never been one for prizes, Winnie, you know me. It's the fun of taking part that counts.'

The other witch gave her a skewed look.

'You almost made that sound believable,' she said.

Gammer Beavis hurried over. 'On you go, Gytha', she said. 'Do your best, eh? The only contender so far is Mrs Weavitt and her whistling frog, and it wasn't as if it could even carry a tune. Poor thing was a bundle of nerves.'

Nanny Ogg shrugged, and walked out into the roped-off area. Somewhere in the distance someone was having hysterics, punctuated by an occasional worried whistle.

Unlike the magic of wizards, the magic of witches did not usually involve the application of much raw power. The difference is between hammers and levers. Witches generally tried to find the small point where a little changes made a lot of result. To make an avalanche you can either shake the mountain, or maybe you can just find exactly the right place to drop a snowflake.

This year Nanny had been idly working on the Man of Straw. It was an ideal trick for her. It got a laugh, it was a bit suggestive, it was a lot easier than it looked but showed she was joining in, and it was unlikely to win.

Damn! She'd been relying on that frog to beat her. She'd heard it whistling quite beautifully on the summer evenings.

She concentrated.

Pieces of straw rustled through the stubble. All she had to

do was use the little bits of wind that drifted across the field, allowed to move *here* and *here*, spiral up and –

She tried to stop her hands from shaking. She'd done this a hundred times, she could tie the damn stuff in *knots* by now. She kept seeing the face of Esme Weatherwax, and the way she'd just sat there, looking puzzled and hurt, while for a few seconds Nanny had been ready to kill –

For a moment she managed to get the legs right, and a suggestion of arms and head. There was a smattering of applause from the watchers. Then an errant eddy caught the thing before she could concentrate on its first step, and it spun down, just a lot of useless straw.

She made some frantic gestures to get it to rise again. It flopped about, tangled itself, and lay still.

There was a bit more applause, nervous and sporadic.

'Sorry . . . don't seem to be able to get the hang of it today,' she muttered, walking off the field.

The judges went into a huddle.

'I reckon that frog did *really well*,' said Nanny, more loudly than was necessary.

The wind, so contrary a little while ago, blew sharper now. What might be called the psychic darkness of the event was being enhanced by real twilight.

The shadow of the bonfire loomed on the far side of the field. No one as yet had the heart to light it. Almost all the non-witches had gone home. Anything good about the day had long drained away.

The circle of judges broke up and Mrs Earwig advanced on the nervous crowd, her smile only slightly waxen at the corners.

'Well, *what* a difficult decision it has been,' she said brightly. 'But what a marvellous turnout, too! It really *has* been a *most* tricky choice –'

Between me and a frog that lost its whistle and got its foot stuck in its banjo, thought Nanny. She looked sidelong at the faces of her sister witches. She'd known some of them for sixty years. If she'd ever read books, she'd have been able to read the faces just like one.

'We all know who won, Mrs Earwig,' she said, interrupting the flow.

'What *do* you mean, Mrs Ogg?'

'There's not a witch here who could get her mind right today,' said Nanny. 'And most of 'em have bought lucky charms, too. Witches? Buying lucky charms?' Several women stared at the ground.

'I don't know why everyone seems so afraid of Miss Weatherwax! I certainly am not! You think she's put a spell on you, then?'

'A pretty sharp one, by the feel of it,' said Nanny. 'Look, Mrs Earwig, no one's won, not with the stuff we've managed today. We all know it. So let's just all go home, eh?'

'Certainly not! I paid ten dollars for this cup and I mean to present it –'

The dying leaves shivered on the trees.

The witches drew together.

Branches rattled.

'It's the *wind*,' said Nanny Ogg. 'That's all . . .'

And then Granny was simply *there*. It was as if they'd just not noticed that she'd been there all the time. She had the knack of fading out of the foreground.

'I jus' thought I'd come to see who won,' she said. 'Join in the applause, and so on . . .'

Letice advanced on her, wild with rage.

'Have you been getting into people's heads?' she shrieked.

'An' how could I do that, Mrs Earwig?' said Granny meekly. 'Past all them lucky charms?'

'You're lying!'

Nanny Ogg heard the indrawn breaths, and hers was loudest. Witches lived by their words.

'I don't lie, Mrs Earwig.'

'Do you *deny* that you set out to ruin my day?'

Some of the witches at the edge of the crowd started to back away.

'I'll grant my jam ain't to everyone's taste but I never –' Granny began, in a modest little tone.

'You've been putting a 'fluence on everyone!'

'I just set out to help, you can ask anyone –'

'You did! Admit it!' Mrs Earwig's voice was as shrill as a gull.

'– and I certainly didn't do any –'

Granny's head turned as the slap came.

For the moment no one breathed, no one moved.

She lifted a hand slowly and rubbed her cheek.

'You know you could have done it easily!'

It seemed to Nanny that Letice's scream echoed off the mountains.

The cup dropped from her hands and crunched on the stubble.

Then the tableau unfroze. A couple of her sister witches stepped forward, put their hands on Letice's shoulders and she was pulled, gently and unprotesting, away . . .

Everyone else waited to see what Granny Weatherwax would do. She raised her head.

'I hope Mrs Earwig is all right,' she said. 'She seemed a bit . . . distraught.'

There was silence. Nanny picked up the abandoned cup and tapped it with a forefinger.

'Hmm,' she said. 'Just plated, I reckon. If she paid ten dollars for it, the poor woman was robbed.' She tossed it to Gammer Beavis, who fumbled it out of the air. 'Can you give it back to her tomorrow, Gammer?'

Gammer nodded, trying not to catch Granny's eye.

'Still, we don't have to let it spoil everything,' Granny said pleasantly. 'Let's have the proper ending to the day, eh? Traditional, like. Roast potatoes and marshmallows and old stories round the fire. And forgiveness. And let's let bygones be bygones.'

Nanny could feel the sudden relief spreading out like a fan. The witches seemed to come alive, at the breaking of the spell that had never actually been there in the first place. There was a general straightening up and the beginnings of a bustle as they headed for the saddlebags on their broomsticks.

'Mr Hopcroft gave me a whole sack of spuds,' said Nanny, as

conversation rose around them. 'I'll go and drag 'em over. Can you get the fire lit, Esme?'

A sudden change in the air made her look up. Granny's eyes gleamed in the dusk.

Nanny knew enough to fling herself to the ground.

Granny Weatherwax's hand curved through the air like a comet and the spark flew out, crackling.

The bonfire exploded. A blue-white flame shot up through the stacked branches and danced into the sky, etching shadows on the forest. It blew off hats and overturned tables and formed figures and castles and scenes from famous battles and joined hands and danced in a ring. It left a purple image on the eye that burned into the brain –

And settled down, and was just a bonfire.

'I never said nothin' about *forgettin'*,' said Granny.

When Granny Weatherwax and Nanny Ogg walked home through the dawn, their boots kicked up the mist. It had, on the whole, been a good night.

After some while, Nanny said: 'That wasn't nice, what you done.'

'I done nothin'.'

'Yeah, well . . . it wasn't nice, what you didn't do. It was like pullin' away someone's chair when they're expecting to sit down.'

'People who don't look where they're sitting should stay stood up,' said Granny.

There was a brief pattering on the leaves, one of those very brief showers you get when a few raindrops don't want to bond with the group.

'Well, all right,' Nanny conceded. 'But it was a little bit cruel.'

'Right,' said Granny.

'And some people might think it was a little bit nasty.'

'Right.'

Nanny shivered. The thoughts that'd gone through her head in those few seconds after Pewsey had screamed –

'I gave you no cause,' said Granny. 'I put *nothin'* in anyone's head that weren't there already.'

'Sorry, Esme.'

'Right.'

'But . . . Letice didn't *mean* to be cruel, Esme. I mean, she's spiteful and bossy and silly, but –'

'You've known me since we was girls, right?' Granny interrupted. 'Through thick and thin, good and bad?'

'Yes, of course, but –'

'And you never sank to sayin' "I'm telling you this as a friend", did you?'

Nanny shook her head. It was a telling point. No one even remotely friendly would say a thing like that.

'What's empowerin' about witchcraft anyway?' said Granny. 'It's a daft sort of a word.'

'Search me,' said Nanny. 'I *did* start out in witchcraft to get boys, to tell you the truth.'

'Think I don't know that?'

'What did you start out to get, Esme?'

Granny stopped, and looked up at the frosty sky and then down at the ground.

'Dunno,' she said, at last. 'Even, I suppose.'

And that, Nanny thought, was that.

Deer bounded away as they arrived at Granny's cottage.

There was a stack of firewood piled up neatly by the back door, and a couple of sacks on the doorstep. One contained a large cheese.

'Looks like Mr Hopcroft and Mr Poorchick have been here,' said Nanny.

'Hmph.' Granny looked at the carefully yet badly written piece of paper attached to the second sack: '"Dear Misftresf Weatherwax, I would be moft grateful if you would let me name thif new championfhip Variety Efme Weatherwax. Yours in hopefully good health, Percy Hopcroft. "Well, well, *well*. I wonder what gave him that idea?'

'Can't imagine,' said Nanny.

'I would just bet you can't,' said Granny.

She sniffed suspiciously, tugged at the sack's string, and pulled out an Esme Weatherwax.

It was rounded, very slightly flattened, and pointy at one end. It was an onion.

Nanny Ogg swallowed. 'I *told* him not –'

'I'm sorry?'

'Oh . . . nothing . . .'

Granny Weatherwax turned the onion round and round, while the world, via the medium of Nanny Ogg, awaited its fate. Then she seemed to reach a decision she was comfortable with.

'A very useful vegetable, the onion,' she said, at last. 'Firm. Sharp.'

'Good for the system,' said Nanny.

'Keeps well. Adds flavour.'

'Hot and spicy,' said Nanny, losing track of the metaphor in the flood of relief. 'Nice with cheese –'

'We don't need to go that far,' said Granny Weatherwax, putting it carefully back in the sack. She sounded almost amicable. 'You comin' in for a cup of tea, Gytha?'

'Er . . . I'd better be getting along –'

'Fair enough.'

Granny started to close the door, and then stopped and opened it again. Nanny could see one blue eye watching her through the crack.

'I was *right* though, wasn't I,' said Granny. It wasn't a question.

Nanny nodded.

'Right,' she said.

'That's nice.'

Pern

ANNE McCAFFREY

PERN

ANNE McCAFFREY

Dragonriders of Pern trilogy:

Dragonflight (1969)
Dragonquest (1971)
The White Dragon (1978)

Harper Hall trilogy:

Dragonsong (1976)
Dragonsinger (1977)
Dragondrums (1978)

Other Pern novels:

Moreta, Dragonlady of Pern (1983)
Nerilka's Story (1986)
Dragonsdawn (1988)
The Renegades of Pern (1989)
All the Weyrs of Pern (1991)
The Chronicles of Pern (1992)
The Dolphins of Pern (1994)
Dragonseye (1996)
The Masterharper of Pern (1998)

Dissatisfied with life on technologically-advanced Earth, hundreds of colonists travelled through space to the star Rukbat, which held six planets in orbit around it, five in stable trajectories, and one that looped wildly around the others. The third planet was capable of sustaining life, and the spacefarers settled there, naming it Pern. They cannibalized their spaceships for matérial and began building their homes.

Pern was ideal for settlement, except for one thing. At irregular intervals, the sixth planet of its system would swing close to it and release swarms of deadly mycorrhizoid spores, which devoured anything they touched and rendered the ground where they landed barren for years. The colonists immediately began searching for a way to combat the Thread, as the spores were named. For defence, they turned to the dragonets, small flying lizards that the colonists had tamed when they first landed. The fire-breathing ability of these reptiles had been a great help in the first Threadfall. By genetically enhancing and selectively breeding these reptiles through the generations, the colonists created a race of full-sized dragons.

With the dragons and their riders working together, the Pern colonists were able to fight Thread effectively and establish a firm hold on the planet. They settled into a quasi-feudal agricultural society, building Holds for the administrators and field workers, Halls for the craftsmen, and Weyrs for the dragons and riders to inhabit.

Many of the Pern novels detail the politics of the Holds and Weyrs between Threadfalls. The entire line of books spans over 2,500 years, from the first landing of the settlers to their descendants' discovery of the master ship's computer centuries later.

Dragonflight, the first of the Dragonriders of Pern books, tells of a time 2500 years after the initial landing. The Thread has not been seen in four centuries, and people are starting to be sceptical of the old warnings. Three dragonriders, Lessa, F'lar, and F'nor, believe that the Thread is coming back, and try to mobilize the planetary defences. Lessa, knowing that there are not enough dragons to combat the Thread effectively, time-travels back four hundred years to a point just after the last Threadfall, when that era's Dragonriders are growing restless and bored from lack of activity. Lessa convinces most of them to come back with her to combat Thread in her time. They arrive and fight off the Thread.

Dragonquest, the second book, picks up seven years after the end of the first book. Relations between the Oldtimers, as the time-travelling dragonriders are called, and the current generation are growing tense. After getting into a fight with one of the old dragonriders, F'nor is sent to Pern's southern continent to recover from his wound. There he discovers a grub that neutralizes the Thread after it burrows into the ground. Realizing they have discovered a powerful new weapon against Thread, F'nor begins planning to seed the grubs over both continents.

Meanwhile, an unexpected Threadfall is the catalyst for a duel between F'lar, the Benden Weyrleader, and T'ron, the leader of the Oldtimers. F'lar wins and banishes all dragonriders who will not accept his role as overall Weyrleader. The banished go to the southern continent. The book ends with the grubs being bred for distribution over Pern.

The third book, *The White Dragon*, chronicles the trials of young Jaxom as he raises the only white dragon on Pern, a genetic anomaly. Jaxom encounters prejudice and scorn from other dragonriders because his dragon is smaller than the rest. He is also scheduled to take command of one of the oldest Holds on Pern, and there are those who doubt his ability to govern. Both Jaxom and his dragon Ruth rise to the challenges and succeed in proving that bigger is not necessarily better. Jaxom commands his Hold, gets the girl, and all is set right with the world.

The Harper Hall trilogy (*Dragonsong, Dragonsinger, Dragondrums*) is aimed at young readers, and deals with a girl named Menolly and her rise from unappreciated daughter to Journeywoman Harper and keeper of fire-lizards.

In many subsequent novels, and in the short novel published here, McCaffrey has examined various other aspects of life on Pern from the earliest days of its colonization by humans.

◆

Runner of Pern

BY ANNE McCAFFREY

Tenna topped the rise and paused to catch her breath, leaning forward, hands on her knees to ease her back muscles. Then, as she had been taught, she walked along the top on what flat space there was, kicking out her legs and shaking the thigh muscles, breathing through her mouth until she stopped panting. Taking her water bottle from her belt, she allowed herself a swig, swishing it around in her mouth to moisturize the dry tissues. She spat out that mouthful and took another, letting this one slowly trickle down her throat. The night was cool enough to keep her from sweating too heavily. But she wouldn't be standing around long enough to get a chill.

It didn't take long for her breath to return to normal and she was pleased by that. She was in good shape. She kicked out her legs to ease the strain she had put on them to make the height. Then, settling her belt and checking the message pouch, she started down the hill at a rapid walking pace. It was too dark – Belior had not yet risen above the plain to give her full light for the down side of the hill – to be safe to run in shadows. She only knew this part of the trace by word of mouth, not actually footing it. She'd done well so far this, her second Turn of running, and had made most of her first Cross by the suggested easy laps. Runners watched out for each other and no station manager would overtax a novice. With any luck, she'd've made it all the way to the Western Sea in the next sevenday. This was the first big test of her apprenticeship as an express runner. And really she'd only the Western Range left to cross once she got to Fort Hold.

Halfway down from the top of the rise, she met the ridge crest she'd been told about and, with the usual check of the pouch she carried, she picked up her knees and started the ground-eating lope that was the pride of a Pernese runner.

Of course, the legendary 'lopers' – the ones who had been able to do a hundred miles in a day – had perished ages ago but their memory was kept alive. Their endurance and dedication were examples to everyone who ran the traces of Pern. There hadn't been many of them, according to the legend, but they had started the runner stations when the need for the rapid delivery of messages occurred, during the First Fall of Thread. Lopers had been able to put themselves in some sort of trance which allowed them not only to run extended distances but kept them warm during snowstorms and freezing temperatures. They had also planted the original traces which now were a network crisscrossing the entire continent.

While Lord Holders and CraftMasters could afford to keep runnerbeasts for their couriers, the average person, wanting to contact crafthalls, relatives, or friends across Pern, could easily afford to express a letter across the continent in runner pouches, carried from station to station. Others might call them 'holds' but runners had always had 'stations' and station agents, as part of *their* craft history. Drum messages were great for short messages, if the weather was right and the winds didn't interrupt the beat, but as long as folks wanted to send a written message, there'd be runners to take them.

Tenna often thought proudly of the tradition she was carrying on. It was a comfort on long solitary journeys. Right now, the running was good: the ground was firm but springy, a surface that had been assiduously maintained since the ancient runners had planted it. Not only did the mossy stuff make running easier but it identified a runner's path. A runner would instantly feel the difference in the surface, if he, or she, strayed off the trace.

Slowly, as full Belior rose behind her, her way became illuminated by the moon's light and she picked up her pace, running easily, breathing freely, her hands carried high, chest height, with elbows tucked in. No need to leave a 'handle', as her father called it, to catch the wind and slow the pace. At times like these, with good footing, a fair light, and a cool evening, you felt like you could run for ever. If there weren't a sea to stop you.

She ran on, able to see the flow of the ridge and, by the time the trace started to descend again, Belior was high enough to light her way. She saw the stream ahead and slowed cautiously – though she'd been told that the ford had a good pebbly surface – and splashed through the ankle-high cold water, up on to the bank, veering slightly south, picking up the trace again by its springy surface.

She'd be over halfway now to Fort Hold and should make it by dawn. This was a well-travelled route, southwest along the coast to the farther Holds. All of what she carried right now was destined for Fort Holders, so it was the end of the line for both the pouch and herself. She'd heard so much about the facilities at Fort that she didn't quite believe them. Runners tended to understatement, rather than exaggeration. If a runner told you a trace was dangerous, you believed it! But what they said about Fort was truly amazing.

Tenna came from a running family: father, uncles, cousins, grandfathers, brothers, sisters and two aunts were all out and about the traces that crisscrossed Pern from Nerat Tip to High Reaches Hook, from Benden to Boll.

'It's bred in us,' her mother had said, answering the queries of her younger children. Cesila managed a large runner station, just at the northern Lemos end of the Keroon plains where the immense sky-broom trees began. Strange trees that flourished only in that region of Pern. Trees, which a much younger Tenna had been sure, were where the Benden Weyr dragons took a rest in their flights across the continent. Cesila had laughed at Tenna's notion.

'The Dragons of Pern don't need to rest anywhere, dear. They just go *between* to wherever they need to go. You probably saw some of them out hunting their weekly meal.'

In her running days, Cesila had completed nine full Crosses a Turn until she'd married another runner and started producing her own bag of runners-to-be.

'Lean we are in the breeding, and leggy, most of us, with big lungs and strong bones. Ah, there now, a few come out who're more for speed than distance but they're handy enough at Gathers, passing the winning line before the others have left the starting ribbon. We have our place on the world same as holders and even weyrfolk. Each to his, or her, own. Weaver and tanner, and farmer, and fisher, and smith and runner and all.'

'That's not the way we was taught to sing the Duty Song,' Tenna's younger brother had remarked.

'Maybe,' Cesila had said with a grin, 'but it's the way I sing it and you can, too. I must have a word with the next harper through here. He can change his words if he wants us to take his messages.' And she gave her head one of her emphatic shakes to end that conversation.

As soon as a runner-bred child had reached full growth, he or she was tested to see if they'd the right Blood for the job. Tenna's legs had stopped growing by the time she'd reached her fifteenth full Turn. That was when she was assessed by a senior runner of another Bloodline. Tenna had been very nervous but her mother, in her usual off-handed way, had given her lanky daughter a long knowing look.

'Nine children I've given your father, Fedri, and four are already runners. You'll be one, too, never fear.'

'But Sedra's –'

Cesila held up her hand. 'I know your sister's mated and breeding but she did two Crosses before she found a man she had to have. So she counts, too. Gotta have proper Bloodlines to breed proper runners and it's us who do that.' Cesila paused to be sure Tenna would not interrupt again. 'I came from a hold with twelve, all of them runners. And all breeding runners. You'll run, girl. Put your mind at ease. You'll run.' Then she'd laughed. 'It's for how long, not will you, for a female.'

Tenna had decided a long time ago – when she had first been considered old enough to mind her younger siblings – that she'd prefer running to raising runners. She'd run until she could no longer lift her knees. She'd an aunt who'd never mated: ran until she was older than Cesila was now and then took over the management of a connecting station down Igen way. Should something happen and she couldn't run any more, Tenna wouldn't mind managing a station. Her mother ran hers proper, always had hot water ready to ease a runner's aching limbs: good food, comfortable beds, and healing skills that rivalled what you could find in any hold. And it was always exciting, for you never knew who might run in that day, or where they'd be going. Runners crossed the continent regularly, bringing with them news from other parts of Pern. Many had interesting tales to tell of problems on the trace and how to cope with them. You heard of all other holds and halls, and the one dragonweyr, as well as what interested runners most specifically: what conditions were like and where traces might need maintenance after a heavy rain or landslide.

She was mightily relieved, however, when her father said he had asked Mallum of the Telgar station to do her assessment. At least Tenna had met the man on those occasions when he'd been through to their place on the edge of Keroon's plains. Like other runners, he was a lanky length of man, with a long face and greying hair that he tied back with his sweatband as most runners did.

Her parents didn't tell her when Mallum was expected, but he turned up one bright morning, handing in a pouch to be logged on the board by the door and then limping to the nearest seat.

'Bruised the heel. We'll have to rock that south trace again. I swear it grows new ones every Turn or two,' he said, mopping his forehead with his orange sweatband and thanking Tenna for the cup of water. 'Cesila, got some of that sheer magic poultice of yours?'

'I do. Put the kettle to heat the moment I saw you struggling up the trace.'

'Was not struggling,' Mallum said in jovial denial. 'Was careful not to put the heel down was all.'

'Don't try to fool me, you spavined gimper,' Cesila replied as she was dipping a poultice sack into the heated water, testing it with a finger.

'Who's to run on? Some orders in that need to be got south smartly.'

'I'm taking it on,' Fedri said, coming out of his room and tying on his sweatband. 'How urgent?' His runner's belt was draped over his shoulder. 'I've others to add from the morning's eastern run.'

'Hmmm. They want to make the Igen Gather.'

'Ha! It'll be there betimes,' Fedri said, reaching for the pouch and carefully adding the other messages to it before he put it through the belt loops. Settling it in the small of his back with one hand, he chalked up the exchange time with the other. 'See you.'

Then he was out the door and turning south, settling into his long-distance stride almost as soon as his foot hit the moss of the trace.

Tenna, knowing what was needed, had already pulled a footstool over to Mallum. She looked up at him for permission and, with his nod, unlaced the right shoe, feeling the fine quality of the leather. Mallum made his own footwear and he had set the stitching fine and tight.

Cesila knelt beside her daughter, craning her head to see the bruise.

'Hmmm. Hit it early on, didn't cha?'

'I did,' Mallum said, drawing his breath in with a hiss as Cesila slapped the poultice on. 'Oooooh! Shards . . . you didn't get it too hot, didja?'

Cesila sniffed denial in reply as she neatly and deftly tied the packet to his foot.

'And is this the lass of yours as is to be taken for a run?' he asked, relaxing his expression from the grimace he'd made when the poultice was first applied. 'Prettiest of the bunch.' And he grinned at Tenna.

'Handsome is as handsome does,' Cesila said. 'Looks is all right but long legs is better. Tenna's her name.'

'Handsome's not a bad thing to be, Cesila, and it's obvious your daughter takes after you.'

Cesila sniffed again but Tenna could see that her mother

didn't mind Mallum's remarks. And Cesila was a handsome woman: lithe still and slender, with graceful hands and feet. Tenna wished she were more like her mother.

'Nice long line of leg,' Mallum went on approvingly. He beckoned for Tenna to come closer and had a good look at the lean muscles, then asked to see her bare feet. Runners tended to walk bare-footed a lot. Some even ran bare-footed. 'Good bone. Hmmm. Nice lean frame. Hmm. Not a pick on you, girl. Hope you can keep warm enough in winter like that.' That was such an old runner comment, but his jollity was encouraging and Tenna was ever so glad that Mallum was her assessor. He was always pleasant on his short stops at Station 97. 'We'll take a short one tomorrow when this foot's eased.'

More runners came in so Cesila and Tenna were busy, checking in messages, sorting the packets for the change-overs, serving food, heating water for baths, tending scratched legs. It was spring of the year and most runners only used leggings during the coldest months.

Enough stayed the night so there was good chatter and gossip to entertain. And prevent Tenna from worrying about satisfying her assessor in the morning.

A runner had come in late that night, on her way north, with some messages to be transferred to an eastern route. His heel bruise much eased, Mallum thought he could take those on.

'It's a good testing trot,' he said and gestured for Tenna to slip the message pouch on her belt. 'I'll travel light, girl.' His grin was teasing, for the pouch weighed little more than the wherhide it was made from. 'First, lemme see what you wear on your feet.'

She showed him her shoes, the most important part of a runner's gear. She'd used her family's special oils to soften the wherhide and then formed it on the lasts that had been carved for her feet by her uncle who did them for her Bloodline. Her stitches were neat but not as fine as Mallum's. She intended to improve. Meanwhile, this pair wasn't a bad effort and fitted her feet like gloves. The spikes were medium length as fit for the present dry trace conditions. Most long-distance runners carried an extra pair with shorter spikes for harder ground, especially during spring and summer. She was working on her winter footwear, hoping she'd need it, for those boots came up to mid-calf and required a lot more conditioning. Even they were lighter weight than the footgear holders would use. But then most holders plodded and the thicker leather was suitable for their tasks as fine soft hide was right for a runner's foot.

Mallum nodded in approval as he handed back her shoes. Now he checked the fit of her belt to be sure it was snug enough not to rub against the small of her back as she ran: that her short trunks would not pull against her legs and that her sleeveless top covered her backside well below her waist to help prevent her getting a kidney chill. Stopping often from a need to relieve one's self ruined the rhythm of a run.

'We'll go now,' Mallum said, having assured himself she was properly accoutred.

Cesila stood in the door, gave her daughter a reassuring nod, and saw them off, up the eastern trace. Before they were out of sight, she gave the particular runner yodel that stopped them in their tracks. They saw her pointing skyward: at the arrow formation of dragons in the sky, a most unusual sight these days when the Dragons of Benden Weyr were so rarely seen.

To see dragons in the sky was the best sort of omen. They were there . . . and then they weren't! She smiled. Too bad runners couldn't just *think* themselves to their destinations the way dragons could. As if he had shared her thought, Mallum grinned back at her and then turned to face the direction in which they were headed and any nervousness Tenna had felt disappeared. When he sprang off again, she was in step with him by the third stride. He nodded again approvingly.

'Running's not just picking up your heels and showing them to those behind you,' Mallum said, his eyes watching the trace ahead, though he must have known it as well as Tenna did. 'A good bit of proper running is learning to pace yourself and your stride. It's knowing the surfaces of the traces you have to traverse. It's knowing how to save your strength so you'll last the longer hauls. When to ease back to a walk, when and how to drink and eat so's you're not too gutty to run right. It's learning the routes of the various Crosses and what sort of weather you might have to run through . . . and learning to manoeuvre on snowrunners on the northern Crosses. And, most important, when to take cover and just let the weather have its way with the world and you safe out of it. So's the messages and the packets you carry will get through as soon as possible.'

She had responded with a nod of appreciation. Not that she hadn't heard the same lecture time and again in the station from every relative and runner. But this time it was for her benefit and she owed Mallum the courtesy of listening closely. She did watch Mallum's stride though, to be sure his heel wasn't bothering him. He caught her glance once and gave her a grin.

'Be sure you carry a wedge of that poultice on any long laps, girl. You never know, you know, when you might need it. As I just did.' And he grimaced, reminding Tenna that even the best runner can put a foot wrong.

While no runner carries much, the long-tailed orange sweat-band runners invariably wore could be used to strap a strain or sprain. An oiled packet, no larger than the palm of a hand, had a cloth soaked in numbweed which both cleansed and eased the scratches one can acquire from time to time. Simple remedies for the most common problems. A wedge of poultice could be added to such travel gear and be well worth its weight.

Tenna had no trouble making that lap with Mallum even when he picked up the pace on the flat section.

'Running with a pretty girl's not hard to do,' he told her when they took one brief pause.

She wished he didn't make so much of her looks. They wouldn't help her run any better and that's what she wanted to be: a top runner.

By the time they reached Irma's station at midday, she was not even breathing very hard. But the moment Mallum slowed, he limped slightly with his full weight on the heel.

'Hmm. Well, I can wait out the day here with more poultice,' he said, pulling the little wedge from one of the pockets of his belt. 'See,' and he displayed it to Tenna, 'handy enough.'

She tapped her aid pocket and smiled.

Old Irma came out with a grin on her sun-dried face for them.

'Will she do, Mallum?' the old woman asked, handing each a cup.

'Oh, aye, she'll do. A credit to her Bloodline and not a bother to run with!' Mallum said with a twinkle in his eyes.

'I pass, do I, Mallum?' Tenna asked, needing to have a direct answer.

'Oh, aye,' and he laughed, walking about and shaking his legs to get the kinks out even as she was doing. 'No fear on that. Any hot water for m'poultice, Irm?'

'Coming up,' and she ducked back into her station and came out with a bowl of steaming water which she set down on the long bench that was an inevitable fixture of every station. The overhang of the roof provided a shelter from sun and rain. Most runners were obsessed with watching the traces to see who was coming and going. The long bench, its surface smoothed by generations of bums sliding across it, was placed so that it commanded a good view of the four traces linking at Irma's.

Automatically, Tenna pulled a footstool from under the bench and held out her hand to receive Mallum's right foot. She untied the shoe, placed the now moistened poultice on the bruise while Irma handed her a bandage to fix it in place, taking a good look at the injury in the process.

'Nother day'll do it. Shoulda stayed off it this mornin', too.'

'Not when I'd a chance to run with such a pretty girl,' Mallum said.

'Just like a man,' Irma said dismissively.

Tenna felt herself blushing, although she was beginning to believe he wasn't just teasing. No one else had ever commented on her looks.

'It wasn't a taxing leg, Irma. It's level most of the way and a good surface,' she said, grinning shyly at Mallum as she tried to divert Irma's criticism.

'Humph! Well, a hill run would've been downright foolish and it is flat this-a-way.'

'Anything for Tenna to take back?' Mallum asked, getting back to business, 'to make her first round trip as a runner?'

'Should be,' Irma said, winking at Tenna for this informal inclusion into the ranks of Pern Runner. 'You could eat now . . . soup's ready and so's the bread.'

'Wouldn't mind a bit myself,' Mallum said, carefully shifting his position as if easing the heat from the poultice, since the heat probably penetrated even the toughened sole of his foot.

By the time Tenna had eaten the light meal, two runners came in, a man she didn't know by sight on a long leg from Bitra with a pouch to go farther west and one of Irma's sons.

'I can run it to 97,' she said, the official designation of her family's station.

'That'll do,' the man said, panting and heaving from his long haul. 'That'll do fine.' He gasped for more breath. 'It's an urgent,' he got out. 'Your name?'

'Tenna.'

'One . . . of . . . Fedri's?' he asked and she nodded. 'That's good . . . enough for me. Ready to . . . hit the trace?'

'Sure,' and she held out her hand for the pouch that he slipped off his belt, pausing only to mark the pass-over time on the flap as he gave it into her keeping. 'You are?' she asked, sliding the pouch on to her own belt and settling it in the small of her back.

'Masso,' he said, reaching now for the cup of water Irma had hastened to bring him. He whooshed her off to the westward trace. With a final grateful farewell wave to Mallum, she picked up her heels as Mallum cheered her on with the traditional runner's 'yo-ho'.

She made it home in less time than it had taken her to reach Irma's and one of her brothers was there to take the pouch on the next westward lap. Silan nodded approval at the pass-over time, marked his own receipt and was off.

'So, girl, you're official,' her mother said and embraced her daughter. 'And no need to sweat it at all, was there?'

'Running's not always as easy,' her father said from the bench, 'but you made good time and that's a grand way to start. I hadn't expected you back before mid-afternoon.'

Tenna did the short legs all around Station 97 for the first summer and into that winter, building her stamina for longer runs and becoming known at all the connecting stations. She made her longest run to Greystones on the coast, just ahead of a very bad snowstorm. Then, because she was the only runner available in Station 18 when the exhausted carrier of an urgent message came in, she had to carry it two stations north. A fishing sloop would be delayed back to port until a new mast could be stepped. Since the vessel was overdue, there were those who'd be very glad to get the message she carried.

Such emergency news should have been drummed ahead but the high winds would tear such a message to nonsense. It was a tough run, with cold as well as wind and snow across a good bit of the low-lying trace. Pacing herself, she did take an hour's rest in one of the Thread shelters that dotted a trace. She made the distance in such good time in those conditions that she got extra stitches on her belt, marking her rise towards journeyman rank.

This run to Fort Hold would be two more stitches on her belt if she finished in good time. And she was sure she would . . . with the comforting sort of certainty which older runners said you began to sense when you'd been travelling the traces a while. She was also now accustomed to judging how long she had run by the feeling in her legs. None of the leaden feeling that accompanied real fatigue; she was still running easily. So long as she had no leg cramp, she knew she could continue effortlessly at this good pace until she reached Station 300 at Fort. Leg cramp was always a hazard and could strike you without warning. She was careful to renew the tablets a runner chewed to ease off a cramp but a bad one could bench a runner for weeks so she was careful to avoid them. And was not too slow about grabbing a handful of any useful herbs she spotted which helped prevent the trouble.

She oughtn't to be letting her mind wander like this, but

with an easy stride and a pleasant night in which to travel, it was hard to keep her mind on the job. She would, smartly enough, if there were complications like bad weather or poor light. This was also far too well travelled country for there to be dangers like tunnel snakes, which were about the worst risk that runners encountered: usually at dawn or dusk when the creatures were out hunting. Of course renegades, while not as common as tunnel snakes, were more dangerous, since they were human, not animal. Although that distinction was often moot. As runners rarely carried marks, they were not as likely to be waylaid as messengers on runnerbeasts or other solitary travellers. Tenna hadn't heard of any renegade attacks this far west but sometimes those people were so vicious that they might just pull up a runner for spite and malice. In the past three Turns, there had been two cases – and those up in northern Lemos and Bitra – where the runners had been hamstrung out of sheer malevolence.

Once in a while, in a bad winter, a flock of very hungry wherries might attack a runner in the open but the instances were rare enough. Snakes were the most likely danger encountered. Particularly mid-summer when there were newly-hatched clutches.

Her father had had injuries two summers back with such a hazard. He'd been amazed at how fast the adult tunnel snake could move when alarmed. Mostly they were torpid creatures, only hunger quickening them. But he'd stepped in the midst of an ill-placed nest and had had the hatchlings swarming up his legs, pricking the skin in innumerable places and even managing to get as high as his crotch. (Her mother had stifled a giggle and remarked that it had been more than her father's pride that had been wounded.) But he'd scars from claw and tooth that he could show.

Moon-lit nights like this one were a joy to run in, with the air cool enough to dry the sweat on her face and chest, the trace springy underfoot and clear ahead of her. And her thoughts could wander.

There would be a Gather shortly after she reached her destination: she knew she was carrying some orders for Crafts displaying at Fort Hold. Pouches were invariably fuller going to or coming from a Gather: orders from those unable to attend, wishing to contact a MasterCraftsman. Maybe, if she was lucky, she could stay over for the Gather. She hadn't been to one in a long while and she did want to find well-tanned leathers for a new pair of running shoes. She'd enough money to her credit to give a fair price for the right hides: she'd checked the books her mother kept of her laps. Most Halls were quite willing to take a runner station chit. She'd one in a belt pocket. If she found just the right skins, she'd a bit of leeway to bargain, above and beyond the surface value of the chit.

A Gather would be fun, too. She loved dancing, and was very good at the Toss dance, if she could find someone who could properly partner her in it. Fort was a good hold. And the music would be special, seeing as how the Harper Hall was right there in Fort. She ran on, tunes of harper melodies flitting through her mind even if she'd no breath to sing them.

She was running along a long curve now, around an upthrust of rock – most traces were straight as possible – and brought her mind back to her directions. Just around this curve, she should find a trace turning off to the right, inland, towards Fort. She must pay attention now so she wouldn't have to break stride and backtrack.

Suddenly she could feel vibrations through her feet, though she could see nothing around the vegetation banking the curve. Listening intently, she could now hear an odd phuff-phuff sound, coming closer, getting louder. The sound was just enough of a warning for her to move left, out of the centre of the trace, where she'd have just that much more of a glimpse of what was making the sound and the vibrations. This was a runner track, not a trail or road. No runner made those sounds, or hit the ground that hard to make vibrations. She saw the dark mass bearing down on her, and flung herself into the undergrowth as runnerbeast and rider came within a finger span of knocking into her. She could feel the wind of their passing and smell the sweat of the beast.

'STUPID!' she shouted after them, getting branches and leaves in her mouth as she fell, feeling needly gouges in the hands she had put out to break her fall. She spent the next minute struggling to her feet and spitting bitter leaves and twigs out of her mouth. They left behind an acrid, drying taste: sticklebush! She'd fallen into a patch of sticklebush. At this time of the Turn, there were no leaves yet to hide the hair-like thorns that coated twig and branch. A nuisance which balanced out their gift of succulent berries in the autumn.

Nor did the rider pull up, or even falter, when the least he could have done was return to be sure she hadn't been injured. Surely he'd seen her? Surely he'd heard her outraged shout? And what was *he* doing, using a runner's trace in the first place? There was a good road north for ordinary travellers.

'I'll get you!' she called, shaking her fist and stamping her feet with frustration.

She was shaking with reaction to such a near miss. Then she became uncomfortably aware of the scratches on hands, arms, legs, chest, and two on one cheek. Stamping with outrage and fury, she got the numbweed from her belt pocket and daubed at the cuts, hissing as the solution stung. But she didn't want the sap to get into her blood. Nor did she want the slivers to work in. She managed to pick the ones out of her hands, daubing the numbweed into those. She couldn't really see the extent of her injuries, some being down the back of her arm. She picked out what slivers she could and carefully pressed in the pad until all the moisture was gone from it. Even if she had avoided infection, she was likely to be teased about falling when she got to the station. Runners were supposed to keep on their feet and in balance. Not that a rider could be expected on the trace at this very early hour. Surely that would also help her find out who the rider had been, besides being bold enough to ride a runner's trace. And if she weren't around to give him a fat lip, maybe another runner would give the lesson in her place. Runners were not above complaining to Lord Holders or their stewards if someone abused their rights.

Having done as much as she could then, she stifled her anger: that didn't get the pouch to its destination. And she mustn't let her anger get the better of common sense. The brush with disaster, close as it was, had resulted in very minor problems, she told herself firmly. What were scratches! But she found it hard to regain her stride. She'd been going so smoothly, too, and so close to the end of this lap.

She could have been killed, smacking into a runnerbeast at the speeds they'd both been travelling. If she hadn't thought to move out of the centre of the trace – where she had every right to be, not him – if she hadn't felt the hoofbeats through her shoes and heard the animal's high breathing. Why, both sets of messages could have been delayed! Or lost.

Her legs felt tired and heavy and she had to concentrate hard to try to regain the rhythm. Reluctantly she realized that she was unlikely to and settled for conserving her energy.

Running into the end of night, the dawn behind her, was not as much a pleasure as it could have been and that annoyed Tenna even more. Just wait till she found out who that rider was! She'd tell him a thing or two. Though common sense told her that she was unlikely to encounter him. He was outbound and she was inbound. If he'd been in that much of a hurry, he might be a relay rider, bound for a distant location. Lord Holders could afford such services and the stabling of fast runnerbeasts along the way. But he shouldn't have been on a runner trace. There were roads for beasts! Hooves could tear up the surface of the trace and the station manager might have to spend hours replacing divots torn up by shod hooves. Traces were for runners. She kept returning to that indignant thought. She just hoped any other runner on the trace would hear him in time! That's one reason you keep your mind on your run, Tenna. Even if you'd no reason to suspect you weren't alone with the night and the moon on a runner trace.

The runner station was just below the main entrance to Fort Hold. History had it that Fort had started runners as short-distance messengers, hundreds and hundreds of Turns ago, even before drum-towers were built. Fort Hold had utilized the skills of runners for many tasks, especially during Threadfall when runners had accompanied all ground crews, vital as couriers in emergencies. The installation of the drum-towers and the development of runnerbeasts had not put an end to the need for the runners of Pern. This main connecting hold was the largest ever built just to house and care for runners. Three levels high, she'd been told, and several back into the Fort cliff. It also boasted one of the best bathing facilities on the continent: hot running water in deep tubs that had eased centuries of runner aches and pains. Cesila had highly recommended that Tenna try for Fort when she got that far west. And here she was and right ready to appreciate the accommodations.

She was very weary and not only out of pace but jarring herself with every step down the broader avenue that led to her destination. Her hands stung from the sap and she hoped she hadn't any slivers left in them. But hands were a long way from the feet.

Beastholders, up early to feed stock, gave her cheery waves and smiles and their courtesies somewhat restored her good humour. She did not care to arrive petulant as well as scratched, not on her first visit here.

Almost as if the manager had a special sensitivity to incoming runners, the double door was thrown open as she came to a rough, gasping halt, hand raised to catch the bell cord.

'Thought I heard someone coming.' The man, welcoming grin on his face, put out both hands to steady her. He was one of the oldest men she had ever seen: his skin a network of wrinkles and grooves, but his eyes were bright – for this hour – and he looked to be a merry man. 'New one, too, at that, for all you look familiar to me. A pretty face is a great sight on a fine morning.'

Sucking in breath enough to give her name, Tenna paced into the large entry room. She unbuckled her message pouch as she eased the tension in her leg muscles.

'Tenna passing 208 with eastern messages. Fort's the destination for all.'

'Welcome to 300, Tenna,' he said, taking the pouch from her and immediately chalking up her arrival on the heavy old board to the left of the station door. 'All for here, huh?' He passed her a cup before he opened the pouch, to check the recipients.

With cup in her hand, she went out again, still flicking her legs to ease the muscles. First she rinsed her mouth, spitting out that first mouthful on to the cobbles. Then she would sip to swallow. Nor was this just water but some sort of fresh-tasting drink that refreshed dry tissues.

'You're a mite the worse for the run,' the man said, standing in the door and pointing to the bloody smears on her bare skin. 'What'd you run into?'

'Sticklebush,' she said through gritted teeth. 'Runnerbeast run me off round the hill curve . . . galloping along a *runner* trace like he must know he shouldn't.' She was astonished at the anger in her voice when she'd meant to sound matter-of-fact.

'That'd be Haligon, more'n likely,' the station keeper said, nodding with a disapproving scowl. 'Saw him peltin' down to the beast hold an hour or so ago. I've warned him myself about using the traces but he says it cuts half an hour off a trip and he's conducting an ex-per-I-ment.'

'He might have killed me,' she said, her anger thoroughly fanned.

'You'd better tell him. Maybe a pretty runner'll get it through his thick skull because the odd crack or two hasn't.'

His reaction made Tenna feel that her anger was righteous. It's one thing to be angry on your own, another to have confirmation of your right to be angry. She felt redeemed. Though she couldn't see why being pretty would be an advantage if you were giving someone what-for. She could hit just as hard as the ugliest runner she'd ever met.

'You'll need a long soak with sticklebush slivers in you. You did have something to put on 'em right then, didn't you?' When she nodded, now annoyed because he implied that she might not have that much sense, he added, 'I'll send m'mate to look at those cuts. Wrong time of the Turn to fall into sticklebush, ya know.' And she nodded her head vigorously. 'All in all, you made a good time from 208,' he added, approvingly. 'Like that in a young runner. Shows you're not just a pretty face. Now, go up the stairs there, take your first right, go along the corridor, fourth door on the left. No one else's up. Towels on the shelves. Leave your clothes: they'll be washed and dry by evening. You'll want a good feed after a night run and then a good long sleep. We've all for you, runner.'

She thanked him, turned to the stairs and then tried to lift the wooden blocks her legs had become up the steps. Her toes dragged as she made her feet move and she was grateful for the carpeting which saved the wooden stairs from her spikes. But then this place was for runners, shoes, spikes and all.

'Fourth door,' she murmured to herself and pushed against a portal which opened into the most spacious bathing room she'd ever seen. And pungent with something pleasantly astringic. Nothing as grand as this even at Keroon Hold. Five tubs ranged along the back wall with curtains to separate them if one needed privacy. There were two massage tables, sturdy, padded, with shelves of oils and salves underneath. They would account for the nice smells. The room was hot and she began to sweat again, a sweat that made her nicks and scratches itch. There were changing cubicles, too, to the right of the door . . . and behind her she found over-sized towels in stacks higher than her head, and she wasn't short. There were other cubbies holding runner pants and shirts for all weathers and the thick anklets that cushioned and warmed weary feet. She took a towel, her fingers feeling the thick, soft nap. It was as big as a blanket.

In the cubicle nearest the tubs, she shucked off her garments, automatically folding them into a neat pile. Then, looping the towel over the hook set by the side of the tub for that purpose, she eased herself into the warm water. The tub was taller than she was and she let herself down to touch a floor, a full hand of water above her head when she did. Amazing!

This was sheer luxury. She wondered how often she could draw a run to Fort Hold. The water made her scratches sting but that was nothing to the comfort it was giving her tired muscles. Swishing around in the large square tub, her hand connected with a ledge, sort of curved, a few inches below the surface. With a grin she realized that she could rest her head on it and be able to float safely. Which was exactly what she did, arms out to her sides, legs dangling. She hadn't known bathing could be so . . . so splendid. She let every muscle in her body go limp. And lay suspended in the water.

'Tenna?' a woman's voice called gently, as if not to startle the lone bather. 'I'm Penda, Torlo's mate. He sent me up. I've some herbs for the bath that'll help those scratches. Wrong time of the Turn to fall into sticklebush.'

'I know,' Tenna agreed dourly. 'Be glad of any help.' Tenna didn't really want to open her eyes or move but she politely swished herself across the water to the edge of the tub.

'Lemme see them cuts so's I can see didja get any punctures like. That'd be no good with the sap rising,' Penda said. She walked quickly to the tub with a odd sideways gait, so whatever had injured her hip had happened a long time ago and she had learned to cope with it. She grinned at Tenna. 'Pretty runner girl, you are. You give Haligon what-for next time you see him.'

'How'll I know him?' Tenna asked acerbically, though she dearly wished a confrontation with the rider. 'And why is "pretty" a help?'

'Haligon likes pretty girls,' and Penda gave an exaggerated wink. 'We'll see you stay about long enough to give him what-for. *You* might do some good.'

Tenna laughed and, at Penda's gesture, held out her hands and turned her left arm where Penda could see it.

'Hmmm. Mostly surface but there's punctures on the heels of both hands,' and she ran oddly soft fingers across Tenna's hands, catching on three silvers so that Tenna shivered with the unpleasant sensation. 'Soaking'll do the most good. Loosen them up in your skin. Prolly clean 'em all out. Stickle's a clever bush, harming you so, but this'll help,' she said and took a collection of bottles from the deep pocket in her apron and selected one. 'Got to leave nothing to chance, ya know,' she added as she deftly splashed about twenty drops into the tub water. 'Don't worry about emptying the tub, either. It'll run clear and'll be fresh water by the time someone else climbs in. I'll take out the slivers when you've soaked. You want a rub then? Or would you rather sleep first?'

'A bit of a rub would be marvellous, thanks. And before I sleep.'

'I'll be back with some food.'

Tenna thought of the bathing room in her parents' station and grinned. Nothing to compare with this, though she'd always thought her station was lucky to have a tub so long you could lie out flat in it: even the tallest runners could. But you had to keep the fire going under the tank all the time to be sure there was enough for when a bath was needed. Not like this – the water already hot and you only needing to step into the tub. The herbs scented the steamy water, making it feel softer against her skin. She lay back again.

She was nearly asleep when Penda returned with a tray containing klah, fresh-baked bread, a little pot of, appropriately enough, stickleberry preserve and a bowl of porridge.

'Messages've already been handed over to them they was sent to so you can sleep good, knowing the run's well ended.'

Tenna consumed her meal, down to the last scrap. Penda was making quite a mixture with the massage oils and the runner inhaled the scent of them. Then Tenna climbed on the table, letting her body go limp while Penda used a tweezer on the slivers still caught in her flesh. Penda counted as she deposited the wicked hairs. Nine, all told. She applied more medication and the last of the itching and discomfort vanished. Tenna sighed. Then Penda soothed tired muscles and tendons. Her touch was sure but gentle. She did announce there were more punctures on the backs of Tenna's arms and legs and proceeded to go at them with the tweezers to remove the slivers. That done, her motions became more soothing and Tenna relaxed again.

'There y'are. Just go along to the third door down on your left, Tenna,' Penda said softly when she had finished.

Tenna roused enough from the delightful, massage-induced stupor and wrapped the big towel tightly around her chest. Like most runner females, she didn't have much of a bust, but that was an advantage.

'Don't forget these,' Penda said, shoving the laces of her running shoes at her. 'Clothes'll be clean and dry when you wake.'

'Thanks, Penda,' Tenna said sincerely, astonished that she'd been drowsy enough to forget her precious shoes.

She padded down the hall in the thick anklets that Penda had slipped on her feet and pushed in the third door. Light from the corridor showed her where the bed was straight across the narrow space, against the wall. Closing the door, she made her way to it in the dark. Dropping the towel, she leaned down to feel for the edge of the quilt she'd seen folded on the foot of the bed. She pulled it over her as she stretched out. Sighed once and fell asleep.

Good-natured laughter and movement down the hall roused her. Someone had half-opened the glowbasket so she saw her own clothes, clean, dry and neatly folded on the stool where she'd dropped her running shoes. She realized she hadn't even taken off the anklets before she got into bed. She wriggled her toes in them. No tenderness there. Her hands were stiff but cool so Penda'd gotten out all the slivers. The skin of her left arm and leg was stiff though and she threw back the quilt and tried to see the injuries. She couldn't but there was a little too much heat in the skin on the back of her left arm and her right leg for her liking. Five sort of sore spots she couldn't really check at all other than identifying them as 'sore'. And, when she checked her legs, two bad red bumps on her thigh, one in the left calf and two on the fleshy part of her right leg by the shin bone. She had suffered more hurt than she'd realized. And stickle slivers could work their way through your flesh and into your blood. One got to your heart and you could die from it. She groaned and rose. Shook out her legs, testing the feel of her muscles, and, thanks to Penda's massage, they didn't ache. She dressed and then carefully folded the quilt, placing it just as she'd found it on the bed.

Making her way back to the stairs, she passed the bathroom and heard the hum of masculine voices, then a laugh that was clearly from a female runner. As she came down the stairs, she was aware of the smell of roasting meats. Her stomach rumbled. One long narrow window lit the hall that led to the main room and she gauged that she had slept most of the day. Perhaps she ought to have had a healer check out the scratches but Penda knew what to do as well as any Hall-trained healer . . . probably better since she was a station manager's mate.

'Now here's a one who's prompt for her supper,' Torlo said, calling the attention of the runners sitting around the room to Tenna's appearance. He introduced her. 'Had a brush with Haligon early this morning,' he added and Tenna did not fail to note that this brash personage was known to them all from the nods and grimaces on their faces.

'I tol' Lord Groghe myself,' one of the older runners said, nodding his head and looking solemn, 'that there'd be an accident . . . then what'd he say to that? I asked him. Someone hurt because a wild lad won't respect what's our rights and propitty.' Then he nodded directly at Tenna. 'You aren't the only one he's knocked aside. Dinncha hear him coming?'

'Met him on the hill curve, she said,' Torlo answered before Tenna could open her own mouth.

'Bad place, bad place. Runner can't see around it,' a second man said and nodded his sympathy to her. 'See you've scratches? Penda put her good junk on ya?' Tenna nodded. 'You'll be right then. I've seen your kin on the traces, haven't I? Betchur one of Fedri and Cesila's, aincha?' He smiled knowingly at the others. 'You're prettier than she was and she was some pretty woman.'

Tenna decided to ignore the compliment and admitted to her parentage. 'Have you been through Station 97?'

'A time or two, a time or two,' he said, grinning amiably. His runner's belt was covered with stitches.

Torlo had come up beside her and now took her left arm to peer at the side she couldn't really see well.

'Punctures,' he said in a flat tone.

The other runners came to be sure his verdict was correct. They all nodded sagely and resumed their seats.

'Sometimes I wonder if all those berries're worth the risk of them slivers in spring,' the veteran runner said.

'Worse time of the Turn to fall into them,' she was told again.

'Misler, you run over to Healer Hall,' Torlo said to one of them.

'Oh, I don't think that's necessary,' Tenna said, because you had to pay healers and she then wouldn't have enough for good leathers.

'Being as how it was the Lord Holder's runnerbeast knocked you in, he'll pay for it,' Torlo said, sensing her reluctance and winking at her.

'One of these days he'll have to pay out blood money iffen he doesn't bring that Haligon up short and *make* him quit our traces. Did those shod hooves leave many holes?' another man asked her.

'No,' she had to admit. 'Surface sprang right back up.'

'Hmmm, that's what it's supposed to do.'

'But we don't need Haligon galloping up and down like traces was put there for *his* benefit.'

Misler had departed on his errand and then, after each runner spoke his or her name and home station, a glass of wine was poured for her. She started to demur but Torlo eyed her sternly.

'You're not on the run-list this day, girl.'

'I need to finish my first Cross,' she said wistfully as she took the glass and found an empty seat.

'You will, lass, you will,' the first man – Grolly – said so assuredly as he held his glass up that she was heartened. The others all seconded his words.

A few scratches and maybe the three-four punctures were not going to keep her from reaching the western seashore. She sipped her wine.

The runners who'd been bathing descended now and were served their wine by the time Misler came trotting back, a man in healer colours following behind, with a hop and a skip to keep up with his long-legged escort.

Beveny introduced himself and asked for Penda to join him. A nicety which pleased Tenna and gave her a very good opinion of the journeyman. The consultation was conducted right there in the main hall since the injuries were to visible portions of her body. And the other runners were genuinely interested in knowing the worst of her condition and offered suggestions: most of them knowledgeable as to which herbs should be used and how efficacious they had been on such and such an occasion. Beveny kept a grin on his face as if he was well used to runner chaffering. As he probably was.

'I think this one, and the two on your leg, may still have slivers in them,' Beveny said at length. 'Nothing a poultice won't draw out overnight, I'm sure.'

There were approving nods and wise smiles from the audience. Poultices were then discussed again and at length and the appropriate one decided on. During this part of the consultation, Tenna was installed in a comfortable, padded chair, a long stool affair attached to the front of it so her legs could stretch out. She'd never been fussed over so much in her life but it was a runner thing: she'd seen her mother and father take the same personal care of any one arriving at their station with an injury. But to be the centre of so much attention – and at Fort Station – was embarrassing in the extreme for Tenna and she kept trying to discount the urgency of such minor wounds. She did offer her packet of her mother's poultice and three of the runners remarked favourably on Cesila's famous poultice but hers was clearly for bruises, not infections, so the healer told her to keep it for emergencies.

'Which I hope you won't have, of course,' he said, smiling at her as he mixed – with the hot water Penda fetched – an aromatic concoction which everyone now in the room had to approve.

Keenly aware that she must be properly modest and forbearing, as well as brave, Tenna braced herself for the treatment. Hot poultices, however therapeutic, could be somewhat uncomfortable. Then the mixture was ready. With deft fingers, Healer Beveny deposited neat blobs, no larger than his thumbnail, on the sore spots. He must have judged the heat just right because none was too hot. He made sure to position the patches right over each blob before securing them with bandage strips which Penda produced. Tenna felt each of the ten hot spots but the sensation was not all that unpleasant.

'I'll check tomorrow, Tenna, but I don't think we have to worry about any of them,' Beveny said with such conviction that Tenna was relieved.

'Nor do you, here at Fort Station with the Healer Hall a stretch away,' said Torlo and courteously saw Beveny to the door and watched a polite few moments until the healer was halfway to his Hall.

'Nice fella,' he said to anyone listening and smiled at Tenna. 'Ah, here's the food.'

Evidently that meal had been held up for her to be treated because now Penda led in the drudge carrying the roast platter with others behind him, laden with large bowls of steaming food.

'Rosa,' she said, pointing to one of the female runners, 'get the board. Spacia, grab a fork and spoon for Tenna. She's not to move. Grolly, her glass is empty . . .' and, as she directed the others to serve the injured runner, she herself carved fine slices from the roasted ribs of herdbeast. 'The rest of you, get on line.'

Tenna's embarrassment returned, waited on as she was by Rosa and Spacia, who cheerfully performed their assigned tasks. Always she had been the one to help, so this situation was quite novel. Of course it was also a runner thing, to be cosseted in need, but she'd never been the recipient before.

Two more batches of runners arrived in from south and east. When they came back from bathing, they had to be told all about Haligon's forcing Tenna off the trace and how she had sticklebush punctures that were severe enough to require a healer. She got the distinct impression that almost everyone had had a run-in, or knew someone who had, with this infamous Haligon. Eventually the tale had been told to everyone and the conversation changed to talk of the Gather three days hence.

Tenna sighed softly to herself. Three days? She'd be fully recovered by then and have to run on. She really did want to get the extra stitches for her first Cross. A Gather, even one at Fort, was not as important as upgrading herself. Well, nearly. It wasn't as if this was the last Gather she'd ever have a chance to attend even if it was the first for her at the First Hold on Pern.

This was home station for two girls. Rosa had a cap of very tight dark curls and a pert face with mischievous eyes. Spacia, with long blonde hair tied back, runner-wise, had a more dignified way about her although she kept up a wickedly bantering conversation with the younger male runners among others there. Then there was an informal concert for Tenna, some of the newer songs that the Harper Hall was airing. Rosa led, Spacia adding an alto line while three of the other runners joined in, one with a little whistle and the others with their voices. The evening became quite enjoyable, especially as either Grolly or Torlo kept filling Tenna's wine glass.

Rosa and Spacia helped her up the stairs, one on either side of her, with the excuse that the bandages mustn't loosen. They chattered about what they intended to wear to the Gather and who they hoped to dance with.

'We're on line tomorrow,' Rosa said as they got her to her bed, 'so we'll probably be off before you get down. Those poultices ought to do the trick.'

They both wished her a good night's sleep. Her head was spinning as she lay down, but pleasantly, and she drifted into sleep very quickly.

Torlo arrived with a tray of food just as she was waking up.

'Not as sore today?'

'Not all over but my leg . . .' She pulled the quilt back so he could see.

'Hmmm. Need more on that one. Went in at an angle. I'm calling Beveny.'

'Oh, really . . . I'd rather . . . Surely Penda knows what the healer made up for me . . .'

'She does but we want the healer to speak about your injuries to Lord Groghe.'

Tenna was dismayed now. A runner didn't go to the Lord Holder without *real* cause for complaint and her injuries were not that serious.

'Now, see here, young runner,' and Torlo waggled a finger at her, 'I'm station master and I say we take this to the Lord Holder on account of it shouldna happened at all.'

Beveny recommended a long soak in the tub and provided her with an astringent to use in the water.

'I'll leave more poultice with Penda. We want that final sliver out. See . . .' and he pointed to the thin, almost invisible hairs of the sticklebush which had come from the arm puncture. 'We want another of these fellows on the pad, not in you.'

Two more had also erupted from the puncture wounds and he carefully covered all three pads with glass slides which he tied together.

'Soak at least an hour, Tenna,' he told her. 'You're to take it very handy today, too. Don't want that sliver to work any further down in your flesh.'

She shuddered at the thought of an evil-looking hair loose in her body.

'Don't worry. It'll be out by evening,' Beveny said, grinning reassuringly. 'And you'll be dancing with us.'

'Oh, I'll have to run on as soon as I'm able,' she said earnestly.

Beveny's grin broadened. 'What? And do me out of my dance with you?' Then his expression turned professional. 'I can't release you as fit to run yet, you know. I'd want to see those puncture marks healing. Especially in the shin where just the dirt and dust of a run could be imbedded and cause a repeat infection. The wounds may seem,' and he emphasized the word, 'insignificant but I've tended a lot of runners and I know the hazards of the trace.'

'Oh,' Tenna said meekly.

'Right. Oh!' And he grinned again, pressing her shoulder with a kindly squeeze. 'You will make your first Cross. Now rest. You runners are a breed apart, you know.'

With that reminder, he left her to make her way to the bathroom.

Rosa, Spacia, Grolly – in fact, all the runners at the Fort Station – were in and out, groaning over the special messages that needed to be delivered to the Fort Crafthalls, the Lord Holder, the Harper Hall, coming from the 'backside of beyond' as Rosa termed it.

'Don't mind us,' Rosa said when Tenna began to feel as if she ought to be doing her share. 'It's always like this just before a Gather and we always complain, but the Gather makes up for it. Which reminds me, you don't have anything to wear.'

'Oh, no, don't worry about me . . .'

'Nonsense,' Spacia said. 'We will if we want to and we do.' She gave Tenna's long frame an intent look and then shook her head. 'Well, nothing we have would fit.' Both girls were shorter than Tenna by a full head and, while neither carried much flesh, they were stockier than the eastern girl.

Then both turned to each other in the same instant and snapped their fingers. 'Silvina!' they exclaimed in chorus.

'C'mon,' Spacia said and reached for Tenna's hand. 'You can walk, can't you?'

'Oh, yes but –'

'On your feet then, runner,' Rosa said and took Tenna's other arm, assisting her to an upright position. 'Silvina's headwoman at the Harper Hall and she always has good things.'

'But . . . I . . .' and then Tenna gave up protesting. It was obvious from the determined expressions on the two runners' faces that they would brook no argument.

'You're taking her to Silvina?' Penda asked, sidling out of the kitchen. 'Good. I've nothing here to fit her and she's got to look her best when she meets that wretch, Haligon.'

'Why?' Tenna suspiciously wanted to know. Why would she need to look her best just to give Haligon what-for?

'Why, to maintain the reputation of Fort Station, of course,' Rosa said with an impish grin. 'We've our pride, you know, and you may be a visitor but you're here, now,' and she pointed emphatically to the ground, 'and must be presentable.'

'Not that you aren't,' Spacia hastily added, being slightly more tactful than Rosa, 'except we want you more so than ever.'

'After all, it *is* your first Fort Gather . . .'

'And you nearly finishing your first Cross, too.'

Their chatter was impossible to resist and there was no way Tenna could appear at a Gather in runner gear which was all she had of her own to wear.

At this evening hour, they found Silvina checking day-records in her office at the Harper Hall and she was more than delighted that she had been approached. She led them down to the storage rooms underneath the Harper Hall.

'We keep quite a few performance dresses in case a soloist wants to wear Harper colours. You wouldn't mind wearing blue, would you?' Silvina said as she paused by the second of a line of locked doors. 'Actually, I think blue would be a very good colour for you.' She had such a lovely speaking voice that Tenna was listening more to her tone than what she was saying. 'And I've one that I think might be just the thing for you.'

She opened a large wardrobe and, from the many there, she brought out a long gown with full sleeves and some fine embroidered trim that made all three girls gasp.

'It's lovely. Oh, I couldn't wear something this valuable,' Tenna exclaimed, backing away.

'Nonsense,' Silvina said and gestured for Tenna to slip out of her runner top.

When Tenna carefully slipped on the dress, the softness of the fabric against her skin made her feel . . . special. She tried a little spin and the long skirt swirled about her ankles while the full sleeves billowed about her arms. It was the most flattering dress she'd worn and she examined it thoroughly, committing the details of its design to her mind so that she could reproduce it the next time she had marks enough for a Gather dress. The one she had at home was nowhere near as splendid as this. Could she, should she dance, in something as elegant as this? What if she spilled something on it?

'I'm not sure . . .' she began as she faced her companions.

'Not SURE!' Rosa was indignant. 'Why, that deep blue shows

up your lovely skin and your eyes . . . they are blue, aren't they, or is it the dress makes them so? And it fits like it was made for YOU!'

Tenna looked down at the low-cut front of the bodice. Whoever it had been made for had had a lot more breast. She didn't fill it out properly. Silvina was rummaging through another box.

'Here,' she said, and stuffed two pads in the front, settling them with such a practised hand that the adjustment was done before Tenna could protest.

'There! That's much better,' Spacia said and then giggled. 'I have to pad, too. But it'd be worse for us as runners to be heavy, bumping around all the time.'

Tenna tentatively felt her newly improved form but, as she looked at herself in the mirror, she could see that the fit of the top was vastly improved and she looked more . . . more . . . well, it fitted better. The fabric was so smooth to the touch, it was a pleasure just to feel the dress on her. And this shade of blue . . .

'This is Harper Blue,' she said with surprise.

'Of course it is,' Silvina said with a laugh. 'Not that it matters. You'll be wearing runner cords . . . though right now,' and Silvina's appreciative grin broadened, 'you don't look runnerish . . . if you'll forgive my frankness.'

Tenna couldn't help admiring how much better her figure looked with that little alteration. She had a slim waist and the dress hugged it before flaring out over hips which she knew to be too bony and best covered.

'The pads won't . . . pop out . . . will they, when I'm dancing?'

'If you'll take off the dress, I'll put a few stitches to secure them where they should stay,' Silvina said.

That was done so quickly that Silvina was folding the lovely dress over Tenna's arm before she realized it.

'Now, shoes?' Spacia asked. 'She can't wear spikes.'

'She might better wear them,' Rosa said dourly, 'with some of those louts who come to a Fort Gather. Haligon's not the only one who'll home in on her, looking that way.'

Silvina had cast a measuring glance at Tenna's long narrow feet and now took a long box down from one of the many shelves in this huge storeroom.

'Should have something to fit even narrow runner feet . . .' she murmured and came up with a pair of soft, ankle-high, black suede boots. 'Try these.'

They did not fit. But the fourth pair – in dark red – were only slightly too long.

'Wear thick anklets and they'll fit fine,' Spacia suggested.

And the three girls left, Tenna carefully transporting the dress to the station. Rose and Spacia insisted on sharing the burden of the shoes and the underskirt which Silvina offered to complete the costume.

The last sliver of sticklebush was on the pad the next morning and Beveny added it to the others, handing the evidence packet over to Torlo who grinned in satisfaction.

'This'll make Lord Groghe see that we've a legitimate complaint,' he said and nodded emphatically at Tenna. She was about to protest when he added, 'But not until after the Gather for he's too busy to be approached right now. And he'll be in a much better mood after a good Gather.' He turned to Tenna. 'So you have to stay till after and that's that.'

'But I could run short distances now, couldn't I?'

'Mmm,' Torlo said, nodding. 'Iffen a run comes up. Don't like to be idle, do you, girl?' She shook her head. 'Wal, Healer, is she fit?'

'Short run and no hills,' Beveny said, 'and nowhere Haligon might ride.' He grinned mischievously at her and took his leave.

Just before midday, Torlo called her from the front bench where she'd been watching the Gather stalls being erected.

'Run down to the Port for me, will you? A ship just was drummed in and has cargo for the Gather. We're to get its manifests.' He took her by the arm and showed the route to her on the big map of Fort Hold that displayed local traces and roads. 'Straight run . . . downhill all the way to the Port. And not too steep on the way back.'

It was good to be running again and, though the spring weather had turned chilly, she soon worked up enough heat to keep warm. The captain was muchly relieved to deliver the manifests to her. The cargo was being unloaded and he was anxious to get it up the road to the hold in time for the Gather. He was equally anxious to receive payment for the deliveries and she could promise she'd have the manifests in the designated hands before dinner time.

He also had a pouch of letters from the eastern sea coast on board which were addressed to Fort Hold. So she carried a full belt back. Her legs felt the slight incline but she didn't decrease her pace despite a slight soreness in the right leg at the shin.

Well, a warm bath in one of those incredible tubs would take care of that. And the Gather was tomorrow.

Fort Station was full that night, with runners coming from other stations for the Gather the next day. Tenna bunked in with Rosa and Spacia and a southern runner, Delfie, took the fourth bed in their room. It was a front room with a window, and you heard the traffic on the road, but Tenna was tired enough to sleep through anything.

'Which is as well because the comings and goings up the main track kept up all night long,' Rosa said with cheerful disgust. 'Let's eat outside. It's so crowded in here.' So they all sat on the front benches to eat.

Spacia gave Tenna a conspiratorial wink as Tenna followed the others outside. There had been a few spare seats but not all together. It would be nicer to eat outside instead of the packed tables. Penda and her drudges had their hands full pouring klah and distributing bread, cheese and porridge.

Actually, it was much more interesting to sit outside to eat. There was so much going on. Gather wagons kept arriving from both directions and rolled on to the field set aside for their use. Stalls which had been bare boards and uprights last night were being decorated with Hall colours and craft insignia. And more stalls were being erected on the wide court in front of the hold. The long tongue and groove boards for the dancing surface were being slotted into place in the centre and the harpers' platform erected. Tenna wanted to hug herself with delight at all the activity. She'd never actually seen a Gather gathering before . . . especially in such a big hold as Fort. Since she had run yesterday, she felt a little better about not having made a push to finish her first Cross. And she had the chance to see the dragonriders pop into the air above Fort Hold.

'Oh, they are so beautiful,' she said, noticing that Rosa and Spacia were also watching the graceful creatures landing, and the elegantly-clad dragonriders dismounting.

'Yes, they are,' Rosa said in an odd tone. 'I just wish they wouldn't keep going on about Thread coming back.' She shuddered.

'You don't think it will?' Tenna said, for she had recently had several runs into the Benden Station and knew that weyrfolk were certain that Thread would return. Hadn't the Red Star been seen in the Eye Rock at the Winter Solstice?

Rosa shrugged. 'It can for all of me but it's going to interfere with running something fierce.'

'I noticed that the Benden Thread halts are all repaired,' Tenna said.

Spacia shrugged. 'We'd be fools to take any chances, wouldn't we?' Then she grimaced. 'I'd really hate to be stuck in one of those boxes with Thread falling all around me. Why, the wardrobe in Silvina's storeroom is larger. What if it got in a crack, Thread got in, and I couldn't get out?' She pantomimed terror and revulsion.

'It'll never come to that,' Rosa said confidently.

'Lord Groghe certainly got rid of all the greenery around the hold,' Spacia remarked, gesturing around.

'That was as much for the Gather as because the dragonriders said he had to,' Rosa said dismissively. 'Oh, here come the Boll runners . . .' and she jumped to her feet, waving at the spearhead of runners who had just appeared on the southern road.

They were running effortlessly, their legs moving as if they had drilled that matched stride. They certainly made a fine sight, Tenna thought, pride swelling in her chest and catching her breath!

'They must have started last night,' Rosa said. 'Oh, d'you see Cleve, Spacia?'

'Third rank from the rear,' Spacia said pointing. 'As if anyone could miss *him*!' she added in a slightly derisive tone, winking at Tenna. Then murmured behind her hand for Tenna's ears only. 'She's been so sure he wouldn't come . . . Ha!'

Tenna grinned, now understanding why Rosa had wanted to sit outside that morning and why she had sent Spacia in when they needed more klah.

Then, all of a sudden, as if the arrival of that contingent had been the signal, the Gather was ready. All stalls were up and furnished, the first shift of harpers on the platform and ready to entertain. Then Rosa pointed to the wide steps leading down from the entrance to the hold and there were the Lord and Lady, looking exceedingly grand in brown Gather finery, descending to the court to formally open the Gather Square. They were accompanied by the dragonriders as well as a clutch of folk, young and old and all related to the Lord Holder. According to Rosa, Lord Groghe had a large family.

'Oh, let's not miss the opening,' Spacia told Tenna. Rosa had accompanied Cleve into the station and was helping Penda serve the Boll group a second breakfast after their long run.

So the two girls had excellent seats to watch the two Lord Holders do the official walk through the Gather.

'There's Haligon,' Spacia said, her tone hard, pointing.

'Which one?'

'He's wearing brown,' Spacia said.

Tenna was none the wiser. 'There are a lot of people wearing brown.'

'He's walking just behind Lord Groghe.'

'So are a lot of other people.'

'He's got the curliest head of hair,' Spacia added.

There were two who answered that description but Tenna decided it was the shorter of the young men, the one who walked with a definite swagger. That had to be Haligon. He was handsome enough, though she liked the appearance of the taller man in brown more: not as attractive perhaps, but with a nicer grin on his face. Haligon obviously thought himself very much the lad, from the smug expression on *his* face.

Tenna nodded. She'd give him what-for, so she would.

'C'mon, we should change before the mob get upstairs,' Spacia said, touching Tenna's arm to get her attention.

Now that she had identified Haligon, Tenna was quite ready to be looking her very best. Spacia was also determined to assist and took pains with Tenna's appearance, fluffing her hair so that it framed her face, helping her with lip colour and a touch of eye shadow.

'Bring out the blue in 'em, though your eyes are really grey, aren't they?'

'Depends on what I'm wearing.' Tenna gave a little twirl in front of the long miror in the room, watching the bias-cut swirl around her ankles. As Spacia had suggested, the anklets took up the spare room in the toes of the borrowed boots. Nor did they look ungainly on the end of her legs as her long feet usually did. She was really quite pleased with her looks. And had to admit, with a degree of satisfaction, that she looked 'pretty'.

Then Spacia stood beside her, the yellow of her gown an attractive contrast to Tenna's deep blue.

'Ooops, I'd better find you some spare runner cords or everyone'll think you're new in the Harper Hall.'

No spare cords were found, though Spacia turned out all the drawers.

'Maybe I should be Harper Hall,' Tenna said thoughtfully. 'That way I can deal with Haligon as he deserves before he suspects.'

'Hmm, that might be the wiser idea, you know,' Spacia agreed.

Rosa came rushing in, pulling at her clothes in a rush to change.

'Need any help?' Spacia asked as Rosa pulled her pink, floral-printed Gather dress from its hanger.

'No, no but get down there and keep Felisha from Cleve. She's determined to get him, you know. Waltzed right in before he'd finished eating and started hanging on his arm as if they were espoused.' Rosa's voice was muffled as she pulled the dress over her head. They all heard a little tearing and Rosa cried out in protest, standing completely still, the dress half-on. 'Oh, no, no! What did I rip? What'll I do? How bad is it? Can you see?'

While the seam had only parted a bit, and Spacia was threading a needle to make the repairs, Rosa was so disturbed at the thought of her rival that Tenna volunteered to go down.

'You know which one Cleve is?' Rosa asked anxiously and Tenna nodded and left the room.

She identified Felisha before she did Cleve. The girl, with a mop of curly black tangles half-covering her face, was flirting outrageously with the tall, lantern-jawed runner. He had an engaging smile, though a trifle absent, as he kept looking towards the stairs. Tenna chuckled to herself. Rosa needn't worry. Cleve was obviously uncomfortable with Felisha's coy looks and the way she kept tossing her hair over her shoulder, letting it flick into his face.

'Cleve?' she asked as she approached them. Felisha glared at her and gave her head a perceptible tilt to indicate to Tenna to move on.

'Yes?' Cleve moved a step closer to Tenna, and further from Felisha who then altered her stance to put her arm through his in a proprietary fashion that obviously annoyed Cleve.

'Rosa told me that you'd had a run in with Haligon, too?'

'Yes, I did,' Cleve said, seizing on the subject and trying to disentangle himself. 'Ran me down on the Boll trace six sevendays ago. Got a nasty sprain out of it. Rosa mentioned he pushed you into sticklebush and you had some mean slivers. Caught you on the hill curve, did he?'

Tenna turned up her hands to show the mottled sliver pricks still visible from that encounter.

'How terrible!' Felisha said insincerely. 'That boy's far too reckless.'

'Indeed,' Tenna said, not liking this girl at all, though she smiled amiably. Surely she was too heavyset to be a runner. Her mop of hair covered whatever hall or hold cords she might be wearing. Tenna turned to Cleve. 'Spacia told me that you know a lot about the local leathers and I need new shoes.'

'Don't they tan hides wherever you come from?' Felisha asked snidely.

'Station 97, isn't it?' Cleve said, grinning. 'Come, I've a mind to look for new leathers myself and the bigger the Gather the more chance at a good price, right?' He brushed free of Felisha and, taking Tenna by the arm, propelled her across to the door.

Tenna had a brief glance at the furious look on Felisha's face as they made their escape.

'Thank *you*, Tenna,' Cleve said, exhaling with exaggeration as they strode across the court to the Gather Square. 'That girl's a menace.'

'Is she a Boll runner? She didn't introduce herself.'

Cleve chuckled. 'No, she's Weaver Hall,' he said dismissively, 'but my station runs messages for her CraftMaster.' He grimaced.

'Tenna?' Torlo called from the door and they both stopped, allowing him to catch up with them.

'Anyone point out Haligon to you yet?' he asked.

'Yes, Rosa and Spacia did. He was behind the Lord Holder. I'll have a word with him when we meet.'

'Good girl, good girl,' Torlo said, pressing her arm firmly in encouragement and then he returned to the station.

'Will you?' Cleve asked, eyes wide with surprise.

'Will I what? Give him what-for? Indeed I will,' Tenna said, firming her mind with purpose. 'A bit of what he gave me.'

'I thought it was sticklebushes you fell into?' Cleve asked, taking it all literally. 'There're none of those in a Square.'

'Measuring his length on a Gather floor will do nicely, I think,' she replied. It ought to be rather easy to trip someone up with such a crowd around. And she had committed herself rather publicly to giving this Haligon a visible lesson. Even Healer Beveny was helping her. She was obliged to act. She certainly didn't wish to lose respect in the station. She took a deep breath. Would tripping him be sufficient? At least on the personal level. There'd still be the charge of reckless behaviour levelled against him with the healer-verified proof of her injuries. These had certainly kept her from running for three days – loss of income.

'Oh!' she said, seeing the display for fabrics draped on the Weaver Hall booth: brilliant colours, and floral prints, as well as stripes in both bold and muted colours. She put her hands behind her back because the temptation to finger the cloth was almost irresistible.

Cleve wrinkled his nose. 'That's Felisha's hall's stuff.'

'Oh, that red is amazing . . .'

'Yeah, it's a good hall . . .'

'In spite of her?' And Tenna chuckled at his reluctant admission.

'Yes . . .' and he grinned ruefully.

They passed the GlassCraft display: mirrors with ornate frames and plain wood; goblets and drinking glasses in all shapes and colours, pitchers in all sizes.

Tenna caught a reflection and almost didn't recognize herself except for that fact that there was Cleve beside her. She straightened her shoulders and smiled back at the unfamiliar girl in the glass.

The next stand was a large Tailor Hall display with finished goods in tempting array, dresses, shirts, trousers, and more intimate garments: enticing merchandise to be sure and this one was already packed out with buyers.

'What's keeping Rosa?' Cleve asked, glancing back over his shoulder towards the station which would be visible until they turned the corner.

'Well, she wanted to look extra nice for you,' Tenna said.

Cleve grinned. 'She always looks nice.' And he blushed suddenly.

'She's a very kind and thoughtful person,' Tenna said sincerely.

'Ah, here we are,' he said, pointing to the hides displayed at the stall on the corner of the Square. 'Though I think there are several stalls. Fort Gathers're big enough to attract a lot of CraftHalls. Let's see what's available every place. Are you good at haggling? If you're not, we can leave it to Rosa. She's very good.

And they'd know she means business. You being unknown, they might think they could put one over on you.'

Tenna grinned slyly. 'I plan to get the most for my mark, I assure you.'

'I shouldn't teach you how to run traces, then, should I?' Cleve said with a tinge of rueful apology in his voice.

Tenna smiled back and began to saunter aimlessly past the leather stall. Just then Rosa caught up with them, giving Tenna a kiss as if they hadn't parted company fifteen minutes before. Cleve threw one arm about Rosa's shoulders and whispered in her ear, making her giggle. Other shoppers walked around the three, standing in the middle of the wide aisle. Tenna didn't object to the chance to examine the leather goods without appearing to do so. The journeyman behind the counter pretended not to see her not looking at his wares. She was also trying to see if she could spot Haligon among those promenading about the Square.

By the time the three of them had done their first circuit of the Gather, it was almost impossible to move for the crowds. But a goodly crowd also added to the 'gather feeling' and the trio of runners were exhilarated by the atmosphere. They spent so many hours in work that was solitary and time-consuming: often at hours when most other folk had finished their labours and were enjoying companionship and family life. True, they had the constant satisfaction of knowing that they provided an important service but you didn't think of that running through a chilling rain or battling against a fierce gale. You thought more of what you *didn't* have and what you were missing.

Refreshment stalls displayed all kinds of drink and finger edibles. So, when they had finished their circuit, they bought food and drink and sat at the tables about the dance Square.

'There he is!' Rosa said suddenly, pointing across the Square where a group of young men were surveying girls parading in their Gather finery. It was a custom to take a Gather partner – someone with whom to spend the occasion – which could include the day, the evening meal, the dancing and whatever else was mutually decided. Everyone recognized the limitation and made sure that the details were arranged ahead of time so that there wouldn't be a misunderstanding of intent.

This would an ideal situation in which to make Haligon suffer indignity. The area where he was standing with his friends was at the roadside, dusty and spotted with droppings from all the draught animals pulling Gather wagons past it. He'd look silly, his good clothes mussed. With any luck, she could get his fancy Gather clothing soiled as well as dusty.

'Excuse me,' Tenna said, putting down her drink. 'I've a score to settle.'

'Oh!' Rosa's eyes went wide but an encouraging 'yo-ho' followed Tenna as she cut diagonally across the wooden dancing floor. Haligon was still in the company of the taller man, laughing at something said and eyeing the girls who were parading conspicuously along that side of the Gather Square. Yes, this was the time to repay him for her fall.

Tenna went right up to him, tapped him on the shoulder, and when he turned around in response, the arch smile on his face turned to one of considerable interest at her appearance, his eyes lighting as he gave her a sweeping look of appreciation. He was looking so boldly that he did not see Tenna cock her right arm. Putting her entire body into the swing, she connected her fist smartly to his chin. He dropped like a felled herdbeast, flat on his back and unconscious. And right on top of some droppings. Although the impact of her fist on his chin had rocked her back on her heels, she brushed her hands together with great satisfaction and, pivoting on the heel of her borrowed red shoe, retraced her steps.

She was halfway back to Rosa and Cleve when she heard someone rapidly overtaking her. So she was ready when her arm was seized and her progress halted.

'What was that all about?' It was the tall lad in brown who pulled her about, a look of genuine surprise on his face. And his eyes, too, surveyed her in her form-fitting blue dress.

'I thought he ought to have a little of what he deals out so recklessly,' she said, and proceeded.

'Wait a minute. What was he supposed to have done to you?

I've never seen you around Fort before and he's never mentioned meeting someone like you. And he would!' His eyes glinted with appreciation.

'Oh?' and Tenna cocked her head at him. They were nearly at eye-level. 'Well, he pushed me into sticklebushes.' She showed him her hands and his expression altered to one of real concern.

'Sticklebushes? They're dangerous at this season.'

'I do know that . . . the hard way,' she replied caustically.

'But where? When?'

'That doesn't matter. I've evened the score.'

'Indeed,' and his grin was respectful. 'But are you sure it was my brother?'

'Do you know all Haligon's friends?'

'Haligon?' He blinked. After a pause in which his eyes reflected a rapid series of considerations, he said, 'I thought I did.' And he laughed nervously. Then he gestured for her to continue on her way. She could see that he was being careful not to annoy her and that provided her further amused satisfaction.

'There is a lot about Haligon that he would want kept quiet,' she said. 'He's a reckless sort.'

'And you're the one to teach him manners?' He had to cover his mouth, but she could see that his eyes were brimming with laughter.

'Someone has to.'

'Oh? Just what offence did he give you? It's not often . . . Haligon . . . measures his length. Couldn't you have found a less public spot to deliver your lesson? You've ruined his Gather clothes with muck.'

'Actually, I chose the spot deliberately. Let him feel what it's like to be flattened unexpectedly.'

'Yes, I'm sure. But where did you encounter him?'

'He was using a runner trace, at the gallop, in the middle of the night . . .'

'Oh,' and he stopped dead in his tracks, an odd, almost guilty look on his face. 'When was this?' he asked, all amusement gone from his face.

'Four nights ago, at the hill curve.'

'And?'

'I was knocked into sticklebushes.' With those words, she held out her right leg and pulled her skirt up high enough to expose the red dots of the healing injuries. And again displayed her free hand and its healing rack of punctures.

'They got infected?' He was really concerned now and obviously knew the dangers of the sticklebush.

'I've saved the slivers,' she said in a firm tone. 'Healer Beveny has them for proof. I wasn't able to continue working and I've been laid up three days.'

'I'm sorry to hear that.' And he sounded sincere, his expression sombre. Then he gave his head a little shake and smiled at her, a trifle warily, but there was a look in his eyes that told her he found her attractive. 'If you promise not to drop me, may I say that you don't look at all like most runners I've met.' His eyes lingered only briefly on her bodice and then he hastily cleared his throat. 'I'd better get back and see . . . if Haligon's come to.'

Tenna spared a glance at the little knot of people clustered around her victim and, giving him a gracious nod, continued on her way back to Rosa and Cleve.

They were looking pale and shocked.

'There! Honour is satisfied,' she said, slipping into her seat.

Rosa and Cleve exchanged looks.

'No,' Rosa said and leaned towards her, one hand on her forearm. 'It wasn't Haligon you knocked down.'

'It wasn't? But that's the fellow you pointed out to me. He's in brown . . .'

'So is Haligon. He's the one followed you across the dance floor. The one you were talking to and I don't think you were giving him any what-for.'

'OH!' Tenna slumped weakly against the back of her chair. 'I hit the wrong man?'

'Uhhuh,' Rosa said as both she and Cleve nodded their heads.

'Oh dear,' and she made a start to get up but Rosa hastily put out a restraining hand.

'I don't think apologies will help.'

'No? Who did I hit?'

'His twin brother, Horon, who's bad enough in his own way.'

'Quite likely, with the lewd look he gave me.' Tenna was halfway to convincing herself that she had at least hit someone who needed a put-down.

'Horon's a bit of a bully and nice girls won't have anything to do with him. Especially at a Gather.' Then Rosa giggled, covering her mouth with her hand. 'He was sure looking you up and down. That's why we thought you'd hit him.'

Remembering the force of her punch, Tenna rubbed her sore knuckles.

'You may have done someone a favour,' Cleve said, grinning. 'That was some punch.'

'My brothers taught me how,' Tenna said absently, watching the group across the Square. She was a trifle relieved when Horon was helped to his feet. And pleased that he staggered and needed assistance. Then, as the group around Horon moved about, she saw Haligon's figure striding up to the station. 'Uh oh. Why's he going to the station?'

'I wouldn't worry about that,' Rosa said, standing up. 'Torlo would love to remind him of all the harm he's been doing runners.'

'Even if they weren't as pretty as you are,' Cleve said. 'Let's see about your leathers.'

They took their empty glasses back to the refreshment stand. Tenna managed one more look at the station but there was no sign of Haligon or Torlo, though there was a lot of coming and going. There would be, on a Gather day. Would she have to knock Haligon down, too? To satisfy runner honour? It wouldn't be as easy, for he had been wary enough of her when he had caught up with her on the dance floor.

After a second round of the Gather stalls, they all decided to find out what prices were being asked. At the first Tanner's stall, Cleve did more of the talking so that the real buyer was protected from the blandishments of the Tanner journeyman, a man named Ligand.

'Blue for a Harper singer?' Ligand had begun, glancing at Tenna. 'Thought I saw you eyeing the stall earlier.'

'I'm Runner,' Tenna said.

'She just happens to look her best in blue,' Rosa said quickly in case Tenna might be embarrassed to admit she wore a borrowed gown.

'She does indeed,' Ligand said. 'I'd never have guessed her for a runner.'

'Why not?' Rosa asked, bridling.

'Because she's wearing blue,' Ligand said deferentially. 'So what colour is your delight this fine Gather day?'

'I'd like a dark green,' and Tenna pointed to a stack of hides dyed various shades of that colour in the shelves behind him.

'Good choice for a runner,' he said and, with a deft lift, transferred the heavy stack of hides to the front counter. Then he moved off to the other end of his stall where two holders were examining heavy belts.

'Not that trace moss leaves stains,' Rosa remarked as Tenna began flipping through the pile, fingering the leather as she went along.

'We go for the reddy-browns in Boll,' Cleve said. 'So much of the soil down in Boll is that shade. And trace moss doesn't do as well in the heat as it does in the north.'

'Does fine in Igen,' Tenna said, having run trace there.

'So it does,' Cleve said reflectively. 'I like that one,' he added, spreading his hand over the hide before Tenna could flip to the next one. 'Good deep emerald green.'

Tenna had also been considering it. 'Enough here for boots. I only need enough for summer shoes. He wouldn't want to divide it.'

'Ah, and you've found one you like, huh? Good price on that.' And Ligand was obviously aware of all that went on at his booth. He flipped up the hide to see the markings on the underside. 'Give it to you for nine marks.'

Rosa gasped. 'At five it's robbery.' Then she looked chagrined to have protested when Tenna was the prospective purchaser.

'I'd agree with that,' Tenna said, having only four to spend.

She gave the skin one more pat and, smiling courteously at Ligand, walked off, her companions hastily following her.

'You won't find better quality anywhere,' Ligand called after them.

'It was good quality,' Tenna murmured as they walked away. 'But four marks is my limit.'

'Oh, we should be able to find a smaller hide for that much, though maybe not the same green,' Rosa said airily.

However, by the time they had done a third circuit and seen all the green hides available, they had not found either the same green or the same beautifully softened hide.

'I just don't have five. Even if we could bargain him down to that price,' Tenna said. 'That brown at the third stand would be all right. Shall we try that?'

'Oho,' Rosa said, stopping in her tracks, her expression alarmed.

Cleve, too, stopped and Tenna couldn't see what caused their alarm when suddenly a man appeared out of the crowd and stood directly in their path. She recognized the tall, white-haired man from the morning's ceremony as Lord Holder Groghe.

'Runner Tenna?' he asked formally. But the expression in his wide-set eyes was pleasant.

'Yes,' she said, raising her chin slightly. Was he about to give *her* what-for for punching his son, Horon? She certainly couldn't admit to having hit the wrong one.

'Shall we sit over here, with your friends?' Lord Groghe said, gesturing towards a free table. He put a hand on her elbow and guided her gently in that direction, away from the stream of folk.

Tenna thought confusedly that neither his expression nor his tone was peremptory. He was unexpectedly gracious. A heavyset man with a full face and the beginning of jowls, he smiled to everyone as they made their way to the table, for there were many curious glances at the four of them. He caught the eye of the wineman and held up four fingers. The wineman nodded and hastened to serve them.

'I have an apology to make to you, Runner Tenna.' He kept his voice low and for their ears alone.

'You do?' And, at Rosa's startled expression, Tenna added courteously with only a short hesitation, 'Lord Groghe?'

'I have verified that my son, Haligon, ran you down four nights ago and you were sufficiently injured so that you were unable to run.' Groghe's brows met in a scowl which was for the circumstances, not her part in them. 'I confess that I have heard rumours of other complaints about his use of runner traces. Station Master Torlo informed me of several near-collisions. You may be sure that, from now on, Haligon will leave the traces for the runners who made them. You're from Station 97? Keroon Hold?'

Tenna could only nod. She couldn't believe this was happening. A Lord Holder was apologizing to her?

'My son, Haligon, had no idea that he had nearly run you down the other night. He may be reckless,' and Groghe smiled somewhat indulgently, 'but he would never knowingly cause injury.'

Rosa prodded Tenna in the ribs, and Tenna realized that she must make as much as she could of this opportunity, not just for herself but for all runners.

'Lord Groghe, I . . . we all,' and she included Rosa and Cleve, 'would be grateful to know that we may run the traces without interference. I had only the briefest warning that someone else was using the path. The hill hid his approach and there was wind, too, covering the sound of his approach. I could have been severely injured. Traces are not wide, you know.' He nodded, and she went on boldly. 'And they were made for runners, not riders.' He nodded again. 'I think Fort Station would be grateful for your help in keeping just runners on the traces.'

Then she couldn't think of anything else to say. And just sat there, smiling with nervous twitches in the corners of her mouth.

'I have been well and truly told off, Runner Tenna.' He smiled back at her, his eyes dropping for a split second to her bodice. 'You're a very pretty girl. Blue becomes you.' He reached over and gave her hand a pat before he rose. 'I've told Torlo that the incursions will cease.' Then, in his usual booming voice, he added, 'Enjoy the Gather, runners, and the wine.'

With that he rose and walked off, nodding and smiling as he went, leaving the three runners stunned. Rosa was the first to recover. She took a good swig of the wine.

'Torlo was right. You did it,' Rosa said. 'And this is *good* wine.'

'What else would they serve Lord Groghe?' Cleve said and surreptitiously eased the glass left at the Lord Holder's seat closer to his. The level of wine had not been much reduced by the sip that Lord Groghe had taken. 'We can split this one.'

'I can't believe that Lord Holder apologized to . . .' and Tenna shook her head, hand on her chest, 'me. Tenna.'

'You were the one injured, weren't you?' Rosa said.

'Yes, but . . .'

'How did Lord Groghe know?' Cleve finished for Tenna who was puzzling such an answer.

'We all saw Haligon go up to the station,' Rosa said before taking another sip of the wine. She rolled her eyes in appreciation of the taste. 'But Lord Groghe's a fair man, even if he usually thinks women are halfwits. But he's fair.' Then she giggled again. 'And he said how pretty you are so that helped, you know. Haligon likes his girls pretty. So does Lord Groghe, but he only looks.'

The three runners had been so intent on their own conversation that they did not notice Haligon's approach until he unrolled the green hide from Ligand's stall in front of Tenna.

'In apology, Runner Tenna, because I really didn't know there was someone on the curve of the trace the other night,' Haligon said and gave a courteous bow, his eyes fixed on Tenna's face. Then his contrite expression altered to chagrin. 'The station master gave me what-for in triples. So did my father.'

'Oh, didn't you believe Tenna?' Rosa asked him pertly.

'How could I doubt the injuries she showed me?' Haligon said. Now he waved for the wineman to serve their table.

Cleve gestured for him to be seated.

'Is . . . your brother all right?' Tenna asked, a question she hadn't quite dared ask Lord Groghe.

Haligon's eyes twinkled with merriment. 'You have taught him a lesson, too, you know.'

'I don't usually go around knocking people down,' Tenna began and received another surreptitious jab in her ribs from Rosa, sitting beside her. 'Except when they need it.' She leaned forward, away from Rosa. 'I meant to hit *you.*'

Haligon rubbed his jaw. 'I'm as glad enough you didn't. When Master Torlo told me that you'd been kept from running for three days, I knew I was very much at fault. Then he told me of the other near-misses. Will you accept this leather in compensation, with my apology?'

'Your father has already apologized.'

'I make my own, Runner Tenna,' he said with an edge to his voice and a solemn expression.

'I accept, but . . .' and she was about to refuse the leather when, once again, Rosa jabbed her. She'd have sore ribs at this rate. 'I accept.'

'Good, for I should have a miserable Gather without your forgiveness,' Haligon said, his expression lightening. Lifting the glass he had just been served, he tilted it in her direction and drank. 'Will you save me a dance?'

Tenna pretended to consider. But she was secretly thrilled for, despite their first encounter, there was something about Haligon that she found very attractive. Just in case, she shifted in her chair, moving her upper body away from Rosa to avoid another peremptory jab.

'I was hoping to be able to do the Toss dance,' she began and, when Haligon eagerly opened his mouth to claim that, she added, 'but my right leg isn't entirely sound.'

'But sound enough surely for the quieter dances?' Haligon asked. 'You seemed to be walking well enough.'

'Yes, walking's no strain for me . . .' and Tenna hesitated a little longer, 'but I would enjoy having a partner.' Which allowed him to ask for more than one dance.

'The slow ones, then?'

'Beveny asked for one, remember,' Rosa said casually.

'When does the dancing start?' Tenna asked.

'Not until full dark, after the meal,' Haligon said. 'Would you be my supper partner?'

She heard Rosa inhale sharply but she really did find him an agreeable sort. Certainly the invitation was acceptable. 'I would be delighted to,' she said graciously.

It was so arranged and Haligon toasted the agreement with the last of his wine, rose, bowed to them all and left the table.

'Yo-ho, Tenna,' Rosa murmured as they watched his tall figure disappear in the Gather crowd.

Cleve, too, grinned. 'Neatly done. Do hope you'll be back on another Cross soon in case we have some more problems you can help us with.'

'Oh, run off, will you?' Tenna replied flippantly. Now she allowed herself to finger the dark green leather hide. 'Was he watching us, do you suppose? How'd he know?'

'Oh, no one's ever said Haligon was a dimwit,' Rosa said. 'Though he is, riding runner traces like he has.'

'*He* must have told his father, then,' Cleve said. 'Owning up to all that shows an honest nature. I might end up liking him after all.'

'Proper order,' Rosa said. 'Though he never admitted using the traces before when Torlo braced him on that.' She grinned at Tenna. 'It's sure true that a pretty girl gets more attention than a plain one like me.'

'You are not plain,' Cleve said indignantly and realized he had fallen into Rosa's neatly-laid trap to elicit a compliment from him.

'I'm not?' she replied, smiling archly.

'Oh, you!' he said with the wordless disgust of the well-baited. Then he laughed and carefully split Groghe's glass between their glasses. 'Much too good to waste.'

Tenna returned to the station long enough to put away the beautiful leather. And long enough to get many requests for dances and to be supper partner from other runners who congratulated her.

'Told ya so, dinnit I?' Penda said, catching Tenna's arm as she was leaving. The woman was grinning from ear to ear. 'Pretty girl's always heard, ya know.'

Tenna laughed. 'And Haligon's going to stay off the traces.'

'So his father promised,' Penda said, 'but we'll have to see does he.'

'I'll see that he does,' Tenna promised airily and returned to the Gather Square. She'd never had such a marvellous time before.

The supper lines were now forming down the road at the roasting pits and she began to wonder if Haligon had just been funning her and had never intended, Lord Holder's son that he was, to honour his invitation. Then he appeared beside her, offering his arm.

'I didn't forget,' he murmured, taking her by the arm.

Being partnered with a Holder's son allowed them to patronize a different line at the roasting pits and so they were served well before Cleve and Rosa. The wine Haligon ordered was more of the excellent one she'd sampled in the afternoon so Tenna was quite merry and relaxed by the time the dancing began.

What surprised her, because she'd given the first dance to Grolly – as much because he didn't expect to get any dances from such a pretty girl as because he asked her first – was that Haligon did not dance it with someone else. He waited at the table for a breathless Grolly to bring her back. It was a sprightly enough tune for dancing but not as fast or complicated as the Toss was. The next dance was at a slower tempo and she held out her hand to Haligon, despite the fact that half the male runners at the Gather were now crowding about for a chance to dance with her.

He pulled her into his arms with a deft movement and they were suddenly cheek to cheek. He was only a little taller than she was so their steps matched effortlessly. One circuit of the room and she had perfect confidence in his leading.

Since they were dancing cheek to cheek she could feel his face muscles lifting in a smile. And he gave her a quick pressure with both hands.

'Do you know when you're running again?'

'I've already had a short leg, down to the Port,' she said. 'Enough for a good warm-up.'

'How *do* you manage such long distances on your own legs?' he asked, holding her out slightly to see her face in the light of the glowbaskets that lined the dance floor. He really wanted to know, too.

'Part of it's training, of course. Part that my Blood is bred to produce runners.'

'Could you have done anything else with your life?'

'I could but I like running. There's a sort of . . . magic to it. Sometimes you feel you could run round the world. And I like night running. You feel like you're the only one awake and alive and moving.'

'Quite likely you are, save for dimwits on mounts on traces they shouldn't be using,' he said in a wry tone. 'How long *have* you been running?'

He sounded genuinely interested. She had thought perhaps she had made a mistake, being sentimental about something as commonplace as running.

'Almost two whole Turns. This is my first Cross.'

'And I was a dimglowed idiot who interrupted it,' he said in an apologetic tone.

Tenna was almost embarrassed at his continued references to his mistake.

'How often do I have to say I've forgiven you?' she said, putting her lips closer to his ear. 'That green leather is going to make fine shoes for me. By the way, how you'd know that was the hide I wanted? Were you following us about?'

'Father said I had to make amends in some way more personal than handing you marks . . .'

'You didn't give Tanner Ligand what he asked for, did you?' Her query was sharp because she didn't want him to have had to spend more than she felt necessary. And she leaned away from his guiding arm enough so that she could see his face as he answered.

'I won't tell you how much, Tenna, but we struck a fair bargain. Trouble was,' and now Haligon's voice was rueful, 'he knew just how much I needed that particular hide. It's the talk of the Gather, you know.'

Tenna suspected that it was and she hoped she could tell it to her own station before they heard rumour which always exaggerated.

'Hmmm. I should have expected that,' she said ruefully. 'I shall be able to make two pairs of summer shoes out of that much leather and I'll think of you every time I wear them.' She grinned up at him.

'Fair enough,' and, evidently satisfied by this exchange, he resettled his arms about her, drawing her just that much closer. 'You didn't seem as interested in any other hide, you know. So I'd got off more lightly than I thought I might. I didn't know runners made their own footwear.'

'We do, and it's much better to make them for yourself. Then you've only yourself to blame if you've blisters.'

'Blisters? They would be bad for a runner.'

'Almost as bad as sticklebush slivers.'

He groaned. 'Will I ever be able to live that down?'

'You can try.' Maybe she could get him to dance with her all night. He was possibly the best partner she'd ever had. Not that she ever lacked for them. But he was subtly different. In his dancing, too, for he seemed to know many combinations of the dance steps and she really had to keep her attention on her feet and following his lead. Maybe it was him being a Holder's son.

'Maybe it's being a runner,' and his remark startled her, it being near what she'd just been thinking, 'but you're the lightest thing on your feet.' He reset his hands more firmly about her, drawing her as close as he could.

They were both silent, each concentrating on the complexities of the dance. It ended all too soon for Tenna. She didn't really wish to release him. Nor he, her. So they stood on the dance floor, arms at their sides but not with much distance between them. The music began again: a faster dance and before she could say a word, Haligon had swung her into his arms and moved off in the rhythm of this tune. This time they had to concentrate not only on the steps but also to avoid collisions with more erratic dancers whirling about the floor.

Three dances to a set and Haligon whisked her off the floor during the change of musicians on the pretext of needing a drink. With glasses of chilled white wine, he guided her into the shadow of a deserted stall.

She smiled to herself, rehearsing a number of deft rejections if she needed them.

'I don't think you're at all lame, Tenna,' he said conversationally. 'Especially if the station master let you take a run down to the Port. Care to have a go at the first Toss dance after all?'

His expression dared her.

'We'll see.'

Pause.

'So, will you run on tomorrow?'

'I'll be careful with the wine in case I do,' she said, half-warning him as she lifted the glass.

'Will you make it to the sea from here in one run?'

'Quite likely. It's spring and there'd be no snow on the Pass trace.'

'Would you still go if there were?'

'No one said anything about snow on the Pass trace at the station.'

'Keep your ears open, don't you?'

'A runner always needs to know conditions on the trace.' She gave him a stern look.

'All right, I've got the message.'

'Fair enough.'

Pause.

'You're not at all what I expected, you know,' Haligon said respectfully.

'I can quite candidly say the same of you, Haligon,' she replied.

The new musicians played the first bar of the next song, to acquaint people with a sample of the dance to come.

So, when Tenna felt his arm about her shoulders, she did not resist the pressure. Nor did she when both arms enfolded her and his mouth found hers. It was a nice kiss, not sloppy as others had been, but well placed on her lips, as if he knew what he was about in kissing. His arms about her were sure, too, not crushing her needlessly against him. Respectful, she thought . . . and then, as the kiss deepened with her cooperation, she didn't think of anything but enjoying the experience.

Haligon monopolized her all evening, rather deftly, she realized. Always whisking her off the dance floor before any one else could find her. They kissed quite a bit between dances. He was far more respectful of her person than she expected. And she said so.

'With the punch you can deliver, my girl,' he answered, 'you can bet your last mark I'm not about to risk my brother's fate.'

He also found other chilled drinks for her to drink instead of more wine. She appreciated that even more. Especially when the music of the Toss dance began. The floor cleared of all save a few hardy couples.

'Shall we?' and Haligon's grin was all the challenge she needed.

The ache in her right shin was really minor and her confidence in his partnering had grown throughout the evening otherwise she would not have taken his dare.

During the pattern of the dance, the female partner was to be swung as high as possible, and if she was very clever, she would twirl mid-air before being caught by the male. It would be a dangerous dance, but it was ever so much fun. Tenna's older brother had taught her and given her enough practice so that she was well able to make the turns. It had ensured her partners at any Gather in the east once it was known how light she was and what a good dancer.

From the very first toss, she knew that Haligon was the best partner she'd ever had. There was great cheering for them when she managed a full two turns in the air before he caught her. In one of the rare close movements of the dance, he whispered swift instructions so that she was prepared for the final Toss. And able to execute it, sure he would be there to keep her from crashing on the floor. She was close enough to being missed so that the spectators gasped just as he caught her caught half a handspan above the floor. Another girl was not so lucky but suffered no more than the indignity of the fall.

Cleve, Rosa, Spacia, Grolly and most of the station crowded about them when they left the dance floor, congratulating them on such a performance. They were offered drinks, meat rolls and other delicacies.

'Upholding the honour of the station,' Cleve loudly proclaimed. 'And the hold, of course,' he magnanimously added, bowing to Haligon.

'Tenna's the best partner I've ever had,' Haligon replied sincerely, mopping his face.

'Well, you had the chance to find out,' muttered Grolly.

Then Torlo reached through the crowd and tapped Tenna's shoulder.

'You're on the run list, Tenna,' he said, emphasizing the warning with a nod.

'To the coast?'

'Aye, as you wished.' Torlo gave Haligon a severe look.

'I'll escort you to the station, then, Tenna?' Haligon asked.

The harpers had struck up another slow dance. Rosa and Spacia were looking intensely at Tenna but she couldn't interpret their glances. She also knew her duty as a runner.

'This is the last dance then.' And she took Haligon by the arm and led him to the floor.

Haligon tucked her in against him and she let her body relax against his and to his leading. She had never had such a Gather in her life. She could almost be glad that he'd run her off the trace and so started the events that had culminated in this lovely night.

They said nothing, both enjoying the flow of the dance and the sweet music. When it ended, Haligon led her from the floor, holding her right hand in his, and towards the station, its glowbasket shining at the door.

'So, Runner Tenna, you finish your first Cross. It won't be your last, will it?' Haligon asked as they paused just beyond the circle of light. He lifted his hand and lightly brushed back the curls.

'No, it's unlikely to. I'm going to run as long as I'm able.'

'But you'll be Crossing often, won't you?' he asked and she nodded. 'So, if sometime in the future, when I've got my own holding . . . I'm going to breed runners . . . beasts, that is,' he qualified hastily, and she almost laughed at his urgent correction. 'I've been trying to find the strain I want to breed, you see, and used the traces as sort of the best footing for comparison. I mean, is there any chance you might . . . possibly . . . consider running more often on this side of the world?'

Tenna cocked her head at him, surprised by the intensity and roughness in his pleasant voice.

'I might.' She smiled up at him. This Haligon was more of a temptation to her than he knew.

Now he smiled back at her, a challenge sparkling in his eyes. 'We'll just have to see, won't we?'

'Yes, I guess we will.'

With that answer, she gave him a quick kiss on the cheek and ducked into the station before she could say more than she ought right now after such a limited acquaintance . . . But maybe raising runners, both kinds – four-legged and two – in the west wasn't a bad idea at all.

A Song of Ice and Fire

GEORGE
R. R. MARTIN

A Song of Ice and Fire

GEORGE
R. R. MARTIN

A Game of Thrones (1996)
A Clash of Kings (1998)
A Storm of Swords (forthcoming)
A Dance with Dragons (forthcoming)
The Winds of Winter (forthcoming)

One of the most recent of the great multi-volume fantasy epics is George R. R. Martin's *A Song of Ice and Fire*, which when complete will span six volumes. This immense saga is set in the world of the Seven Kingdoms, a land where seasons have been thrown out of balance, with summer and winter both lasting for years.

As the first book opens, the reader learns that three noble families had conspired to depose their insane king and take control of the kingdom. The Lannisters, the Baratheons, and the Starks all exist in an uneasy truce that is soon broken when the current king, Robert Baratheon, asks Ned Stark to come down from the northern city of Winterfell and help him to rule, giving him the coveted title of Hand of the King, which makes him the second most powerful man of the Seven Kingdoms. Ned's efforts to solve the murder of his predecessor in that post soon embroil him in conflict with the queen and her brothers. The balance of power among the great families is thus unsettled. As the game of thrones grows deadly, even more sinister forces are stirring in the north, behind the great ice-wall that protects the Seven Kingdoms and all the realms of men.

A civil war threatens to sweep the land when the Lannisters

kill Robert and attempt to seize power, opposed only by the Starks and Baratheons. Meanwhile, the head of the Targaryen family, Viserys, sells his sister into marriage in return for armies that will help him reconquer the Seven Kingdoms.

The forthcoming volumes of the series will depict the gradual unfolding and resolution of the terrible many-sided conflict that will rack this troubled world.

The story offered here, 'The Hedge Knight', takes place about a hundred years prior to the events described in *A Game of Thrones*.

The Hedge Knight

BY GEORGE R. R. MARTIN

The spring rains had softened the ground, so Dunk had no trouble digging the grave. He chose a spot on the western slope of a low hill, for the old man had always loved to watch the sunset. 'Another day done,' he would sigh, 'and who knows what the morrow will bring us, eh, Dunk?'

Well, one morrow had brought rains that soaked them to the bones, and the one after had brought wet gusty winds, and the next a chill. By the fourth day the old man was too weak to ride. And now he was gone. Only a few days past, he had been singing as they rode, the old song about going to Gulltown to see a fair maid, but instead of Gulltown he'd sung of Ashford. *Off to Ashford to see the fair maid, heigh-ho, heigh-ho,* Dunk thought miserably as he dug.

When the hole was deep enough, he lifted the old man's body in his arms and carried him there. He had been a small man, and slim; stripped of hauberk, helm, and swordbelt, he seemed to weigh no more than a bag of leaves. Dunk was hugely tall for his age, a shambling, shaggy, big-boned boy of sixteen or seventeen years (no one was quite certain which) who stood closer to seven feet than to six, and had only just begun to fill out his frame. The old man had often praised his strength. He had always been generous in his praise. It was all he had to give.

Dunk laid him out in the bottom of the grave and stood over him for a time. The smell of rain was in the air again, and he knew he ought to fill the hole before it broke, but it was hard to throw dirt down on that tired old face. *There ought to be a septon here, to say some prayers over him, but he only has me.* The old man had taught Dunk all he knew of swords and shields and lances, but had never been much good at teaching him words.

'I'd leave your sword, but it would rust in the ground,' he said at last, apologetic. 'The gods will give you a new one, I guess. I wish you didn't die, ser.' He paused, uncertain what else needed to be said. He didn't know any prayers, not all the way through; the old man had never been much for praying. 'You were a true knight, and you never beat me when I didn't deserve it,' he finally managed, 'except that one time in Maidenpool. It was the inn boy who ate the widow-woman's pie, not me, I told you. It don't matter now. The gods keep you, ser.' He kicked dirt in the hole, then began to fill it methodically, never looking at the thing at the bottom. *He had a long life,* Dunk thought. *He must have been closer to sixty than to fifty, and how many men can say that?* At least he had lived to see another spring.

The sun was westering as he fed the horses. There were three; his swaybacked stot, the old man's palfrey, and Thunder, his warhorse, who was ridden only in tourney and battle. The big brown stallion was not as swift nor strong as he had once been, but he still had his bright eye and fierce spirit, and he was more valuable than everything else Dunk owned. *If I sold Thunder and old Chestnut, and the saddles and bridles too, I'd come away with enough silver to . . .* Dunk frowned. The only life he knew was the life of a hedge knight, riding from keep to keep, taking service with this lord and that lord, fighting in their battles and eating in their halls until the war was done, then moving on. There were tourneys from time to time as well, though less often, and he knew that some hedge knights turned robber during lean winters, though the old man never had.

I could find another hedge knight in need of a squire to tend his animals and clean his mail, he thought, *or might be I could go to some city, to Lannisport or King's Landing, and join the City Watch. Or else . . .*

He had piled the old man's things under an oak. The cloth purse contained three silver stags, nineteen copper pennies, and a chipped garnet; as with most hedge knights, the greatest part of his worldly wealth had been tied up in his horses and weapons. Dunk now owned a chain-mail hauberk that he had scoured the rust off a thousand times. An iron halfhelm with a broad nasal and a dent on the left temple. A swordbelt of cracked brown leather, and a longsword in a wood-and-leather scabbard. A dagger, a razor, a whetstone. Greaves and gorget, an eight-foot war lance of turned ash topped by a cruel iron point, and an oaken shield with a scarred metal rim, bearing the sigil of Ser Arlan of Pennytree: a winged chalice, silver on brown.

Dunk looked at the shield, scooped up the swordbelt, and looked at the shield again. The belt was made for the old man's skinny hips. It would never do for him, no more than the hauberk would. He tied the scabbard to a length of hempen rope, knotted it around his waist, and drew the longsword.

The blade was straight and heavy, good castle-forged steel, the grip soft leather wrapped over wood, the pommel a smooth polished black stone. Plain as it was, the sword felt good in his hand, and Dunk knew how sharp it was, having worked it with whetstone and oilcloth many a night before they went to sleep. *It fits my grip as well as it ever fitted his,* he thought to himself, *and there is a tourney at Ashford Meadow.*

Sweetfoot had an easier gait than old Chestnut, but Dunk was still sore and tired when he spied the inn ahead, a tall daub-and-timber building beside a stream. The warm yellow light spilling from its windows looked so inviting that he could not pass it by. *I have three silvers,* he told himself, *enough for a good meal and as much ale as I care to drink.*

As he dismounted, a naked boy emerged dripping from the stream and began to dry himself on a roughspun brown cloak. 'Are you the stableboy?' Dunk asked him. The lad looked to be no more than eight or nine, a pasty-faced skinny thing, his bare feet caked in mud up to the ankle. His hair was the queerest thing about him. He had none. 'I'll want my palfrey rubbed down. And oats for all three. Can you tend to them?'

The boy looked at him brazenly. 'I could. If I wanted.'

Dunk frowned. 'I'll have none of that. I am a knight, I'll have you know.'

'You don't look to be a knight.'

'Do all knights look the same?'

'No, but they don't look like you, either. Your swordbelt's made of rope.'

'So long as it holds my scabbard, it serves. Now see to my horses. You'll get a copper if you do well, and a clout in the ear if you don't.' He did not wait to see how the stableboy took that, but turned away and shouldered through the door.

At this hour, he would have expected the inn to be crowded, but the common room was almost empty. A young lordling in a fine damask mantle was passed out at one table, snoring softly into a pool of spilled wine. Otherwise there was no one. Dunk looked around uncertainly until a stout, short, whey-faced woman emerged from the kitchens and said, 'Sit where you like. Is it ale you want, or food?'

'Both.' Dunk took a chair by the window, well away from the sleeping man.

'There's good lamb, roasted with a crust of herbs, and some ducks my son shot down. Which will you have?'

He had not eaten at an inn in half a year or more. 'Both.'

The woman laughed. 'Well, you're big enough for it.' She drew a tankard of ale and brought it to his table. 'Will you be wanting a room for the night as well?'

'No.' Dunk would have liked nothing better than a soft straw mattress and a roof above his head, but he needed to be careful with his coin. The ground would serve. 'Some food, some ale, and it's on to Ashford for me. How much further is it?'

'A day's ride. Bear north when the road forks at the burned mill. Is my boy seeing to your horses, or has he run off again?'

'No, he's there,' said Dunk. 'You seem to have no custom.'

'Half the town's gone to see the tourney. My own would as well, if I allowed it. They'll have this inn when I go, but the boy would sooner swagger about with soldiers, and the girl turns to sighs and giggles every time a knight rides by. I swear I couldn't tell you why. Knights are built the same as other men, and I never knew a joust to change the price of eggs.' She eyed Dunk curiously; his sword and shield told her one thing, his rope belt and roughspun tunic quite another. 'You're bound for the tourney yourself?'

He took a sip of the ale before he answered. A nut-brown colour it was, and thick on the tongue, the way he liked it. 'Aye,' he said. 'I mean to be a champion.'

'Do you, now?' the innkeep answered, polite enough.

Across the room, the lordling raised his head from the wine puddle. His face had a sallow, unhealthy cast to it beneath a rat's nest of sandy brown hair, and blond stubble crusted his chin. He rubbed his mouth, blinked at Dunk, and said, 'I dreamed of you.' His hand trembled as he pointed a finger. 'You stay away from me, do you hear? You stay *well* away.'

Dunk stared at him uncertainly. 'My lord?'

The innkeep leaned close. 'Never you mind that one, ser. All he does is drink and talk about his dreams. I'll see about that food.' She bustled off.

'Food?' The lordling made the word an obscenity. He staggered to his feet, one hand on the table to keep himself from falling. 'I'm going to be sick,' he announced. The front of his tunic was crusty red with old wine-stains. 'I wanted a whore, but there's none to be found here. All gone to Ashford Meadow. Gods be good, I need some wine.' He lurched unsteadily from the common room, and Dunk heard him climbing steps, singing under his breath.

A sad creature, thought Dunk. *But why did he think he knew me?* He pondered that a moment over his ale.

The lamb was as good as any he had ever eaten, and the duck was even better, cooked with cherries and lemons and not near as greasy as most. The innkeep brought buttered pease as well, and oaten bread still hot from her oven. *This is what it means to be a knight,* he told himself as he sucked the last bit of meat off the bone. *Good food, and ale whenever I want it, and no one to clout me in the head.* He had a second tankard of ale with the meal, a third to wash it down, and a fourth because there was no one to tell him he couldn't, and when he was done he paid the woman with a silver stag and still got back a fistful of coppers.

It was full dark by the time Dunk emerged. His stomach was

full and his purse was a little lighter, but he felt good as he walked to the stables. Ahead, he heard a horse whicker. 'Easy, lad,' a boy's voice said. Dunk quickened his step, frowning.

He found the stableboy mounted on Thunder and wearing the old man's armour. The hauberk was longer than he was, and he'd had to tilt the helm back on his bald head or else it would have covered his eyes. He looked utterly intent, and utterly absurd. Dunk stopped in the stable door and laughed.

The boy looked up, flushed, vaulted to the ground. 'My lord, I did not mean –'

'Thief,' Dunk said, trying to sound stern. 'Take off that armour, and be glad that Thunder didn't kick you in that fool head. He's a warhorse, not a boy's pony.'

The boy took off the helm and flung it to the straw. 'I could ride him as well as you,' he said, bold as you please.

'Close your mouth, I want none of your insolence. The hauberk too, take it off. What did you think you were doing?'

'How can I tell you, with my mouth closed?' The boy squirmed out of the chain-mail and let it fall.

'You can open your mouth to answer,' said Dunk. 'Now pick up that mail, shake off the dirt, and put it back where you found it. And the halfhelm too. Did you feed the horses, as I told you? And rub down Sweetfoot?'

'Yes,' the boy said, as he shook straw from the mail. 'You're going to Ashford, aren't you? Take me with you, ser.'

The innkeep had warned him of this. 'And what might your mother say to that?'

'My mother?' The boy wrinkled up his face. 'My mother's dead, she wouldn't say anything.'

He was surprised. Wasn't the innkeep his mother? Perhaps he was only 'prenticed to her. Dunk's head was a little fuzzy from the ale. 'Are you an orphan boy?' he asked uncertainly.

'Are you?' the boy threw back.

'I was once,' Dunk admitted. *Till the old man took me in.*

'If you took me, I could squire for you.'

'I have no need of a squire,' he said.

'Every knight needs a squire,' the boy said. 'You look as though you need one more than most.'

Dunk raised a hand threateningly. 'And you look as though you need a clout in the ear, it seems to me. Fill me a sack of oats. I'm off for Ashford . . . alone.'

If the boy was frightened, he hid it well. For a moment he stood there defiant, his arms crossed, but just as Dunk was about to give up on him the lad turned and went for the oats.

Dunk was relieved. *A pity I couldn't . . . but he has a good life here at the inn, a better one than he'd have squiring for a hedge knight. Taking him would be no kindness.*

He could still feel the lad's disappointment, though. As he mounted Sweetfoot and took up Thunder's lead, Dunk decided that a copper penny might cheer him. 'Here, lad, for your help.' He flipped the coin down at him with a smile, but the stableboy made no attempt to catch it. It fell in the dirt between his bare feet, and there he let it lay.

He'll scoop it up as soon as I am gone, Dunk told himself. He turned the palfrey and rode from the inn, leading the other two horses. The trees were bright with moonlight, and the sky was cloudless and speckled with stars. Yet as he headed down the road he could feel the stableboy watching his back, sullen and silent.

The shadows of the afternoon were growing long when Dunk reined up on the edge of broad Ashford Meadow. Threescore pavilions had already risen on the grassy field. Some were small, some large; some square, some round; some of sailcloth, some of linen, some of silk; but all were brightly coloured, with long banners streaming from their centre poles, brighter than a field of wildflowers with rich reds and sunny yellows, countless shades of green and blue, deep blacks and greys and purples.

The old man had ridden with some of these knights; others Dunk knew from tales told in common rooms and round campfires. Though he had never learned the magic of reading or writing, the old man had been relentless when it came to teaching him heraldry, often drilling him as they rode. The nightingales belonged to Lord Caron of the Marches, as skilled with the high harp as he was with a lance. The crowned stag was for Ser Lyonel Baratheon, the Laughing Storm. Dunk picked out the Tarly huntsman, House Dondarrion's purple lightning, the red apple of the Fossoways. There roared the lion of Lannister, gold on crimson, and there the dark green sea-turtle of the Estermonts swam across a pale green field. The brown tent beneath a red stallion could only belong to Ser Otho Bracken, who was called the Brute of Bracken since slaying Lord Quentyn Blackwood three years past during a tourney at King's Landing. Dunk heard that Ser Otho struck so hard with the blunted longaxe that he stove in the visor of Lord Blackwood's helm and the face beneath it. He saw some Blackwood banners as well, on the west edge of the meadow, as distant from Ser Otho as they could be. Marbrand, Mallister, Cargyll, Westerling, Swann, Mullendore, Hightower, Florent, Frey, Penrose, Stokeworth, Darry, Parren, Wylde; it seemed as though every lordly house of the west and south had sent a knight or three to Ashford to see the fair maid and brave the lists in her honour.

Yet however fine their pavilions were to look upon, he knew there was no place there for him. A threadbare wool cloak would be all the shelter he had tonight. While the lords and great knights dined on capons and suckling pigs, Dunk's supper would be a hard, stringy piece of salt beef. He knew full well that if he made his camp upon that gaudy field, he would need to suffer both silent scorn and open mockery. A few perhaps would treat him kindly, yet in a way that was almost worse.

A hedge knight must hold tight to his pride. Without it, he was no more than a sellsword. *I must earn my place in that company. If I fight well, some lord may take me into his household. I will ride in noble company then, and eat fresh meat every night in a castle hall, and raise my own pavilion at tourneys. But first I must do well.* Reluctantly, he turned his back on the tourney grounds and led his horses into the trees.

On the outskirts of the great meadow a good half-mile from

town and castle he found a place where a bend in a brook had formed a deep pool. Reeds grew thick along its edge, and a tall leafy elm presided over all. The spring grass there was as green as any knight's banner and soft to the touch. It was a pretty spot, and no one had yet laid claim to it. *This will be my pavilion,* Dunk told himself, *a pavilion roofed with leaves, greener even than the banners of the Tyrells and the Estermonts.*

His horses came first. After they had been tended, he stripped and waded into the pool to wash away the dust of travel. 'A true knight is cleanly as well as godly,' the old man always said, insisting that they wash themselves head to heels every time the moon turned, whether they smelled sour or not. Now that he was a knight, Dunk vowed he would do the same.

He sat naked under the elm while he dried, enjoying the warmth of the spring air on his skin as he watched a dragonfly move lazily among the reeds. *Why would they name it a dragonfly?* he wondered. *It looks nothing like a dragon.* Not that Dunk had ever seen a dragon. The old man had, though. Dunk had heard the story half a hundred times, how Ser Arlan had been just a little boy when his grandfather had taken him to King's Landing, and how they'd seen the last dragon there the year before it died. She'd been a green female, small and stunted, her wings withered. None of her eggs had ever hatched. 'Some say King Aegon poisoned her,' the old man would tell. 'The third Aegon that would be, not King Daeron's father, but the one they named Dragonbane, or Aegon the Unlucky. He was afraid of dragons, for he'd seen his uncle's beast devour his own mother. The summers have been shorter since the last dragon died, and the winters longer and crueller.'

The air began to cool as the sun dipped below the tops of the trees. When Dunk felt gooseflesh prickling his arms, he beat his tunic and breeches against the trunk of the elm to knock off the worst of the dirt, and donned them once again. On the morrow he could seek out the master of the games and enrol his name, but he had other matters he ought to look into tonight if he hoped to challenge.

He did not need to study his reflection in the water to know that he did not look much like a knight, so he slung Ser Arlan's shield across his back to display the sigil. Hobbling the horses, Dunk left them to crop the thick green grass beneath the elm as he set out on foot for the tourney grounds.

In normal times the meadow served as a commons for the folk of Ashford town across the river, but now it was transformed. A second town had sprung up overnight, a town of silk instead of stone, larger and fairer than its elder sister. Dozens of merchants had erected their stalls along the edge of the field, selling felts and fruits, belts and boots, hides and hawks, earthenware, gemstones, pewterwork, spices, feathers, and all manner of other goods. Jugglers, puppeteers, and magicians wandered amongst the crowds plying their trades . . . as did the whores and cutpurses. Dunk kept a wary hand on his coin.

When he caught the smell of sausages sizzling over a smoky fire, his mouth began to water. He bought one with a copper from his pouch, and a horn of ale to wash it down. As he ate he watched a painted wooden knight battle a painted wooden dragon. The puppeteer who worked the dragon was good to watch too; a tall drink of water, with the olive skin and black hair of Dorne. She was slim as a lance with no breasts to speak of, but Dunk liked her face and the way her fingers made the dragon snap and slither at the end of its strings. He would have tossed the girl a copper if he'd had one to spare, but just now he needed every coin.

There were armourers among the merchants, as he had hoped. A Tyroshi with a forked blue beard was selling ornate helms, gorgeous fantastical things wrought in the shapes of birds and beasts and chased with gold and silver. Elsewhere he found a swordmaker hawking cheap steel blades, and another whose work was much finer, but it was not a sword he lacked.

The man he needed was all the way down at the end of the row, a shirt of fine chain-mail and a pair of lobstered steel gauntlets displayed on the table before him. Dunk inspected them closely. 'You do good work,' he said.

'None better.' A stumpy man, the smith was no more than five feet tall, yet wide as Dunk about the chest and arms. He had a black beard, huge hands, and no trace of humility.

'I need armour for the tourney,' Dunk told him. 'A suit of good mail, with gorget, greaves, and greathelm.' The old man's halfhelm would fit his head, but he wanted more protection for his face than a nasal bar alone could provide.

The armourer looked him up and down. 'You're a big one, but I've armoured bigger.' He came out from behind the table. 'Kneel, I want to measure those shoulders. Aye, and that thick neck o' yours.' Dunk knelt. The armourer laid a length of knotted rawhide along his shoulders, grunted, slipped it about his throat, grunted again. 'Lift your arm. No, the right.' He grunted a third time. 'Now you can stand.' The inside of a leg, the thickness of his calf, and the size of his waist elicited further grunts. 'I have some pieces in me wagon that might do for you,' the man said when he was done. 'Nothing prettied up with gold nor silver, mind you, just good steel, strong and plain. I make helms that look like helms, not winged pigs and queer foreign fruits, but mine will serve you better if you take a lance in the face.'

'That's all I want,' said Dunk. 'How much?'

'Eight hundred stags, for I'm feeling kindly.'

'Eight hundred?' It was more than he had expected. 'I . . . I could trade you some old armour, made for a smaller man . . . a halfhelm, a mail hauberk . . .'

'Steely Pate sells only his own work,' the man declared, 'but it might be I could make use of the metal. If it's not too rusted, I'll take it and armour you for six hundred.'

Dunk could beseech Pate to give him the armour on trust, but he knew what sort of answer that request would likely get. He had travelled with the old man long enough to learn that merchants were notoriously mistrustful of hedge knights, some of whom were little better than robbers. 'I'll give you two silvers now, and the armour and the rest of the coin on the morrow.'

The armourer studied him a moment. 'Two silvers buys you a day. After that, I sell me work to the next man.'

Dunk scooped the stags out of his pouch and placed them in the armourer's calloused hand. 'You'll get it all. I mean to be a champion here.'

'Do you?' Pate bit one of the coins. 'And these others, I suppose they all came just to cheer you on?'

The moon was well up by the time he turned his steps back towards his elm. Behind him, Ashford Meadow was ablaze with torchlight. The sounds of song and laughter drifted across the grass, but his own mood was sombre. He could think of only one way to raise the coin for his armour. And if he should be defeated . . . 'One victory is all I need,' he muttered aloud. 'That's not so much to hope for.'

Even so, the old man would never have hoped for it. Ser Arlan had not ridden a tilt since the day he had been unhorsed by the Prince of Dragonstone in a tourney at Storm's End, many years before. 'It is not every man who can boast that he broke seven lances against the finest knight in the Seven Kingdoms,' he would say. 'I could never hope to do better, so why should I try?'

Dunk had suspected that Ser Arlan's age had more to do with it than the Prince of Dragonstone did, but he never dared say as much. The old man had his pride, even at the last. *I am quick and strong, he always said so, what was true for him need not be true for me,* he told himself stubbornly.

He was moving through a patch of weed, chewing over his chances in his head, when he saw the flicker of firelight through the bushes. *What is this?* Dunk did not stop to think. Suddenly his sword was in his hand and he was crashing through the grass.

He burst out roaring and cursing, only to jerk to a sudden halt at the sight of the boy beside the campfire. 'You!' He lowered the sword. 'What are you doing here?'

'Cooking a fish,' said the bald boy. 'Do you want some?'

'I meant, how did you *get* here? Did you steal a horse?'

'I rode in the back of a cart, with a man who was bringing some lambs to the castle for my lord of Ashford's table.'

'Well, you'd best see if he's gone yet, or find another cart. I won't have you here.'

'You can't make me go,' the boy said, impertinent. 'I'd had enough of that inn.'

'I'll have no more insolence from you,' Dunk warned. 'I should throw you over my horse right now and take you home.'

'You'd need to ride all the way to King's Landing,' said the boy. 'You'd miss the tourney.'

King's Landing. For a moment Dunk wondered if he were being mocked, but the boy had no way of knowing that he had been born in King's Landing as well. *Another wretch from Flea Bottom, like as not, and who can blame him for wanting out of that place?*

He felt foolish standing there with sword in hand over an eight-year-old orphan. He sheathed it, glowering so the boy would see that he would suffer no nonsense. *I ought to give him a good beating at the least,* he thought, but the child looked so pitiful he could not bring himself to hit him. He glanced around the camp. The fire was burning merrily within a neat circle of rocks. The horses had been brushed, and clothes were hanging from the elm, drying above the flames. 'What are those doing there?'

'I washed them,' the boy said. 'And I groomed the horses, made the fire, and caught this fish. I would have raised your pavilion, but I couldn't find one.'

'There's my pavilion.' Dunk swept a hand above his head, at the branches of the tall elm that loomed above them.

'That's a tree,' the boy said, unimpressed.

'It's all the pavilion a true knight needs. I would sooner sleep under the stars than in some smoky tent.'

'What if it rains?'

'The tree will shelter me.'

'Trees leak.'

Dunk laughed. 'So they do. Well, if truth be told, I lack the coin for a pavilion. And you'd best turn that fish, or it will be burned on the bottom and raw on the top. You'd never make a kitchen boy.'

'I would if I wanted,' the boy said, but he turned the fish.

'What happened to your hair?' Dunk asked of him.

'The maesters shaved it off.' Suddenly self-conscious, the boy pulled up the hood of his dark brown cloak, covering his head.

Dunk had heard that they did that sometimes, to treat lice or rootworms or certain sicknesses. 'Are you ill?'

'No,' said the boy. 'What's your name?'

'Dunk,' he said.

The wretched boy laughed aloud, as if that was the funniest thing he'd ever heard. *'Dunk?'* he said. 'Ser Dunk? That's no name for a knight. Is it short for Duncan?'

Was it? The old man had called him just *Dunk* for as long as he could recall, and he did not remember much of his life before. 'Duncan, yes,' he said. 'Ser Duncan of . . .' Dunk had no other name, nor any house; Ser Arlan had found him living wild in the stews and alleys of Flea Bottom. He had never known his father or mother. What was he to say? 'Ser Duncan of Flea Bottom' did not sound very knightly. He could take Pennytree, but what if they asked him where it was? Dunk had never been to Pennytree, nor had the old man talked much about it. He frowned for a moment, and then blurted out, 'Ser Duncan the Tall.' He *was* tall, no one could dispute that, and it sounded puissant.

Though the little sneak did not seem to think so. 'I have never heard of any Ser Duncan the Tall.'

'Do you know every knight in the Seven Kingdoms, then?'

The boy looked at him boldly. 'The good ones.'

'I'm as good as any. After the tourney, they'll all know that. Do *you* have a name, thief?'

The boy hesitated. 'Egg,' he said.

Dunk did not laugh. *His head does look like an egg. Small boys can be cruel, and grown men as well.* 'Egg,' he said, 'I should beat you bloody and send you on your way, but the truth is, I have no pavilion and I have no squire either. If you'll swear to do as you're told, I'll let you serve me for the tourney. After that, well, we'll see. If I decide you're worth your keep, you'll have clothes on your back and food in your belly. The clothes might be roughspun and the food salt beef and salt fish, and maybe some venison from time to time where there are no foresters about, but you won't go hungry. And I promise not to beat you except when you deserve it.'

Egg smiled. 'Yes, my lord.'

'*Ser*,' Dunk corrected. 'I am only a hedge knight.' He wondered if the old man was looking down on him. *I will teach him the arts of battle, the same as you taught me, ser. He seems a likely lad, might be one day he'll make a knight.*

The fish was still a little raw on the inside when they ate it, and the boy had not removed all the bones, but it still tasted a world better than hard salt beef.

Egg soon fell asleep beside the dying fire. Dunk lay on his back nearby, his big hands behind his head, gazing up at the night sky. He could hear distant music from the tourney grounds, half a mile away. The stars were everywhere, thousands and thousands of them. One fell as he was watching, a bright green streak that flashed across the black and then was gone.

A falling star brings luck to him who sees it, Dunk thought. *But the rest of them are all in their pavilions by now, staring up at silk instead of sky. So the luck is mine alone.*

In the morning, he woke to the sound of a cock crowing. Egg was still there, curled up beneath the old man's second-best cloak. *Well, the boy did not run off during the night, that's a start.* He prodded him awake with his foot. 'Up. There's work to do.' The boy rose quick enough, rubbing his eyes. 'Help me saddle Sweetfoot,' Dunk told him.

'What about breakfast?'

'There's salt beef. *After* we're done.'

'I'd sooner eat the horse,' Egg said. 'Ser.'

'You'll eat my fist if you don't do as you're told. Get the brushes. They're in the saddle sack. Yes, that one.'

Together they brushed out the palfrey's sorrel coat, hefted Ser Arlan's best saddle over her back, and cinched it tight. Egg was a good worker once he put his mind to it, Dunk saw.

'I expect I'll be gone most of the day,' he told the boy as he mounted. 'You're to stay here and put the camp in order. Make sure no *other* thieves come nosing about.'

'Can I have a sword to run them off with?' Egg asked. He had blue eyes, Dunk saw, very dark, almost purple. His bald head made them seem huge, somehow.

'No,' said Dunk. 'A knife's enough. And you had best be here when I come back, do you hear me? Rob me and run off and I'll hunt you down, I swear I will. With dogs.'

'You don't have any dogs,' Egg pointed out.

'I'll get some,' said Dunk. 'Just for you.' He turned Sweetfoot's head towards the meadow and moved off at a brisk trot, hoping the threat would be enough to keep the boy honest. Save for the clothes on his back, the armour in his sack, and the horse beneath him, everything Dunk owned in the world was back at that camp. *I am a great fool to trust the boy so far, but it is no more than the old man did for me,* he reflected. *The Mother must have sent him to me so that I could pay my debt.*

As he crossed the field, he heard the ring of hammers from the riverside, where carpenters were nailing together jousting barriers and raising a lofty viewing stand. A few new pavilions were going up as well, while the knights who had come earlier slept off last night's revels or sat to break their fasts. Dunk could smell woodsmoke, and bacon as well.

To the north of the meadow flowed the River Cockleswent, a vassal stream to the mighty Mander. Beyond the shallow ford lay town and castle. Dunk had seen many a market town during his journeys with the old man. This was prettier than most; the whitewashed houses with their thatched roofs had an inviting aspect to them. When he was smaller, he used to wonder what it would be like to live in such a place; to sleep every night with a roof over your head, and wake every morning with the same walls wrapped around you. *It may be that soon I'll know. Aye, and Egg too.* It could happen. Stranger things happened every day.

Ashford Castle was a stone structure built in the shape of a triangle, with round towers rising thirty feet tall at each point and thick crenellated walls running between. Orange banners flew from its battlements, displaying the white sun-and-chevron sigil of its lord. Men-at-arms in orange-and-white livery stood outside the gates with halberds, watching people come and go, seemingly more intent on joking with a pretty milkmaid than in keeping anyone out. Dunk reined up in front of the short, bearded man he took for their captain and asked for the master of the games.

'It's Plummer you want, he's steward here. I'll show you.'

Inside the yard, a stableboy took Sweetfoot for him. Dunk slung Ser Arlan's battered shield over a shoulder and followed the guards captain back of the stables to a turret built into an angle of the curtain wall. Steep stone steps led up to the wallwalk. 'Come to enter your master's name for the lists?' the captain asked as they climbed.

'It's my own name I'll be putting in.'

'Is it now?' Was the man smirking? Dunk was not certain. 'That door there. I'll leave you to it and get back to my post.'

When Dunk pushed open the door, the steward was sitting at a trestle table, scratching on a piece of parchment with a quill. He had thinning grey hair and a narrow pinched face. 'Yes?' he said, looking up. 'What do you want, man?'

Dunk pulled shut the door. 'Are you Plummer the steward? I came for the tourney. To enter the lists.'

Plummer pursed his lips. 'My lord's tourney is a contest for knights. Are you a knight?'

He nodded, wondering if his ears were red.

'A knight with a name, mayhaps?'

'Dunk.' Why had he said *that*? 'Ser Duncan. The Tall.'

'And where might you be from, Ser Duncan the Tall?'

'Everyplace. I was squire to Ser Arlan of Pennytree since I was five or six. This is his shield.' He showed it to the steward. 'He was coming to the tourney, but he caught a chill and died, so I came in his stead. He knighted me before he passed, with his own sword.' Dunk drew the longsword and laid it on the scarred wooden table between them.

The master of the lists gave the blade no more than a glance. 'A sword it is, for a certainty. I have never heard of this Arlan of Pennytree, however. You were his squire, you say?'

'He always said he meant for me to be a knight, as he was. When he was dying he called for his longsword and bade me kneel. He touched me once on my right shoulder and once on my left, and said some words, and when I got up he said I was a knight.'

'Hmpf.' The man Plummer rubbed his nose. 'Any knight can make a knight, it is true, though it is more customary to stand a vigil and be anointed by a septon before taking your vows. Were there any witnesses to your dubbing?'

'Only a robin, up in a thorn tree. I heard it as the old man was saying the words. He charged me to be a good knight and true, to obey the seven gods, defend the weak and innocent, serve my lord faithfully and defend the realm with all my might, and I swore that I would.'

'No doubt.' Plummer did not deign to call him *ser*, Dunk could not help but notice. 'I shall need to consult with Lord Ashford. Will you or your late master be known to any of the good knights here assembled?'

Dunk thought a moment. 'There was a pavilion flying the banner of House Dondarrion? The black, with purple lightning?'

'That would be Ser Manfred, of that House.'

'Ser Arlan served his lord father in Dorne, three years past. Ser Manfred might remember me.'

'I would advise you to speak to him. If he will vouch for you, bring him here with you on the morrow, at this same time.'

'As you say, m'lord.' He started for the door.

'Ser Duncan,' the steward called after him.

Dunk turned back.

'You are aware,' the man said, 'that those vanquished in tourney forfeit their arms, armour, and horse to the victors, and must needs ransom them back?'

'I know.'

'And do you have the coin to pay such ransom?'

Now he *knew* his ears were red. 'I won't have need of coin,' he said, praying it was true. *All I need is one victory. If I win my first tilt, I'll have the loser's armour and horse, or his gold, and I can stand a loss myself.*

He walked slowly down the steps, reluctant to get on with

what he must do next. In the yard, he collared one of the stableboys. 'I must speak with Lord Ashford's master of horse.'

'I'll find him for you.'

It was cool and dim in the stables. An unruly grey stallion snapped at him as he passed, but Sweetfoot only whickered softly and nuzzled his hand when he raised it to her nose. 'You're a good girl, aren't you?' he murmured. The old man always said that a knight should never love a horse, since more than a few were like to die under him, but he never heeded his own counsel either. Dunk had often seen him spend his last copper on an apple for old Chestnut or some oats for Sweetfoot and Thunder. The palfrey had been Ser Arlan's riding horse, and she had borne him tirelessly over thousands of miles, all up and down the Seven Kingdoms. Dunk felt as though he was betraying an old friend, but what choice did he have? Chestnut was too old to be worth much of anything, and Thunder must carry him in the lists.

Some time passed before the master of horse deigned to appear. As he waited, Dunk heard a blare of trumpets from the walls, and a voice in the yard. Curious, he led Sweetfoot to the stable door to see what was happening. A large party of knights and mounted archers poured through the gates, a hundred men at least, riding some of the most splendid horses that Dunk had ever seen. *Some great lord has come.* He grabbed the arm of a stableboy as he ran past. 'Who are they?'

The boy looked at him queerly. 'Can't you see the banners?' He wrenched free and hurried off.

The banners . . . As Dunk turned his head, a gust of wind lifted the black silk pennon atop the tall staff, and the fierce three-headed dragon of House Targaryen seemed to spread its wings, breathing scarlet fire. The banner-bearer was a tall knight in white scale armour chased with gold, a pure white cloak streaming from his shoulders. Two of the other riders were armoured in white from head to heel as well. *Kingsguard knights with the royal banner.* Small wonder Lord Ashford and his sons came hurrying out the doors of the keep, and the fair maid too, a short girl with yellow hair and a round pink face. *She does not seem so fair to me,* Dunk thought. The puppet girl was prettier.

'Boy, let go of that nag and see to my horse.'

A rider had dismounted in front of the stables. *He is talking to me,* Dunk realized. 'I am not a stableboy, m' lord.'

'Not clever enough?' The speaker wore a black cloak bordered in scarlet satin, but underneath was raiment bright as flame, all reds and yellows and golds. Slim and straight as a dirk, though only of middling height, he was near Dunk's own age. Curls of silver-gold hair framed a face sculpted and imperious; high brow and sharp cheekbones, straight nose, pale smooth skin without blemish. His eyes were a deep violet colour. 'If you cannot manage a horse, fetch me some wine and a pretty wench.'

'I . . . m'lord, pardons, I'm no serving man either. I have the honour to be a knight.'

'Knighthood has fallen on sad days,' said the princeling, but then one of the stableboys came rushing up, and he turned away to hand him the reins of his palfrey, a splendid blood bay. Dunk was forgotten in an instant. Relieved, he slunk back inside the stables to wait for the master of horse. He felt ill at ease enough around the lords in their pavilions, he had no business speaking to princes.

That the beautiful stripling was a prince he had no doubt. The Targaryens were the blood of lost Valyria across the seas, and their silver-gold hair and violet eyes set them apart from common men. Dunk knew Prince Baelor was older, but the youth might well have been one of his sons: Valarr, who was often called 'the Young Prince' to set him apart from his father, or Matarys, 'the Even Younger Prince', as old Lord Swann's fool had named him once. There were other princelings as well, cousins to Valarr and Matarys. Good King Daeron had four grown sons, three with sons of their own. The line of the dragonkings had almost died out during his father's day, but it was commonly said that Daeron II and his sons had left it secure for all time.

'You. Man. You asked for me.' Lord Ashford's master of horse had a red face made redder by his orange livery, and a brusque manner of speaking. 'What is it? I have no time for –'

'I want to sell this palfrey,' Dunk broke in quickly, before the man could dismiss him. 'She's a good horse, sure of foot –'

'I have no time, I tell you.' The man gave Sweetfoot no more than a glance. 'My lord of Ashford has no need of such. Take her to the town, perhaps Henly will give you a silver or three.' That quick, he was turning away.

'Thank you, m'lord,' Dunk said before he could go. 'M'lord, has the king come?'

The master of horse laughed at him. 'No, thank the gods. This infestation of princes is trial enough. Where am I going to find the stalls for all these animals? And fodder?' He strode off shouting at his stableboys.

By the time Dunk left the stable, Lord Ashford had escorted his princely guests into the hall, but two of the Kingsguard knights in their white armour and snowy cloaks still lingered in the yard, talking with the captain of the guard. Dunk halted before them. 'M'lords, I am Ser Duncan the Tall.'

'Well met, Ser Duncan,' answered the bigger of the white knights. 'I am Ser Roland Crakehall, and this is my Sworn Brother, Ser Donnel of Duskendale.'

The seven champions of the Kingsguard were the most puissant warriors in all the Seven Kingdoms, saving only perhaps the crown prince, Baelor Breakspear himself. 'Have you come to enter the lists?' Dunk asked anxiously.

'It would not be fitting for us to ride against those we are sworn to protect,' answered Ser Donnel, red of hair and beard.

'Prince Valarr has the honour to be one of Lady Ashford's champions,' explained Ser Roland, 'and two of his cousins mean to challenge. The rest of us have come only to watch.'

Relieved, Dunk thanked the white knights for their kindness, and rode out through the castle gates before another prince should think to accost him. *Three princelings*, he pondered as he turned the palfrey towards the streets of Ashford town. Valarr was the eldest son of Prince Baelor, second in line to the Iron Throne, but Dunk did not know how much of his father's fabled prowess with lance and sword he might have inherited. About the other Targaryen princes he knew even less. *What will I do if*

I have to ride against a prince? Will I even be allowed to challenge one so high-born? He did not know the answer. The old man had often said he was thick as a castle wall, and just now he felt it.

Henly liked the look of Sweetfoot well enough until he heard Dunk wanted to sell her. Then all the stableman could see in her were faults. He offered three hundred silvers. Dunk said he must have three thousand. After much arguing and cursing, they settled at seven hundred fifty silver stags. That was a deal closer to Henly's starting price than to Dunk's, which made him feel the loser in the tilt, but the stableman would go no higher, so in the end he had no choice but to yield. A second argument began when Dunk declared that the price did not include the saddle, and Henly insisted that it had.

Finally it was all settled. As Henly left to fetch his coin, Dunk stroked Sweetfoot's mane and told her to be brave. 'If I win, I'll come back and buy you again, I promise.' He had no doubt that all the palfrey's flaws would vanish in the intervening days, and she would be worth twice what she was today.

The stableman gave him three gold pieces and the rest in silver. Dunk bit one of the gold coins and smiled. He had never tasted gold before, nor handled it. 'Dragons', men called the coins, since they were stamped with the three-headed dragon of House Targaryen on one side. The other bore the likeness of the king. Two of the coins Henly gave him had King Daeron's face; the third was older, well-worn, and showed a different man. His name was there under his head, but Dunk could not read the letters. Gold had been shaved off its edges too, he saw. He pointed this out to Henly, and loudly. The stableman grumbled, but handed over another few silvers and a fistful of coppers to make up the weight. Dunk handed a few of the coppers right back, and nodded at Sweetfoot. 'That's for her,' he said. 'See that she has some oats tonight. Aye, and an apple too.'

With the shield on his arm and the sack of old armour slung over his shoulder, Dunk set out on foot through the sunny streets of Ashford town. The heft of all that coin in his pouch made him feel queer; almost giddy on one hand, and anxious on the other. The old man had never trusted him with more than a coin or two at a time. He could live a year on this much money. *And what will I do when it's gone, sell Thunder?* That road ended in beggary or outlawry. *This chance will never come again, I must risk all.*

By the time he splashed back across the ford to the south bank of the Cockleswent, the morning was almost done and the tourney grounds had come to life once more. The wine-sellers and sausage-makers were doing a brisk trade, a dancing bear was shuffling along to his master's playing as a singer sang 'The Bear, the Bear, and the Maiden Fair', jugglers were juggling, and the puppeteers were just finishing another fight.

Dunk stopped to watch the wooden dragon slain. When the puppet knight cut its head off and the red sawdust spilled out on to the grass, he laughed aloud and threw the girl two coppers. 'One for last night,' he called. She caught the coins in the air and threw him back a smile as sweet as any he had ever seen.

Is it me she smiles at, or the coins? Dunk had never been with a girl, and they made him nervous. Once, three years past, when the old man's purse was full after half a year in the service of blind Lord Florent, he'd told Dunk the time had come to take him to a brothel and make him a man. He'd been drunk, though, and when he was sober he did not remember. Dunk had been too embarrassed to remind him. He was not certain he wanted a whore anyway. If he could not have a highborn maiden like a proper knight, he wanted one who at least liked him more than his silver.

'Will you drink a horn of ale?' he asked the puppet girl as she was scooping the sawdust blood back into her dragon. 'With me, I mean? Or a sausage? I had a sausage last night, and it was good. They're made with pork, I think.'

'I thank you, m'lord, but we have another show.' The girl rose, and ran off to the fierce fat Dornishwoman who worked the puppet knight while Dunk stood there feeling stupid. He liked the way she ran, though. *A pretty girl, and tall. I would not have to kneel to kiss that one.* He knew how to kiss. A tavern girl had showed him one night in Lannisport, a year ago, but she'd been so short she had to sit on the table to reach his lips. The memory made his ears burn. What a great fool he was. It was jousting he should be thinking about, not kissing.

Lord Ashford's carpenters were whitewashing the waist-high wooden barriers that would separate the jousters. Dunk watched them work a while. There were five lanes, arrayed north to south so none of the competitors would ride with the sun in his eyes. A three-tiered viewing stand had been raised on the eastern side of the lists, with an orange canopy to shield the lords and ladies from rain and sun. Most would sit on benches, but four high-backed chairs had been erected in the centre of the platform, for Lord Ashford, the fair maid, and the visiting princes.

On the eastern verge of the meadow, a quintain had been set up and a dozen knights were tilting at it, sending the pole arm spinning every time they struck the splintered shield suspended from one end. Dunk watched the Brute of Bracken take his turn, and then Lord Caron of the Marches. *I do not have as good a seat as any of them*, he thought uneasily.

Elsewhere, men were training afoot, going at each other with wooden swords while their squires stood shouting ribald advice. Dunk watched a stocky youth try to hold off a muscular knight who seemed lithe and quick as a mountain cat. Both had the red apple of the Fossoways painted on their shields, but the younger man's was soon hacked and chipped to pieces. 'Here's an apple that's not ripe yet,' the older said as he slammed the other's helm. The younger Fossoway was bruised and bloody by the time he yielded, but his foe was hardly winded. He raised his visor, looked about, saw Dunk, and said, 'You there. Yes, you, the big one. Knight of the winged chalice. Is that a longsword you wear?'

'It is mine by rights,' Dunk said defensively. 'I am Ser Duncan the Tall.'

'And I Ser Steffon Fossoway. Would you care me try me, Ser Duncan the Tall? It would be good to have someone new to cross swords with. My cousin's not ripe yet, as you've seen.'

'Do it, Ser Duncan,' urged the beaten Fossoway as he removed his helm. 'I may not be ripe, but my good cousin is rotten to the core. Knock the seeds out of him.'

Dunk shook his head. Why were these lordlings involving him in their quarrel? He wanted no part of it. 'I thank you, ser, but I have matters to attend.' He was uncomfortable carrying so much coin. The sooner he paid Steely Pate and got his armour, the happier he would be.

Ser Steffon looked at him scornfully. 'The hedge knight has matters.' He glanced about and found another likely opponent loitering nearby. 'Ser Grance, well met. Come try me. I know every feeble trick my cousin Raymun has mastered, and it seems that Ser Duncan needs to return to the hedges. Come, come.'

Dunk stalked away red-faced. He did not have many tricks himself, feeble or otherwise, and he did not want anyone to see him fight until the tourney. The old man always said that the better you knew your foe, the easier it was to best him. Knights like Ser Steffon had sharp eyes to find a man's weakness at a glance. Dunk was strong and quick, and his weight and reach were in his favour, but he did not believe for a moment that his skills were the equal of these others. Ser Arlan had taught him as best he could, but the old man had never been the greatest of knights even when young. Great knights did not live their lives in the hedges, nor die by the side of a muddy road. *That will not happen to me*, Dunk vowed. *I will show them that I can be more than a hedge knight.*

'Ser Duncan.' The younger Fossoway hurried to catch him. 'I should not have urged you to try my cousin. I was angry with his arrogance, and you are so large, I thought . . . well, it was wrong of me. You wear no armour. He would have broken your hand if he could, or a knee. He likes to batter men in the training yard, so they will be bruised and vulnerable later, should he meet them in the lists.'

'He did not break you.'

'No, but I am his own blood, though his is the senior branch of the apple tree, as he never ceases to remind me. I am Raymun Fossoway.'

'Well met. Will you and your cousin ride in the tourney?'

'He will, for a certainty. As to me, would that I could. I am only a squire as yet. My cousin has promised to knight me, but insists that I am not ripe yet.' Raymun had a square face, a pug nose, and short woolly hair, but his smile was engaging. 'You have the look of a challenger, it seems to me. Whose shield do you mean to strike?'

'It makes no difference,' said Dunk. That was what you were supposed to say, though it made all the difference in the world. 'I will not enter the lists until the third day.'

'And by then some of the champions will have fallen, yes,' Raymun said. 'Well, may the Warrior smile on you, ser.'

'And you.' *If he is only a squire, what business do I have being a knight? One of us is a fool.* The silver in Dunk's pouch clinked with every step, but he could lose it all in a heartbeat, he knew. Even the rules of this tourney worked against him, making it very unlikely that he would face a green or feeble foe.

There were a dozen different forms a tourney might follow, according to the whim of the lord who hosted it. Some were mock battles between teams of knights, others wild mêlées where the glory went to the last fighter left standing. Where individual combats were the rule, pairings were sometimes determined by lot, and sometimes by the master of the games.

Lord Ashford was staging this tourney to celebrate his daughter's thirteenth nameday. The fair maid would sit by her father's side as the reigning Queen of Love and Beauty. Five champions wearing her favours would defend her. All others must perforce be challengers, but any man who could defeat one of the champions would take his place and stand as a champion himself, until such time as another challenger unseated him. At the end of three days of jousting, the five who remained would determine whether the fair maid retain the crown of Love and Beauty, or whether another would wear it in her place.

Dunk stared at the grassy lists and the empty chairs on the viewing stand and pondered his chances. One victory was all he needed; then he could name himself one of the champions of Ashford Meadow, if only for an hour. The old man had lived nigh on sixty years and had never been a champion. *It is not too much to hope for, if the gods are good.* He thought back on all the songs he had heard, songs of blind Symeon Star-Eyes and noble Serwyn of the Mirror Shield, of Prince Aemon the Dragonknight, Ser Ryam Redwyne, and Florian the Fool. They had all won victories against foes far more terrible than any he would face. *But they were great heroes, brave men of noble birth, except for Florian. And what am I? Dunk of Flea Bottom? Or Ser Duncan the Tall?*

He supposed he would learn the truth of that soon enough. He hefted the sack of armour and turned his feet towards the merchants' stalls, in search of Steely Pate.

Egg had worked manfully at the campsite. Dunk was pleased; he had been half afraid his squire would run off again. 'Did you get a good price for your palfrey?' the boy asked.

'How did you know I'd sold her?'

'You rode off and walked back, and if robbers had stolen her you'd be more angry than you are.'

'I got enough for this.' Dunk took out his new armour to show the boy. 'If you're ever to be a knight, you'll need to know good steel from bad. Look here, this is fine work. This mail is double-chain, each link bound to two others, see? It gives more protection than single chain. And the helm, Pate's rounded the top, see how it curves? A sword or an axe will slide off, where they might bite through a flat-topped helm.' Dunk lowered the greathelm over his head. 'How does it look?'

'There's no visor,' Egg pointed out.

'There's air holes. Visors are points of weakness.' Steely Pate had said as much. 'If you knew how many knights have taken an arrow in the eye as they lifted their visor for a suck o' cool air, you'd never want one,' he'd told Dunk.

'There's no crest either,' said Egg. 'It's just plain.'

Dunk lifted off the helm. 'Plain is fine for the likes of me. See how bright the steel is? It will be your task to keep it that way. You know how to scour mail?'

'In a barrel of sand,' said the boy, 'but you don't have a barrel. Did you buy a pavilion too, ser?'

'I didn't get *that* good a price.' *The boy is too bold for his own good, I ought to beat that out of him.* He knew he would not, though. He liked the boldness. He needed to be bolder himself. *My squire is braver than I am, and more clever.* 'You did well here, Egg,' Dunk told him. 'On the morrow, you'll come with me. Have a look at the tourney grounds. We'll buy oats for the horses and fresh bread for ourselves. Maybe a bit of cheese as well, they were selling good cheese at one of the stalls.'

'I won't need to go into the castle, will I?'

'Why not? One day, I mean to live in a castle. I hope to win a place above the salt before I'm done.'

The boy said nothing. *Perhaps he fears to enter a lord's hall,* Dunk reflected. *That's no more than might be expected. He will grow out of it in time.* He went back to admiring his armour, and wondering how long he would wear it.

Ser Manfred was a thin man with a sour look on his face. He wore a black surcoat slashed with the purple lightning of House Dondarrion, but Dunk would have remembered him anyway by his unruly mane of red-gold hair. 'Ser Arlan served your lord father when he and Lord Caron burned the Vulture King out of the Red Mountains, ser,' he said from one knee. 'I was only a boy then, but I squired for him. Ser Arlan of Pennytree.'

Ser Manfred scowled. 'No. I know him not. Nor you, boy.'

Dunk showed him the old man's shield. 'This was his sigil, the winged chalice.'

'My lord father took eight hundred knights and near four thousand foot into the mountains. I cannot be expected to remember every one of them, nor what shields they carried. It may be that you were with us, but . . .' Ser Manfred shrugged.

Dunk was struck speechless for an instant. *The old man took a wound in your father's service, how can you have forgotten him?* 'They will not allow me to challenge unless some knight or lord will vouch for me.'

'And what is that to me?' said Ser Manfred. 'I have given you enough of my time, ser.'

If he went back to the castle without Ser Manfred, he was lost. Dunk eyed the purple lightning embroidered across the black wool of Ser Manfred's surcoat and said, 'I remember your father telling the camp how your house got its sigil. One stormy night, as the first of your line bore a message across the Dornish Marches, an arrow killed his horse beneath him and spilled him on the ground. Two Dornishmen came out of the darkness in ring-mail and crested helms. His sword had broken beneath him when he fell. When he saw that, he thought he was doomed. But as the Dornishmen closed to cut him down, lightning cracked from the sky. It was a bright burning purple, and it split, striking the Dornishmen in their steel and killing them both where they stood. The message gave the Storm King victory over the Dornish, and in thanks he raised the messenger to lordship. He was the first Lord Dondarrion, so he took for his arms a forked purple lightning bolt, on a black field powdered with stars.'

If Dunk thought the tale would impress Ser Manfred, he could not have been more wrong. 'Every potboy and groom who has ever served my father hears that story soon or late. Knowing it does not make you a knight. Begone with you, ser.'

It was with a leaden heart that Dunk returned to Ashford Castle, wondering what he might say so that Plummer would grant him the right of challenge. The steward was not in his turret chamber, however. A guard told him he might be found in the Great Hall. 'Shall I wait here?' Dunk asked. 'How long will he be?'

'How should I know? Do what you please.'

The Great Hall was not so great, as halls went, but Ashford was a small castle. Dunk entered through a side door, and spied the steward at once. He was standing with Lord Ashford and a dozen other men at the top of the hall. He walked towards them, beneath a wall hung with wool tapestries of fruits and flowers.

'. . . more concerned if they were *your* sons, I'll wager,' an angry man was saying as Dunk approached. His straight hair and square-cut beard were so fair they seemed white in the dimness of the hall, but as he got closer he saw that they were in truth a pale silvery colour touched with gold.

'Daeron has done this before,' another replied. Plummer was standing so as to block Dunk's view of the speaker. 'You should never have commanded him to enter the lists. He belongs on a tourney field no more than Aerys does, or Rhaegel.'

'By which you mean he'd sooner ride a whore than a horse,' the first man said. Thickly-built and powerful, the prince – he was surely a prince – wore a leather brigantine covered with silver studs beneath a heavy black cloak trimmed with ermine. Pox scars marked his cheeks, only partly concealed by his silvery beard. 'I do not need to be reminded of my son's failings, brother. He has only eighteen years. He can change. He *will* change, gods be damned, or I swear I'll see him dead.'

'Don't be an utter fool. Daeron is what he is, but he is still your blood and mine. I have no doubt Ser Roland will turn him up, and Aegon with him.'

'When the tourney is over, perhaps.'

'Aerion is here. He is a better lance than Daeron in any case, if it is the tourney that concerns you.' Dunk could see the speaker now. He was seated in the high seat, a sheaf of parchments in one hand, Lord Ashford hovering at his shoulder. Even seated, he looked to be a head taller than the other, to judge from the long straight legs stretched out before him. His short-cropped hair was dark and peppered with grey, his strong jaw clean-shaven. His nose looked as though it had been broken more than once. Though he was dressed very plainly, in green doublet, brown mantle, and scuffed boots, there was a weight to him, a sense of power and certainty.

It came to Dunk that he had walked in on something that he ought never have heard. *I had best go and come back later, when they are done*, he decided. But it was already too late. The prince with the silvery beard suddenly took note of him.

'Who are you, and what do you mean by bursting in on us?' he demanded harshly

'He is the knight that our good steward was expecting,' the seated man said, smiling at Dunk in a way that suggested he had been aware of him all the time. 'You and I are the intruders here, brother. Come closer, ser.'

Dunk edged forward, uncertain what was expected of him. He looked at Plummer, but got no help there. The pinch-faced steward who had been so forceful yesterday now stood silent, studying the stones of the floor. 'My lords,' he said, 'I asked Ser Manfred Dondarrion to vouch for me so I might enter the lists, but he refuses. He says he knows me not. Ser Arlan served him, though, I swear it. I have his sword and shield, I –'

'A shield and a sword do not make a knight,' declared Lord Ashford, a big bald man with a round red face. 'Plummer has spoken to me of you. Even if we accept that these arms belonged to this Ser Arlan of Pennytree, it may well be that you found him dead and stole them. Unless you have some better proof of what you say, some writing or –'

'I remember Ser Arlan of Pennytree,' the man in the high seat said quietly. 'He never won a tourney that I know, but he never shamed himself either. At King's Landing sixteen years ago, he overthrew Lord Stokeworth and the Bastard of Harrenhal in the mêlée, and many years before at Lannisport he unhorsed the Grey Lion himself. The lion was not so grey then, to be sure.'

'He told me about that, many a time,' said Dunk.

The tall man studied him. 'Then you will remember the Grey Lion's true name, I have no doubt.'

For a moment there was nothing in Dunk's head at all. *A thousand times the old man had told that tale, a thousand times, the lion, the lion, his name, his name, his name . . .* He was near despair when suddenly it came. 'Ser Damon Lannister!' he shouted. 'The Grey Lion! He's Lord of Casterly Rock now.'

'So he is,' said the tall man pleasantly, 'and he enters the lists on the morrow.' He rattled the sheaf of papers in his hand.

'How can you possibly remember some insignificant hedge

knight who chanced to unhorse Damon Lannister many years ago?' said the prince with the silver beard, frowning.

'I make it a practice to learn all I can of my foes.'

'Why would you deign to joust with a hedge knight?'

'It was nine years past, at Storm's End. Lord Baratheon held a hastilude to celebrate the birth of a grandson. The lots made Ser Arlan my opponent in the first tilt. We broke four lances before I finally unhorsed him.'

'*Seven*,' insisted Dunk, 'and that was against the Prince of Dragonstone!' No sooner were the words out than he wanted them back. *Dunk the lunk, thick as a castle wall*, he could hear the old man chiding.

'So it was.' The prince with the broken nose smiled gently. 'Tales grow in the telling, I know. Do not think ill of your old master, but it was four lances only, I fear.'

Dunk was grateful that the hall was dim; he knew his ears were red. 'My lord.' *No, that's wrong too.* 'Your Grace.' He fell to his knees and lowered his head. 'As you say, four, I meant no . . . I never . . . the old man, Ser Arlan, he used to say I was thick as a castle wall and slow as an aurochs.'

'And strong as an aurochs, by the look of you,' said Baelor Breakspear. 'No harm was done, ser. Rise.'

Dunk got to his feet, wondering if he should keep his head down or if he was allowed to look a prince in the face. *I am speaking with Baelor Targaryen, Prince of Dragonstone, Hand of the King, and heir apparent to the Iron Throne of Aegon the Conqueror.* What could a hedge knight dare say to such a person? 'Y-you gave him back his horse and armour and took no ransom, I remember,' he stammered. 'The old – Ser Arlan, he told me you were the soul of chivalry, and that one day the Seven Kingdoms would be safe in your hands.'

'Not for many a year still, I pray,' Prince Baelor said.

'No,' said Dunk, horrified. He almost said, *I didn't mean that the king should die*, but stopped himself in time. 'I am sorry, m'lord. Your Grace, I mean.'

Belatedly he recalled that the stocky man with the silver beard had addressed Prince Baelor as brother. *He is blood of the dragon as well, damn me for a fool.* He could only be Prince Maekar, the youngest of King Daeron's four sons. Prince Aerys was bookish and Prince Rhaegel mad, meek, and sickly. Neither was like to cross half the realm to attend a tourney, but Maekar was said to be a redoubtable warrior in his own right, though ever in the shadow of his eldest brother.

'You wish to enter the lists, is that it?' asked Prince Baelor. 'That decision rests with the master of the games, but I see no reason to deny you.'

The steward inclined his head. 'As you say, my lord.'

Dunk tried to stammer out thanks, but Prince Maekar cut him off. 'Very well, ser, you are grateful. Now be off with you.'

'You must forgive my noble brother, ser,' said Prince Baelor. 'Two of his sons have gone astray on their way here, and he fears for them.'

'The spring rains have swollen many of the streams,' said Dunk. 'Perhaps the princes are only delayed.'

'I did not come here to take counsel from a hedge knight,' Prince Maekar declared to his brother.

'You may go, ser,' Prince Baelor told Dunk, not unkindly.

'Yes, my lord.' He bowed and turned.

But before he could get away, the prince called after him. 'Ser. One thing more. You are not of Ser Arlan's blood?'

'Yes, m'lord. I mean, no. I'm not.'

The prince nodded at the battered shield Dunk carried, and the winged chalice upon its face. 'By law, only a trueborn son is entitled to inherit a knight's arms. You must needs find a new device, ser, a sigil of your own.'

'I will,' said Dunk. 'Thank you again, Your Grace. I will fight bravely, you'll see.' *As brave as Baelor Breakspear*, the old man would often say.

The wine-sellers and sausage-makers were doing a brisk trade, and whores walked brazenly amongst the stalls and pavilions. Some were pretty enough, one red-haired girl in particular. He could not help staring at her breasts, the way they moved under her loose shift as she sauntered past. He thought of the silver in his pouch. *I could have her, if I liked. She'd like the clink of my coin well enough, I could take her back to my camp and have her, all night if I wanted.* He had never lain with a woman, and for all he knew he might die in his first tilt. Tourneys could be dangerous . . . but whores could be dangerous too, the old man had warned him of that. *She might rob me while I slept, and what would I do then?* When the red-haired girl glanced back over her shoulder at him, Dunk shook his head and walked away.

He found Egg at the puppet show, sitting crosslegged on the ground with the hood of his cloak pulled all the way forward to hide his baldness. The boy had been afraid to enter the castle, which Dunk put down to equal parts shyness and shame. *He does not think himself worthy to mingle with lords and ladies, let alone great princes.* It had been the same with him when he was little. The world beyond Flea Bottom had seemed as frightening as it was exciting. *Egg needs time, that's all.* For the present, it seemed kinder to give the lad a few coppers and let him enjoy himself among the stalls than to drag him along unwilling into the castle.

This morning the puppeteers were doing the tale of Florian and Jonquil. The fat Dornishwoman was working Florian in his armour made of motley, while the tall girl held Jonquil's strings. 'You are no knight,' she was saying as the puppet's mouth moved up and down. 'I know you. You are Florian the Fool.'

'I am, my lady,' the other puppet answered, kneeling. 'As great a fool as ever lived, and as great a knight as well.'

'A fool *and* a knight?' said Jonquil. 'I have never heard of such a thing.'

'Sweet lady,' said Florian, 'all men are fools, and all men are knights, where women are concerned.'

It was a good show, sad and sweet both, with a sprightly swordfight at the end, and a nicely-painted giant. When it was over, the fat woman went among the crowd to collect coins while the girl packed away the puppets.

Dunk collected Egg and went up to her.

'M'lord?' she said, with a sideways glance and a half-smile.

She was a head shorter than he was, but still taller than any other girl he had ever seen.

'That was good,' Egg enthused. 'I like how you make them move, Jonquil and the dragon and all. I saw a puppet show last year, but they moved all jerky. Yours are more smooth.'

'Thank you,' she told the boy politely.

Dunk said, 'Your figures are well carved too. The dragon, especially. A fearsome beast. You make them yourself?'

She nodded. 'My uncle does the carving. I paint them.'

'Could you paint something for me? I have the coin to pay.' He slipped the shield off his shoulder and turned it to show her. 'I need to paint something over the chalice.'

The girl glanced at the shield, and then at him. 'What would you want painted?'

Dunk had not considered that. If not the old man's winged chalice, what? His head was empty. *Dunk the lunk, thick as a castle wall.* 'I don't . . . I'm not certain.' His ears were turning red, he realized miserably. 'You must think me an utter fool.'

She smiled. 'All men are fools, and all men are knights.'

'What colour paint do you have?' he asked, hoping that might give him an idea.

'I can mix paints to make any colour you want.'

The old man's brown had always seemed drab to Dunk. 'The field should be the colour of sunset,' he said suddenly. 'The old man liked sunsets. And the device . . .'

'An elm tree,' said Egg. 'A big elm tree, like the one by the pool, with a brown trunk and green branches.'

'Yes,' Dunk said. 'That would serve. An elm tree . . . but with a shooting star above. Could you do that?'

The girl nodded. 'Give me the shield. I'll paint it this very night, and have it back to you on the morrow.'

Dunk handed it over. 'I am called Ser Duncan the Tall.'

'I'm Tanselle,' she laughed. 'Tanselle Too-Tall, the boys used to call me.'

'You're not too tall,' Dunk blurted out. 'You're just right for . . .' He realized what he had been about to say, and blushed furiously.

'For?' said Tanselle, cocking her head inquisitively.

'Puppets,' he finished lamely.

The first day of the tourney dawned bright and clear. Dunk bought a sackful of foodstuffs, so they were able to break their fast on goose eggs, fried bread, and bacon, but when the food was cooked he found he had no appetite. His belly felt hard as a rock, even though he knew he would not ride today. The right of first challenge would go to knights of higher birth and greater renown, to lords and their sons and champions from other tourneys.

Egg chattered all though their breakfast, talking of this man and that man and how they might fare. *He was not japing me when he said he knew every good knight in the Seven Kingdoms*, Dunk thought ruefully. He found it humbling to listen so intently to the words of a scrawny orphan boy, but Egg's knowledge might serve him should he face one of these men in a tilt.

The meadow was a churning mass of people, all trying to elbow their way closer for a better view. Dunk was as good an elbower as any, and bigger than most. He squirmed forward to a rise six yards from the fence. When Egg complained that all he could see were arses, Dunk sat the boy on his shoulders. Across the field, the viewing stand was filling up with high-born lords and ladies, a few rich townfolk, and a score of knights who had decided not to compete today. Of Prince Maekar he saw no sign, but he recognized Prince Baelor at Lord Ashford's side. Sunlight flashed golden off the shoulder clasp that held his cloak and the slim coronet about his temples, but otherwise he dressed far more simply than most of the other lords. *He does not look a Targaryen in truth, with that dark hair*. Dunk said as much to Egg.

'It's said he favours his mother,' the boy reminded him. 'She was a Dornish princess.'

The five champions had raised their pavilions at the north end of the lists with the river behind them. The smallest two were orange, and the shields hung outside their doors displayed the white sun-and-chevron. Those would be Lord Ashford's sons

Androw and Robert, brothers to the fair maid. Dunk had never heard other knights speak of their prowess, which meant they would likely be the first to fall.

Beside the orange pavilions stood one of deep-dyed green, much larger. The golden rose of Highgarden flapped above it, and the same device was emblazoned on the great green shield outside the door. 'That's Leo Tyrell, Lord of Highgarden,' said Egg.

'I knew that,' said Dunk, irritated. 'The old man and I served at Highgarden before you were ever born.' He hardly remembered that year himself, but Ser Arlan had often spoken of Leo Longthorn, as he was sometimes called; a peerless jouster, for all the silver in his hair. 'That must be Lord Leo beside the tent, the slender greybeard in green and gold.'

'Yes,' said Egg. 'I saw him at King's Landing once. He's not one you'll want to challenge, ser.'

'Boy, I do not require your counsel on who to challenge.'

The fourth pavilion was sewn together from diamond-shaped pieces of cloth, alternating red and white. Dunk did not know the colours, but Egg said they belonged to a knight from the Vale of Arryn named Ser Humfrey Hardyng. 'He won a great mêlée at Maidenpool last year, ser, and overthrew Ser Donnel of Duskendale and the Lords Arryn and Royce in the lists.'

The last pavilion was Prince Valarr's. Of black silk it was, with a line of pointed scarlet pennons hanging from its roof like long red flames. The shield on its stand was glossy black, emblazoned with the three-headed dragon of House Targaryen. One of the Kingsguard knights stood beside it, his shining white armour stark against the black of the tentcloth. Seeing him there, Dunk wondered whether any of the challengers would dare to touch the dragon shield. Valarr was the king's grandson, after all, and son to Baelor Breakspear.

He need not have worried. When the horns blew to summon the challengers, all five of the maid's champions were called forth to defend her. Dunk could hear the murmur of excitement in the crowd as the challengers appeared one by one at the south end of the lists. Heralds boomed out the name of each knight in turn. They paused before the viewing stand to dip their lances in salute to Lord Ashford, Prince Baelor, and the fair maid, then circled to the north end of the field to select their opponents. The Grey Lion of Casterly Rock struck the shield of Lord Tyrell, while his golden-haired heir Ser Tybolt Lannister challenged Lord Ashford's eldest son. Lord Tully of Riverrun tapped the diamond-patterned shield of Ser Humfrey Hardyng, Ser Abelar Hightower knocked upon Valarr's, and the younger Ashford was called out by Ser Lyonel Baratheon, the knight they called the Laughing Storm.

The challengers trotted back to the south end of the lists to await their foes: Ser Abelar in silver-and-smoke colours, a stone watchtower on his shield, crowned with fire; the two Lannisters all crimson, bearing the golden lion of Casterly Rock; the Laughing Storm shining in cloth-of-gold, with a black stag on breast and shield and a rack of iron antlers on his helm; Lord Tully wearing a striped blue-and-red cloak clasped with a silver trout at each shoulder. They pointed their twelve-foot lances skyward, the gusty winds snapping and tugging at the pennons.

At the north end of the field, squires held brightly barded destriers for the champions to mount. They donned their helms and took up lance and shield, in splendour the equal of their foes: the Ashfords' billowing orange silks, Ser Humfrey's red-and-white diamonds, Lord Leo on his white charger with green satin trappings patterned with golden roses, and of course Valarr Targaryen. The Young Prince's horse was black as night, to match the colour of his armour, lance, shield, and trappings. Atop his helm was a gleaming three-headed dragon, wings spread, enamelled in a rich red; its twin was painted upon the glossy black surface of his shield. Each of the defenders had a wisp of orange silk knotted about an arm, a favour bestowed by the fair maid.

As the champions trotted into position, Ashford Meadow grew almost still. Then a horn sounded, and stillness turned to tumult in half a heartbeat. Ten pairs of gilded spurs drove into the flanks of ten great warhorses, a thousand voices began to scream and shout, forty ironshod hooves pounded and tore the grass, ten lances dipped and steadied, the field seemed almost to shake, and champions and challengers came together in a rending crash of wood and steel. In an instant, the riders were beyond each other, wheeling about for another pass. Lord Tully reeled in his saddle but managed to keep his seat. When the commons realized that all ten of the lances had broken, a great roar of approval went up. It was a splendid omen for the success of the tourney, and a testament to the skill of the competitors.

Squires handed fresh lances to the jousters to replace the broken ones they cast aside, and once more the spurs dug deep. Dunk could feel the earth trembling beneath the soles of his feet. Atop his shoulders, Egg shouted happily and waved his pipestem arms. The Young Prince passed nearest to them. Dunk saw the point of his black lance kiss the watchtower on his foe's shield and slide off to slam into his chest, even as Ser Abelar's own lance burst into splinters against Valarr's breastplate. The grey stallion in the silver-and-smoke trappings reared with the force of the impact, and Ser Abelar Hightower was lifted from his stirrups and dashed violently to the ground.

Lord Tully was down as well, unhorsed by Ser Humfrey Hardyng, but he sprang up at once and drew his longsword, and Ser Humfrey cast aside his lance – unbroken – and dismounted to continue their fight afoot. Ser Abelar was not so spritely. His squire ran out, loosened his helm, and called for help, and two serving men lifted the dazed knight by the arms to help him back to his pavilion. Elsewhere on the field, the six knights who had remained ahorse were riding their third course. More lances shattered, and this time Lord Leo Tyrell aimed his point so expertly he ripped the Grey Lion's helm cleanly off his head. Barefaced, the Lord of Casterly Rock raised his hand in salute and dismounted, yielding the match. By then Ser Humfrey had beaten Lord Tully into surrender, showing himself as skilled with a sword as he was with a lance.

Tybolt Lannister and Androw Ashford rode against each other thrice more before Ser Androw finally lost shield, seat, and match all at once. The younger Ashford lasted even longer, breaking no less than nine lances against Ser Lyonel Baratheon, the Laughing Storm. Champion and challenger both lost their saddles on their tenth course, only to rise together to fight on, sword against mace. Finally a battered Ser Robert Ashford admitted defeat, but on the viewing stand his father looked anything but dejected. Both Lord Ashford's sons had been ushered from the ranks of the champions, it was true, but they had acquitted themselves nobly against two of the finest knights in the Seven Kingdoms.

I must do even better, though, Dunk thought as he watched victor and vanquished embrace and walk together from the field. *It is not enough for me to fight well and lose. I must win at least the first challenge, or I lose all.*

Ser Tybolt Lannister and the Laughing Storm would now take their places among the champions, replacing the men they had defeated. Already the orange pavilions were coming down. A few feet away, the Young Prince sat at his ease in a raised camp chair before his great black tent. His helm was off. He had dark hair like his father, but a bright streak ran through it. A serving man brought him a silver goblet and he took a sip. *Water, if he is wise,* Dunk thought, *wine if not.* He found himself wondering if Valarr had indeed inherited a measure of his father's prowess, or whether it had only been that he had drawn the weakest opponent.

A fanfare of trumpets announced that three new challengers had entered the lists. The heralds shouted their names. 'Ser Pearse of House Caron, Lord of the Marches.' He had a silver harp emblazoned on his shield, though his surcoat was patterned with nightingales. 'Ser Joseth of House Mallister, from Seagard.' Ser Joseth sported a winged helm; on his shield, a silver eagle flew across an indigo sky. 'Ser Gawen of House Swann, Lord of Stonehelm on the Cape of Wrath.' A pair of swans, one black and one white, fought furiously on his arms. Lord Gawen's armour, cloak, and horse bardings were a riot of black and white as well, down to the stripes on his scabbard and lance.

Lord Caron, harper and singer and knight of renown, touched

the point of his lance to Lord Tyrell's rose. Ser Joseth thumped on Ser Humfrey Hardyng's diamonds. And the black-and-white knight, Lord Gawen Swann, challenged the black prince with the white guardian. Dunk rubbed his chin. Lord Gawen was even older than the old man, and the old man was dead. 'Egg, who is the least dangerous of these challengers?' he asked the boy on his shoulders, who seemed to know so much of these knights.

'Lord Gawen,' the boy said at once. 'Valarr's foe.'

'*Prince* Valarr,' he corrected. 'A squire must keep a courteous tongue, boy.'

The three challengers took their places as the three champions mounted up. Men were making wagers all around them and calling out encouragement to their choices, but Dunk had eyes only for the prince. On the first pass he struck Lord Gawen's shield a glancing blow, the blunted point of the lance sliding aside just as it had with Ser Abelar Hightower, only this time it was deflected the other way, into empty air. Lord Gawen's own lance broke clean against the prince's chest, and Valarr seemed about to fall for an instant before he recovered his seat.

The second time through the lists, Valarr swung his lance left, aiming for his foe's breast, but struck his shoulder instead. Even so, the blow was enough to make the older knight lose his lance. One arm flailed for balance and Lord Gawen fell. The Young Prince swung from the saddle and drew his sword, but the fallen man waved him off and raised his visor. 'I yield, Your Grace,' he called. 'Well fought.' The lords in the viewing stand echoed him, shouting, '*Well fought! Well fought!*' as Valarr knelt to help the grey-haired lord to his feet.

'It was not either,' Egg complained.

'Be quiet, or you can go back to camp.'

Further away, Ser Joseth Mallister was being carried off the field unconscious, while the harp lord and the rose lord were going at each other lustily with blunted longaxes, to the delight of the roaring crowd. Dunk was so intent on Valarr Targaryen that he scarcely saw them. *He is a fair knight, but no more than that,* he found himself thinking. *I would have a chance against him. If the gods were good, I might even unhorse him, and once afoot my weight and strength would tell.*

'Get him!' Egg shouted merrily, shifting his seat on Dunk's back in his excitement. 'Get him! Hit him! Yes! He's right there, he's *right there*!' It seemed to be Lord Caron he was cheering on. The harper was playing a different sort of music now, driving Lord Leo back and back as steel sang on steel. The crowd seemed almost equally divided between them, so cheers and curses mingled freely in the morning air. Chips of wood and paint were flying from Lord Leo's shield as Lord Pearse's axe knocked the petals off his golden rose, one by one, until the shield finally shattered and split. But as it did, the axehead hung up for an instant in the wood . . . and Lord Leo's own axe crashed down on the haft of his foe's weapon, breaking it off not a foot from his hand. He cast aside his broken shield, and suddenly he was the one on the attack. Within moments, the harper knight was on one knee, singing his surrender.

For the rest of the morning and well into the afternoon, it was more of the same, as challengers took the field in twos and threes, and sometimes five together. Trumpets blew, the heralds called out names, warhorses charged, the crowd cheered, lances snapped like twigs, and swords rang against helms and mail. It was, smallfolk and high lord alike agreed, a splendid day of jousting. Ser Humfrey Hardyng and Ser Humfrey Beesbury, a bold young knight in yellow and black stripes with three beehives on his shield, splintered no less than a dozen lances apiece in an epic struggle the smallfolk soon began calling, 'The Battle of Humfrey'. Ser Tybolt Lannister was unhorsed by Ser Jon Penrose and broke his sword in his fall, but fought back with shield alone to win the bout and remain a champion. One-eyed Ser Robyn Rhysling, a grizzled old knight with a salt-and-pepper beard, lost his helm to Lord Leo's lance in their first course, yet refused to yield. Three times more they rode at each other, the wind whipping Ser Robyn's hair while the shards of broken lances flew round his bare face like wooden knives, which Dunk thought all the more wondrous when Egg told him that Ser Robyn had lost his eye to a splinter from a broken lance not five years earlier. Leo Tyrell was too chivalrous to aim another lance at Ser Robyn's unprotected head, but even so Rhysling's stubborn courage (or was it folly?) left Dunk astounded. Finally the Lord of Highgarden struck Ser Robyn's breastplate a solid thump right over the heart and sent him cartwheeling to the earth.

Ser Lyonel Baratheon also fought several notable matches. Against lesser foes, he would often break into booming laughter the moment they touched his shield, and laugh all the time he was mounting and charging and knocking them from their stirrups. If his challengers wore any sort of crest on their helm, Ser Lyonel would strike it off and fling it into the crowd. The crests were ornate things, made of carved wood or shaped leather, and sometimes gilded and enamelled or even wrought in pure silver, so the men he beat did not appreciate this habit, though it made him a great favourite of the commons. Before long, only crestless men were choosing him. As loud and often as Ser Lyonel laughed down a challenger, though, Dunk thought the day's honours should go to Ser Humfrey Hardyng, who humbled fourteen knights, each one of them formidable.

Meanwhile the Young Prince sat outside his black pavilion, drinking from his silver goblet and rising from time to time to mount his horse and vanquish yet another undistinguished foe. He had won nine victories, but it seemed to Dunk that every one was hollow. *He is beating old men and upjumped squires, and a few lords of high birth and low skill. The truly dangerous men are riding past his shield as if they do not see it.*

Late in the day, a brazen fanfare announced the entry of a new challenger to the lists. He rode in on a great red charger whose black bardings were slashed to reveal glimpses of yellow, crimson, and orange beneath. As he approached the viewing stand to make his salute, Dunk saw the face beneath the raised visor, and recognized the prince he'd met in Lord Ashford's stables.

Egg's legs tightened around his neck. 'Stop that,' Dunk snapped, yanking them apart. 'Do you mean to choke me?'

'Prince Aerion Brightflame,' a herald called. *'Of the Red Keep*

of King's Landing, son of Maekar Prince of Summerhall of House Targaryen, grandson to Daeron the Good, the Second of His Name, King of the Andals, the Rhoynar, and the First Men, and Lord of the Seven Kingdoms.'

Aerion bore a three-headed dragon on his shield, but it was rendered in colours much more vivid than Valarr's; one head was orange, one yellow, one red, and the flames they breathed had the sheen of gold leaf. His surcoat was a swirl of smoke and fire woven together, and his blackened helm was surmounted by a crest of red enamel flames.

After a pause to dip his lance to Prince Baelor, a pause so brief that it was almost perfunctory, he galloped to the north end of the field, past Lord Leo's pavilion and the Laughing Storm's, slowing only when he approached Prince Valarr's tent. The Young Prince rose and stood stiffly beside his shield, and for a moment Dunk was certain that Aerion meant to strike it . . . but then he laughed and trotted past, and banged his point hard against Ser Humfrey Hardyng's diamonds. 'Come out, come out, little knight,' he sang in a loud clear voice, 'it's time you faced the dragon.'

Ser Humfrey inclined his head stiffly to his foe as his destrier was brought out, and then ignored him while he mounted, fastened his helm, and took up lance and shield. The spectators grew quiet as the two knights took their places. Dunk heard the *clang* of Prince Aerion dropping his visor. The horn blew.

Ser Humfrey broke slowly, building speed, but his foe raked the red charger hard with both spurs, coming hard. Egg's legs tightened again. *'Kill him!'* he shouted suddenly. *'Kill him, he's right there, kill him, kill him, kill him!'* Dunk was not certain which of the knights he was shouting to.

Prince Aerion's lance, gold-tipped and painted in stripes of red, orange, and yellow, swung down across the barrier. *Low, too low*, thought Dunk the moment he saw it. *He'll miss the rider and strike Ser Humfrey's horse, he needs to bring it up*. Then, with dawning horror, he began to suspect that Aerion intended no such thing. *He cannot mean to . . .*

At the last possible instant, Ser Humfrey's stallion reared

away from the oncoming point, eyes rolling in terror, but too late. Aerion's lance took the animal just above the armour that protected his breastbone, and exploded out of the back of his neck in a gout of bright blood. Screaming, the horse crashed sideways, knocking the wooden barrier to pieces as he fell. Ser Humfrey tried to leap free, but a foot caught in a stirrup and they heard his shriek as his leg was crushed between the splintered fence and falling horse.

All of Ashford Meadow was shouting. Men ran on to the field to extricate Ser Humfrey, but the stallion, dying in agony, kicked at them as they approached. Aerion, having raced blithely around the carnage to the end of the lists, wheeled his horse and came galloping back. He was shouting too, though Dunk could not make out the words over the almost human screams of the dying horse. Vaulting from the saddle, Aerion drew his sword and advanced on his fallen foe. His own squires and one of Ser Humfrey's had to pull him back. Egg squirmed on Dunk's shoulders. 'Let me down,' the boy said. 'The poor horse, *let me down.*'

Dunk felt sick himself. *What would I do if such a fate befell Thunder?* A man-at-arms with a poleaxe dispatched Ser Humfrey's stallion, ending the hideous screams. Dunk turned and forced his way through the press. When he came to open ground, he lifted Egg off his shoulders. The boy's hood had fallen back and his eyes were red. 'A terrible sight, aye,' he told the lad, 'but a squire must needs be strong. You'll see worse mishaps at other tourneys, I fear.'

'It was no mishap,' Egg said, mouth trembling. 'Aerion meant to do it. You saw.'

Dunk frowned. It had looked that way to him as well, but it was hard to accept that any knight could be so unchivalrous, least of all one who was blood of the dragon. 'I saw a knight green as summer grass lose control of his lance,' he said stubbornly, 'and I'll hear no more of it. The jousting is done for the day, I think. Come, lad.'

He was right was about the end of the day's contests. By the time the chaos had been set to rights, the sun was low in the west, and Lord Ashford had called a halt.

As the shadows of evening crept across the meadow, a hundred torches were lit along the merchants' row. Dunk bought a horn of ale for himself and half a horn for the boy, to cheer him. They wandered for a time, listening to a spritely air on pipes and drums and watching a puppet show about Nymeria, the warrior queen with the ten thousand ships. The puppeteers had only two ships, but managed a rousing sea battle all the same. Dunk wanted to ask the girl Tanselle if she had finished painting his shield, but he could see that she was busy. *I'll wait until she is done for the night*, he resolved. *Perhaps she'll have a thirst then.*

'Ser Duncan,' a voice called behind him. And then again, 'Ser Duncan.' Suddenly Dunk remembered that was him. 'I saw you among the smallfolk today, with this boy on your shoulders,' said Raymun Fossoway as he came up, smiling. 'Indeed, the two of you were hard to miss.'

'The boy is my squire. Egg, this is Raymun Fossoway.' Dunk had to pull the boy forward, and even then Egg lowered his head and stared at Raymun's boots as he mumbled a greeting.

'Well met, lad,' Raymun said easily. 'Ser Duncan, why not watch from the viewing gallery? All knights are welcome there.'

Dunk was at ease among smallfolk and servants; the idea of claiming a place amongst the lords, ladies, and landed knights made him uncomfortable. 'I would not have wanted any closer view of that last tilt.'

Raymun grimaced. 'Nor I. Lord Ashford declared Ser Humfrey the victor and awarded him Prince Aerion's courser, but even so, he will not be able to continue. His leg was broken in two places. Prince Baelor sent his own maester to tend him.'

'Will there be another champion in Ser Humfrey's place?'

'Lord Ashford had a mind to grant the place to Lord Caron, or perhaps the other Ser Humfrey, the one who gave Hardyng such a splendid match, but Prince Baelor told him that it would not be seemly to remove Ser Humfrey's shield and pavilion under the circumstances. I believe they will continue with four champions in place of five.'

Four champions, Dunk thought. *Leo Tyrell, Lyonel Baratheon, Tybolt Lannister, and Prince Valarr.* He had seen enough this first day to know how little chance he would stand against the first three. Which left only . . .

A hedge knight cannot challenge a prince. Valarr is second in line to the Iron Throne. He is Baelor Breakspear's son, and his blood is the blood of Aegon the Conquerer and the Young Dragon and Prince Aemon the Dragonknight, and I am some boy the old man found behind a pot shop in Flea Bottom.

His head hurt just thinking about it. 'Who does your cousin mean to challenge?' he asked Raymun.

'Ser Tybolt, all things being equal. They are well matched. My cousin keeps a sharp watch on every tilt, though. Should any man be wounded on the morrow, or show signs of exhaustion or weakness, Steffon will be quick to knock on his shield, you may count on it. No one has ever accused him of an excess of chivalry.' He laughed, as if to take the sting from his words. 'Ser Duncan, will you join me for a cup of wine?'

'I have a matter I must attend to,' said Dunk, uncomfortable with the notion of accepting hospitality he could not return.

'I could wait here and bring your shield when the puppet show is over, ser,' said Egg. 'They're going to do Symeon Star-Eyes later, and make the dragon fight again as well.'

'There, you see, your matter is attended to, and the wine awaits,' said Raymun. 'It's an Arbor vintage, too. How can you refuse me?'

Bereft of excuses, Dunk had no choice but to follow, leaving Egg at the puppet show. The apple of House Fossoway flew above the gold-coloured pavilion where Raymun attended his cousin. Behind it, two servants were basting a goat with honey and herbs over a small cookfire. 'There's food as well, if you're hungry,' Raymun said negligently as he held the flap for Dunk. A brazier of coals lit the interior and made the air pleasantly warm. Raymun filled two cups with wine. 'They say Aerion is in a rage at Lord Ashford for awarding his charger to Ser

Humfrey,' he commented as he poured, 'but I'll wager it was his uncle who counselled it.' He handed Dunk a wine cup.

'Prince Baelor is an honourable man.'

'As the Bright Prince is not?' Raymun laughed. 'Don't look so anxious, Ser Duncan, there's none here but us. It is no secret that Aerion is a bad piece of work. Thank the gods that he is well down in the order of succession.'

'You truly believe he meant to kill the horse?'

'Is there any doubt of it? If Prince Maekar had been here, it would have gone differently, I promise you. Aerion is all smiles and chivalry so long as his father is watching, if the tales be true, but when he's not . . .'

'I saw that Prince Maekar's chair was empty.'

'He's left Ashford to search for his sons, along with Roland Crakehall of the Kingsguard. There's a wild tale of robber knights going about, but I'll wager the prince is just off drunk again.'

The wine was fine and fruity, as good a cup as he had ever tasted. He rolled it in his mouth, swallowed, and said, 'Which prince is this now?'

'Maekar's heir. Daeron, he's named, after the king. They call him Daeron the Drunken, though not in his father's hearing. The youngest boy was with him as well. They left Summerhall together but never reached Ashford.' Raymun drained his cup and set it aside. 'Poor Maekar.'

'Poor?' said Dunk, startled. 'The king's son?'

'The king's *fourth* son,' said Raymun, 'not quite as bold as Prince Baelor, nor as clever as Prince Aerys, nor as gentle as Prince Rhaegel. And now he must suffer seeing his own sons overshadowed by his brother's. Daeron is a sot, Aerion is vain and cruel, the third son was so unpromising they gave him to the Citadel to make a maester of him, and the youngest –'

'*Ser! Ser Duncan!*' Egg burst in panting. His hood had fallen back, and the light from the brazier shone in his big dark eyes. 'You have to run, he's hurting her!'

Dunk lurched to his feet, confused. 'Hurting? Who?'

'*Aerion!*' the boy shouted. 'He's *hurting* her. The puppet girl. *Hurry!*' Whirling, he darted back out into the night.

Dunk made to follow, but Raymun caught his arm. 'Ser Duncan. *Aerion,* he said. A prince of the blood. Be careful.'

It was good counsel, he knew. The old man would have said the same. But he could not listen. He wrenched free of Raymun's hand and shouldered his way out of the pavilion. He could hear shouting off in the direction of the merchants' row. Egg was almost out of sight. Dunk ran after him. His legs were long and the boy's short; he quickly closed the distance.

A wall of watchers had gathered around the puppeteers. Dunk shouldered through them, ignoring their curses. A man-at-arms in the royal livery stepped up to block him. Dunk put a big hand on his chest and shoved, sending the man flailing backwards to sprawl on his arse in the dirt.

The puppeteers' stall had been knocked on its side. The fat Dornishwoman was on the ground weeping. One man-at-arms was dangling the puppets of Florian and Jonquil from his hands as another set them afire with a torch. Three more men were opening chests, spilling more puppets on the ground and stamping on them. The dragon puppet was scattered all about them, a broken wing here, its head there, its tail in three pieces. And in the midst of it all stood Prince Aerion, resplendent in a red velvet doublet with long dagged sleeves, twisting Tanselle's arm in both hands. She was on her knees, pleading with him. Aerion ignored her. He forced open her hand and seized one of her fingers. Dunk stood there stupidly, not quite believing what he saw. Then he heard a *crack*, and Tanselle screamed.

One of Aerion's men tried to grab him, and went flying. Three long strides, then Dunk grabbed the prince's shoulder and wrenched him around hard. His sword and dagger were forgotten, along with everything the old man had ever taught him. His fist knocked Aerion off his feet, and the toe of his boot slammed into the prince's belly. When Aerion went for his knife, Dunk stepped on his wrist and then kicked him again, right in the mouth. He might have kicked him to death right then and there, but the princeling's men swarmed over him. He had a man on each arm and another pounding him across the back. No sooner had he wrestled free of one than two more were on him.

Finally they shoved him down and pinned his arms and legs. Aerion was on his feet again. The prince's mouth was bloody. He pushed inside it with a finger. 'You've loosened one of my teeth,' he complained, 'so we'll start by breaking all of yours.' He pushed his hair from his eyes. 'You look familiar.'

'You took me for a stableboy.'

Aerion smiled redly. 'I recall. You refused to take my horse. Why did you throw your life away? For this whore?' Tanselle was curled up on the ground, cradling her maimed hand. He gave her a shove with the toe of his boot. 'She's scarcely worth it. A traitor. The dragon ought never lose.'

He is mad, thought Dunk, *but he is still a prince's son, and he means to kill me.* He might have prayed then, if he had known a prayer all the way through, but there was no time. There was hardly even time to be afraid.

'Nothing more to say?' said Aerion. 'You bore me, ser.' He poked at his bloody mouth again. 'Get a hammer and break all his teeth out, Wate,' he commanded, 'and then let's cut him open and show him the colour of his entrails.'

'*No!*' a boy's voice said. 'Don't hurt him!'

Gods be good, the boy, the brave foolish boy, Dunk thought. He fought against the arms restraining him, but it was no good. 'Hold your tongue, you stupid boy. Run away. They'll hurt you!'

'No they won't.' Egg moved closer. 'If they do, they'll answer to my father. And my uncle as well. Let go of him, I said. Wate, Yorkel, you know me. Do as I say.'

The hands holding his left arm were gone, and then the others. Dunk did not understand what was happening. The men-at-arms were backing away. One even knelt. Then the crowd parted for Raymun Fossoway. He had donned mail and helm, and his hand was on his sword. His cousin Ser Steffon, just behind him, had already bared his blade, and with them were a half-dozen men-at-arms with the red apple badge sewn on their breasts.

Prince Aerion paid them no mind. 'Impudent little wretch,'

he said to Egg, spitting a mouthful of blood at the boy's feet. 'What happened to your hair?'

'I cut it off, brother,' said Egg. 'I didn't want to look like you.'

The second day of the tourney was overcast, with a gusty wind blowing from the west. *The crowds should be less on a day like this,* Dunk thought. It would have been easier for them to find a spot near the fence to see the jousting up close. *Egg might have sat on the rail, while I stood behind him.*

Instead Egg would have a seat in the viewing box, dressed in silks and furs, while Dunk's view would be limited to the four walls of the tower cell where Lord Ashford's men had confined him. The chamber had a window, but it faced in the wrong direction. Even so, Dunk crammed himself into the window seat as the sun came up, and stared gloomily off across town and field and forest. They had taken his hempen swordbelt, and his sword and dagger with it, and they had taken his silver as well. He hoped Egg or Raymun would remember Chestnut and Thunder.

'Egg,' he muttered low under his breath. His squire, a poor lad plucked from the streets of King's Landing. Had ever a knight been made such a fool? *Dunk the lunk, thick as a castle wall and slow as an aurochs.*

He had not been permitted to speak to Egg since Lord Ashford's soldiers had scooped them all up at the puppet show. Nor Raymun, nor Tanselle, nor anyone, not even Lord Ashford himself. He wondered if he would ever see any of them again. For all he knew, they meant to keep him in this small room until he died. *What did I think would happen?* he asked himself bitterly. *I knocked down a prince's son and kicked him in the face.*

Beneath these grey skies, the flowing finery of the high-born lords and great champions would not seem quite so splendid as it had the day before. The sun, walled behind the clouds, would not brush their steel helms with brilliance, nor make their gold and silver chasings glitter and flash, but even so,

Dunk wished he was in the crowd to watch the jousting. It would be a good day for hedge knights, for men in plain mail on unbarded horses.

He could *hear* them, at least. The horns of the heralds carried well, and from time to time a roar from the crowd told him that someone had fallen, or risen, or done something especially bold. He heard faint hoofbeats too, and once in a great while the clash of swords or the *snap* of a lance. Dunk winced whenever he heard that last; it reminded him of the noise Tanselle's finger had made when Aerion broke it. There were other sounds too, closer at hand: footfalls in the hall outside his door, the stamp of hooves in the yard below, shouts and voices from the castle walls. Sometimes they drowned out the tourney. Dunk supposed that was just as well.

'A hedge knight is the truest kind of knight, Dunk,' the old man had told him, a long long time ago. 'Other knights serve the lords who keep them, or from whom they hold their lands, but we serve where we will, for men whose causes we believe in. Every knight swears to protect the weak and innocent, but we keep the vow best, I think.' Queer how strong that memory seemed. Dunk had quite forgotten those words. And perhaps the old man had as well, towards the end.

The morning turned to afternoon. The distant sounds of the tourney began to dwindle and die. Dusk began to seep into the cell, but Dunk still sat in the window seat, looking out on the gathering dark and trying to ignore his empty belly.

And then he heard footsteps and a jangling of iron keys. He uncoiled and rose to his feet as the door opened. Two guards pushed in, one bearing an oil lamp. A serving man followed with a tray of food. Behind came Egg. 'Leave the lamp and the food and go,' the boy told them.

They did as he commanded, though Dunk noticed that they left the heavy wooden door ajar. The smell of the food made him realize how ravenous he was. There was hot bread and honey, a bowl of pease porridge, a skewer of roast onions and well-charred meat. He sat by the tray, pulled apart the bread with his hands, and stuffed some into his mouth. 'There's no knife,' he observed. 'Did they think I'd stab you, boy?'

'They didn't tell me what they thought.' Egg wore a close-fitting black wool doublet with a tucked waist and long sleeves lined with red satin. Across his chest was sewn the three-headed dragon of House Targaryen. 'My uncle says I must humbly beg your forgiveness for deceiving you.'

'Your uncle,' said Dunk. 'That would be Prince Baelor.'

The boy looked miserable. 'I never meant to lie.'

'But you did. About everything. Starting with your name. I never heard of a Prince Egg.'

'It's short for Aegon. My brother Aemon named me Egg. He's off at the Citadel now, learning to be a maester. And Daeron sometimes calls me Egg as well, and so do my sisters.'

Dunk lifted the skewer and bit into a chunk of meat. Goat, flavoured with some lordly spice he'd never tasted before. Grease ran down his chin. 'Aegon,' he repeated. 'Of course it would be Aegon. Like Aegon the Dragon. How many Aegons have been king?'

'Four,' the boy said. 'Four Aegons.'

Dunk chewed, swallowed, and tore off some more bread. 'Why did you do it? Was it some jape, to make a fool of the stupid hedge knight?'

'No.' The boy's eyes filled with tears, but he stood there manfully. 'I was supposed to squire for Daeron. He's my oldest brother. I learned everything I had to learn to be a good squire, but Daeron isn't a very good knight. He didn't want to ride in the tourney, so after we left Summerhall he stole away from our escort, only instead of doubling back he went straight on towards Ashford, thinking they'd never look for us that way. It was him shaved my head. He knew my father would send men hunting us. Daeron has common hair, sort of a pale brown, nothing special, but mine is like Aerion's and my father's.'

'The blood of the dragon,' Dunk said. 'Silver-gold hair and purple eyes, everyone knows that.' *Thick as a castle wall, Dunk.*

'Yes. So Daeron shaved it off. He meant for us to hide until the tourney was over. Only then you took me for a stableboy, and . . .' He lowered his eyes. 'I didn't care if Daeron fought or not, but I wanted to be *somebody's* squire. I'm sorry, ser. I truly am.'

Dunk looked at him thoughtfully. He knew what it was like to want something so badly that you would tell a monstrous lie just to get near it. 'I thought you were like me,' he said. 'Might be you are. Only not the way I thought.'

'We're both from King's Landing still,' the boy said hopefully.

Dunk had to laugh. 'Yes, you from the top of Aegon's Hill and me from the bottom.'

'That's not so far, ser.'

Dunk took a bite from an onion. 'Do I need to call you *m'lord* or *Your Grace* or something?'

'At court,' the boy admitted, 'but other times you can keep on calling me Egg if you like. Ser.'

'What will they do with me, Egg?'

'My uncle wants to see you. After you're done eating, ser.'

Dunk shoved the platter aside, and stood. 'I'm done now, then. I've already kicked one prince in the mouth, I don't mean to keep another waiting.'

Lord Ashford had turned his own chambers over to Prince Baelor for the duration of his stay, so it was to the lord's solar that Egg – no, *Aegon*, he would have to get used to that – conducted him. Baelor sat reading by the light of a beeswax candle. Dunk knelt before him. 'Rise,' the prince said. 'Would you care for wine?'

'As it please you, Your Grace.'

'Pour Ser Duncan a cup of the sweet Dornish red, Aegon,' the prince commanded. 'Try not to spill it on him, you've done him sufficient ill already.'

'The boy won't spill, Your Grace,' said Dunk. 'He's a good boy. A good squire. And he meant no harm to me, I know.'

'One need not intend harm to do it. Aegon should have come to me when he saw what his brother was doing to these puppeteers. Instead he ran to you. That was no kindness. What you did, ser . . . well, I might have done the same in your place, but I am a prince of the realm, not a hedge knight. It is never wise to strike a king's grandson in anger, no matter the cause.'

Dunk nodded grimly. Egg offered him a silver goblet, brimming with wine. He accepted it and took a long swallow.

'I *hate* Aerion,' Egg said with vehemence. 'And I had to run for Ser Duncan, uncle, the castle was too far.'

'Aerion is your brother,' the prince said firmly, 'and the septons say we must love our brothers. Aegon, leave us now, I would speak with Ser Duncan privately.'

The boy put down the flagon of wine and bowed stiffly. 'As you will, Your Grace.' He went to the door of the solar and closed it softly behind him.

Baelor Breakspear studied Dunk's eyes for a long moment. 'Ser Duncan, let me ask you this – how good a knight are you, truly? How skilled at arms?'

Dunk did not know what to say. 'Ser Arlan taught me sword and shield, and how to tilt at rings and quintains.'

Prince Baelor seemed troubled by that answer. 'My brother Maekar returned to the castle a few hours ago. He found his heir drunk in an inn a day's ride to the south. Maekar would never admit as much, but I believe it was his secret hope that his sons might outshine mine in this tourney. Instead they have both shamed him, but what is he to do? They are blood of his blood. Maekar is angry, and must needs have a target for his wrath. He has chosen you.'

'Me?' Dunk said miserably.

'Aerion has already filled his father's ear. And Daeron has not helped you either. To excuse his own cowardice, he told my brother that a huge robber knight, chance met on the road, made off with Aegon. I fear you have been cast as this robber knight, ser. In Daeron's tale, he has spent all these days pursuing you hither and yon, to win back his brother.'

'But Egg will tell him the truth. Aegon, I mean.'

'Egg *will* tell him, I have no doubt,' said Prince Baelor, 'but the boy has been known to lie too, as you have good reason to recall. Which son will my brother believe? As for the matter of these puppeteers, by the time Aerion is done twisting the tale it will be high treason. The dragon is the sigil of the royal House. To portray one being slain, sawdust blood spilling from its neck . . . well, it was doubtless innocent, but it was far from wise. Aerion calls it a veiled attack on House Targaryen, an incitement to revolt. Maekar will likely agree. My brother has a prickly nature, and he has placed all his best hopes on Aerion, since Daeron has been such a grave disappointment to him.' The prince took a sip of wine, then set the goblet aside. 'Whatever my brother believes or fails to believe, one truth is beyond dispute. You laid hands upon the blood of the dragon. For that offence, you must be tried, and judged, and punished.'

'Punished?' Dunk did not like the sound of that.

'Aerion would like your head, with or without teeth. He will not have it, I promise you, but I cannot deny him a trial. As my royal father is hundreds of leagues away, my brother and I must sit in judgement of you, along with Lord Ashford, whose domains these are, and Lord Tyrell of Highgarden, his liege lord. The last time a man was found guilty of striking one of royal blood, it was decreed that he should lose the offending hand.'

'My *hand*?' said Dunk, aghast.

'And your foot. You kicked him too, did you not?'

Dunk could not speak.

'To be sure, I will urge my fellow judges to be merciful. I am the King's Hand and the heir to the throne, my word carries some weight. But so does my brother's. The risk is there.'

'I,' said Dunk, 'I . . . Your Grace, I . . .' *They meant no treason, it was only a wooden dragon, it was never meant to be a royal prince,* he wanted to say, but his words had deserted him once and all. He had never been any good with words.

'You have another choice, though,' Prince Baelor said quietly. 'Whether it is a better choice or a worse one, I cannot say, but I remind you that any knight accused of a crime has the right to demand trial by combat. So I ask you once again, Ser Duncan the Tall – how good a knight are you? Truly?'

* * *

'A trial of seven,' said Prince Aerion, smiling. 'That is *my* right, I do believe.'

Prince Baelor drummed his fingers on the table, frowning. To his left, Lord Ashford nodded slowly. 'Why?' Prince Maekar demanded, leaning forward towards his son. 'Are you afraid to face this hedge knight alone, and let the gods decide the truth of your accusations?'

'Afraid?' said Aerion. 'Of such as this? Don't be absurd, father. My thought is for my beloved brother. Daeron has been wronged by this Ser Duncan as well, and has first claim to his blood. A trial of seven allows both of us to face him.'

'Do me no favours, brother,' muttered Daeron Targaryen. The eldest son of Prince Maekar looked even worse than he had when Dunk had encountered him in the inn. He seemed to be sober this time, his red-and-black doublet unstained by wine, but his eyes were bloodshot, and a fine sheen of sweat covered his brow. 'I am content to cheer you on as you slay the rogue.'

'You are too kind, sweet brother,' said Prince Aerion, all smiles, 'but it would be selfish of me to deny you the right to prove the truth of your words at the hazard of your body. I must insist upon a trial of seven.'

Dunk was lost. 'Your Grace, my lords,' he said to the dais. 'I do not understand. What is this trial of seven?'

Prince Baelor shifted uncomfortably in his seat. 'It is another form of trial by combat. Ancient, seldom invoked. It came across the narrow sea with the Andals and their seven gods. In any trial by combat, the accuser and accused are asking the gods to decide the issue between them. The Andals believed that if seven champions fought on each side, the gods, being thus honoured, would be more like to take a hand and see that a just result was achieved.'

'Or mayhaps they simply had a taste for swordplay,' said Lord Leo Tyrell, a cynical smile touching his lips. 'Regardless, Ser Aerion is within his rights. A trial of seven it must be.'

'I must fight *seven men*, then?' Dunk asked hopelessly.

'Not alone, ser,' Prince Maekar said impatiently. 'Don't play the fool, it will not serve. It must be seven against seven. You must needs find six other knights to fight beside you.'

Six knights, Dunk thought. They might as well have told him to find six thousand. He had no brothers, no cousins, no old comrades who had stood beside him in battle. Why would six strangers risk their own lives to defend a hedge knight against two royal princelings? 'Your Graces, my lords,' he said, 'what if no one will take my part?'

Maekar Targaryen looked down on him coldly. 'If a cause is just, good men will fight for it. If you can find no champions, ser, it will be because you are guilty. Could anything be more plain?'

Dunk had never felt so alone as he did when he walked out of the gates of Ashford Castle and heard the portcullis rattle down behind him. A soft rain was falling, light as dew on his skin, and yet he shivered at the touch of it. Across the river, coloured rings haloed the scant few pavilions where fires still burned. The night was half-gone, he guessed. Dawn would be on him in a few hours. *And with dawn comes death.*

They had given him back his sword and silver, yet as he waded across the ford, his thoughts were bleak. He wondered if they expected him to saddle a horse and flee. He could, if he wished. That would be the end of his knighthood, to be sure; he would be no more than an outlaw henceforth, until the day some lord took him and struck off his head. *Better to die a knight than live like that*, he told himself stubbornly. Wet to the knee, he trudged past the empty lists. Most of the pavilions were dark, their owners long asleep, but here and there a few candles still burned. Dunk heard soft moans and cries of pleasure coming from within one tent. It made him wonder whether he would die without ever having known a maid.

Then he heard the snort of a horse, a snort he somehow knew for Thunder's. He turned his steps and ran, and there he was, tied up with Chestnut outside a round pavilion lit from within by a vague golden glow. On its centre pole the banner hung sodden, but Dunk could still make out the dark curve of the Fossoway apple. It looked like hope.

'A trial by combat,' Raymun said heavily. 'Gods be good, Duncan, that means lances of war, morning-stars, battle-axes . . . the swords won't be blunted, do you understand that?'

'Raymun the Reluctant,' mocked his cousin Ser Steffon. An apple made of gold and garnets fastened his cloak of yellow wool. 'You need not fear, cousin, this is a knightly combat. As you are no knight, your skin is not at risk. Ser Duncan, you have one Fossoway at least. The ripe one. I saw what Aerion did to those puppeteers. I am for you.'

'And I,' snapped Raymun angrily. 'I only meant –'

His cousin cut him off. 'Who else fights with us, Ser Duncan?'

Dunk spread his hands hopelessly. 'I know no one else. Well, except for Ser Manfred Dondarrion. He wouldn't even vouch that I was a knight, he'll never risk his life for me.'

Ser Steffon seemed little perturbed. 'Then we need five more good men. Fortunately, I have more than five friends. Leo Longthorn, the Laughing Storm, Lord Caron, the Lannisters, Ser Otho Bracken . . . aye, and the Blackwoods as well, though you will never get Blackwood and Bracken on the same side of a mêlée. I shall go and speak with some of them.'

'They won't be happy at being woken,' his cousin objected.

'Excellent,' declared Ser Steffon. 'If they are angry, they'll fight all the more fiercely. You may rely on me, Ser Duncan. Cousin, if I do not return before dawn, bring my armour and see that Wrath is saddled and barded for me. I shall meet you both in the challengers' paddock.' He laughed. 'This will be a day long remembered, I think.' When he strode from the tent, he looked almost happy.

Not so Raymun. 'Five knights,' he said glumly after his cousin had gone. 'Duncan, I am loath to dash your hopes, but . . .'

'If your cousin can bring the men he speaks of . . .'

'Leo Longthorn? The Brute of Bracken? The Laughing Storm?' Raymun stood. 'He knows all of them, I have no doubt, but I would be less certain that any of them know *him*. Steffon sees this as a chance for glory, but it means your life. You should find your own men. I'll help. Better you have too many champions than too few.' A noise outside made Raymun turn his head. 'Who goes there?' he demanded, as a boy ducked through the flap, followed by a thin man in a rain-sodden black cloak.

'Egg?' Dunk got to his feet. 'What are you doing here?'

'I'm your squire,' the boy said. 'You'll need someone to arm you, ser.'

'Does your lord father know you've left the castle?'

'Gods be good, I hope not.' Daeron Targaryen undid the clasp of his cloak and let it slide from his thin shoulders.

'*You?* Are you mad, coming here?' Dunk pulled his knife from his sheath. 'I ought to shove this through your belly.'

'Probably,' Prince Daeron admitted. 'Though I'd sooner you poured me a cup of wine. Look at my hands.' He held one out and let them all see how it shook.

Dunk stepped towards him, glowering. 'I don't care about your hands. You lied about me.'

'I had to say *something* when my father demanded to know where my little brother had got to,' the prince replied. He seated himself, ignoring Dunk and his knife. 'If truth be told, I hadn't even realized Egg was gone. He wasn't at the bottom of my wine cup, and I hadn't looked anywhere else, so . . .' He sighed.

'Ser, my father is going to join the seven accusers,' Egg broke in. 'I begged him not to, but he won't listen. He says it is the only way to redeem Aerion's honour, and Daeron's.'

'Not that I ever asked to have my honour redeemed,' said Prince Daeron sourly. 'Whoever has it can keep it, so far as I'm concerned. Still, here we are. For what it's worth, Ser Duncan, you have little to fear from me. The only thing I like less than horses are swords. Heavy things, and beastly sharp. I'll do my best to look gallant in the first charge, but after that . . . well, perhaps you could strike me a nice blow to the side of the helm. Make it ring, but not *too* loud, if you take my meaning. My brothers have my measure when it comes to fighting and dancing and thinking and reading books, but none of them is half my equal at lying insensible in the mud.'

Dunk could only stare at him, and wonder whether the princeling was trying to play him for a fool. 'Why did you come?'

'To warn you of what you face,' Daeron said. 'My father has commanded the Kingsguard to fight with him.'

'The Kingsguard?' said Dunk, appalled.

'Well, the three who are here. Thank the gods uncle Baelor left the other four at King's Landing with our royal grandfather.'

Egg supplied the names. 'Ser Roland Crakehall, Ser Donnel of Duskendale, and Ser Willem Wylde.'

'They have small choice in the matter,' said Daeron. 'They are sworn to protect the lives of the king and royal family, and my brothers and I are blood of the dragon, gods help us.'

Dunk counted on his fingers. 'That makes six. Who is the seventh man?'

Prince Daeron shrugged. 'Aerion will find someone. If need be, he will buy a champion. He has no lack of gold.'

'Who do you have?' Egg asked.

'Raymun's cousin Ser Steffon.'

Daeron winced. 'Only one?'

'Ser Steffon has gone to some of his friends.'

'I can bring people,' said Egg. 'Knights. I can.'

'Egg,' said Dunk, 'I will be fighting your own brothers.'

'You won't hurt Daeron, though,' the boy said. 'He *told* you he'd fall down. And Aerion . . . I remember, when I was little, he used to come into my bedchamber at night and put his knife between my legs. He had too many brothers, he'd say, maybe one night he'd make me his sister, then he could marry me. He threw my cat in the well too. He says he didn't, but he always lies.'

Prince Daeron gave a weary shrug. 'Egg has the truth of it. Aerion's quite the monster. He thinks he's a dragon in human form, you know. That's why he was so wroth at that puppet show. A pity he wasn't born a Fossoway, then he'd think himself an apple and we'd all be a deal safer, but there you are.' Bending, he scooped up his fallen cloak and shook the rain from it. 'I must steal back to the castle before my father wonders why I'm taking so long to sharpen my sword, but before I go, I would like a private word, Ser Duncan. Will you walk with me?'

Dunk looked at the princeling suspiciously a moment. 'As you wish, Your Grace.' He sheathed his dagger. 'I need to get my shield too.'

'Egg and I will look for knights,' promised Raymun.

Prince Daeron knotted his cloak around his neck and pulled up the hood. Dunk followed him back out into the soft rain. They walked towards the merchants' wagons.

'I dreamed of you,' said the prince.

'You said that at the inn.'

'Did I? Well, it's so. My dreams are not like yours, Ser Duncan. Mine are true. They frighten me. *You* frighten me. I dreamed of you and a dead dragon, you see. A great beast, huge, with wings so large they could cover this meadow. It had fallen on top of you, but you were alive and the dragon was dead.'

'Did I kill it?'

'That I could not say, but you were there, and so was the dragon. We were the masters of dragons once, we Targaryens. Now they are all gone, but we remain. I don't care to die today. The gods alone know why, but I don't. So do me a kindness if you would, and make certain it is my brother Aerion you slay.'

'I don't care to die either,' said Dunk.

'Well, I shan't kill you, ser. I'll withdraw my accusation as well, but it won't serve unless Aerion withdraws his.' He sighed. 'It may be that I've killed you with my lie. If so, I am sorry. I'm doomed to some hell, I know. Likely one without wine.' He shuddered, and on that they parted, there in the cool soft rain.

The merchants had drawn up their wagons on the western verge of the meadow, beneath a stand of birch and ash. Dunk stood under the trees and looked helplessly at the empty place where the puppeteers' wagon had been. *Gone.* He had feared they might be. *I would flee as well, if I were not thick as a castle wall.* He wondered what he would do for a shield now. He had the silver to buy one, he supposed, *if* he could find one for sale . . .

'Ser Duncan,' a voice called out of the dark. Dunk turned to find Steely Pate standing behind him, holding an iron lantern. Under a short leather cloak, the armourer was bare from the waist up, his broad chest and thick arms covered with coarse black hair. 'If you are come for your shield, she left it with me.' He looked Dunk up and down. 'Two hands and two feet, I count. So it's to be trial by combat, is it?'

'A trial of seven. How did you know?'

'Well, they might have kissed you and made you a lord, but it didn't seem likely, and if it went t'other way, you'd be short some parts. Now follow me.'

His wagon was easy to distinguish by the sword and anvil painted on its side. Dunk followed Pate inside. The armourer hung the lantern on a hook, shrugged out of his wet cloak, and pulled a roughspun tunic down over his head. A hinged board dropped down from one wall to make a table. 'Sit,' he said, shoving a low stool towards him.

Dunk sat. 'Where did she go?'

'They make for Dorne. The girl's uncle, there's a wise man. Well gone is well forgot. Stay and be seen, and belike the dragon remembers. Besides, he did not think she ought to see you die.' Pate went to the far end of the wagon, rummaged about in the shadows a moment, and returned with the shield. 'Your rim was old cheap steel, brittle and rusted,' he said. 'I've made you a new one, twice as thick, and put some bands across the back. It will be heavier now, but stronger too. The girl did the paint.'

She had made a better job of it than he could ever have hoped for. Even by lantern light, the sunset colours were rich and bright, the tree tall and strong and noble. The falling star was a bright slash of paint across the oaken sky. Yet now that Dunk held it in his hands, it seemed all wrong. The star was *falling*, what sort of sigil was that? Would he fall just as fast? And sunset heralds night. 'I should have stayed with the chalice,' he said miserably. 'It had wings, at least, to fly away, and Ser Arlan said the cup was full of faith and fellowship and good things to drink. This shield is all painted up like death.'

'The elm's alive,' Pate pointed out. 'See how green the leaves are? Summer leaves, for certain. And I've seen shields blazoned with skulls and wolves and ravens, even hanged men and bloody heads. They served well enough, and so will this. You know the old shield rhyme? *Oak and iron, guard me well . . .*'

'*. . . or else I'm dead, and doomed to hell,*' Dunk finished. He had not thought of that rhyme in years. The old man had taught it to him, a long time ago. 'How much do you want for the new rim and all?' he asked Pate.

'From you?' Pate scratched his beard. 'A copper.'

The rain had all but stopped as the first wan light suffused the eastern sky, but it had done its work. Lord Ashford's men had removed the barriers, and the tourney field was one great morass of grey-brown mud and torn grass. Tendrils of fog were writhing along the ground like pale white snakes as Dunk made his way back towards the lists. Steely Pate walked with him.

The viewing stand had already begun to fill, the lords and ladies clutching their cloaks tight about them against the morning chill. Smallfolk were drifting towards the field as well, and hundreds of them already stood along the fence. *So many come to see me die*, thought Dunk bitterly, but he wronged them. A few steps further on, a woman called out, 'Good fortune to you.' An old man stepped up to take his hand and said, 'May the gods give you strength, ser.' Then a begging brother in a tattered brown robe said a blessing on his sword, and a maid kissed his cheek. *They are for me.*

'Why?' he asked Pate. 'What am I to them?'

'A knight who remembered his vows,' the smith said.

They found found Raymun outside the challengers' paddock at the south end of the lists, waiting with his cousin's horse and Dunk's. Thunder tossed restlessly beneath the weight of chinet, chamfron, and blanket of heavy mail. Pate inspected the armour and pronounced it good work, even though someone else had forged it. Wherever the armour had come from, Dunk was grateful.

Then he saw the others; the one-eyed man with the salt-and-pepper beard, the young knight in the striped yellow-and-black surcoat with the beehives on the shield. *Robyn Rhysling and Humfrey Beesbury,* he thought in astonishment. *And Ser Humfrey Hardyng as well.* Hardyng was mounted on Aerion's red charger, now barded in his red-and-white diamonds.

He went to them. 'Sers, I am in your debt.'

'The debt is Aerion's,' Ser Humfrey Hardyng replied, 'and we mean to collect it.'

'I had heard your leg was broken.'

'You heard the truth,' Hardyng said. 'I cannot walk. But so long as I can sit a horse, I can fight.'

Raymun took Dunk aside. 'I hoped Hardyng would want another chance at Aerion, and he did. As it happens, the other Humfrey is his brother by marriage. Egg is responsible for Ser Robyn, whom he knew from other tourneys. So you are five.'

'Six,' said Dunk in wonder, pointing. A knight was entering the paddock, his squire leading his charger behind him. 'The Laughing Storm.' A head taller than Ser Raymun and almost of a height with Dunk, Ser Lyonel wore a cloth-of-gold surcoat bearing the crowned stag of House Baratheon, and carried his antlered helm under his arm. Dunk reached for his hand. 'Ser Lyonel, I cannot thank you enough for coming, nor Ser Steffon for bringing you.'

'Ser Steffon?' Ser Lyonel gave him a puzzled look. 'It was your squire who came to me. The boy, Aegon. My own lad tried to chase him off, but he slipped between his legs and turned a flagon of wine over my head.' He laughed. 'There has not been a trial of seven for more than a hundred years, do you know that? I was not about to miss a chance to fight the Kingsguard knights, and tweak Prince Maekar's nose in the bargain.'

'Six,' Dunk said hopefully to Raymun Fossoway as Ser Lyonel joined the others. 'Your cousin will bring the last, surely.'

A roar went up from the crowd. At the north end of the meadow, a column of knights came trotting out of the river mist. The three Kingsguard came first, like ghosts in their gleaming white enamel armour, long white cloaks trailing behind them. Even their shields were white, blank and clean as a field of new-fallen snow. Behind rode Prince Maekar and his sons. Aerion was mounted on a dapple grey, orange and red flickering through the slashes in the horse's caparison at each stride. His brother's destrier was a smaller bay, armoured in overlapping black and gold scales. A green silk plume trailed from Daeron's helm. It was their father who made the most fearsome appearance, however. Black curved dragon teeth ran across his shoulders, along the crest of his helm, and down his back, and the huge spiked mace strapped to his saddle was as deadly-looking a weapon as any Dunk had ever seen.

'Six,' Raymun exclaimed suddenly. 'They are only six.'

It was true, Dunk saw. *Three black knights and three white. They are a man short as well.* Was it possible that Aerion had not been able to find a seventh man? What would that mean? Would they fight six against six if neither found a seventh?

Egg slipped up beside him as he was trying to puzzle it out. 'Ser, it's time you donned your armour.'

'Thank you, squire. If you would be so good?'

Steely Pate lent the lad a hand. Hauberk and gorget, greaves and gauntlet, coif and codpiece, they turned him into steel, checking each buckle and each clasp thrice. Ser Lyonel sat sharpening his sword on a whetstone while the Humfreys talked quietly, Ser Robyn prayed, and Raymun Fossoway paced back and forth, wondering where his cousin had got to.

Dunk was fully armoured by the time Ser Steffon finally appeared. 'Raymun,' he called, 'my mail, if you please.' He had changed into a padded doublet to wear beneath his steel.

'Ser Steffon,' said Dunk, 'what of your friends? We need another knight to make our seven.'

'You need two, I fear,' Ser Steffon said. Raymun laced up the back of the hauberk.

'M'lord?' Dunk did not understand. 'Two?'

Ser Steffon picked up a gauntlet of fine lobstered steel and slid his left hand into it, flexing his fingers. 'I see five here,' he said while Raymun fastened his swordbelt. 'Beesbury, Rhysling, Hardyng, Baratheon, and yourself.'

'And you,' said Dunk. 'You're the sixth.'

'I am the seventh,' said Ser Steffon, smiling, 'but for the other side. I fight with Prince Aerion and the accusers.'

Raymun had been about to hand his cousin his helm. He stopped as if struck. 'No.'

'Yes.' Ser Steffon shrugged. 'Ser Duncan understands, I am sure. I have a duty to my prince.'

'You told him to rely on you.' Raymun had gone pale.

'Did I?' He took the helm from his cousin's hands. 'No doubt I was sincere at the time. Bring me my horse.'

'Get him yourself,' said Raymun angrily. 'If you think I wish any part of this, you're as thick as you are vile.'

'Vile?' Ser Steffon *tsk*ed. 'Guard your tongue, Raymun. We're both apples from the same tree. And you are my squire. Or have you forgotten your vows?'

'No. Have you forgotten yours? You swore to be a knight.'

'I shall be more than a knight before this day is done. *Lord* Fossoway. I like the sound of that.' Smiling, he pulled on his other gauntlet, turned away, and crossed the paddock to his horse. Though the other defenders stared at him with contemptuous eyes, no one made a move to stop him.

Dunk watched Ser Steffon lead his destrier back across the field. His hands coiled into fists, but his throat felt too raw for speech. *No words would move the likes of him anyway.*

'Knight me.' Raymun put a hand on Dunk's shoulder and turned him. 'I will take my cousin's place. Ser Duncan, knight me.' He went to one knee.

Frowning, Dunk moved a hand to the hilt of his longsword, then hesitated. 'Raymun, I . . . I should not.'

'You must. Without me, you are only five.'

'The lad has the truth of it,' said Ser Lyonel Baratheon. 'Do it, Ser Duncan. Any knight can make a knight.'

'Do you doubt my courage?' Raymun asked.

'No,' said Dunk. 'Not that, but . . .' Still he hesitated.

A fanfare of trumpets cut the misty morning air. Egg came running up to them. 'Ser, Lord Ashford summons you.'

The Laughing Storm gave an impatient shake of the head. 'Go

to him, Ser Duncan. I'll give squire Raymun his knighthood.' He slid his sword out of his sheath and shouldered Dunk aside. 'Raymun of House Fossoway,' he began solemnly, touching the blade to the squire's right shoulder, 'in the name of the Warrior I charge you to be brave.' The sword moved from his right shoulder to his left. 'In the name of the Father I charge you to be just.' Back to the right. 'In the name of the Mother I charge you to defend the young and innocent.' The left. 'In the name of the Maid I charge you to protect all women . . .'

Dunk left them there, feeling as relieved as he was guilty. *We are still one short,* he thought as Egg held Thunder for him. *Where will I find another man?* He turned the horse and rode slowly towards the viewing stand, where Lord Ashford stood waiting. From the north end of the lists, Prince Aerion advanced to meet him. 'Ser Duncan,' he said cheerfully, 'it would seem you have only five champions.'

'Six,' said Dunk. 'Ser Lyonel is knighting Raymun Fossoway. We will fight you six against seven.' Men had won at far worse odds, he knew.

But Lord Ashford shook his head. 'That is not permitted, ser. If you cannot find another knight to take your side, you must be declared guilty of the crimes of which you stand accused.'

Guilty, thought Dunk. *Guilty of loosening a tooth, and for that I must die.* 'M'lord, I beg a moment.'

'You have it.'

Dunk rode slowly along the fence. The viewing stand was crowded with knights. *'M'lords,'* he called to them, *'do none of you remember Ser Arlan of Pennytree? I was his squire. We served many of you. Ate at your tables and slept in your halls.'* He saw Manfred Dondarrion seated in the highest tier. *'Ser Arlan took a wound in your lord father's service.'* The knight said something to the lady beside him, paying no heed. Dunk was forced to move on. *'Lord Lannister, Ser Arlan unhorsed you once in tourney.'* The Grey Lion examined his gloved hands, studiedly refusing to raise his eyes. *'He was a good man, and he taught me how to be a knight. Not only sword and lance, but honour. A knight defends the innocent, he said. That's all I did. I need one more knight to fight beside me. One, that's all. Lord Caron? Lord Swann?'* Lord Swann laughed softly as Lord Caron whispered in his ear.

Dunk reined up before Ser Otho Bracken, lowering his voice. 'Ser Otho, all know you for a great champion. Join us, I beg you. In the names of the old gods and the new. My cause is just.'

'That may be,' said the Brute of Bracken, who had at least the grace to reply, 'but it is your cause, not mine. I know you not, boy.'

Heartsick, Dunk wheeled Thunder and raced back and forth before the tiers of pale cold men. Despair made him shout. '*Are there no true knights among you?*'

Only silence answered.

Across the field, Prince Aerion laughed. 'The dragon is not mocked,' he called out.

Then came a voice. 'I will take Ser Duncan's side.'

A black stallion emerged from out of the river mists, a black knight on his back. Dunk saw the dragon shield, and the red enamel crest upon his helm with its three roaring heads. *The Young Prince. Gods be good, it is truly him?*

Lord Ashford made the same mistake. 'Prince Valarr?'

'No.' The black knight lifted the visor of his helm. 'I did not think to enter the lists at Ashford, my lord, so I brought no armour. My son was good enough to lend me his.' Prince Baelor smiled almost sadly.

The accusers were thrown into confusion, Dunk could see. Prince Maekar spurred his mount forward. 'Brother, have you taken leave of your senses?' He pointed a mailed finger at Dunk. 'This man attacked my son.'

'This man protected the weak, as every true knight must,' replied Prince Baelor. 'Let the gods determine if he was right or wrong.' He gave a tug on his reins, turned Valarr's huge black destrier, and trotted to the south end of the field.

Dunk brought Thunder up beside him, and the other defenders gathered round them; Robyn Rhysling and Ser Lyonel, the Humfreys. *Good men all, but are they good enough?* 'Where is Raymun?'

'*Ser* Raymun, if you please.' He cantered up, a grim smile

lighting his face beneath his plumed helm. 'My pardons, ser. I needed to make a small change to my sigil, lest I be mistaken for my dishonourable cousin.' He showed them all his shield. The polished golden field remained the same, and the Fossoway apple, but this apple was green instead of red. 'I fear I am still not ripe . . . but better green than wormy, eh?'

Ser Lyonel laughed, and Dunk grinned despite himself. Even Prince Baelor seemed to approve.

Lord Ashford's septon had come to the front of the viewing stand and raised his crystal to call the throng to prayer.

'Attend me, all of you,' Baelor said quietly. 'The accusers will be armed with heavy war lances for the first charge. Lances of ash, eight feet long, banded against splitting and tipped with a steel point sharp enough to drive through plate with the weight of a warhorse behind it.'

'We shall use the same,' said Ser Humfrey Beesbury. Behind him, the septon was calling on the Seven to look down and judge this dispute, and grant victory to the men whose cause was just.

'No,' Baelor said. 'We will arm ourselves with tourney lances instead.'

'Tourney lances are made to break,' objected Raymun.

'They are also made twelve feet long. If our points strike home, theirs cannot touch us. Aim for helm or chest. In a tourney it is a gallant thing to break your lance against a foe's shield, but here it may well mean death. If we can unhorse them and keep our own saddles, the advantage is ours.' He glanced to Dunk. 'If Ser Duncan is killed, it is considered that the gods have judged him guilty, and the contest is over. If both of his accusers are slain, or withdraw their accusations, the same is true. Elsewise, all seven of one side or the other must perish or yield for the trial to end.'

'Prince Daeron will not fight,' Dunk said.

'Not well, anyway,' laughed Ser Lyonel. 'Against that, we have three of the White Swords to contend with.'

Baelor took that calmly. 'My brother erred when he demanded that the Kingsguard fight for his son. Their oath forbids them to harm a prince of the blood. Fortunately, I am such.' He gave them a faint smile. 'Keep the others off me long enough, and I shall deal with the Kingsguard.'

'My prince, is that chivalrous?' asked Ser Lyonel Baratheon as the septon was finishing his invocation.

'The gods will let us know,' said Baelor Breakspear.

A deep expectant silence had fallen across Ashford Meadow. Eighty yards away, Aerion's grey stallion trumpeted with impatience and pawed the muddy ground. Thunder was very still by comparison; he was an older horse, veteran of half a hundred fights, and he knew what was expected of him. Egg handed Dunk up his shield. 'May the gods be with you, ser,' the boy said.

The sight of his elm tree and shooting star gave him heart. Dunk slid his left arm through the strap and tightened his fingers around the grip. *Oak and iron, guard me well, or else I'm dead and doomed to hell.* Steely Pate brought his lance to him, but Egg insisted that it must be him who put it into Dunk's hand.

To either side, his companions took up their own lances and spread out in a long line. Prince Baelor was to his right and Ser Lyonel to his left, but the narrow eyeslit of the greathelm limited Dunk's vision to what was directly ahead of him. The viewing stand was gone, and likewise the smallfolk crowding the fence; there was only the muddy field, the pale blowing mist, the river, town, and castle to the north, and the princeling on his grey charger with flames on his helm and a dragon on his shield. Dunk watched Aerion's squire hand him a war lance, eight feet long and black as night. *He will put that through my heart if he can.*

A horn sounded.

For a heartbeat Dunk sat as still as a fly in amber, though all the horses were moving. A stab of panic went through him. *I have forgotten,* he thought wildly, *I have forgotten all, I will shame myself, I will lose everything.*

Thunder saved him. The big brown stallion knew what to

do, even if his rider did not. He broke into a slow trot. Dunk's training took over then. He gave the warhorse a light touch of spur and couched his lance. At the same time he swung his shield until it covered most of the left side of his body. He held it at an angle, to deflect blows away from him. *Oak and iron guard me well, or else I'm dead and doomed to hell.*

The noise of the crowd was no more than the crash of distant waves. Thunder slid into a gallop. Dunk's teeth jarred together with the violence of the pace. He pressed his heels down, tightening his legs with all his strength and letting his body become part of the motion of the horse beneath. *I am Thunder and Thunder is me, we are one beast, we are joined, we are one.* The air inside his helm was already so hot he could scarce breathe.

In a tourney joust, his foe would be to his left across the tilting barrier, and he would need to swing his lance across Thunder's neck. The angle made it more likely that the wood would split on impact. But this was a deadlier game they played today. With no barriers dividing them, the destriers charged straight at one another. Prince Baelor's huge black was much faster than Thunder, and Dunk glimpsed him pounding ahead through the corner of his eyeslit. He sensed more than saw the others. *They do not matter, only Aerion matters, only him.*

He watched the dragon come. Spatters of mud sprayed back from the hooves of Prince Aerion's grey, and Dunk could see the horse's nostrils flaring. The black lance still angled upwards. A knight who holds his lance high and brings it on line at the last moment always risks lowering it too far, the old man had told him. He brought his own point to bear on the centre of the princeling's chest. *My lance is part of my arm,* he told himself. *It's my finger, a wooden finger. All I need do is touch him with my long wooden finger.*

He tried not to see the sharp iron point at the end of Aerion's black lance, growing larger with every stride. *The dragon, look at the dragon,* he thought. The great three-headed beast covered the prince's shield, red wings and gold fire. *No, look only where you mean to strike,* he remembered suddenly, but his lance had already begun to slide off line. Dunk tried to correct, but it was too late. He saw his point strike Aerion's shield, taking the dragon between two of its heads, gouging into a gout of painted flame. At the muffled *crack*, he felt Thunder recoil under him, trembling with the force of the impact, and half a heartbeat later something smashed into his side with awful force. The horses slammed together violently, armour crashing and clanging as Thunder stumbled and Dunk's lance fell from his hand. Then he was past his foe, clutching at his saddle in a desperate effort to keep his seat. Thunder lurched sideways in the sloppy mud and Dunk felt his hind legs slip out from under. They were sliding, spinning, and then the stallion's hindquarters slapped down hard. '*Up!*' Dunk roared, lashing out with his spurs. '*Up, Thunder!*' And somehow the old warhorse found his feet again.

He could feel a sharp pain under his rib, and his left arm was being pulled down. Aerion had driven his lance through oak, wool, and steel; three feet of splintered ash and sharp iron stuck from his side. Dunk reached over with his right hand, grasped the lance just below the head, clenched his teeth, and pulled it out of him with one savage yank. Blood followed, seeping through the rings of his mail to redden his surcoat. The world swam and he almost fell. Dimly, through the pain, he could hear voices calling his name. His beautiful shield was useless now. He tossed it aside, elm tree, shooting star, broken lance, and all, and drew his sword, but he hurt so much he did not think he could swing it.

Turning Thunder in a tight circle, he tried to get a sense of what was happening elsewhere on the field. Ser Humfrey Hardyng clung to the neck of his mount, obviously wounded. The other Ser Humfrey lay motionless in a lake of bloodstained mud, a broken lance protruding from his groin. He saw Prince Baelor gallop past, lance still intact, and drive one of the Kingsguard from his saddle. Another of the white knights was already down, and Maekar had been unhorsed as well. The third of the Kingsguard was fending off Ser Robyn Rhysling.

Aerion, where is Aerion? The sound of drumming hooves

behind him made Dunk turn his head sharply. Thunder bugled and reared, hooves lashing out futilely as Aerion's grey stallion barrelled into him at full gallop.

This time there was no hope of recovery. His longsword went spinning from his grasp, and the ground rose up to meet him. He landed with a bruising impact that jarred him to the bone and drove the breath from his lungs. Pain stabbed through him, so sharp he sobbed. For a moment it was all he could do to lie there. The taste of blood filled his mouth. *Dunk the lunk, thought he could be a knight.* He knew he had to find his feet again, or die. Groaning, he forced himself to hands and knees. He could not breathe, nor could he see. The eyeslit of his helm was packed with mud. Lurching blindly to his feet, Dunk scraped at the mud with a mailed finger. *There, that's . . .*

Through his fingers, he glimpsed a dragon flying, and a spiked morning-star whirling on the end of a chain. Then his head seemed to burst to pieces.

When his eyes opened he was on the ground again, sprawled on his back. The mud had all been knocked from his helm, but now one eye was closed by blood. Above was nothing but dark grey sky. His face throbbed, and he could feel cold wet metal pressing in against cheek and temple. *He broke my head, and I'm dying.* What was worse was the others who would die with him, Raymun and Prince Baelor and the rest. *I've failed them. I am no champion. I'm not even a hedge knight. I am nothing.* He remembered Prince Daeron boasting that no one could lie insensible in the mud as well as he did. *He never saw Dunk the lunk, though, did he?* The shame was worse than the pain.

The dragon appeared above him.

Three heads it had, and wings bright as flame, red and yellow and orange. It was laughing. 'Are you dead yet, hedge knight?' it asked. 'Cry for quarter and admit your guilt, and perhaps I'll only claim a hand and a foot. Oh, and those teeth, but what are a few teeth? A man like you can live years on pease porridge.' The dragon laughed again. 'No? Eat *this*, then.' The spiked ball whirled round and round the sky, and fell towards his head as fast as a shooting star.

Dunk rolled.

Where he found the strength he did not know, but he found it. He rolled into Aerion's legs, threw a steel-clad arm around his thigh, dragged him cursing into the mud, and rolled on top of him. *Let him swing his bloody morning-star now.* The prince tried forcing the lip of his shield up at Dunk's head, but his battered helm took the brunt of the impact. Aerion was strong, but Dunk was stronger, and larger and heavier as well. He grabbed hold of the shield with both hands and twisted until the straps broke. Then he brought it down on the top of the princeling's helm, again and again and again, smashing the enamelled flames of his crest. The shield was thicker than Dunk's had been, solid oak banded with iron. A flame broke off. Then another. The prince ran out of flames long before Dunk ran out of blows.

Aerion finally let go the handle of his useless morning-star and clawed for the poniard at his hip. He got it free of its sheath, but when Dunk whanged his hand with the shield the knife sailed off into the mud.

He could vanquish Ser Duncan the Tall, but not Dunk of Flea Bottom. The old man had taught him jousting and swordplay, but this sort of fighting he had learned earlier, in shadowy wynds and crooked alleys behind the city's winesinks. Dunk flung the battered shield away and wrenched up the visor of Aerion's helm. *A visor is a weak point,* he remembered Steely Pate saying. The prince had all but ceased to struggle. His eyes were purple and full of terror. Dunk had a sudden urge to grab one and pop it like a grape between two steel fingers, but that would not be knightly. '*YIELD!*' he shouted.

'I yield,' the dragon whispered, pale lips barely moving. Dunk blinked down at him. For a moment he could not credit what his ears had heard. *Is it done, then?* He turned his head slowly from side to side, trying to see. His vision slit was partly closed by the blow that had smashed in the left side of his face. He glimpsed Prince Maekar, mace in hand, trying to fight his way to his son's side. Baelor Breakspear was holding him off.

Dunk lurched to his feet and pulled Prince Aerion up after him. Fumbling at the lacings of his helm, he tore it off and flung it away. At once he was drowned in sights and sounds; grunts and curses, the shouts of the crowd, one stallion screaming while another raced riderless across the field. Everywhere steel rang on steel. Raymun and his cousin were slashing at each other in front of the viewing stand, both afoot. Their shields were splintered ruins, the green apple and the red had both been hacked to tinder. One of the Kingsguard knights was carrying a wounded brother from the field. They looked alike in their white armour and white cloaks. The third of the white knights was down, and the Laughing Storm had joined Prince Baelor against Prince Maekar. Mace, battle-axe, and longsword clashed and clanged, ringing against helm and shield. Maekar was taking three blows for every one he landed, and Dunk could see that it would be over soon. *I must make an end to it before more of us are killed.*

Prince Aerion made a sudden dive for his morning-star. Dunk kicked him in the back and knocked him face down, then grabbed hold of one of his legs and dragged him across the field. By the time he reached the viewing stand where Lord Ashford sat, the Bright Prince was brown as a privy. Dunk hauled him on to his feet and rattled him, shaking some of the mud on to Lord Ashford and the fair maid. 'Tell him!'

Aerion Brightflame spat out a mouthful of grass and dirt. 'I withdraw my accusation.'

Afterwards Dunk could not have said whether he walked from the field under his own power or had required help. He hurt everywhere, and some places worse than others. *I am a knight now in truth?* he remembered wondering. *Am I a champion?*

Egg helped him remove his greaves and gorget, and Raymun as well, and even Steely Pate. He was too dazed to tell them apart. They were fingers and thumbs and voices. Pate was the one complaining, Dunk knew. 'Look what he's done to me armour,' he said. 'All dinted and banged and scratched. Aye, I ask you, why do I bother? I'll have to cut that mail off him, I fear.'

'Raymun,' Dunk said urgently, clutching at his friend's hands.

'The others. How did they fare?' He had to know. 'Has anyone died?'

'Beesbury,' Raymun said. 'Slain by Donnel of Duskendale in the first charge. Ser Humfrey is gravely wounded as well. The rest of us are bruised and bloody, no more. Save for you.'

'And them? The accusers?'

'Ser Willem Wylde of the Kingsguard was carried from the field insensate, and I think I cracked a few of my cousin's ribs. At least I hope so.'

'And Prince Daeron?' Dunk blurted. 'Did he survive?'

'Once Ser Robyn unhorsed him, he lay where he fell. He may have a broken foot. His own horse trod on him while running loose about the field.'

Dazed and confused as he was, Dunk felt a huge sense of relief. 'His dream was wrong, then. The dead dragon. Unless Aerion died. He didn't though, did he?'

'No,' said Egg. 'You spared him. Don't you remember?'

'I suppose.' Already his memories of the fight were becoming confused and vague. 'One moment I feel drunk. The next it hurts so bad I know I'm dying.'

They made him lie down on his back and talked over him as he gazed up into the roiling grey sky. It seemed to Dunk that it was still morning. He wondered how long the fight had taken.

'Gods be good, the lance point drove the rings deep into his flesh,' he heard Raymun saying. 'It will mortify unless . . .'

'Get him drunk and pour some boiling oil into it,' someone suggested. 'That's how the maesters do it.'

'Wine.' The voice had a hollow metallic ring to it. '*Not* oil, that will kill him, boiling wine. I'll send Maester Yormwell to have a look at him when he's done tending my brother.'

A tall knight stood above him, in black armour dinted and scarred by many blows. *Prince Baelor.* The scarlet dragon on his helm had lost a head, both wings, and most of its tail. 'Your Grace,' Dunk said, 'I am your man. Please. Your man.'

'My man.' The black knight put a hand on Raymun's shoulder to steady himself. 'I need good men, Ser Duncan. The realm

. . .' His voice sounded oddly slurred. Perhaps he'd bitten his tongue.

Dunk was very tired. It was hard to stay awake. 'Your man,' he murmured once more.

The prince moved his head slowly from side to side. 'Ser Raymun . . . my helm, if you'd be so kind. Visor . . . visor's cracked, and my fingers . . . fingers feel like wood . . .'

'At once, Your Grace.' Raymun took the prince's helm in both hands and grunted. 'Goodman Pate, a hand.'

Steely Pate dragged over a mounting stool. 'It's crushed down at the back, Your Grace, towards the left side. Smashed into the gorget. Good steel, this, to stop such a blow.'

'Brother's mace, most like,' Baelor said thickly. 'He's strong.' He winced. 'That . . . feels queer, I . . .'

'Here it comes.' Pate lifted the battered helm away. 'Gods be good. *Oh gods oh gods oh gods preserve . . .*'

Dunk saw something red and wet fall out of the helm. Someone was screaming, high and terrible. Against the bleak grey sky swayed a tall, tall prince in black armour with only half a skull. He could see red blood and pale bone beneath and something else, something blue-grey and pulpy. A queer troubled look passed across Baelor Breakspear's face, like a cloud passing before a sun. He raised his hand and touched the back of his head with two fingers, oh so lightly. And then he fell.

Dunk caught him. 'Up,' they say he said, just as he had with Thunder in the mêlée, 'up, up.' But he never remembered that afterwards, and the prince did not rise.

Baelor of House Targaryen, Prince of Dragonstone, Hand of the King, Protector of the Realm, and heir apparent to the Iron Throne of the Seven Kingdoms of Westeros, went to the fire in the yard of Ashford Castle on the north bank of the River Cockleswent. Other great houses might choose to bury their dead in the dark earth or sink them in the cold green sea, but the Targaryens were the blood of the dragon, and their ends were writ in flame.

He had been the finest knight of his age, and some argued

that he should have gone to face the dark clad in mail and plate, a sword in his hand. In the end though, his royal father's wishes prevailed, and Daeron II had a peaceable nature. When Dunk shuffled past Baelor's bier, the prince wore a black velvet tunic with the three-headed dragon picked out in scarlet thread upon his breast. Around his throat was a heavy gold chain. His sword was sheathed by his side, but he did wear a helm, a thin golden helm with an open visor so men could see his face.

Valarr, the Young Prince, stood vigil at the foot of the bier while his father lay in state. He was a shorter, slimmer, handsomer version of his sire, without the twice-broken nose that had made Baelor seem more human than royal. Valarr's hair was brown, but a bright streak of silver-gold ran through it. The sight of it reminded Dunk of Aerion, but he knew that was not fair. Egg's hair was growing back as bright as his brother's, and Egg was a decent enough lad, for a prince.

When he stopped to offer awkward sympathies, well larded with thanks, Prince Valarr blinked cool blue eyes at him and said, 'My father was only nine-and-thirty. He had it in him to be a great king, the greatest since Aegon the Dragon. Why would the gods take him, and leave *you*?' He shook his head. 'Begone with you, Ser Duncan. Begone.'

Wordless, Dunk limped from the castle, down to the camp by the green pool. He had no answer for Valarr. Nor for the questions he asked himself. The maesters and the boiling wine had done their work, and his wound was healing cleanly, though there would be a deep puckered scar between his left arm and his nipple. He could not see the wound without thinking of Baelor. *He saved me once with his sword, and once with a word, even though he was a dead man as he stood there*. The world made no sense when a great prince died so a hedge knight might live. Dunk sat beneath his elm and stared morosely at his feet.

When four guardsmen in the royal livery appeared in his camp late one day, he was sure they had come to kill him after all. Too weak and weary to reach for a sword, he sat with his back to the elm, waiting.

'Our prince begs the favour of a private word.'

'Which prince?' asked Dunk, wary.

'This prince,' a brusque voice said before the captain could answer. Maekar Targaryen walked out from behind the elm.

Dunk got slowly to his feet. *What would he have of me now?*

Maekar motioned, and the guards vanished as suddenly as they had appeared. The prince studied him a long moment, then turned and paced away from him to stand beside the pool, gazing down at his reflection in the water. 'I have sent Aerion to Lys,' he announced abruptly. 'A few years in the Free Cities may change him for the better.'

Dunk had never been to the Free Cities, so he did not know what to say to that. He was pleased that Aerion was gone from the Seven Kingdoms, and hoped he never came back, but that was not a thing you told a father of his son. He stood silent.

Prince Maekar turned to face him. 'Some men will say I meant to kill my brother. The gods know it is a lie, but I will hear the whispers till the day I die. And it was my mace that dealt the fatal blow, I have no doubt. The only other foes he faced in the mêlée were three Kingsguard, whose vows forbade them to do any more than defend themselves. So it was me. Strange to say, I do not recall the blow that broke his skull. Is that a mercy or a curse? Some of both, I think.'

From the way he looked at Dunk, it seemed the prince wanted an answer. 'I could not say, Your Grace.' Perhaps he should have hated Maekar, but instead he felt a queer sympathy for the man. 'You swung the mace, m'lord, but it was for me Prince Baelor died. So I killed him too, as much as you.'

'Yes,' the prince admitted. 'You'll hear them whisper as well. The king is old. When he dies, Valarr will climb the Iron Throne in place of his father. Each time a battle is lost or a crop fails, the fools will say, "Baelor would not have let it happen, but the hedge knight killed him."'

Dunk could see the truth in that. 'If I had not fought, you would have had my hand off. And my foot. Sometimes I sit under that tree there and look at my feet and ask if I couldn't have spared one. How could my foot be worth a prince's life?

And the other two as well, the Humfreys, they were good men too.' Ser Humfrey Hardyng had succumbed to his wounds only last night.

'And what answer does your tree give you?'

'None that I can hear. But the old man, Ser Arlan, every day at evenfall he'd say, "I wonder what the morrow will bring?" He never knew, no more than we do. Well, mighten it be that some morrow will come when I'll have need of that foot? When the *realm* will need that foot, even more than a prince's life?'

Maekar chewed on that a time, mouth clenched beneath the silvery-pale beard that made his face seem so square. 'It's not bloody likely,' he said harshly. 'The realm has as many hedge knights as hedges, and all of them have feet.'

'If Your Grace has a better answer, I'd want to hear it.'

Maekar frowned. 'It may be that the gods have a taste for cruel japes. Or perhaps there are no gods. Perhaps none of this had any meaning. I'd ask the High Septon, but the last time I went to him he told me that no man can truly understand the workings of the gods. Perhaps he should try sleeping under a tree.' He grimaced. 'My youngest son seems to have grown fond of you, ser. It is time he was a squire, but he tells me he will serve no knight but you. He is an unruly boy, as you will have noticed. Will you have him?'

'Me?' Dunk's mouth opened and closed and opened again. 'Egg . . . Aegon, I mean . . . he is a good lad, but, Your Grace, I know you honour me, but . . . I am only a hedge knight.'

'That can be changed,' said Maekar. 'Aegon is to return to my castle at Summerhall. There is a place there for you, if you wish. A knight of my household. You'll swear your sword to me, and Aegon can squire for you. While you train him, my master-at-arms will finish your own training.' The prince gave him a shrewd look. 'Your Ser Arlan did all he could for you, I have no doubt, but you still have much to learn.'

'I know, m'lord.' Dunk looked about him. At the green grass and the reeds, the tall elm, the ripples dancing across the surface of the sunlit pool. Another dragonfly was moving across the water, or perhaps it was the same one. *What shall it be, Dunk?*

he asked himself. *Dragonflies or dragons?* A few days ago he would have answered at once. It was all he had ever dreamed, but now that the prospect was at hand it frightened him. 'Just before Prince Baelor died, I swore to be his man.'

'Presumptuous of you,' said Maekar. 'What did he say?'

'That the realm needed good men.'

'That's true enough. What of it?'

'I will take your son as squire, Your Grace, but not at Summerhall. Not for a year or two. He's seen sufficient of castles, I would judge. I'll have him only if I can take him on the road with me.' He pointed to old Chestnut. 'He'll ride my stot, wear my old cloak, and he'll keep my sword sharp and my mail scoured. We'll sleep in inns and stables, and now and again in the halls of some landed knight or lesser lordling, and maybe under trees when we must.'

Prince Maekar gave him an incredulous look. 'Did the trial addle your wits, man? Aegon is a prince of the realm. The blood of the dragon. Princes are not made for sleeping in ditches and eating hard salt beef.' He saw Dunk hesitate. 'What is it you're afraid to tell me? Say what you will, ser.'

'Daeron never slept in a ditch, I'll wager,' Dunk said, very quietly, 'and all the beef that Aerion ever ate was thick and rare and bloody, like as not.'

Maekar Targaryen, Prince of Summerhall, regarded Dunk of Flea Bottom for a long time, his jaw working silently beneath his silvery beard. Finally he turned and walked away, never speaking a word. Dunk heard him riding off with his men. When they were gone, there was no sound but the faint thrum of the dragonfly's wings as it skimmed across the water.

The boy came the next morning, just as the sun was coming up. He wore old boots, brown breeches, a brown wool tunic, and an old traveller's cloak. 'My lord father says I am to serve you.'

'Serve you, *ser*,' Dunk reminded him. 'You can start by saddling the horses. Chestnut is yours, treat her kindly. I don't want to find you on Thunder unless I put you there.'

Egg went to get the saddles. 'Where are we going, ser?'

Dunk thought for a moment. 'I have never been over the Red Mountains. Would you like to have a look at Dorne?'

Egg grinned. 'I hear they have good puppet shows,' he said.

Memory, Sorrow, and Thorn

TAD WILLIAMS

Memory, Sorrow, and Thorn

TAD WILLIAMS

The Dragonbone Chair (1988)
Stone of Farewell (1990)
To Green Angel Tower (1993)

Tad Williams's trilogy takes place all across the lands of Osten Ard, from the marshes of the southern Wran to Yiqanuc, the icy northern home of the trolls, but its heart is in the great high keep known as the Hayholt.

The story begins when the death of Prester John, the powerful human king who has been the castle's master for many years, and who has extended his empire out from Erkynland to rule nearly all the nations of Osten Ard, sets in motion a falling-out between his royal sons – a war that eventually brings the entire world to the edge of actual extinction as the undead immortal Ineluki exploits the conflict for his own purposes. Among those caught up in this vast apocalyptic struggle are the scullion Simon Snowlock; Miriamele, the daughter of one of the royal brothers; Binabik the troll; the mysterious witch-woman known as Geloe; and several members of Ineluki's own Sithi – the near-immortal people he once gave his life to protect.

Five centuries before Prester John's era, in the failing days of his race's multimillennial empire, Ineluki had been the lord of the Hayholt, known then by its ancient name of Asu'a. As mortals besieged his castle, he had cast a terrible spell, a final and suicidal attempt to defeat the human upstarts. Ineluki and his followers had died in the conflagration, and Asu'a had been largely destroyed, but the mortals who survived merely rebuilt on the ruins of the Sithi's great keep, making it their own. Several mortal kings of different lands claimed the castle over the centuries, among them the Heron King, Holly King, and Fisher King of Osten Ard's legends, but none ever held it long until Prester John began his storied reign.

◆

The Burning Man

BY TAD WILLIAMS

Years and years later, I still start up in the deepest part of night with his agonized face before me. And always, in these terrible dreams, I am helpless to ease his suffering.

I will tell the tale then, in hope the last ghosts may be put to rest, if such a thing can ever happen in this place where there are more ghosts than living souls. But you will have to listen closely – this is a tale that the teller herself does not fully understand.

I will tell you of Lord Sulis, my famous stepfather.

I will tell you what the witch foretold to me.

I will tell you of the love that I had and I lost.

I will tell you of the night I saw the burning man.

Tellarin gifted me with small things, but they were not small to me. My lover brought me sweetmeats, and laughed to see me eat them so greedily.

'Ah, little Breda,' he told me. 'It is strange and wonderful that a mere soldier should have to smuggle honeyed figs to a king's daughter.' And then he kissed me, put his rough face against me and kissed me, and that was a sweeter thing than any fig that God ever made.

But Sulis was not truly a king, nor was I his true daughter.

Tellarin was not wrong about everything. The gladness I felt when I saw my soldier or heard him whistling below the window was strange and wonderful indeed.

My true father, the man from whose loins I sprang, died in

the cold waters of the Kingslake when I was very small. His companions said that a great pikefish became caught in the nets and dragged my father Ricwald to a drowning death, but others whispered that it was his companions themselves who murdered him, then weighted his body with stones.

Everyone knew that my father would have been gifted with the standard and spear of Great Thane when all the thanes of the Lake People next met. His father and uncle had both been Great Thane before him, so some whispered that God had struck down my poor father because one family should not hold power so long. Others believed that my father's companions on the boat had simply been paid shame-gold to drown him, to satisfy the ambition of one of the other families.

I know these things only from my mother Cynethrith's stories. She was young when my father died, and had two small children – me, not yet five years old, and my brother Aelfric, two years my elder. Together we went to live in the house of my father's father because we were the last of his line, and among the Lake People of Erkynland it was blood of high renown. But it was not a happy house. Godric, my grandfather, had himself been Great Thane for twice ten years before illness ended his rule, and he had high hopes that my father would follow him, but after my father died, Godric had to watch a man from one of the other families chosen to carry the spear and standard instead. From that moment, everything that happened in the world only seemed to prove to my grandfather that the best days of Erkynland and the Lake People had passed.

Godric died before I reached seven years, but he made those years between my father's death and his own very unhappy ones for my mother, with many complaints and sharp rebukes at how she managed the household and how she raised Aelfric and me, his dead son's only children. My grandfather spent much time with Aelfric, trying to make him the kind of man who would bring the spear and standard back to our family, but my brother was small and timid – it must have been clear he would never rule more than his own household. This

Godric blamed on my mother, saying she had taught the boy womanish ways.

Grandfather was less interested in me. He was never cruel to me, only fierce and short-spoken, but he was such a frightening figure, with bristling white beard, growling voice, and several missing fingers, that I could never do anything but shrink from him. If that was another reason he found little savour in life, then I am sorry for it now.

In any case, my mother's widowhood was a sad, bitter time for her. From mistress of her own house, and prospective wife of the Great Thane, she now became only one of three grown daughters in the house of a sour old man, for one of my father's sisters had also lost her husband, and the youngest had been kept at home, unmarried, to care for her father in his dotage.

I believe that had even the humblest of fishermen courted my mother, she would have looked upon him kindly, as long as he had a house of his own and no living relatives. But instead a man who has made the entire age tremble came to call.

'What is he like?' Tellarin once asked me. 'Tell me about your stepfather.'

'He is your lord and commander,' I smiled. 'What can I tell you that you do not know?'

'Tell me what he says when he is in his house, at his table, what he does.' Tellarin looked at me then, his long face suddenly boyish and surprised. 'Hah! It feels like sacrilege even to wonder!'

'He is just a man,' I told him, and rolled my eyes. Such silly things men feel about other men – that this one is so large and important, while they themselves are so small! 'He eats, he sleeps, he breaks wind. When my mother was alive, she used to say that he took up more room in a bed than any three others might, because he thrashed so, and talked aloud in his sleep.' I made my stepfather sound ordinary on purpose, because I did not like it when Tellarin seemed as interested in him as he was in me.

My Nabbanai soldier became serious then. 'How it must have

grieved him when your mother died. He must have loved her very much.'

As if it had not grieved me! I resisted the temptation to roll my eyes again, and instead told him, with all the certainty of youth, 'I do not think he loved her at all.'

My mother once said that when my stepfather and his household first appeared across the meadowlands, riding north towards the Kingslake, it was as though the heavenly host itself had descended to earth. Trumpets heralded their approach, drawing people from every town as though to witness a pilgrimage passing, or the procession of a saint's relic. The knights' armour and lances were polished to a sparkle, and their lord's heron crest gleamed in gold thread on all the tall banners. Even the horses of the Nabban-men were larger and prouder than our poor Erkynlandish ponies. The small army was followed by sheep and cattle in herds, and by dozens and dozens of wagons and oxcarts, a train so vast that their rutted path is still visible on the face of the land threescore years later.

I was a child, though, and saw none of it – not then. Within my grandfather's hall, I heard only rumours, things whispered by my aunts and my mother over their sewing. The powerful lord who had come was a Nabbanai nobleman, they reported, called by many Sulis the Apostate. He claimed that he came in peace, and wanted only to make a home for himself here beside the Kingslake. He was an exile from his own country – a heretic, some claimed, driven forth by the Lector under threat of excommunication because of his impertinent questions about the life of Usires Aedon, our blessed Ransomer. No, he had been forced from his home by the conniving of the escritors, said others. Angering a churchman is like treading on a serpent, they said.

Mother Church still had an unsolid grip on Erkynland in those days, and even though most had been baptized into the Aedonite faith, very few of the Lake People trusted the Sancellan Aedonitis. Many called it 'that hive of priests', and said that its chief aim was not God's work, but increasing its own power.

Many still think so, but they no longer speak ill of the church where strangers can hear them.

I know far more of these things today than I did when they happened. I understand much and much, now that I am old and everyone in my story is dead. Of course, I am not the first to have travelled this particular sad path. Understanding always comes too late, I think.

Lord Sulis had indeed fallen out with the church, and in Nabban the church and the state were so closely tied, he had made an enemy of the Imperator in the Sancellan Mahistrevis as well, but so powerful and important was the family of my stepfather-to-be that he was not imprisoned or executed, but instead strongly encouraged to leave Nabban. His countrymen thought he took his household to Erkynland because any nobleman could be king in that backward country – my country – but Sulis had his own reasons, darker and stranger than anyone could guess. So it was that he had brought his entire household, his knights and kerns and all their women and children, a small city's worth of folk, to the shores of the Kingslake.

For all the sharpness of their swords and strength of their armour, the Nabbanai treated the Lake People with surprising courtesy, and for the first weeks there was trade and much good fellowship between their camp and our towns. It was only when Lord Sulis announced to the thanes of the Lake People that he meant to settle in the High Keep, the deserted castle on the headlands, that the Erkynlanders became uneasy.

Huge and empty, the domain only of wind and shadows, the High Keep had looked down on our lands since the beginnings of the oldest tales. No one remembered who had built it – some said giants, but some swore the fairy-folk had built it themselves. The Northmen from Rimmersgard were said to have held it for a while, but they were long gone, driven out by a dragon from the fortress the Rimmersmen had stolen from the Peaceful Ones. So many tales surrounded that castle! When I was small, one of my mother's bondwomen told me that it was now the haunt of frost-witches and restless ghosts. Many a night I had thought of it standing deserted on the windy clifftop, only a half-day's ride away, and frightened myself so that I could not sleep.

The idea of someone rebuilding the ruined fortress made the thanes uneasy, but not only for fear of waking its spirits. The High Keep held a powerful position, perhaps an impregnable one – even in their crumbling condition, the walls would be almost impossible to storm if armed men held them. But the thanes were in a difficult spot. Though the men of the Lake People might outnumber those of Sulis, the heron knights were better armed, and the discipline of Nabbanai fighting men was well-known – a half-legion of the Imperator's Sea Wolves had slaughtered ten times that number of Thrithings-men in a battle just a few years before. And Osweard, the new Great Thane, was young and untested as a war leader. The lesser thanes asked my grandfather Godric to lend his wisdom, to speak to this Nabbanai lord and see what he could grasp of the man's true intention.

So it was that Lord Sulis came to my grandfather's steading, and saw my mother for the first time.

When I was a little girl, I liked to believe that Sulis fell in love with my mother Cynethrith the moment he saw her, as she stood quietly behind her father-in-law's chair in Godric's great hall. She was beautiful, that I know – before my father died, all the people of the household used to call her Ricwald's Swan, because of her long neck and white shoulders. Her hair was a pale, pale gold, her eyes as green as the summer Kingslake. Any ordinary man would have loved her on sight. But 'ordinary' must be the least likely of all the words that could be used to describe my stepfather.

When I was a young woman, and falling in love myself for the first time, I knew for certain that Sulis could not have loved her. How could anyone who loved have been as cold and distant as he was? As heavily polite? Aching then at the mere thought of Tellarin, my secret beloved, I knew that a man who acted as my stepfather had acted towards my mother could not feel anything like love.

Now I am not so sure. So many things are different when I look at them now. In this extremity of age, I am farther away, as though I looked at my own life from a high hilltop, but in some ways it seems I see things much more closely.

Sulis was a clever man, and could not have failed to notice how my grandfather Godric hated the new Great Thane – it was in everything my grandfather said. He could not speak of the weather without mentioning how the summers had been warmer and the winters shorter in the days when he himself had been Great Thane, and had his son been allowed to succeed him, he as much as declared, every day would have been the first day of Maia-month. Seeing this, Sulis made compact with the bitter old man, first by the gifts and subtle compliments he gave him, but soon in the courting of Godric's daughter-in-law as well.

While my grandfather became more and more impressed by this foreign nobleman's good sense, Sulis made his master stroke. Not only did he offer a bride price for my mother – for a widow! – that was greater than would have been paid even for the virgin daughter of a ruling Great Thane, a sizable fortune of swords and proud Nabban horses and gold plate, but Sulis told Godric that he would even leave my brother and myself to be raised in our grandfather's house.

Godric had still not given up all hope of Aelfric, and this idea delighted him, but he had no particular use for me. My mother would be happier, both men eventually decided, if she were allowed to bring at least one of her children to her new home on the headlands.

Thus it was settled, and the powerful foreign lord married into the household of the old Great Thane. Godric told the rest of the thanes that Sulis meant only good, that by this gesture he had proved his honest wish to live in peace with the Lake People. There were priests in Sulis' company who would cleanse the High Keep of any unquiet spirits, Godric explained to the thanes – as Sulis himself had assured my grandfather – and thus, he argued, letting Sulis take the ancient keep for his own would bring our folk a double blessing.

What Osweard and the lesser thanes thought of this, I do not know. Faced with Godric's enthusiasm, with the power of the Nabbanai lord, and perhaps even with their own secret shame in the matter of my father's death, they chose to give in. Lord Sulis and his new bride were gifted with the deserted High Keep, with its broken walls and its ghosts.

Did my mother love her second husband? I cannot answer that any better than I can say what Sulis felt, and they are both so long dead that I am now the only living person who knew them both. When she first saw him in the doorway at Godric's house, he would certainly have been the light of every eye. He was not young – like my mother, he had already lost a spouse, although a decade had passed since his widowing, while hers was still fresh – but he was a great man from the greatest city of all. He wore a mantle of pure white over his armour, held at the shoulder by a lapis badge of his family's heron crest. He had tucked his helmet under his arm when he entered the hall and my mother could see that he had very little hair, only a fringe of curls at the back of his head and over his ears, so that his forehead gleamed in the firelight. He was tall and strongly-made, his unwhiskered jaw square, his nose wide and prominent. His strong, heavy features had a deep and contemplative look, but also a trace of sadness – almost, my mother once told me, the sort of face she thought God Himself might show on the Day of Weighing-Out.

He frightened her and he excited her – both of these things I know from the way she spoke of that first meeting. But did she love him, then or in the days to come? I cannot say. Does it matter? So many years later, it is hard to believe that it does.

Her time in her father-in-law's house had been hard, though. Whatever her deepest feelings about him, I do not doubt that she was happy to wed Sulis.

In the month that my mother died, when I was in my thirteenth year, she told me that she believed Sulis had been afraid to love her. She never explained this – she was in her final weakness, and it was difficult for her to speak – and I still do not know what she meant.

The next to the last thing she ever said to me made even less sense. When the weakness in her chest was so terrible that she would lose the strength to breathe for long moments, she still summoned the strength to declare, 'I am a ghost.'

She may have spoken of her suffering – that she felt she only clung to the world, like a timid spirit that will not take the road to Heaven, but lingers ever near the places it knew. Certainly her last request made it clear that she had grown weary of the circles of this world. But I have wondered since if there might be some other meaning to her words. Did she mean that her own life after my father's death had been nothing more than a ghost-life? Or did she perhaps intend to say that she had become a shade in her own house, something that waited in the dark, haunted corridors of the High Keep for her second husband's regard to give it true life – a regard that would never come from that silent, secret-burdened man?

My poor mother. Our poor, haunted family!

I remember little of the first year of my mother's marriage to Lord Sulis, but I cannot forget the day we took possession of our new home. Others had gone before us to make our arrival as easeful as possible – I know they had, because a great tent had already been erected on the green in the Inner Bailey, which was where we slept for the first months – but to the child I was, it seemed we were riding into a place where no mortals had ever gone. I expected witches or ogres around every corner.

We came up the cliff road beside the Kingslake until we reached the curtain wall and began to circle the castle itself. Those who had gone before had hacked a crude road in the shadow of the walls, so we had a much easier passage than we would have only days earlier. We rode in a tunnel cut between the wall and forest. Where the trees and brush had not been chopped away, the Kingswood grew right to the castle's edge, striving with root and tendril to breach the great stones of the wall.

At the castle's northern gate we found nothing but a cleared place on the hillside, a desolation of tree stumps and burn-blackened grass – the thriving town of Erkynchester that today sprawls all around the castle's feet had not even been imagined. Not all the forest growth had been cleared. Vines still clung to the pillars of the shattered gatehouse, rooted in the cracks of the odd, shiny stone which was all that remained of the original gateway, hanging in great braids across the opening to make a tangled, living arbour.

'Do you see?' Lord Sulis spread his strong arms as if he had designed and crafted the wilderness himself. 'We will make our home in the greatest and oldest of all houses.'

As he led her across that threshold and into the ruins of the ancient castle, my mother made the sign of the Tree upon her breast.

I know many things now that I did not know on the first day we came to the High Keep. Of all the many tales about the place, some I now can say are false, but others I am now certain are true. For one thing, there is no question that the Northmen lived here. Over the years I have found many of their coins, struck with the crude *'F'* rune of their King Fingil, and they also left the rotted remains of their wooden longhouses in the Outer Bailey, which my stepfather's workmen found during the course of other diggings. So I came to realize that if the story of the Northmen living here was a true one, it stood to reason that the legend of the dragon might also be true, as well as the terrible tale of how the Northmen slaughtered the castle's immortal inhabitants.

But I did not need such workaday proofs as coins or ruins to show me that our home was full of unquiet ghosts. That I learned for myself beyond all dispute, on the night I saw the burning man.

Perhaps someone who had grown up in Nabban or one of

the other large cities of the south would not have been so astonished by their first sight of the High Keep, but I was a child of the Lake People. Before that day, the largest building I had ever approached was the great hall of our town where the thanes met every spring – a building that could easily have been hidden in any of several parts of the High Keep and then never discovered again. On that first day, it was clear to me that the mighty castle could only have been built by giants.

The curtain wall was impressive enough to a small girl – ten times my own height and made of huge, rough stones that I could not imagine being hauled into place by anything smaller than the grandest of ogres – but the inner walls, in the places where they still stood, were not just vast but also beautiful. They were shaped of shining white stone which had been polished like jewellery, the blocks of equal size to those of the outer wall but with every join so seamless that from a distance each wall appeared to be a single thing, a curving piece of ivory or bone erupting from the hillside.

Many of the keep's original buildings had been burned or torn down, some so that the men from Rimmersgard could pillage the stones to build their own tower, squat as a barrel but very tall. In any other place the Northmen's huge construction would have loomed over the whole landscape and would certainly have been the focus of my amazement. But in any other place, there would not have been the Angel Tower.

I did not know its name then – in fact, it had no name, since the shape at its very peak could scarcely be seen – but the moment I saw it I knew there could be nothing else like it on earth, and for once childish exaggeration was correct. Its entrance was blocked by piles of rubble the Northmen had never finished clearing, and much of the lower part of its façade had cracked and fallen away in some unimaginable cataclysm, so that its base was raw stone, but it still thrust into the sky like a great white fang, taller than any tree, taller than anything mortals have ever built.

Excited but also frightened, I asked my mother whether the tower might not fall down on us. She tried to reassure me, saying it had stood for a longer time than I could imagine, perhaps since before there had even been people living beside the Kingslake, but that only made me feel other, stranger things.

The last words my mother ever spoke to me were, 'Bring me a dragon's claw.'

I thought at first that in the final hours of her illness she was wandering in her thoughts back to our early days at the castle.

The story of the High Keep's dragon, the creature who had driven out the last of the Northmen, was so old it had lost much of its power to frighten, but it was still potent to a little girl. The men of my stepfather's company used to bring me bits of polished stone – I learned after a while that they were shards of crumbled wall-carvings from the oldest parts of the castle – and tell me, 'See, here is a broken piece of the great red dragon's claw. He lives down in the caves below the castle, but sometimes at night he comes up to sniff around. He is sniffing for little girls to eat!'

The first few times, I believed them. Then, as I grew older and less susceptible, I learned to scorn the very idea of the dragon. Now that I am an old woman, I am plagued by dreams of it again. Sometimes even when I am awake, I think I can sense it down in the darkness below the castle, feel the moments of restlessness that trouble its long, deep sleep.

So on that night long ago, when my dying mother told me to bring her a dragon's claw, I thought she was remembering something from our first year in the castle. I was about to go look for one of the old stones, but her bondwoman Ulca – what the Nabbanai called her handmaiden or body servant – told me that was not what my mother wanted. A dragon's claw, she explained to me, was a charm to help those who suffered find the ease of a swift death. Ulca had tears in her eyes, and I think she was Aedonite enough to be troubled by the idea, but she was a sensible young woman and did not waste time arguing the right or wrong of it. She told me that the only way

I could get such a thing swiftly would be from a woman named Xanippa who lived in the settlement that had sprung up just outside the High Keep's walls.

I was barely into womanhood, but I felt very much a child. The idea of even such a short journey outside the walls after dark frightened me, but my mother had asked, and to refuse a deathbed request was a sin long before Mother Church arrived to parcel up and name the rights and wrongs of life. I left Ulca at my mother's side and hurried across the rainy, nightbound castle.

The woman Xanippa had once been a whore, but as she had become older and fatter she had decided she needed another profession, and had developed a name as a herbwife. Her tumbledown hut, which stood against the keep's southeast curtain wall, overlooking the Kingswood, was full of smoke and bad smells. Xanippa had hair like a bird's nest, tied with what had once been a pretty ribbon. Her face might have been round and comely once, but years and fat had turned it into something that looked as though it had been brought up in a fishing net. She was also so large she did not move from her stool by the fire during the time I was there – or on most other occasions, I guessed.

Xanippa was very suspicious of me at first, but when she found out who I was and what I wanted, and saw my face as proof, she accepted the three small coins I gave her and gestured for me to fetch her splintered wooden chest from the fireplace corner. Like its mistress, the chest had clearly once been in better condition and more prettily painted. She set it on the curve of her belly and began to search through it with a painstaking care that seemed at odds with everything else about her.

'Ah, here,' she said at last. 'Dragon's claw.' She held out her hand to show me the curved, black thing. It was certainly a claw, but far too small to belong to any dragon I could imagine. Xanippa saw my hesitation. 'It is an owl's toe, you silly girl. "Dragon's claw" is just a name.' She pointed to a tiny ball of glass over the talon's tip. 'Do not pull that off or break it. In fact, do not touch it at all. Do you have a purse?'

I showed her the small bag that hung always on a cord around my neck. Xanippa frowned. 'The cloth is very thin.' She found some rags in one of the pockets of her shapeless robe and wrapped the claw, then dropped it into my purse and tucked it back in my bodice. As she did so, she squeezed my breast so hard that I murmured in pain, then patted my head. 'Merciful Rhiap,' she growled, 'was I ever so young as this? In any case, be careful, my little sweetmeat. This is heartsbane on the tip of this claw, from the marshes of the Wran. If you are careless, this is one prick that will make sure you die a virgin.' She laughed. 'You don't want that, do you?'

I backed to the door. Xanippa grinned to see my fright. 'And you had better give your stepfather a message from me. He will not find what he seeks among the womenfolk here or among the herbwives of the Lake People. Tell him he can believe me, because if I could solve his riddle, I would – and, oh, but I would make him pay dearly for it! No, he will have to find the Witch of the Forest and put his questions to her.'

She was laughing again as I got the door open at last and escaped. The rain was even stronger now, and I slipped and fell several times, but still ran all the way back to the Inner Bailey.

When I reached my mother's bed, the priest had already come and gone, as had my stepfather, who Ulca told me had never spoken a word. My mother had died only a short time after I left on my errand. I had failed her – had left her to suffer and die with no family beside her. The shame and sorrow burned so badly that I could not imagine the pain would ever go away. As the other women prepared her for burial, I could do nothing but weep. The dragon's claw dangled next to my heart, all but forgotten.

I spent weeks wandering the castle, lost and miserable. I only remembered the message Xanippa had given me when my mother had been dead and buried almost a month.

I found my stepfather on the wall overlooking the Kingslake, and told him what Xanippa had said. He did not ask me how I came to be carrying messages for such a woman. He did not even signify he had heard me. His eyes were fixed on something in the far distance – on the boats of the fisher-folk, perhaps, dim in the fog.

The first years in the ruined High Keep were hard ones, and not just for my mother and me. Lord Sulis had to oversee the rebuilding, a vast and endlessly complicated task, as well as keep up the spirits of his own people through the first bleak winter.

It is one thing for soldiers, in the initial flush of loyal indignity, to swear they will follow their wronged commander anywhere. It is another thing entirely when that commander comes to a halt, when following becomes true exile. As the Nabbanai troops came to understand that this cold backwater of Erkynland was to be their home for ever, problems began – drinking and fighting among the soldiers, and even more unhappy incidents between Sulis' men and the local people . . . *my* people, although it was hard for me to remember that sometimes. After my mother died, I sometimes felt as if I were the true exile, surrounded by Nabbanai names and faces and speech even in the middle of my own land.

If we did not enjoy that first winter, we survived it, and continued as we had begun, a household of the dispossessed. But if ever a man was born to endure that state, it was my stepfather.

When I see him now in my memory, when I picture again that great heavy brow and that stern face, I think of him as an island, standing by himself on the far side of dangerous waters, near but for ever unvisited. I was too young and too shy to try to shout across the gulf that separated us, but it scarcely mattered – Sulis did not seem like a man who regretted his own solitude. In the middle of a crowded room his eyes were always on the walls instead of the people, as though he could see through stone to some better place. Even in his happiest and most festive moods, I seldom heard him laugh, and his swift, distracted smiles suggested that the jokes he liked best could never truly be explained to anyone else.

He was not a bad man, or even a difficult man, as my grandfather Godric had been, but when I saw the immense loyalty of his soldiers it was sometimes hard for me to understand it. Tellarin said that when he had joined Avalles' company, the others had told him of how Lord Sulis had once carried two of his wounded bondmen from the field, one trip for each, through a storm of Thrithings arrows. If that is true, it is easy to understand why his men loved him, but there were few opportunities for such obvious sorts of bravery in the High Keep's echoing halls.

While I was still young, Sulis would pat me on the head when we met, or ask me questions that were meant to show a paternal interest, but which often betrayed an uncertainty as to how old I was and what I liked to do. When I began to grow a womanish form, he became even more correct and formal, and would offer compliments on my clothes or my stitchery in the same studied way that he greeted the High Keep's tenants at Aedonmansa, when he called each man by his name – learned from the seneschal's accounting books – as he filed past, and wished each a good year.

Sulis grew even more distant in the year after my mother died, as though losing her had finally untethered him from the daily tasks he had always performed in such a stiff, practised way. He spent less and less time seeing to the matters of government, and instead sat reading for hours – sometimes all through the night, wrapped in heavy robes against the midnight chill, burning candles faster than the rest of the house put together.

The books that had come with him from his family's great house in Nabban were mostly tomes of religious instruction, but also some military and other histories. He occasionally allowed me to look at one, but although I was learning, I still read only slowly, and could make little of the odd names and devices in the accounts of battle. Sulis had other books that he would never even let me glance at, plainbound volumes that he kept locked in wooden boxes. The first time I ever saw one go back into its chest, I found the memory returning to me for days afterward. What sort of books were they, I wondered, that must be kept sealed away?

One of the locked boxes contained his own writings, but I did not find that out for two more years, until the night of Black Fire was almost upon us.

It was in the season after my mother's death, on a day when I found him reading in the grey light that streamed into the throne room, that Lord Sulis truly looked at me for the one and only time I remember.

When I shyly asked what he was doing, he allowed me to examine the book in his lap, a beautiful illuminated history of the prophet Varris with the heron of Honsa Sulis worked in gilt on the binding. I traced with my finger an illustration of Varris being martyred on the wheel. 'Poor, poor man,' I said. 'How he must have suffered. And all because he stayed true to his God. The Lord must have given him sweet welcome to Heaven.'

The picture of Varris in his agony jumped a little – I had startled my stepfather into a flinch. I looked up to find him gazing at me intently, his brown eyes so wide with feelings I could not recognize that for a moment I was terrified that he would strike me. He lifted his huge, broad hand, but gently. He touched my hair, then curled the hand into a fist, never once shifting that burning stare from me.

'They have taken everything from me, Breda.' His voice was tight-clenched with a pain I could not begin to understand. 'But I will never bend my back. Never.'

I held my breath, uncertain and still a little frightened. A moment later my stepfather recovered himself. He brought his fist to his mouth and pretended to cough – he was the least able dissembler I have ever known – and then bade me let him finish his reading while the light still held. To this day I do not know who he believed had taken everything from him – the Imperator and his court in Nabban? The priests of Mother Church? Or perhaps even God and His army of angels?

What I do know was that he tried to tell me of what burned inside him, but could not find the words. What I also know is that at least for that moment, my heart ached for the man.

My Tellarin asked me once, 'How could it be possible that no other man has made you his own? You are beautiful, and the daughter of a king.'

But as I have said before, Lord Sulis was not my father, nor was he king. And the evidence of the mirror that had once been my mother's suggested that my soldier overspoke my comeliness as well. Where my mother had been fair and full of light, I was dark. Where she was long of neck and limb and ample of hip, I was made small, like a young boy. I have never taken up much space on the earth – nor will I below it, for that matter. Wherever my grave is made, the digging will not shift much soil.

But Tellarin spoke with the words of love, and love is a kind of spell which banishes all sense.

'How can you care for a rough man like me?' he asked me. 'How can you love a man who can bring you no lands but the farm a soldier's pension can buy? Who can give your children no title of nobility?'

Because love does not do sums, I should have told him. Love makes choices, and then gives its all.

Had he seen himself as I first saw him, though, he could have had no questions.

It was an early spring day in my fifteenth year, and the sentries had seen the boats coming across the Kingslake at first light of morning. These were no ordinary fishing-craft, but barges loaded with more than a dozen men and their warhorses. Many of the castle folk had gathered to see the travellers come in and to learn their news.

After they had brought all their goods ashore on the lakefront, Tellarin and the rest of the company mounted and rode up the hill path and in through the main gates. The gates themselves had only lately been rebuilt – they were crude things of heavy, undressed timbers, but enough to serve in case of war. My stepfather had reason to be cautious, as the delegation that arrived that day was to prove.

It was actually Tellarin's friend Avalles who was called master of these men, because Avalles was an equestrian knight, one of the Sulean family nephews, but it was not hard to see which of the two truly held the soldiers' loyalty. My Tellarin was barely twenty years old on the first day I saw him. He was not handsome – his face was too long and his nose too impudent to grace one of the angels painted in my stepfather's books – but I thought him quite, quite beautiful. He had taken off his helmet to feel the morning sun as he rode, and his golden hair streamed in the wind off the lake. Even my inexperienced eye could see that he was still young for a fighting man, but I could also see that the men who rode with him admired him too.

His eyes found me in the crowd around my father and he smiled as though he recognized me, although we had never seen each other before. My blood went hot inside me, but I knew so little of the world, I did not recognize the fever of love.

My stepfather embraced Avalles, then allowed Tellarin and the others to kneel before him as each swore his fealty in turn, although I am sure Sulis wanted only to be finished with ceremony so he could return to his books.

The company had been sent by my stepfather's family council in Nabban. A letter from the council, carried by Avalles, reported that there had been a resurgence of talk against Sulis in the imperatorial court at Nabban, much of it fanned by the Aedonite priests. A poor man who held odd, perhaps irreligious beliefs was one thing, the council wrote, but when the same beliefs belonged to a nobleman with money, land, and a famous name, many powerful people would consider him a threat. In fear for my stepfather's life, his family had thus sent this carefully picked troop and warnings to Sulis to be more cautious than ever.

Despite the company's grim purpose, news from home was always welcome, and many of the new troop had fought beside other members of my stepfather's army. There were many glad reunions.

When Lord Sulis had at last been allowed to retreat to his reading, but before Ulca could hurry me back indoors, Tellarin asked Avalles if he could be introduced to me. Avalles himself was a dark, heavy-faced youth with a fledgling beard, only a few years Tellarin's elder, but with so much of the Sulean family's gravity in him that he seemed a sort of foolish old uncle. He gripped my hand too tightly and mumbled several clumsy compliments about how fair the flowers grew in the north, then introduced me to his friend.

Tellarin did not kiss my hand, but held me far more firmly with just his bright eyes. He said, 'I will remember this day always, my lady,' then bowed. Ulca caught my elbow and dragged me away.

Even in the midst of love's fever, which was to spread all through my fifteenth year, I could not help but notice that the changes which had begun in my stepfather when my mother died were growing worse.

Lord Sulis now hardly left his chambers at all, closeting himself with his books and his writings, being drawn out only to attend to the most pressing of affairs. His only regular conversations were with Father Ganaris, the plain-spoken military chaplain who was the sole priest to have accompanied Lord Sulis out of Nabban. Sulis had installed his old battlefield comrade in the castle's newly-built chapel, and it was one of the few places the master of the High Keep would still go. His visits did not seem to bring the old chaplain much pleasure, though. Once I watched them bidding each other farewell, and as Sulis turned and shouldered his way through the wind, heading back across the courtyard to our residence, Ganaris sent a look after him that was grim and sad – the expression, I thought, of a man whose old friend has a mortal illness.

Perhaps if I had tried, I could have done something to help my stepfather. Perhaps there could have been some other path than the one that led us to the base of the tree that grows in darkness. But the truth is that although I saw all these signs, I gave them little attention. Tellarin, my soldier, had begun to court me – at first only with glances and greetings, later with small gifts – and all else in my life shrank to insignificance by comparison.

In fact, so changed was everything that a newer, larger sun might have risen into the sky above the High Keep, warming every corner with its light. Even the most workaday tasks took fresh meaning because of my feelings for bright-eyed Tellarin. My catechisms and my reading lessons I now pursued diligently, so that my beloved might not find me lacking in conversation . . . except on those days when I could scarcely attend to them at all for dreaming about him. My walks in the castle grounds became excuses to look for him, to hope for a shared glance across a courtyard or down a hallway. Even the folktales Ulca told me over our stitchery, which before had been only a means to make the time pass pleasantly, now seemed completely new. The princes and princesses who fell in love were Tellarin and me. Their every moment of suffering burned me like fire, their ultimate triumphs thrilled me so deeply that some days I feared I might actually faint.

After a time, Ulca, who guessed but did not know, refused to tell me any tale that had kissing in it.

But I had my own story by then, and I was living it fully. My own first kiss came as we were walking in the sparse, windy garden that lay in the shadow of the Northmen's tower. That ugly building was ever after beautiful to me, and even on the coldest of days, if I could see that tower, it would warm me.

'Your stepfather could have my head,' my soldier told me, his cheek touching lightly against mine. 'I have betrayed both his trust and my station.'

'Then if you are a condemned man,' I whispered, 'you may as well steal again.' And I pulled him back farther into the shadows and kissed him until my mouth was sore. I was alive in a way I had never been, and almost mad with it. I was hungry for him, for his kisses, his breath, the sound of his voice.

He gifted me with small things that could not be found in Lord Sulis' drab and careful household – flowers, sweetmeats, small baubles he found at the markets in the new town of

Erkynchester, outside the castle gates. I could hardly bring myself to eat the honeyed figs he bought for me, not because they were too rich for his purse, although they were – he was not wealthy like his friend Avalles – but because they were gifts from him, and thus precious. To do something as destructive as eat them seemed unimaginably wasteful.

'Eat them slowly, then,' he told me. 'They will kiss your lips when I cannot.'

I gave myself to him, of course, completely and utterly. Ulca's dark hints about soiled women drowning themselves in the Kingslake, about brides sent back to their families in disgrace, even about bastardy as the root of a dozen dreadful wars, were all ignored. I offered Tellarin my body as well as my heart. Who would not? And if I were that young girl once more, coming out of the shadows of her sorrowful childhood into that bright day, I would do it again, with equal joy. Even now that I see the foolishness, I cannot fault the girl I was. When you are young and your life stretches so far ahead of you, you are also without patience – you cannot understand that there will be other days, other times, other chances. God has made us this way. Who knows why He chose it so?

As for me, I knew nothing in those days but the fever in my blood. When Tellarin rapped at my door in the dark hours, I brought him to my bed. When he left me, I wept, but not from shame. He came to me again and again as autumn turned to winter, and as winter crept past we built a warm, secret world all our own. I could not imagine a life without him in it every moment.

Again, youth was foolish, for I have now managed to live without him for many years. There has even been much that was pleasing in my life since I lost him, although I would never have been able to believe such a thing then. But I do not think I have ever again lived as deeply, as truly, as in that first year of reckless discovery. It was as though I somehow knew that our time together would be short.

Whether it is called fate, or our weird, or the will of Heaven,

I can look back now and see how each of us was set on to the track, how we were all made ready to travel in deep, dark places.

It was a night in late Feyever-month of that year when I began to realize that something more than simple distraction had overtaken my stepfather. I was reeling back down the corridor to my chamber – I had just kissed Tellarin farewell in the great hall, and was mad with the excitement of it – I nearly stumbled into Lord Sulis. I was first startled, then terrified. My crime, I felt sure, must be as plain as blood on a white sheet. I waited trembling for him to denounce me. Instead he only blinked and held his candle higher.

'Breda?' he said. 'What are you doing, girl?'

He had not called me 'girl' since before my mother died. His fringe of hair was astrew, as though he had just clambered from some assignation of his own, but if that was so, his stunned gaze suggested it had not been a pleasant one. His broad shoulders sagged, and he seemed so tired he could barely hold up his head. The man who had so impressed my mother on that first day in Godric's hall had changed almost beyond recognizing.

My stepfather was wrapped in blankets, but his legs showed naked below the knee. Could this be the same Sulis, I wondered, who as long as I had known him had dressed each day with the same care as he had once used to set his lines of battle? The sight of his pale bare feet was unspeakably disturbing.

'I . . . I was restless and could not sleep, sire. I wished some air.'

His glance flicked across me and then began to rove the shadows again. He looked not just confused but actually frightened. 'You should not be out of your chamber. It is late, and these corridors are full of . . .' He hesitated, then seemed to stop himself from saying something. 'Full of draughts,' he said at last. 'Full of cold air. Go on with you, girl.'

Everything about him made me uneasy. As I backed away, I felt compelled to say, 'Goodnight, sire, and God bless you.'

He shook his head – it almost seemed a shudder – then turned and padded away.

A few days later the witch was brought to the High Keep in chains.

I only learned the woman had been brought to the castle when Tellarin told me. As we lay curled in my bed after lovemaking, he suddenly announced, 'Lord Sulis has captured a witch.'

I was startled. Even with my small experience, I knew this was not the general run of pillow talk. 'What do you mean?'

'She is a woman who lives in the Aldheorte forest,' he said, pronouncing the Erkynlandish name with his usual charming clumsiness. 'She comes often to the market in a town down the Ymstrecca, east of here. She is well-known there – she makes herbal cures, I think, charms away warts, nonsense such as that. That is what Avalles said, anyway.'

I remembered the message that the once-whore Xanippa had bade me give my stepfather on the night my mother died. Despite the warm night, I pulled the blanket up over our damp bodies. 'Why should Lord Sulis want her?' I asked.

Tellarin shook his head, unconcerned. 'Because she is a witch, I suppose, and so she is against God. Avalles and some of the other soldiers arrested her and brought her in this evening.'

'But there are dozens of root-peddlers and conjure-women in the town on the lakeshore where I grew up, and more living outside the castle walls. What does he want with her?'

'My lord does not think she is any old harmless conjure-woman,' Tellarin said. 'He has put her in one of the deep cells underneath the throne room, with chains on her arms and legs.'

I had to see, of course, as much out of curiosity as out of worry about what seemed my stepfather's growing madness.

In the morning, while Lord Sulis was still abed, I went down to the cells. The woman was the only prisoner – the deep cells were seldom used, since those kept in them were likely to die from the chill and damp before they had served a length of term instructive to others – and the guard on duty there was perfectly willing to let the stepdaughter of the castle's master gawk at the witch. He pointed me to the last cell door in the underground chamber.

I had to stand on my toes to see through the barred slot in the door. The only light was a single torch burning on the wall behind me, so the witch was mostly hidden in shadows. She wore chains on wrists and ankles, just as Tellarin had said, and sat on the floor near the back of the windowless cell, her hunched shoulders giving her the shape of a rain-soaked hawk.

As I stared, the chains rattled ever so slightly, although she did not look up. 'What do you want, little daughter?' Her voice was surprisingly deep.

'Lord . . . Lord Sulis is my stepfather,' I said at last, as if it explained something.

Her eyes snapped open, huge and yellow. I had already thought her shaped like a hunting bird – now I almost feared she would fly at me and tear me with sharp talons. 'Do you come to plead his case?' she demanded. 'I tell you the same thing I told him – there is no answer to his question. None that I can give, anyway.'

'What question?' I asked, hardly able to breathe.

The witch peered at me in silence for a moment, then clambered to her feet. I could see that it was a struggle for her to lift the chains. She shuffled forward until the light from the door slot fell on her squarely. Her dark hair was cut short as a man's. She was neither pretty nor ugly, neither tall nor short, but there was a power about her, and especially in the unblinking yellow lamps of her eyes, that drew my gaze and held it. She was something I had not seen before and did not at all understand. She spoke like an ordinary woman, but she had wildness in her like the crack of distant thunder, like the flash of a deer in flight. I felt so helpless to turn away that I feared she had cast a spell upon me.

At last she shook her head. 'I will not involve you in your father's madness, child.'

'He is not my father. He married my mother.'

Her laugh was almost a bark. 'I see.'

I moved uneasily from foot to foot, face still pressed against the bars. I did not know why I spoke to the woman at all, or what I wanted from her. 'Why are you chained?'

'Because they fear me.'

'What is your name?' She frowned but said nothing, so I tried another. 'Are you really a witch?'

She sighed. 'Little daughter, go away. If you have nothing to do with your stepfather's foolish ideas, then the best you can do is stay far from all this. It does not take a sorceress to see that it will not end happily.'

Her words frightened me, but I still could not pull myself away from the cell door. 'Is there something you want? Food? Drink?'

She eyed me again, the large eyes almost fever-bright. 'This is an even stranger household than I guessed. No, child. What I want is the open sky and my forest, but that is what I will not get from you or anyone. But your father says he has need of me – he will not starve me.'

The witch turned her back on me then and shuffled to the rear of the cell, dragging her chains across the stone. I climbed the stairs with my head full to aching – excited thoughts, sorrowful thoughts, frightened thoughts, all were mixed together and full of fluttering confusion, like birds in a sealed room.

My stepfather kept the witch prisoned as Marris-month turned into Avrel and the days of spring paced by. Whatever he wished from her, she would not give it. I visited her many times, but although she was kind enough in her way, she would speak to me only of meaningless things. Often she asked me to describe how the frost on the ground had looked that morning, or what birds were in the trees and what they sang, since in that deep, windowless cell carved into the stone of the headland, she could see and hear nothing of the world outside.

I do not know why I was so drawn to her. Somehow she seemed to hold the key to many mysteries – my stepfather's madness, my mother's sorrow, my own growing fears that the foundations beneath my new happiness were unsolid.

Although my stepfather did feed her, as she had promised he would, and did not allow her to be mistreated in anything beyond the fact of her imprisonment, the witch-woman still grew markedly thinner by the day, and dark circles formed like bruises beneath her eyes. She was pining for freedom, and like a wild animal kept in a pen, her unhappiness was sickening her. It hurt me to see her, as though my own liberty had been stolen. Each time I found her more drawn and weak than the time before, it brought back to me the agony and shame of my mother's last, horrible days. Each time I left the cells, I went to a spot where I could be alone and I wept. Even my stolen hours with Tellarin could not ease the sadness I felt.

I would have hated my stepfather for what he was doing to her, but he too was growing more sickly with each day, as though he were trapped in some mirror version of her dank cell. Whatever the question was that she had spoken of, it plagued Sulis so terribly that he, a decent man, had stolen her freedom – so terribly that he scarcely slept in the nights at all, but sat up until dawn's first light reading and writing and mumbling to himself in a kind of ecstasy. Whatever the question, I began to fear that both he and the witch would die because of it.

The one time that I worked up the courage to ask my stepfather why he had imprisoned her, he stared over my head at the sky, as though it had turned an entirely new colour, and told me, 'This place has too many doors, girl. You open one, then another, and you find yourself back where you began. I cannot find my way.'

If that was an answer, I could make no sense of it.

I offered the witch death and she gave me a prophecy in return.

The sentries on the wall of the Inner Bailey were calling the midnight watch when I arose. I had been in my bed for hours, but sleep had never once come near. I wrapped myself in my heaviest cloak and slipped into the hallway. I could hear my stepfather through his door, talking as though to a visitor. It hurt to hear his voice, because I knew he was alone.

At this hour, the only guard in the cells was a crippled old soldier who did not even stir in his sleep when I walked past him. The torch in the wall-sconce had burned very low, and at first I could not see the witch's shape in the shadows. I wanted to call to her, but I did not know what to say. The bulk of the great, sleeping castle seemed to press down on me.

At last the heavy chains clinked. 'Is that you, little daughter?' Her voice was weary. After a while she stood and shuffled forward. Even in the faint light, she had a terrible, dying look. My hand stole to the purse that hung around my neck. I touched my golden Tree as I said a silent prayer, then felt the curve of that other thing, which I had carried with me since the night of my mother's death. In a moment that seemed to have its own light, quite separate from the flickering glow of the torch, I pulled out the dragon's claw and extended it to her through the bars.

The witch raised an eyebrow as she took it from me. She carefully turned it over in her palm, then smiled sadly. 'A poisoned owl's claw. Very appropriate. Is this for me to use on my captors? Or on myself?'

I shrugged helplessly. 'You want to be free,' was all I could say.

'Not with this, little daughter,' she said. 'At least, not this time. As it happens, I have already surrendered – or, rather, I have bargained. I have agreed to give your stepfather what he thinks he wants in exchange for my freedom. I must see and feel the sky again.' Gently, she handed me back the claw.

I stared at her, almost sick with the need to know things. 'Why won't you tell me your name?'

Another sad smile. 'Because my true name I give to no one. Because any other name would be a lie.'

'Tell me a lie, then.'

'A strange household, indeed! Very well. The people of the north call me Valada.'

I tried it on my tongue. 'Valada. He will set you free now?'

'Soon, if the bargain is honoured on both sides.'

'What is it, this bargain?'

'A bad one for everyone.' She saw my look. 'You do not want to know, truly. Someone will die because of this madness – I see it as clearly as I see your face peering through the door.'

My heart was a piece of cold stone in my breast. 'Someone will die? Who?'

Her expression became weary, and I could see that standing with the weight of her shackles was an effort for her. 'I do not know. And in my weariness, I have already told you too much, little daughter. These are not matters for you.'

I was dismissed, even more miserable and confused. The witch would be free, but someone else would die. I could not doubt her word – no one could, who had seen her fierce, sad eyes as she spoke. As I walked back to my bedchamber, the halls of the Inner Bailey seemed a place entirely new, a strange and unfamiliar world.

My feelings for Tellarin were still astonishingly strong, but in the days after the witch's foretelling I was so beset with unhappiness that our love was more like a fire that made a cold room habitable than a sun which warmed everything, as it had been. If my soldier had not had worries of his own, he would certainly have noticed.

The cold inside me became a chill like deepest winter when I overheard Tellarin and Avalles speaking about a secret task Lord Sulis had for them, something to do with the witch. It was hard to tell what was intended – my beloved and his friend did not themselves know all that Sulis planned, and they were speaking only to each other, and not for the benefit of their secret listener. I gathered that my stepfather's books had shown him that the time for some important thing had drawn close. They would build or find some kind of fire. It would take them on a short journey by night, but they did not say – or perhaps did not yet know – on what night. Both my beloved and Avalles were clearly disturbed by the prospect.

If I had feared before, when I thought the greatest risk was to my poor, addled stepfather, now I was almost ill with terror. I could barely stumble through the remaining hours of the day, so consumed was I with the thought that something might happen to Tellarin. I dropped my beadwork so many times that Ulca took it away from me at last. When dark came, I could not get to sleep for hours, and when I did I woke up panting and shuddering from a dream in which Tellarin had fallen into flames and was burning just beyond my reach.

I lay tossing in my bed all the night. How could I protect my beloved? Warning him would do no good. He was stubborn, and also saved his deepest beliefs for those things he could grasp and touch, so I knew he would put little stock in the witch's words. In any case, even if he believed me, what could he do? Refuse an order from Lord Sulis because of a warning from me, his secret lover? No, it would be hopeless to try to persuade Tellarin not to go – he spoke of his loyalty to his master almost as often as he did of his feelings for me.

I was in an agony of fearful curiosity. What did my stepfather plan? What had he read in those books, that he now would risk not just his own life, but that of my beloved as well?

Not one of them would tell me anything, I knew. Even the witch had said that the matter was not for me. Whatever I discovered would be by my own hand.

I resolved to look at my stepfather's books, those that he kept hidden from me and everyone else. Once it would have been all but impossible, but now – because he sat reading and writing and whispering to himself all the night's dark hours – I could trust that when Sulis did sleep, he would sleep like the dead.

I stole into my stepfather's chambers early the next morning. He had sent his servants away weeks before, and the castle-folk no longer dared rap on his doors unless summoned. The rooms were empty but for my stepfather and me.

He lay sprawled across his bed, his head hanging back over the edge of the pallet. Had I not known how moderate most of his habits were, I would have thought from his deep, rough breathing and the way he had disordered the blankets that he had drunk himself stuporous, but Sulis seldom took even a single cup of wine.

The key to the locked boxes was on a cord around his neck. As I tugged it out of his shirt with as much care as I could, I could not help but see how much happier he appeared with the blankness of sleep on him. The furrows on his brow had loosened, and his jaw was no longer clenched in the grimace of distraction that had become his constant expression. In that moment, although I hated what he had done to the witch Valada, I pitied him. Whatever madness had overtaken him of late, he had been a kind man in his way, in his time.

He stirred and made an indistinct sound. Heart beating swiftly, I hurried to draw the cord and key over his head.

When I had found the wooden chests and unlocked them, I began to pull out and examine my stepfather's forbidden books, leafing quickly and quietly through each in turn, with one ear cocked for changes in his breathing. Most of the plainbound volumes were written in tongues I did not know, two or three in characters I could not even recognize. Those of which I could understand a little seemed to contain either tales of the fairy-folk or stories about the High Keep during the time of the Northmen.

A good part of an hour had passed when I discovered a loosely-bound book titled *Writings of Vargellis Sulis, Seventh Lord of Honsa Sulis, Now Master of the Sulean House in Exile*. My stepfather's careful hand filled the first pages densely, then grew larger and more imperfect as it continued, until the final pages seemed almost to have been scribed by a child still learning letters.

A noise from the bed startled me, but my stepfather had only grunted and turned on his side. I continued through the book as swiftly as I could. It seemed to be only the most recent of a lifetime's worth of writings – the earliest dates in the volume were from the first year we had lived in the High Keep. The bulk of the pages listed tasks to be performed in the High Keep's rebuilding, and records of important judgements Sulis had made as lord of the keep and its tenant lands. There were other notations of a more personal nature, but they were brief and unelaborated. For that terrible day almost three years earlier, he had written only: *Cynethrith Dead of Chest Fever. She shall be Buried on the Headland.*

The sole mention of me was a single sentence from several months before – *Breda happy Today.* It was oddly painful to me that my sombre stepfather should have noticed that and made a record of it.

The later pages held almost no mention of the affairs of either home or governance, as in daily life Sulis had also lost interest in both. Instead, there were more and more notes that seemed to be about things he had read in other books – one said *Plesinnen claims that Mortality is consumed in God as a Flame consumes Branch or Bough. How then . . .* with the rest smudged – one word might have been *nails*, and further on I could make out *Holy Tree*. Another of his notes listed several *Doorways* that had been located by someone named Nisses, with explanations next to each that explained nothing at all – *Shifted*, read my stepfather's shaky hand beside one, or *from a Time of No Occupation*, or even, *Met a Dark Thing*.

It was only on the last two pages that I found references to the woman in the cell below the throne room.

Have at Last rec'd Word of the woman called Valada, the scrawl stated. *No one else Living North of Perdruin has Knowledge of the Black Fire. She must be Made to Speak what she knows.* Below that, in another day's even less disciplined hand, was written, *The Witch balks me, but I cannot have another Failure as on the Eve of Elysiamansa. Stoning Night will be next Time of Strong Voices beneath the Keep. Walls will be Thin. She will show me the Way of Black Fire or there is no other Hope. Either she will answer, or Death.*

I sat back, trying to make sense of it all. Whatever my stepfather planned, it would happen soon – Stoning Night was the last night of Avrel, only a few days away. I could not tell from his writings if the witch was still in danger – did he mean to kill her if she failed, or only if she tried to cheat his bargain with her? – but I had no doubt that this search for the thing called Black Fire would bring danger to everyone else, most importantly and most frighteningly my soldier, Tellarin.

Again my stepfather murmured in his sleep, an unhappy sound. I locked his books away and stole out again.

All that day I felt distracted and feverish, but this time it was not love that fevered me. I was terrified for my lover and fearful for my stepfather and the witch Valada, but what I knew and how I had discovered it I could not tell to anyone. For the first time since my soldier had kissed me, I felt alone. I was full up with secrets, and unlike Sulis, had not even a book to which they could be confided.

I would follow them, I decided at last. I would follow them into the place my stepfather spoke of, the place beneath the keep where the walls were thin and the voices strong. While they searched for the Black Fire, I would watch for danger. I would protect them all. I would be their angel.

Stoning Night came around at last.

Even had I not read my stepfather's writings, I think I would have known that the hour had come in which they meant to search for Black Fire, because Tellarin was so distracted and full of shadows. Although he admitted nothing to me as we lay together in my bedchamber, I could feel that he was anxious about what would happen that night. But he was bound to my stepfather by honour and blood, and had no choice.

He snapped at me when I kissed his ear and curled my fingers in his hair. 'Give a man some peace, girl.'

'Why are you a man and I am a girl?' I teased him, pretending a lightness I did not truly feel. 'Is there such a difference in our ages? Have I not given to you already that which makes me a woman?'

My soldier was short-tempered and did not hear the love in what I said. 'Anybody who will not leave off when she is asked proves herself still a child. And I am a man because I wear a soldier's badge, and because if my master asks, I must give my life.'

Tellarin was five years my elder, and in those long-ago days I was almost as impressed by the difference as he was, but I think now that all men are younger than their women, especially when their honour has been touched.

As he stared at the ceiling his face turned from angry to solemn, and I knew he was thinking of what he must do that night. I was frightened too, so I kissed him again, softly this time, and apologized.

When he had gone, full of excuses meant to hide his actual task, I prepared for my own journey. I had hidden my thickest cloak and six fat candles where Ulca and the other serving-women would not find them. When I was dressed and ready, I touched my mother's golden Tree where it lay against my heart, and said a prayer for the safety of all who would go with me into darkness.

Stoning Night – the last night of Avrel, on the eve of Maia-month, the black hours when tales say spirits walk until driven back to their graves by dawn and the crowing cock. The High Keep lay silent around me as I followed my beloved and the others through the dark. It did not feel so much that the castle slept as that the great keep held its breath and waited.

There is a stairwell beneath the Angel Tower, and that was where they were bound. I learned of it for the first time on that night, as I stood wrapped in my dark cloak, listening from the shadows of the wall opposite the tower. Those I followed were four – my stepfather, Tellarin and his friend Avalles, and the woman Valada. Despite the bargain she had made, the witch's arms were still chained. It saddened me to see her restrained like an animal.

The workmen who had been repairing the tower had laid a rough wooden floor over the broken stones of the old one – perhaps to make certain no one fell down one of the many holes, perhaps simply to close off any openings into the castle's deepest places. Some had even suggested that all the old castle floor should be sealed under brick, so that nothing would ever come up that way to trouble the sleep of God-fearing folk.

Because of this wooden floor, I waited a long time before following them through the tower's outer portal, knowing it would take some time for my stepfather and his two bondmen to shift the boards. As I lurked in the shadows by the tower wall while the wind prowled the Inner Bailey, I thought about the Angel who stood at the top of the tower, a figure black with the grime of centuries that no rain could wash away, tipped sideways as though about to lose her balance and fall. Who was she? One of the blessed saints? Was it an omen – did she watch over me as I meant to look over Tellarin and the rest? I looked up, but the tower's high top was invisible in the night.

At last I tried the latch of the tower door and found the bolt had not been shot. I hoped that it meant the Angel was indeed looking out for me.

Inside the tower the moonlight ended, so while still in the doorway I lit my first candle from the hidden touchwood, which had nearly burnt down. My footsteps seemed frighteningly loud in the stony entry hall, but no one appeared from the shadows to demand my business in that place. I heard no sound of my stepfather or the rest.

I paused for a moment in front of the great, upward-winding staircase, and could not help but wonder what the workmen would find when they cleared the rubble and reached the top – as I still wonder all these years later, with the painstaking work yet unfinished. I suppose I will not see it in my lifetime. Will they discover treasures left by the fairy-folk? Or perhaps only those ancient beings' frail bones?

Even were it not for the things that happened on that fateful night, still the Angel Tower would haunt me, as it haunts this great keep and all the lands beneath its long shadow. No mortals, I think, will ever know all its secrets.

Once, long ago, I dreamed that my stepfather gave me the Angel herself to clean, but that no matter how I tried, I could not scrub the black muck from her limbs and face. He told me that it was not my fault, that God would have lent me the strength if He truly wanted the Angel's face to be seen, but I still wept at my failure.

I moved from the entry hall to a place where the floor fell away in great broken shards, and tried to imagine what could smash stones so thoroughly and yet leave the tower itself still standing. It was not easy to follow where my stepfather and my beloved had already gone, but I climbed down the rubble, leaning to set my candle before me so that I could have both my hands free. I wished, not for the last time, that I had worn something other than my soft shoes. I clambered down and down, hurting my feet, tearing my dress in several places, until I reached the jumble of smaller broken stones which was the floor, at least a half dozen times my own height below the level of the Inner Bailey. In the midst of this field of shards gaped a great, black hole bigger than the rest, a jagged mouth that waited to swallow me down. As I crunched closer to it, I heard what I knew must be the voices of the others floating up from the depths, although they sounded strange to me.

More stones had been pushed aside to reveal the entrance to the stairwell, a lip of shiny white with steps inside it that vanished into shadow. Another voice floated up, laughing. It belonged to no one I knew.

Even with all that had happened in the previous days, I had never yet felt so frightened, but I knew Tellarin was down there in the dark places. I made the sign of the Tree upon my breast, then stepped on to the stairway.

At first I could find no trace of them.

As I descended, the light of my single candle served only to make the stairwell seem more than ever like a shadowy throat waiting to swallow me, but fear alone could not keep me from my beloved – if anything, it sped my steps. I hurried downward until it seemed I must have gone as far beneath the castle as the Angel Tower loomed above it, but still I had not caught up with them.

Whether it was a trick of sound, or of the winds that are said to blow through the caves of the Kingslake cliffs, I continued to hear unfamiliar voices. Some seemed so close that if I had not had a candle, I would have been certain I could reach out and touch the person who whispered to me, but the flickering light showed me that the stairwell was empty. The voices babbled, and sometimes sang, in a soft, sad tongue I did not understand or even recognize.

I knew I should be too frightened to remain, that I should turn and flee back to moonlight and clean air, but although the bodiless murmurs filled me with dismay, I felt no evil in them. If they were ghosts, I do not think they even knew I was there. It was as though the castle talked to itself, like an old man sitting beside the fire, lost in the memories of days long past.

The stairwell ended in a wide landing with open doorways at either end, and I could not help thinking of the doorways mentioned in my stepfather's book. As I paused to consider which way I should go, I examined the carvings on the walls, delicate vines and flowers whose type I had never seen before. Above one doorframe a nightingale perched on a tree bough. Another tree bough was carved above the far doorway – or rather, I saw as I moved my candle, they were both boughs from one single tree, which had been carved directly above me, spreading across the ceiling of the stairwell as though I myself were the tree's trunk. On the bough above the second doorway twined a slender serpent. I shuddered, and began to move towards the nightingale door, but at that moment words floated up out of the darkness.

'. . . if you have lied to me. I am a patient man, but . . .'

It was my stepfather, and even if I had not recognized his faint voice, I would have known him by the words, for that is what he always said. And he spoke the truth – he *was* a patient man. He had always been like one of the stones of the hilltop rings, cool and hard and in no hurry to move, growing warm only after the sun of an entire summer has beat upon him. I had sometimes felt I would like to break a stick upon him, if only to make him turn and truly look at me.

Only once did he ever do that, I had believed – on that day when he told me that 'they' had taken everything from him. But now I knew he had looked at me another time, perhaps seen me smile on a day when my lover had given me a gift or a kiss, and had written in his book, *Breda happy Today.*

My stepfather's words had drifted up through the other doorway. I lit another candle and placed it on top of the first, which had burned almost to the holder, then followed the voice of Sulis through the serpent door.

Downward I went, and downward still farther – what seemed a journey of hours, through sloping, long-deserted corridors that twisted like yarn spilled from a sack. The light of the candles showed me stone that, although I knew it was even more ancient, seemed newer and brighter than that which I had seen farther above. In places the passageways opened into rooms choked with dirt and rubble, but which must have been massive, with ceilings as high as any of the greatest halls I have ever heard of in Nabban. The carvings I could see were so delicate, so perfect, that they might have been the actual things of nature – birds, plants, trees – frozen into stone by the sort of magical spells that so often had been part of my mother's and Ulca's stories.

It was astonishing to think that this entire world had lain in its tomb of earth below us as long as we had lived in the High Keep, and for generations before that. I knew I was seeing the ancient home of the fairy-folk. With all the stories, and even with the evidence of the tower itself, I had still never imagined they would have such a way with stone, to make it froth like water and shimmer like ice, to make it stretch overhead in slender arcs like the finest branches of a willow tree. Had the Northmen truly killed them all? For the first time, I understood something of what this meant, and a deep, quiet horror stole over me. The creators of all this beauty, slaughtered, and their houses usurped by their slayers – no wonder the darkness was full of unquiet voices. No wonder the High Keep was a place of haunted sadness for everyone who lived in it. The castle of our day was founded on ancient murder. It was built on death.

It pulled at me, that thought. It became tangled in my mind with the memory of my stepfather's distracted stare, of the witch in chains. Good could not come from evil, I felt sure. Not without sacrifice. Not without blood and atonement.

My fear was growing again.

The Peaceful Ones might have been gone, but I was learning that their great house remained lively.

As I hurried downward, following the tracks of my stepfather and his company in the dust of centuries, I found suddenly that I had taken a wrong turning. The passage ended in a pile of broken stone, but when I returned to the last cross-corridor, there was no sign of footprints, and the place itself was not familiar, as though the ruins themselves had shifted around me. I closed my eyes, listening for the sound of Tellarin's voice, for I felt sure that my heart would be able to hear him through all the stone in Erkynland. But nothing came to me but the ghost-murmurs, which blew in like an autumn breeze, full of sighing, rustling nonsense.

I was lost.

For the first time it became clear to me what a foolish thing I had done. I had gone into a place where I should not be. Not one person knew I was there, and when my last candle burned out, I would be lost in the darkness.

Tears started in my eyes, but I wiped them away. Weeping had not brought my father back, or my mother. It would do me no good now.

I did my best to retrace my steps, but the voices flittered around me like invisible birds, and before long I was wandering blindly. Confused by the noises in my head and by the flickering shadows, twice I almost tumbled into great crevices in the passageway floor. I kicked a stone into one that fell without hitting anything until I could not bear to listen any longer.

The darkness seemed to be closing on me, and I might have been lost for ever – might have become another part of the whispering chorus – but by luck or accident or the hand of fate, I made a turning into a corridor I did not recognize and found myself standing at the lip of another stairwell, listening to the voice of the witch Valada drift up from the deeps.

'. . . not an army or a noble household that you can order about, Lord Sulis. Those who lived here are dead, but the place is alive. You must take what you are given . . .'

It was as though she had heard my very thoughts. Even as I shuddered to hear my forebodings spoken aloud, I hurried towards the sound, terrified that if it faded I would never again hear a familiar voice.

What seemed another hour went by, although I had been so long in the haunted dark that I was no judge. My lover and the rest seemed almost to have become phantoms themselves, floating ahead of me like dandelion seeds, always just beyond my reach.

The stairs continued to curl downward, and as my third and fourth candles burned I could see glimpses of the great spaces through which we all descended, level upon level, as if making a pilgrimage down the tiers of Heaven. At times, as the candles flickered on the wooden base, I thought I could see even more. From the corner of my eye the ruins seemed to take on a sort of life. There were moments when the ghost-voices swelled and the shadows seem to take on form. If I half-closed my eyes, I could almost see these bleak spaces full of bright, laughing folk.

Why did the Northmen kill such beauty? And how could a people who built such a place be defeated by any mortals, however bloodthirsty and battle-hungry?

A light bloomed in the depths, red and yellow, making the polished stone of the stairwell seem to quiver. For a moment I thought it only another wisp of my imagination, but then, from so close it seemed we could kiss if we wished, I heard my beloved's voice.

'Do not trust her sire,' Tellarin said, sounding more than a little fearful. 'She is lying again.'

Intensely happy, but with my caution abruptly restored, I shaded the candle with my palm and hurried down the stairs as quietly as I could. As their voices grew louder, and I saw that the light blooming in the darkness came from their torches, I pinched the flame to extinguish my candle completely. However glad I was to find them, I guessed they would not feel the same about me.

I crept closer to the light, but could not see Tellarin and the others because something like a cloud of smoke blocked my view. It was only when I reached the base of the curving stair and stepped silently on to the floor of the great chamber that I could actually see the four shapes.

They stood in the middle of a room so cavernous that even the torches my lover and Avalles held could not carry light to its highest corners. Before them loomed the thing I had thought was smoke. I still could not see it clearly, despite the torch flames burning only an arm's length from it, but now it seemed a vast tree with black leaves and trunk. A shadow cloaked it and hid all but the broadest outline, a dark shroud like the mist that hid the hills on a winter morning, but it was not mist in which the tree-shape crouched, I felt sure. It was pure Darkness.

'You must decide whether to listen to me or a young soldier,' the witch was saying to my stepfather. 'I will tell you again – if you cut so much as a leaf, you will mark yourselves as ravagers and it will not go well with you. Can you not feel that?'

'And I think Tellarin is right,' Avalles proclaimed, but his voice was less sure than his words. 'She seeks to trick us.'

My stepfather looked from the tree-shadow to the witch. 'If we may not take any wood, then why have you brought us here?' he asked slowly, as though it cost great effort just to speak.

I could hear the sour smile in Valada's answer. 'You have held me captive in your damp pile of stones for two moons, seeking my help with your mad questions. If you do not believe that I know what I know, why did you shackle me and bring me here?'

'But the wood . . . ?'

'I did not say you could not take anything to burn, I said that you would be a fool to lift axe or knife to the Great Witchwood. There is deadfall beneath, if you are bold enough to search for it.'

Sulis turned to Avalles. 'Go and gather some dead wood, nephew.'

The young knight hesitated, then handed his torch to my stepfather and walked a little unsteadily towards the great dark tree. He bent beneath the outer branches and vanished from sight. After an interval of silence, Avalles stumbled back out again.

'It is . . . it is too dark to see,' he panted. His eyes were showing white around the edges. 'And there is something in there – an animal, perhaps. I . . . I can feel it breathing.' He turned to my stepfather. 'Tellarin's eyes are better than mine . . .'

No! I wanted to scream. The tree-thing sat and waited, cloaked in shadows no torchlight could penetrate. I was ready to burst from hiding and beg my beloved not to go near it, but as if he had heard my silent cry, Lord Sulis cursed and thrust the torch back into Avalles' hand.

'By Pelippa and her bowl!' my stepfather said. 'I will do it myself.'

Just before he stepped through the branches, I thought I heard the leaves whisper, although there was no wind in the chamber. The quiet hiss and rattle grew louder, perhaps because my stepfather was forcing his way beneath the thick branches. Long moments trudged past, then the rustling became even more violent. At last Sulis emerged, staggering a little, with what seemed a long bar of shadow clasped under each arm. Tellarin and Avalles stepped forward to help him but he waved them off, shaking his head as though he had been dealt a blow. Even in the dark room, I could see that he had gone very pale.

'You spoke the truth, Valada,' he said. 'No axe, no knife.'

While I watched, he bade Avalles and my beloved make a ring on the ground from the broken stones that littered the chamber. He crossed the two pieces of wood he had gathered in the centre of the circle, then he used kindling from a pouch on his belt and one of the torches to set the witchwood alight. As the strange fire sputtered into life, the room seemed to become darker, as though the very light from the torches bent towards the firepit and was sucked away. The flames began to rise.

The rustle of the shadowy tree stilled. Everything grew silent – even the flames made no sound. My heart pounded as I leaned closer, almost forgetting to keep myself hidden. It was indeed a Black Fire that burned now in that deep, lost place, a fire that flickered like any blaze, and yet whose flames were wounds in the very substance of the world, holes as darkly empty as a starless sky.

It is hard to believe, but that is what I saw. I could look through the flames of the Black Fire, not to what stood on the other side of the fire, but to *somewhere else* – into nothingness at first, but then colour and shape began to expand outward in the space above the firepit, as though something turned the very air inside-out.

A face appeared in the fire. It was all I could do not to cry out.

The stranger surrounded by the black flames was like no man I had ever seen. The angles of his face were all somehow wrong, his chin too narrow, the large eyes slanted upward at the corners. His hair was long and white, but he did not look old. He was naked from the waist up, and his pale, glossy skin was marked with dreadful scars, but despite the flames in which he lay, his burns seemed old rather than new.

The Black Fire unshaped even the darkness. All that was around it bent, as though the very world grew stretched and shivery as the reflection on a bubble of river water.

The burning man seemed to slumber in the flames, but it was a horribly unquiet sleep. He pitched and writhed, even brought his hands up before his face, as though to protect himself from some terrible attack. When his eyes at last opened, they were dark as shadow itself, staring at things that I could not see, at shadows far beyond the fire. His mouth stretched in a silent, terrible scream, and despite his alien aspect, despite being so frightened I feared my heart would stop, I still ached to see his suffering. If he was alive, how could his body burn and burn without being consumed? If he was a ghost, why had death not ended his pain?

Tellarin and Avalles backed away from the firepit, wide-eyed and fearful. Avalles made the sign of the Tree.

My stepfather looked at the burning man's writhing mouth and blind eyes, then turned to the witch Valada. 'Why does he not speak to us? Do something!'

She laughed her sharp laugh. 'You wished to meet one of the Sithi, Lord Sulis – one of the Peaceful Ones. You wished to find a doorway, but some doorways open not on elsewhere, but elsewhen. The Black Fire has found you one of the fair folk in his sleep. He is dreaming, but he can hear you across the centuries. Speak to him! I have done what I promised.'

Clearly shaken, Sulis turned to the man in the flames. 'You!' he called. 'Can you understand me?'

The burning man writhed again, but now his dark unseeing eyes turned in my stepfather's direction. 'Who is there?' he asked, and I heard his voice in the chamber of my skull rather than in my ears. 'Who walks the Road of Dreams?' The apparition lifted a hand as though he might reach through the years and touch us. For a moment, astonishment pushed the agony from his odd face. 'You are mortals! But why do you come to me? Why do you disturb the sleep of Hakatri of the House of Year-Dancing?'

'I am Sulis.' The tremble in my stepfather's voice made him seem an old, old man. 'Called by some "the Apostate". I have risked everything I own – have spent years studying – to ask a question which only the Peaceful Ones can answer. Will you help me?'

The burning man did not seem to be listening. His mouth twisted again, and this time his cry of pain had sound. I tried to stop my ears, but it was already inside my head. 'Ah, it burns!' he moaned. 'Still the worm's blood burns me – even when I sleep. Even when I walk the Road of Dreams!'

'The worm's blood . . . ?' My stepfather was puzzled. 'A dragon? What are you saying?'

'She was like a great black snake,' Hakatri murmured. 'My brother and I, we followed her into her deep place and we fought her and slew her, but I have felt her scorching blood upon me and will never be at peace again. By the Garden, it pains me so!' He made a choking sound, then fell silent for a moment. 'Both our swords bit,' he said, and it was almost a chant, a song, 'but my brother Ineluki was the fortunate one. He escaped a terrible burning. Black, black it was, that ichor, and hotter than even the flames of Making! I fear death itself could not ease this agony . . .'

'Be silent!' Sulis thundered, full of rage and misery. 'Witch, is this spell for nothing? Why will he not listen to me?'

'There is no spell, except that which opens the doorway,' she replied. 'Hakatri perhaps came to that doorway because of how the dragon's blood burned him – there is nothing else in all the world like the blood of the great worms. His wounds keep him always close to the Road of Dreams, I think. Ask him your question, Nabban-man. He is as like to answer it as any other of the immortals you might have found.'

I could feel it now – could feel the weird that had brought us here take us all in its grip. I held my breath, caught between a terror that blew like a cold wind inside my head, that screamed at me to leave Tellarin and everything else and run away, and a fierce wondering about what had brought my stepfather to this impossibly strange meeting.

Lord Sulis tilted his chin down towards his chest for a moment, as though now the time had come, he was uncertain of what he wished to say. At last he spoke, quaveringly at first, but with greater strength as he went on.

'Our church teaches us that God appeared in this world, wearing the form of Usires Aedon, performing many miracles, singing up cures for the sick and lame, until at last the Imperator Crexis caused him to be hung from the Execution Tree. Do you know of this, Hakatri?'

The burning man's blind eyes rolled towards Sulis again. He did not answer, but he seemed to be listening.

'The promise of the Aedon the Ransomer is that all who live will be gathered up – that there will be no death,' my stepfather continued. 'And this is proved because he was God made flesh in this world, and that is proved because of the miracles he performed. But I have studied much about your own people, Hakatri. Such miracles as Usires the Aedon performed could have been done by one of your Sithi people, or even perhaps by one of only half-immortal blood.' His smile was as bleak as a skull's. 'After all, even my fiercest critics in Mother Church agree that Usires had no human father.'

Sulis bowed his head again for a moment, summoning up words or strength. I gasped for air – I had forgotten to breathe. Avalles and Tellarin still stared, their fear now mixed with astonishment, but the witch Valada's face was hidden from me in shadow.

'Both my wives have been taken from me by death, both untimely,' my stepfather said. 'My first wife gave me a son before she died, a beautiful boy named Sarellis who died himself in screaming pain because he stepped on a horseshoe nail – a nail! – and caught a death fever. Young men I have commanded were slaughtered in the hundreds, the thousands, their corpses piled on the battlefield like the husks of locusts, and all for a small stretch of land here or there, or sometimes merely over words. My parents are dead, too, with too much unspoken between us. Everyone I ever truly loved has been stolen from me by death.'

His hoarse voice had taken on a disturbing force, a cracked power, as though he meant to shout down the walls of Heaven itself.

'Mother Church tells me to believe that I will be reunited with them,' he said. 'They preach to me, saying, "See the works of Usires our Lord and be comforted, for his task was to show death should hold no fear," they told me. But I cannot be sure – I cannot simply trust! Is the church right? Will I see those I love again? Will we all live on? The masters of the church have called me a heretic and declared me apostate because I would not give up doubting the divinity of the Aedon, but I must know! Tell me, Hakatri, was Usires of your folk? Is the story of his godhood simply a lie to keep us happy, to keep priests fat and rich?' He blinked back tears, his stolid face transfigured by rage and pain. 'Even if God should damn me for ever to hell for it, still I must know – *is our faith a lie?*'

He was shaking so badly now that he took a staggering step

back from the fire and almost fell. No one moved except the man in the flames, who followed Sulis with his blank, dark eyes.

I realized that I was weeping too, and silently rubbed the tears away. Seeing my stepfather's true and terrible pain was like a knife twisted inside me, and yet I was angry too. All for this? For such unknowable things he left my mother lonely, and now had nearly destroyed his own life?

After a long time in which all was silent as the stone around us, Hakatri said slowly, 'Always you mortals have tortured yourselves.' He blinked, and the way his face moved was so alien that I had to turn away and then look at him anew before I could understand what he said. 'But you torture yourself most when you seek answers to things that have none.'

'No answers?' Sulis was still shaking. 'How can that be?'

The burning man raised his long-fingered hands in what I could only guess was a gesture of peace. 'Because that which is meant for mortals is not given to the Zida'ya to know, any more than you can know of our Garden, or where we go when we leave this place.

'Listen to me, mortal. What if your messiah were indeed one of the Dawn Children – would that prove somehow that your God had not chosen that to happen? Would that prove your Ransomer's words any the less true?' Hakatri shook his head with the weird, foreign grace of a shorebird.

'Just tell me whether Usires was one of your folk,' Sulis demanded raggedly. 'Spare me your philosophies and tell me! For I am burning too! I have not been free of the pain in years!'

As the echoes of my stepfather's cry faded, the fairy-lord in his ring of black flames paused, and for the first time he seemed truly to see across the gulf. When he spoke, his voice was full of sadness.

'We Zida'ya know little of the doings of mortals, and there are some of our own blood who have fallen away from us, and whose works are hidden from us as well. I do not think your Usires Aedon was one of the Dawn Children, but more than that I cannot tell you, mortal man, nor could any of my folk.'

He lifted his hands again, weaving the fingers in an intricate, incomprehensible gesture. 'I am sorry.'

A great shudder ran through the creature called Hakatri then – perhaps the pain of his burns returning, a pain that he had somehow held at bay while he listened to my stepfather speak. Sulis did not wait to hear more, but stepped forward and kicked the witchwood fire into a cloud of whirling sparks, then dropped to his knees with his hands over his face.

The burning man was gone.

After a march of silence that seemed endless, the witch called out, 'Will you honour your bargain with me now, Lord Sulis? You said that if I brought you to one of the immortals, you would free me.' Her voice was flat, but there was still a gentleness to it that surprised me.

My stepfather's reply, when it came, was choked and hard to understand. He waved his hand. 'Take off her chains, Avalles. I want nothing more from her.'

In the midst of this great bleak wilderness of sorrow, I felt a moment of sharp happiness as I realized that despite my foreboding, the witch, my beloved, even my tortured stepfather, all would survive this terrible night. As Avalles began to unlock the witch's shackles, shivering so that he could hardly hold the key, I had a moment to dream that my stepfather would return to health, that he would reward my Tellarin for his bravery and loyalty, and that my beloved and I would make a home for ourselves somewhere far away from this ghost-riddled, windswept headland.

My stepfather let out a sudden, startling cry. I turned to see him fall forward on to his belly, his body ashake with weeping. This seizure of grief in stern, quiet Sulis was in some ways the most frightening thing I had yet seen in that long, terrifying night.

Then, even as his cry rebounded in the invisible upper reaches of the chamber and provoked a dim rustle in the leaves of the shadowy tree, something else seized my attention. Two figures were struggling where the witch had stood. At first I thought Avalles and the woman Valada were fighting, but then I saw that the witch had stepped back and was watching the battle, her bright eyes wide with surprise. Instead, it was Avalles and Tellarin who were tangled together, their torches fallen from their hands. Shocked, helpless with surprise, I watched them tumble to the ground. A moment later a dagger rose and fell, then the brief struggle was ended.

I screamed, 'Tellarin!' and rushed forward.

He stood, brushing the dust from his breeks, and stared at me as I came out of the shadows. The end of his knife was blackened with blood. He had a stillness about him that might have been fear, or simply surprise.

'Breda? What are you doing here?'

'Why did he attack you?' I cried. Avalles lay twisted on the ground in a spreading puddle of black. 'He was your friend!'

He said nothing, but leaned to kiss me, then turned and walked to where my stepfather still crouched on the ground in a fit of grief. My beloved put his knee in my stepfather's back, then wrapped his hand in the hair at the back of the older man's head and pulled until his tearstained face was tilted up into the torchlight.

'I did not want to kill Avalles,' my soldier explained, in part to me, in part to Sulis. 'But he insisted on coming, fearing that I would become closer in his uncle's favour if he were not there too.' He shook his head. 'Sad. But it is only your death that was my task, Sulis, and I have been waiting long for such a perfect opportunity.'

Despite the merciless strain of his position, my stepfather smiled, a ghastly, tight-stretched grin. 'Which Sancellan sent you?'

'Does it matter? You have more enemies in Nabban than you can count, Sulis Apostate. You are a heretic and a schismatic, and you are dangerous. You should have known you would not be left here, to build your power in the wilderness.'

'I did not come here to build power,' my stepfather grunted. 'I came here to have my questions answered.'

'Tellarin!' I struggled to make sense where there could be none. 'What are you doing?'

His voice took on a little of its former gentle tone. 'This is nothing to do with you and me, Breda.'

'Did you . . . ?' I could scarcely say it. My tears were making the chamber as blurry as the Black Fire ever did. 'Did you . . . only pretend love for me? Was it all to help you kill him?'

'No! I had no need of you, girl – I was already one of his most trusted men.' He tightened his grip on Sulis then, until I feared my stepfather's neck would break. 'What you and I have, little Breda, that is good and real. I will take you back to Nabban with me – I will be rich now, and you will be my wife. You will learn what a true city is, instead of this devilish, backward pile of stone.'

'You love me? Truly, you love me?' I wanted very much to believe him. 'Then let my stepfather go, Tellarin!'

He frowned. 'I cannot. His death is the task I was given to do before I ever met you, and it is a task that needs doing. He is a madman, Breda! Surely after tonight's horrors, after seeing the demon he called up with forbidden magic, you can see why he cannot be allowed to live.'

'Do not kill him, please! I beg you!'

He lifted his hand to still me. 'I am sworn to my master in Nabban. This one thing I must do, and then we are both free.'

Even an appeal in the name of love could not stop him. Confused and overwhelmed, unable to argue any longer with the man who had brought me so much joy, I turned to the witch, praying that she would do something – but Valada was gone. She had taken her freedom, leaving the rest of us to murder each other if we wished. I thought I saw a movement in the shadows, but it was only some other phantom, some flying thing that drifted above the stairwell on silent wings.

Lord Sulis was silent. He did not struggle against Tellarin's grip, but waited for slaughter like an old bull. When he swallowed, the skin on his neck pulled so tight that watching it made tears spill on to my cheeks once more. My beloved pressed his knife against my stepfather's throat as I stumbled towards them. Sulis looked at me, but still said nothing. Whatever thought was in his eyes, it had gone so deep that I could not even guess what it might be.

'Tell me again that you love me,' I asked as I reached his side. As I looked at my soldier's frightened but exultant face, I could not help thinking of the High Keep, a haunted place built on murder, in whose corrupted, restless depths we stood. For a moment I thought the ghost-voices had returned, for my head was full of roaring, rushing noise. 'Tell me again, Tellarin,' I begged him. 'Please.'

My beloved did not move the blade from Sulis' throat, but said, 'Of course I love you, Breda. We will be married, and all of Nabban will lie at your feet. You will never be cold or lonely again.' He leaned forward, and I could feel the beautiful long muscles of his back tense beneath my hand. He hesitated when he heard the click of the glass ball as it fell to the tiles and rattled away.

'What . . . ?' he asked, then straightened suddenly, grabbing at the spot at his waist where the claw had pricked him. I took a few staggering steps and fell, weeping. Behind me, Tellarin began to wheeze, then to choke. I heard his knife clatter to the stone.

I could not look, but the sound of his last rattling breaths will never leave me.

Now that I am old, I know that this secretive keep will be the place I die. When I have breathed my last, I suppose they will bury me on the headland beside my mother and Lord Sulis.

After that long night beneath the castle had ended, the Heron King, as the Lake People called my stepfather, came to resemble once more the man he had been. He reigned over the High Keep for many more years, and gradually even my own brawling, jealous folk acknowledged him as their ruler, although the kingship did not outlive Sulis himself.

My own mark on the world will be even smaller.

I never married, and my brother Aelfric died of a fall from his horse without fathering any children, so although the Lake People still squabble over who should carry the standard and spear of the Great Thane, none of my blood will ever lead them again. Nor, I expect, will anyone stay on in the great castle that Lord Sulis rebuilt after I am dead – there are few enough left of our household now, and those who stay only do so for love of me. When I am gone, I doubt any will remain even to tend our graves.

I cannot say why I chose to keep this bleak place as my home, any more than I could say why I chose my stepfather's life over that of my beautiful, deceitful Tellarin. Because I feared to build something on blood that should have been founded on something better, I suppose. Because love does not do sums, but instead makes choices, and then gives its all.

Whatever the reasons, I have made those choices.

After he carried me out of the depths and back to daylight, my stepfather scarcely ever mentioned that dreadful night again. He was still distant to the end of his days, still full of shadows, but at times I thought I sensed a peace in him that he had not had before. Why that might be, I could not say.

As he lay at last on his deathbed, breath growing fainter and fainter, I sat by his side for hours of every day and spoke to him of all that happened in the High Keep, talking of the rebuilding, which still continued, and of the tenants, and the herds, as if at any moment he might rise to resume his stewardship. But we both knew he would not.

When the last moment came, there was a kind of quiet expectancy on his face – no fear, but something more difficult to describe. As he strained for his final breath of air, I suddenly remembered something I had read in his book, and realized that I had made a mistake on that night so long ago.

She will show me the Way of Black Fire or there is no other Hope, he had written. *Either she will answer, or Death.*

He had not meant that he would kill her if she did not give him what he needed. He had meant that if she could not help him find an answer, then he would have to wait until death came for him before he could learn the truth.

And now he would finally receive an answer to the question that had tormented him for so long.

* * *

Whatever that answer might be, Sulis did not return to share it with me. Now I am an old, old woman, and I will find it soon enough myself. It is strange, perhaps, but I find I do not much care. In one year with Tellarin, in those months of fierce love, I lived an entire lifetime. Since then I have lived another one, a long, slow life whose small pleasures have largely balanced the moments of suffering. Surely two lives are enough for anyone – who needs the endless span of the immortals? After all, as the burning man made clear, an eternity of pain would be no gift.

And now that I have told my tale, even the ghosts that sometimes still startle me awake at midnight seem more like ancient friends than things to be feared.

I have made my choices.

I think I am content.

The Wheel of Time

ROBERT JORDAN

The Wheel of Time

ROBERT JORDAN

The Eye of the World (1990)
The Great Hunt (1990)
The Dragon Reborn (1991)
The Shadow Rising (1992)
The Fires of Heaven (1993)
Lord of Chaos (1994)
A Crown of Swords (1996)
The Path of Daggers (1998)

The world of Robert Jordan's *The Wheel of Time* lies both in our future and our past, a world of kings and queens and Aes Sedai, women who can tap the True Source and wield the One Power, which turns the Wheel and drives the universe: a world where the war between the Light and the Shadow is fought every day.

At the moment of Creation, the Creator bound the Dark One away from the world of humankind, but more than three thousand years ago Aes Sedai, then both men and women, unknowingly bored into that prison outside of time. The Dark One was only able to touch the world lightly, and the hole was eventually sealed over, but the Dark One's taint settled on *saidin*, the male half of the Power. Eventually every male Aes Sedai went mad, and in the Breaking of the World they destroyed civilization and changed the very face of Earth, sinking mountains beneath the sea and bringing new seas where land had been.

Now only women bear the title Aes Sedai. Commanded by their Amyrlin Seat and divided into seven Ajahs named by colour, they rule the great island city of Tar Valon, where their White Tower is located, and are bound by the Three Oaths, fixed into their bones with *saidar*, the female half of the Power: to speak no word that is not true, to make no weapon for one man to kill another, and never to use the One Power except as a weapon against Shadowspawn or in the last extreme of defending her own life, or that of her Warder or another sister.

Men still are born who can learn to channel the Power, or worse, who will channel one day whether they try to or not. Doomed to madness, destruction, and death by the taint on *saidin*, they are hunted down by Aes Sedai and gentled, cut off for ever from the Power for the safety of the world. No man goes to this willingly. Even if they survive the hunt, they seldom survive long after gentling.

For more than three thousand years, while nations and empires rose and fell, nothing has been so feared as a man who can channel. But for all those three thousand years there have been the Prophecies of the Dragon, that the seals on the Dark One's prison will weaken and he will touch the world once more, and that the Dragon, who sealed up that hole, will be Reborn to face the Dark One again. A child, born in sight of Tar Valon on the slopes of Dragonmount, will grow up to be the Dragon Reborn, the only hope of humanity in the Last Battle – a man who can channel. Few people know more than scraps of the Prophecies, and few want to know more.

A world of kings and queens, nations and wars, where the White Tower rules only Tar Valon but even kings and queens are wary of Aes Sedai machinations. A world where the Shadow and the Prophecies loom together.

The present story takes place before the first volume of the series. The succeeding books should be read in order.

◆

New Spring

BY ROBERT JORDAN

The air of Kandor held the sharpness of new spring when Lan returned to the lands where he had always known he would die. Trees bore the first red of new growth, and a few scattered wildflowers dotted winter-brown grass where shadows did not cling to patches of snow, yet the pale sun offered little warmth after the south, a gusting breeze cut through his coat, and grey clouds hinted at more than rain. He was almost home. Almost.

A hundred generations had beaten the wide road nearly as hard as the stone of the surrounding hills, and little dust rose, though a steady stream of ox-carts was leaving the morning farmers' markets in Canluum and merchant trains of tall wagons, surrounded by mounted guards in steel caps and bits of armour, flowed towards the city's high grey walls. Here and there the chains of the Kandori merchants' guild spanned a chest or an Arafellin wore bells, a ruby decorated this man's ear, a pearl brooch that woman's breast, but for the most part the traders' clothes were as subdued as their manner. A merchant who flaunted too much profit discovered it hard to find bargains. By contrast, farmers showed off their success when they came to town. Bright embroidery decorated the striding country-men's baggy breeches, the women's wide trousers, their cloaks fluttering in the wind. Some wore coloured ribbons in their hair, or a narrow fur collar. They might have been dressed for the coming Bel Tine dances and feasting. Yet country folk eyed strangers as warily as any guard, eyed them and hefted spears or axes and hurried along. The times carried an edge in Kandor, maybe all along the Borderlands. Bandits had sprung up like weeds this past year, and more troubles than usual out of the Blight. Rumour even spoke of a man who channelled the One Power, but then, rumour often did.

Leading his horse toward Canluum, Lan paid as little attention to the stares he and his companion attracted as he did to Bukama's scowls and carping. Bukama had raised him from the cradle, Bukama and other men now dead, and he could not recall seeing anything but a glower on that weathered face, even when Bukama spoke praise. This time his mutters were for a stone-bruised hoof that had him afoot, but he could always find something.

They did attract attention, two very tall men walking their mounts and a packhorse with a pair of tattered wicker hampers, their plain clothes worn and travel-stained. Their harness and weapons were well-tended, though. A young man and an old, hair hanging to their shoulders and held back by a braided leather cord around the temples. The *hadori* drew eyes. Especially here in the Borderlands, where people had some idea what it meant.

'Fools,' Bukama grumbled. 'Do they think we're bandits? Do they think we mean to rob the lot of them, at midday on the high road?' He glared and shifted the sword at his hip in a way that brought considering stares from a number of merchants' guards. A stout farmer prodded his ox wide of them.

Lan kept silent. A certain reputation clung to Malkieri who still wore the *hadori*, though not for banditry, but reminding Bukama would only send him into a black humour for days. His mutters shifted to the chances of a decent bed that night, of a decent meal before. Bukama seldom complained when there actually was no bed or no food, only about prospects and the inconsequential. He expected little, and trusted to less.

Neither food nor lodging entered Lan's thoughts, despite the distance they had travelled. His head kept swinging north. He remained aware of everyone around him, especially those who glanced his way more than once, aware of the jingle of harness and the creak of saddles, the clop of hooves, the snap of wagon-canvas loose on its hoops. Any sound out of place would shout at him. That had been the first lesson Bukama and his friends had imparted in his childhood; be aware of everything, even when asleep. Only the dead could afford oblivion. Lan remained aware, but the Blight lay north. Still miles away across the hills, yet he could feel it, feel the twisted corruption.

Just his imagination, but no less real for that. It had pulled at him in the south, in Cairhien and Andor, even in Tear, almost five hundred leagues distant. Two years away from the Borderlands, his personal war abandoned for another, and every day the tug grew stronger. The Blight meant death to most men. Death and the Shadow, a rotting land tainted by the Dark One's breath, where anything at all could kill. Two tosses of a coin had decided where to begin anew. Four nations bordered the Blight, but his war covered the length of it, from the Aryth Ocean to the Spine of the World. One place to meet death was as good as another. He was almost home. Almost back to the Blight.

A dry moat surrounded Canluum's wall, fifty paces wide and ten deep, spanned by five broad stone bridges with towers at either end as tall as those that lined the wall itself. Raids out of the Blight by Trollocs and Myrddraal often struck much deeper into Kandor than Canluum, but none had ever made it inside the city's wall. The Red Stag waved above every tower. A proud man, was Lord Varan, the High Seat of House Marcasiev; Queen Ethenielle did not fly so many of her own banners even in Chachin itself.

The guards at the outer towers, in helmets with Varan's antlered crest and the Red Stag on their chests, peered into the backs of wagons before allowing them to trundle on to the bridge, or occasionally motioned someone to push a hood further back. No more than a gesture was necessary; the law in every Borderland forbade hiding your face inside village or town, and no one wanted to be mistaken for one of the Eyeless trying to sneak into the city. Hard gazes followed Lan and Bukama on to the bridge. Their faces were clearly visible. And their *hadori*. No recognition lit any of those watching eyes, though. Two years was a long time in the Borderlands. A great many men could die in two years.

Lan noticed that Bukama had gone silent, always a bad sign, and cautioned him. 'I never start trouble,' the older man snapped, but he did stop fingering his swordhilt.

The guards on the wall above the open iron-plated gates and those on the bridge wore only back- and breastplates for armour, yet they were no less watchful, especially of a pair of Malkieri with their hair tied back. Bukama's mouth grew tighter at every step.

'Al'Lan Mandragoran! The Light preserve us, we heard you were dead fighting the Aiel at the Shining Walls!' The exclamation came from a young guard, taller than the rest, almost as tall as Lan. Young, perhaps a year or two less than he, yet the gap seemed ten years. A lifetime. The guard bowed deeply, left hand on his knee. '*Tai'shar Malkier!*' True blood of Malkier. 'I stand ready, Majesty.'

'I am not a king,' Lan said quietly. Malkier was dead. Only the war still lived. In him, at least.

Bukama was not quiet. 'You stand ready for *what*, boy?' The heel of his bare hand struck the guard's breastplate right over the Red Stag, driving the man upright and back a step. 'You cut your hair short and leave it unbound!' Bukama spat the words. 'You're sworn to a Kandori lord! By what right do you claim to be Malkieri?'

The young man's face reddened as he floundered for answers. Other guards started towards the pair, then halted when Lan let his reins fall. Only that, but they knew his name, now. They eyed his bay stallion, standing still and alert behind him, almost as cautiously as they did him. A warhorse was a formidable weapon, and they could not know Cat Dancer was only half-trained yet.

Space opened up as people already through the gates hurried a little distance before turning to watch, while those still on the bridge pressed back. Shouts rose in both directions from people wanting to know what was holding traffic. Bukama ignored it all, intent on the red-faced guard. He had not dropped the reins of the packhorse or his yellow roan gelding.

An officer appeared from the stone guardhouse inside the

gates, crested helmet under his arm, but one hand in a steel-backed gauntlet resting on his swordhilt. A bluff, greying man with white scars on his face, Alin Seroku had soldiered forty years along the Blight, yet his eyes widened slightly at the sight of Lan. Plainly he had heard the tales of Lan's death, too.

'The Light shine upon you, Lord Mandragoran. The son of el'Leanna and al'Akir, blessed be their memories, is always welcome.' Seroku's eyes flickered towards Bukama, not in welcome. He planted his feet in the middle of the gateway. Five horsemen could have passed easily on either side, but he meant himself for a bar, and he was. None of the guards shifted a boot, yet every one had hand on swordhilt. All but the young man meeting Bukama's glares with his own. 'Lord Marcasiev has commanded us to keep the peace strictly,' Seroku went on, half in apology. But no more than half. 'The city is on edge. All these tales of a man channelling are bad enough, but there have been murders in the street this last month and more, in broad daylight, and strange accidents. People whisper about Shadowspawn loose inside the walls.'

Lan gave a slight nod. With the Blight so close, people always muttered of Shadowspawn when they had no other explanation, whether for a sudden death or unexpected crop failure. He did not take up Cat Dancer's reins, though. 'We intend to rest here a few days before riding north.'

For a moment he thought Seroku was surprised. Did the man expect pledges to keep the peace, or apologies for Bukama's behaviour? Either would shame Bukama, now. A pity if the war ended here. Lan did not want to die killing Kandori.

His old friend turned from the young guard, who stood quivering, fists clenched at his sides. 'All fault here is mine,' Bukama announced to the air in a flat voice. 'I had no call for what I did. By my mother's name, I will keep Lord Marcasiev's peace. By my mother's name, I will not draw sword inside Canluum's walls.' Seroku's jaw dropped, and Lan hid his own shock with difficulty.

Hesitating only a moment, the scar-faced officer stepped aside, bowing and touching swordhilt then heart. 'There is always welcome for Lan Mandragoran Dai Shan,' he said formally. 'And for Bukama Marenellin, the hero of Salmarna. May you both know peace, one day.'

'There is peace in the mother's last embrace,' Lan responded with equal formality, touching hilt and heart.

'May she welcome us home, one day,' Seroku finished. No one really wished for the grave, but that was the only place to find peace in the Borderlands.

Face like iron, Bukama strode ahead pulling Sun Lance and the packhorse after him, not waiting for Lan. This was not well.

Canluum was a city of stone and brick, its paved streets twisting around tall hills. The Aiel invasion had never reached the Borderlands, but the ripples of war always diminished trade a long way from any battles, and now that fighting and winter were both finished, the city had filled with people from every land. Despite the Blight practically on the city's doorstep, gemstones mined in the surrounding hills made Canluum wealthy. And, strangely enough, some of the finest clockmakers anywhere. The cries of hawkers and shopkeepers shouting their wares rose above the hum of the crowd even away from the terraced market squares. Colourfully-dressed musicians, or jugglers, or tumblers performed at every intersection. A handful of lacquered carriages swayed through the mass of people and wagons and carts and barrows, and horses with gold- or silver-mounted saddles and bridles picked their way through the throng, their riders' garb embroidered as ornately as the animals' tack and trimmed with fox or marten or ermine. Hardly a foot of street was left bare anywhere. Lan even saw several Aes Sedai, women with serene, ageless faces. Enough people recognized them on sight that they created eddies in the crowd, swirls to clear a way. Respect or caution, awe or fear, there were sufficient reasons for a king to step aside for a sister. Once you might have gone a year without seeing an Aes Sedai even in the Borderlands, but the sisters seemed to be everywhere since their old Amyrlin Seat died a few months earlier. Maybe it was those tales of a man channelling; they would not let him run free long, if he existed. Lan kept his eyes away from them. The *hadori* could be enough to attract the interest of a sister seeking a Warder.

Shockingly, lace veils covered many women's faces. Thin lace, sheer enough to reveal that they had eyes, and no one had ever heard of a female Myrddraal, but Lan had never expected law to yield to mere fashion. Next they would take down the oil-lamps lining the streets and let the nights grow black. Even more shocking than the veils, Bukama looked right at some of those women and did not open his mouth. Then a jut-nosed man named Nazar Kurenin rode in front of Bukama's eyes, and he did not blink. The young guard surely had been born after the Blight swallowed Malkier, but Kurenin, his hair cut short and wearing a forked beard, was twice Lan's age. The years had not erased the marks of his *hadori* completely. There were many like Kurenin, and the sight of him should have set Bukama spluttering. Lan eyed his friend worriedly.

They had been moving steadily towards the centre of the city, climbing towards the highest hill, Stag's Stand. Lord Marcasiev's fortress-like palace covered the peak, with those of lesser lords and ladies on the terraces below. Any threshold up there offered warm welcome for al'Lan Mandragoran. Perhaps warmer than he wanted now. Balls and hunts, with nobles invited from as much as fifty miles away, including from across the border with Arafel. People avid to hear of his 'adventures'. Young men wanting to join his forays into the Blight, and old men to compare their experiences there with his. Women eager to share the bed of a man whom, so fool stories claimed, the Blight could not kill. Kandor and Arafel were as bad as any southland at times; some of those women would be married. And there would be men like Kurenin, working to submerge memories of lost Malkier, and women who no longer adorned their foreheads with the *ki'sain* in pledge that they would swear their sons to oppose the Shadow while they breathed. Lan could ignore the false smiles while they named him al'Lan Dai Shan, diademed battle lord and uncrowned king of a nation betrayed while he was in his cradle. In his present mood, Bukama might do murder. Or worse, given his oaths at the gate. He would keep those to the death.

'Varan Marcasiev will hold us a week or more with ceremony,' Lan said, turning down a narrower street that led away from the Stand. 'With what we've heard of bandits and the like, he will be just as happy if I don't appear to make my bows.' True enough. He had met the High Seat of House Marcasiev only once, years past, but he remembered a man given entirely to his duties.

Bukama followed without complaint about missing a palace bed or the feasts the cooks would prepare. It was worrying.

No palaces rose in the hollows towards the north wall, only shops and taverns, inns and stables and wagonyards. Bustle surrounded the factors' long warehouses, but no carriages came to the Deeps, and most streets were barely wide enough for carts. They were just as jammed with people as the wide ways, though, and every bit as noisy. Here, the street performers' finery was tarnished, yet they made up for it by being louder, and buyers and sellers alike bellowed as if trying to be heard in the next street. Likely some of the crowd were cutpurses, slipfingers, and other thieves, finished with a morning's business higher up or headed there for the afternoon. It would have been a wonder otherwise, with so many merchants in town. The second time unseen fingers brushed his coat in the crowd, Lan tucked his purse under his shirt. Any banker would advance him more against the Shienaran estate he had been granted on reaching manhood, but loss of the gold on hand meant accepting the hospitality of Stag's Stand.

At the first three inns they tried, slate-roofed cubes of grey stone with bright signs out front, the innkeepers had not a cubbyhole to offer. Lesser traders and merchants' guards filled them to the attics. Bukama began to mutter about making a bed in a hayloft, yet he never mentioned the feather mattresses and linens waiting on the Stand. Leaving their horses with ostlers at a fourth inn, The Blue Rose, Lan entered determined to find some place for them if it took the rest of the day.

Inside, a greying woman, tall and handsome, presided over a crowded common room where talk and laughter almost drowned out the slender girl singing to the music of her zither. Pipesmoke wreathed the ceiling beams, and the smell of roasting lamb floated from the kitchens. As soon as the innkeeper saw Lan and Bukama, she gave her blue-striped apron a twitch and strode towards them, dark eyes sharp.

Before Lan could open his mouth, she seized Bukama's ears, pulled his head down, and kissed him. Kandori women were seldom retiring, but even so it was a remarkably thorough kiss in front of so many eyes. Pointing fingers and snickering grins flashed among the tables.

'It's good to see you again, too, Racelle,' Bukama murmured with a small smile when she finally released him. 'I didn't know you had an inn here. Do you think –?' He lowered his gaze rather than meeting her eyes rudely, and that proved a mistake. Racelle's fist caught his jaw so hard that his hair flailed as he staggered.

'Six years without a word,' she snapped. 'Six years!' Grabbing his ears again, she gave him another kiss, longer this time. Took it rather than gave. A sharp twist of his ears met every attempt to do anything besides standing bent over and letting her do as she wished. At least she would not put a knife in his heart if she was kissing him. Perhaps not.

'I think Mistress Arovni might find Bukama a room somewhere,' a man's familiar voice said drily behind Lan. 'And you, too, I suppose.'

Turning, Lan clasped forearms with the only man in the room beside Bukama of a height with him, Ryne Venamar, his oldest friend except for Bukama. The innkeeper still had Bukama occupied as Ryne led Lan to a small table in the corner. Five years older, Ryne was Malkieri too, but his hair fell in two long bell-laced braids, and more silver bells lined the turned-down tops of his boots and ran up the sleeves of his yellow coat. Bukama did not exactly dislike Ryne – not exactly – yet in his present mood, only Nazar Kurenin could have had a worse effect.

While the pair of them were settling themselves on benches, a serving maid in a striped apron brought hot spiced wine. Apparently Ryne had ordered as soon as he saw Lan. Dark-eyed and full-lipped, she stared Lan up and down openly as she set his mug in front of him, then whispered her name, Lira, in his ear, and an invitation, if he was staying the night. All he wanted that night was sleep, so he lowered his gaze, murmuring that she honoured him too much. Lira did not let him finish. With a raucous laugh, she bent to bite his ear, hard, then announced that by tomorrow's sun she would have honoured him till his knees would not hold him up. More laughter flared at the tables around them.

Ryne forestalled any possibility of righting matters, tossing her a fat coin and giving her a slap on the bottom to send her off. Lira offered him a dimpled smile as she slipped the silver into the neck of her dress, but she left sending smoky glances over her shoulder at Lan that made him sigh. If he tried to say no now, she might well pull a knife over the insult.

'So your luck still holds with women, too.' Ryne's laugh had an edge. Perhaps he fancied her himself. 'The Light knows, they can't find you handsome; you get uglier every year. Maybe I ought to try some of that coy modesty, let women lead me by the nose.'

Lan opened his mouth, then took a drink instead of speaking. He should not have to explain, but Ryne's father had taken him to Arafel the year Lan turned ten. The man wore a single blade on his hip instead of two on his back, yet he was Arafellin to his toenails. He actually started conversations with women who had not spoken to him first. Lan, raised by Bukama and his friends in Shienar, had been surrounded by a small community who held to Malkieri ways.

A number of people around the room were watching their table, sidelong glances over mugs and goblets. A plump copper-skinned woman wearing a much thicker dress than Domani women usually did made no effort to hide her stares as she spoke excitedly to a fellow with curled moustaches and a large pearl in his ear. Probably wondering whether there would be trouble over Lira. Wondering whether a man wearing the *hadori* really would kill at the drop of a pin.

'I didn't expect to find you in Canluum,' Lan said, setting the wine-mug down. 'Guarding a merchant train?' Bukama and the innkeeper were nowhere to be seen.

Ryne shrugged. 'Out of Shol Arbela. The luckiest trader in Arafel, they say. Said. Much good it did him. We arrived yesterday, and last night footpads slit his throat two streets over. No return money for me this trip.' He flashed a rueful grin and took a deep pull at his wine, perhaps to the memory of the merchant or perhaps to the lost half of his wages. 'Burn me if I thought to see you here, either.'

'You shouldn't listen to rumours, Ryne. I've not taken a wound worth mentioning since I rode south.' Lan decided to twit Bukama if they did get a room, about whether it was already paid for and how. Indignation might take him out of his darkness.

'The Aiel,' Ryne snorted. 'I never thought *they* could put paid to you.' He had never faced Aiel, of course. 'I expected you to be wherever Edeyn Arrel is. Chachin, now, I hear.'

That name snapped Lan's head back to the man across the table. 'Why should I be near the Lady Arrel?' he demanded softly. Softly, but emphasizing her proper title.

'Easy, man,' Ryne said. 'I didn't mean . . .' Wisely, he abandoned that line. 'Burn me, do you mean to say you haven't heard? She's raised the Golden Crane. In your name, of course. Since the year turned, she's been from Fal Moran to Maradon, and coming back now.' Ryne shook his head, the bells in his braids chiming faintly. 'There must be two or three hundred men right here in Canluum ready to follow her. You, I mean. Some you'd not believe. Old Kurenin wept when he heard her speak. All ready to carve Malkier out of the Blight again.'

'What dies in the Blight is gone,' Lan said wearily. He felt more than cold inside. Suddenly Seroku's surprise that he intended to ride north took on new meaning, and the young guard's assertion that he stood ready. Even the looks here in the common room seemed different. And Edeyn was part of it. Always she liked standing in the heart of the storm. 'I must see to my horse,' he told Ryne, scraping his bench back.

Ryne said something about making a round of the taverns that night, but Lan hardly heard. He hurried through the kitchens, hot from iron stoves and stone ovens and open hearths, into the cool of the stableyard, the mingled smells of horse and hay and woodsmoke. A greylark warbled on the edge of the stable roof. Greylarks came even before robins in the spring. Greylarks had been singing in Fal Moran when Edeyn first whispered in his ear.

The horses had already been stabled, bridles and saddles and packsaddle atop saddle blankets on the stall doors, but the wicker hampers were gone. Plainly Mistress Arovni had sent word to the ostlers that he and Bukama were being given accommodation.

There was only a single groom in the dim stable, a lean, hard-faced woman mucking out. Silently she watched him check Cat Dancer and the other horses as she worked, watched him begin to pace the length of the straw-covered floor. He tried to think, but Edeyn's name kept spinning though his head. Edeyn's face, surrounded by silky black hair that hung below her waist, a beautiful face with large dark eyes that could drink a man's soul even when filled with command.

After a bit the groom mumbled something in his direction, touching her lips and forehead, and hurriedly shoved her half-filled barrow out of the stable, glancing over her shoulder at him. She paused to shut the doors, and did that hurriedly, too, sealing him in shadow broken only by a little light from open hay doors in the loft. Dust motes danced in the pale golden shafts.

Lan grimaced. Was she that afraid of a man wearing the *hadori*? Did she think his pacing a threat? Abruptly he became aware of his hands running over the long hilt of his sword, aware of the tightness in his own face. Pacing? No, he had been in the walking stance called Leopard in High Grass, used when there were enemies on all sides. He needed calm.

Seating himself crosslegged on a bale of straw, he formed the image of a flame in his mind and fed emotion into it, hate, fear, everything, every scrap, until it seemed that he floated in emptiness. After years of practice, achieving *ko'di*, the oneness, needed less than a heartbeat. Thought and even his own body seemed distant, but in this state he was more aware than usual, becoming one with the bale beneath him, the stable, the scabbarded sword folded behind him. He could 'feel' the horses, cropping at their mangers, and flies buzzing in the corners. They were all part of him. Especially the sword. This time, though, it was only the emotionless void that he sought.

From his beltpouch he took a heavy gold signet ring worked with a flying crane and turned it over and over in his fingers. The ring of Malkieri kings, worn by men who had held back the Shadow nine hundred years and more. Countless times it had been remade as time wore it down, always the old ring melted to become part of the new. Some particle might still exist in it of the ring worn by the rulers of Rhamdashar, that had lived before Malkier, and Aramaelle that had been before Rhamdashar. That piece of metal represented over three thousand years fighting the Blight. It had been his almost as long as he had lived, but he had never worn it. Even looking at the ring was a labour, usually. One he disciplined himself to every day. Without the emptiness, he did not think he could have done so today. In *ko'di*, thought floated free, and emotion lay beyond the horizon.

In his cradle he had been given four gifts. The ring in his hands and the locket that hung around his neck, the sword on his hip and an oath sworn in his name. The locket was the most precious, the oath the heaviest. 'To stand against the Shadow so long as iron is hard and stone abides. To defend the Malkieri while one drop of blood remains. To avenge what cannot be defended.' And then he had been anointed with oil and named Dai Shan, consecrated as the next King of Malkier, and sent away from a land that knew it would die. Twenty men began that journey; five survived to reach Shienar.

Nothing remained to be defended now, only a nation to avenge, and he had been trained to that from his first step. With his mother's gift at his throat and his father's sword in his hand, with the ring branded on his heart, he had fought to avenge Malkier from his sixteenth nameday. But never had he led men into the Blight. Bukama had ridden with him, and others, but he would not lead men there. That war was his alone.

The dead could not be returned to life, a land any more than a man. Only, now, Edeyn Arrel wanted to try.

Her name echoed in the emptiness within him. A hundred emotions loomed like stark mountains, but he fed them into the flame until all was still. Until his heart beat time with the slow stamping of the stalled horses, and the flies' wings beat rapid counterpoint to his breath. She was his *carneira*, his first lover. A thousand years of tradition shouted that, despite the stillness that enveloped him.

He had been fifteen, Edeyn more than twice that, when she gathered the hair that had still hung to his waist in her hands and whispered her intentions. Women had still called him beautiful then, enjoying his blushes, and for half a year she had enjoyed parading him on her arm and tucking him into her bed. Until Bukama and the other men gave him the *hadori*. The gift of his sword on his tenth nameday had made him a man by custom along the Border, though years early for it, yet among Malkieri, that band of braided leather had been more important. Once that was tied around his head, he alone decided where he went, and when, and why. And the dark song of the Blight had become a howl that drowned every other sound. The oath that had murmured so long in his heart became a dance his feet had to follow.

Almost ten years past now that Edeyn had watched him ride away from Fal Moran, and been gone when he returned, yet he still could recall her face more clearly than that of any woman who had shared his bed since. He was no longer a boy, to think that she loved him just because she had chosen to become his first lover, yet there was an old saying among Malkieri men. *Your* carneira *wears part of your soul as a ribbon in her hair for ever.* Custom strong as law made it so.

One of the stable doors creaked open to admit Bukama, coatless, shirt tucked raggedly into his breeches. He looked naked without his sword. As if hesitant, he carefully opened both doors wide before coming all the way in. 'What are you going to do?' he said finally. 'Racelle told me about . . . about the Golden Crane.'

Lan tucked the ring away, letting emptiness drain from him. Edeyn's face suddenly seemed everywhere, just beyond the edge of sight. 'Ryne says even Nazar Kurenin is ready to follow,' he said lightly. 'Wouldn't that be a sight to see?' An army could die trying to defeat the Blight. Armies had died trying. But the memories of Malkier already were dying. A nation was memory as much as land. 'That boy at the gates might let his hair grow and ask his father for the *hadori*.' People were forgetting, trying to forget. When the last man who bound his hair was gone, the last woman who painted her forehead, would Malkier truly be gone, too? 'Why, Ryne might even get rid of those braids.' Any trace of mirth dropped from his voice as he added, 'But is it worth the cost? Some seem to think so.' Bukama snorted, yet there had been a pause. He might be one of those who did.

Striding to the stall that held Sun Lance, the older man began to fiddle with his roan's saddle as though suddenly forgetting why he had moved. 'There's always a cost for anything,' he said, not looking up. 'But there are costs, and costs. The Lady Edeyn . . .' He glanced at Lan, then turned to face him. 'She was always one to demand every right and require the smallest obligation be met. Custom ties strings to you, and whatever you choose, she will use them like a set of reins unless you find a way to avoid it.'

Carefully Lan tucked his thumbs behind his swordbelt. Bukama had carried him out of Malkier tied to his back. The last of the five. Bukama had the right of a free tongue even when it touched Lan's *carneira*. 'How do you suggest I avoid my obligations without shame?' he asked more harshly than he had intended. Taking a deep breath, he went on in a milder tone. 'Come; the common room smells much better than this. Ryne suggested a round of the taverns tonight. Unless Mistress Arovni has claims on you. Oh, yes. How much will our rooms cost? Good rooms? Not too dear, I hope.'

Bukama joined him on the way to the doors, his face going red. 'Not too dear,' he said hastily. 'You have a pallet in the attic, and I . . . ah . . . I'm in Racelle's rooms. I'd like to make a round, but I think Racelle . . . I don't think she means to let me

. . . I . . . Young whelp!' he growled. 'There's a lass named Lira in there who's letting it be known you won't be using that pallet tonight, *or* getting much sleep, so don't think you can –!' He cut off as they walked into the sunlight, bright after the dimness inside. The greylark still sang of spring.

Six men were striding across the otherwise empty yard. Six ordinary men with swords at their belts, like any men on any street in the city. Yet Lan knew before their hands moved, before their eyes focused on him and their steps quickened. He had faced too many men who wanted to kill him not to know. And at his side stood Bukama, bound by oaths that would not let him raise a hand even had he been wearing his blade. If they both tried to get back inside the stable, the men would be on them before they could haul the doors shut. Time slowed, flowed like cool honey.

'Inside and bar the doors!' Lan snapped as his hand went to his hilt. 'Obey me, armsman!'

Never in his life had he given Bukama a command in that fashion, and the man hesitated a heartbeat, then bowed formally. 'My life is yours, Dai Shan,' he said in a thick voice. 'I obey.'

As Lan moved forward to meet his attackers, he heard the bar drop inside with a muffled thud. Relief was distant. He floated in *ko'di*, one with the sword that came smoothly out of its scabbard. One with the men rushing at him, boots thudding on the hard-packed ground as they bared steel.

A lean heron of a fellow darted ahead of the others, and Lan danced the forms. Time like cool honey. The greylark sang, and the lean man shrieked as Cutting the Clouds removed his right hand at the wrist, and Lan flowed to one side so the rest could not all come at him together, flowed from form to form. Soft Rain at Sunset laid open a fat man's face, took his left eye, and a ginger-haired young splinter drew a gash across Lan's ribs with Black Pebbles on Snow. Only in stories did one man face six without injury. The Rose Unfolds sliced down a bald man's left arm, and ginger-hair nicked the corner of Lan's eye. Only in stories did one man face six and survive. He had known that from the start. Duty was a mountain, death a feather, and his duty was to Bukama, who had carried an infant on his back. For this moment he lived, though, so he fought, kicking ginger-hair in the head, dancing his way towards death, danced and took wounds, bled and danced the razor's edge of life. Time like cool honey, flowing from form to form, and there could only be one ending. Thought was distant. Death was a feather. Dandelion in the Wind slashed open the now one-eyed fat man's throat – he had barely paused when his face was ruined – a fork-bearded fellow with shoulders like a blacksmith gasped in surprise as Kissing the Adder put Lan's steel through his heart.

And suddenly Lan realized that he alone stood, with six men sprawled across the width of the stableyard. The ginger-haired youth thrashed his heels on the ground one last time, and then only Lan of the seven still breathed. He shook blood from his blade, bent to wipe the last drops off on the blacksmith's too-fine coat, sheathed his sword as formally as if he were in the training yard under Bukama's eye.

Abruptly people flooded out of the inn, cooks and stablemen, maids and patrons shouting to know what all the noise was about, staring at the dead men in astonishment. Ryne was the very first, sword already in hand, his face blank as he came to stand by Lan. 'Six,' he muttered, studying the bodies. 'You really do have the Dark One's own flaming luck.'

Dark-eyed Lira reached Lan only moments before Bukama, the pair of them gently parting slashes in his clothes to examine his injuries. She shivered delicately as each was revealed, but she discussed whether an Aes Sedai should be sent for to give Healing and how much stitching was needed in as calm a tone as Bukama, and disparagingly dismissed his hand on the needle in favour of her own. Mistress Arovni stalked about, holding her skirts up out of patches of bloody mud, glaring at the corpses littering her stableyard, complaining in a loud voice that gangs of footpads would never be wandering in daylight if the Watch was doing its job. The Domani woman who had stared at Lan inside agreed just as loudly, and for her pains received a sharp command from the innkeeper to fetch them, along with a shove to start her on her way. It was a measure of Mistress Arovni's shock that she treated one of her patrons so, a measure of everyone's shock that the Domani woman went running without complaint. The innkeeper began organizing men to drag the bodies out of sight, still going on about footpads.

Ryne looked from Bukama to the stable as though he did not understand – perhaps he did not, at that – but what he said was, 'Not footpads, I think.' He pointed to the fellow who looked like a blacksmith. 'That one listened to Edeyn Arrel when she was here, and he liked what he heard. One of the others did, too, I think.' Bells chimed as he shook his head. 'It's peculiar. The first she said of raising the Golden Crane was after we heard you were dead outside the Shining Walls. Your name brings men, but with you dead, she could be el'Edeyn.' He spread his hands at the looks Lan and Bukama shot him. 'I make no accusations,' he said hastily. 'I'd never accuse the Lady Edeyn of any such thing. I'm sure she is full of all a woman's tender mercy.' Mistress Arovni gave a grunt like a fist, and Lira murmured half under her breath that the pretty Arafellin did not know much about women.

Lan shook his head. Edeyn might decide to have him killed if it suited her purposes, she might have left orders here and there in case the rumours about him proved false, but if she had, that was still no reason to speak her name in connection with this, especially in front of strangers.

Bukama's hands stilled, holding open a slash down Lan's sleeve. 'Where do we go from here?' he asked quietly.

'Chachin,' Lan said after a moment. There was always a choice, but sometimes every choice was grim. 'You'll have to leave Sun Lance. I mean to depart at first light tomorrow.' His gold would stretch to a new mount for the man.

'Six!' Ryne growled, sheathing his sword with considerable force. 'I think I'll ride with you. I'd as soon not go back to Shol Arbela until I'm sure Ceiline Noreman doesn't lay her husband's death at my boots. And it will be good to see the Golden Crane flying again.'

Lan nodded. To put his hand on the banner and abandon what he had promised himself all those years ago, or to stop her, if he could. Either way, he had to face Edeyn. The Blight would have been much easier.

Chasing after prophecy, Moiraine had decided by the end of the first month, involved very little adventure and a great deal of saddlesoreness and frustration. The Three Oaths still made her skin feel too tight. The wind rattled the shutters, and she shifted on the hard wooden chair, hiding impatience behind a sip of honeyless tea. In Kandor, comforts were kept to a minimum in a house of mourning. She would not have been overly surprised to see frost on the leaf-carved furniture or the metal clock above the cold hearth.

'It was all so strange, my Lady,' Mistress Najima sighed, and for the tenth time hugged her daughters. Perhaps thirteen or fourteen, standing close to their mother's chair, Colar and Eselle had her long black hair and large blue eyes still full of loss. Their mother's eyes seemed big, too, in a face shrunken by tragedy, and her plain grey dress appeared made for a larger woman. 'Josef was always careful with lanterns in the stable,' she went on, 'and he never allowed any kind of open flame. The boys must have carried little Jerid out to see their father at his work, and . . .' Another hollow sigh. 'They were all trapped. How could the whole stable be ablaze so fast? It makes no sense.'

'Little is ever senseless,' Moiraine said soothingly, setting her cup on the small table at her elbow. She felt sympathy, but the woman had begun repeating herself. 'We cannot always see the reason, yet we can take some comfort in knowing there is one. The Wheel of Time weaves us into the Pattern as it wills, but the Pattern is the work of the Light.'

Hearing herself, she suppressed a wince. Those words required dignity and weight her youth failed to supply. If only time could pass faster. At least for the next five years or so. Five years should give her her full strength and provide all the dignity and weight she would ever need. But then, the agelessness that came after working long enough with the One Power would only have made her present task more difficult. The last thing she could afford was anyone connecting an Aes Sedai to her visits.

'As you say, my Lady,' the other woman murmured politely, though an unguarded shift of pale eyes spoke her thoughts. This outlander was a foolish child. The small blue stone of a kesiera dangling from a fine golden chain on to Moiraine's forehead and a dark green dress with six slashes of colour across the breast, far fewer than she was entitled to, made Mistress Najima think her merely a Cairhienin noblewoman, one of many wandering since the Aiel ruined Cairhien. A noblewoman of a minor House, named Alys not Moiraine, making sympathy calls in mourning for her own king, killed by the Aiel. The fiction was easy to maintain, though she did not mourn her uncle in the least.

Perhaps sensing that her thoughts had been too clear, Mistress Najima started up again, speaking quickly. 'It's just that Josef was always so lucky, my Lady. Everyone spoke of it. They said if Josef Najima fell down a hole, there'd be opals at the bottom. When he answered the Lady Kareil's call to go fight the Aiel, I worried, but he never took a scratch. When camp fever struck, it never touched us or the children. Josef gained the Lady's favour without trying. Then it seemed the Light truly did shine on us. Jerid was born safe and whole, and the war ended, all in a matter of days, and when we came home to Canluum, the Lady gave us the livery stable for Josef's service, and . . . and . . .' She swallowed tears she would not shed. Colar began to weep, and her mother pulled her closer, whispering comfort.

Moiraine rose. More repetition. There was nothing here for her. Jurine stood, too, not a tall woman, yet almost a hand taller than she. Either of the girls could look her in the eyes. She had grown accustomed to that since leaving Cairhien. Forcing herself to take time, she murmured more condolences and tried to press a washleather purse on the woman as the girls brought her fur-lined cloak and gloves. A small purse. Obtaining coin meant visits to the bankers and a clear trail. Not that the Aiel had left her estates in a condition to provide much money for some years yet. And not that anyone was likely to be looking for her. Still, discovery might be decidedly unpleasant.

The woman's stiff-necked refusal to take the purse irritated Moiraine. No, that was not the real reason. She understood pride, and besides, Lady Kareil had provided. The real irritant was her own desire to be gone. Jurine Najima had lost her husband and three sons in one fiery morning, but her Jerid had been born in the wrong place by almost twenty miles. The search continued. Moiraine did not like feeling relief in connection with the death of an infant. Yet she did.

Outside under a grey sky, she gathered her cloak tightly. Ignoring the cold was a simple trick, but anyone who went about the streets of Canluum with open cloak would draw stares. Any outlander, at least, unless clearly Aes Sedai. Besides, not allowing the cold to touch you did not make you unaware of it. How these people could call this 'new spring' without a hint of mockery was beyond her.

Despite the near freezing wind that gusted over the rooftops, the winding streets were packed, requiring her to pick her way through a milling mass of people and carts and wagons. The world had certainly come to Canluum. A Taraboner with heavy moustaches pushed past her muttering a hasty apology, and an olive-skinned Altaran woman who scowled at Moiraine, then an Illianer with a beard that left his upper lip bare, a very pretty fellow and not too tall.

Another day she might have enjoyed the sight of him, in another city. Now, he barely registered. It was women she watched, especially those well-dressed, in silks or fine woollens. If only so many were not veiled. Twice she saw Aes Sedai strolling through the crowds, neither a woman she had ever met. Neither glanced in her direction, but she kept her head down and stayed to the other side of the street. Perhaps she should put on a veil. A stout woman brushed by, features blurred behind lace. Sierin Vayu herself could have passed unrecognized at ten feet in one of those.

Moiraine shivered at the thought, ridiculous as it was. If the new Amyrlin learned what she was up to . . . Inserting herself into secret plans, unbidden and unannounced, would not go unpunished. No matter that the Amyrlin who had made them was dead in her sleep and another woman sat on the Amyrlin Seat. Being sequestered on a farm until the search was done was the least she could expect.

It was not just. She and her friend Siuan had helped gather the names, in the guise of offering assistance to any woman who had given birth during the days when the Aiel threatened Tar Valon itself. Of all the women involved in that gathering, just they two knew the real reason. They had winnowed those names for Tamra. Only children born outside the city's walls had really been important, though the promised aid went to every woman found, of course. Only boys born on the west bank of the River Erinin, boys who might have been born on the slopes of Dragonmount.

Behind her a woman shouted shrilly, angrily, and Moiraine jumped a foot before she realized it was a wagon-driver, brandishing her whip at a hawker to hustle his pushcart of steaming meat pies out of her way. Light! A farm was the *least* she could expect! A few men around Moiraine laughed raucously at her leap, and one, a dark-faced Tairen in a striped cloak, made a rude joke about the cold wind curling under her skirts. The laughter grew.

Moiraine stalked ahead stiffly, cheeks crimson, hand tight on the silver hilt of her beltknife. Unthinking, she embraced the True Source, and the One Power flooded her with joyous life. A single glance over her shoulder was all she needed; with *saidar* in her, smells became sharper, colours truer. She could have counted the threads in the cloak the Tairen was letting flap while he laughed. She channelled fine flows of the Power, of Air, and the fellow's baggy breeches dropped to his turned-down boots, the laces undone. Bellowing, he snatched his cloak around him amid gales of renewed mirth. Let him see how *he* liked cold breezes and rowdy jokes!

Satisfaction lasted as long as it took to release the Source. Impetuous impulse and a quick temper had always been her downfall. Any woman able to channel would have seen her weaving if close enough, seen the glow of *saidar* surround her. Even those thin flows could have been felt at thirty paces by the weakest sister in the Tower. A fine way to hide.

Quickening her step, she put distance between herself and the incident. Too little too late, but all she could do now. She stroked the small book in her beltpouch, tried to focus on her task. With only one hand, keeping her cloak closed proved impossible. It whipped about in the wind, and after a moment, she let herself feel the knifing chill. Sisters who took on penances at every turn were foolish, yet a penance could serve many purposes, and maybe she needed a reminder. If she could not remember to be careful, she might as well return to the White Tower now and ask where to start hoeing turnips.

Mentally she drew a line through the name of Jurine Najima. Other names in the book already had real lines inked through them. The mothers of five boys born in the wrong place. The mothers of three girls. An army of almost two hundred thousand men had gathered to face the Aiel outside the Shining Walls, and it still astonished her how many women followed along, how many were with child. An older sister had had to explain. The war had not been short, and men who knew they might die tomorrow wanted to leave part of themselves behind. Women who knew their men might die tomorrow wanted that part of them to keep.

Hundreds had given birth during the key ten days, and in that sort of gathering, with soldiers from nearly every land, too often there was only rumour as to exactly where or when a child had been born. Or to where the parents had gone, with the war ended and the Coalition army melting away along with the Coalition. There were too many entries like 'Saera Deosin. Husband Eadwin. From Murandy. A son?' A whole country to search, only a pair of names to go by, and no certainty the woman had borne a boy. Too many like 'Kari al'Thor. From Andor? Husband Tamlin, Second Captain of the Illianer Companions, took discharge.' That pair might have gone anywhere in the world, and there was doubt she had had a child at all. Sometimes only the mother was listed, with six or eight variations on the name of a home village that might lie in one of two or three countries. The list of those easy to find was growing shorter rapidly.

But the child had to be found. An infant who would grow to manhood and wield the tainted male half of the One Power. Moiraine shuddered at the thought despite herself. That was why this search was so secret, why Moiraine and Siuan, still only Accepted when they learned of the child's birth by accident, had been shunted aside and kept in as much ignorance as Tamra could manage. This was a matter for experienced sisters. But who could she trust with the news that the birth of the Dragon Reborn had been Foretold, and more, that somewhere he already suckled at his mother's breast? Had she had the sort of nightmares that had wakened Moiraine and Siuan so many nights? Yet this boychild would grow to manhood and save the world, so the Prophecies of the Dragon said. If he was not found by a Red sister; the Red Ajah's main purpose was hunting down men who could channel, and Moiraine was sure Tamra had not trusted any of them, even with a child. Could a Red be trusted to remember that he would be humankind's salvation while remembering what else he would be? The day suddenly seemed colder to Moiraine, for remembering.

The inn where she had a small room was called The Gates of Heaven, four sprawling storeys of green-roofed stone, Canluum's best and largest. Nearby shops catered to the lords and ladies on the Stand, looming behind the inn. She would not have stopped in it had there been another room to be found in the city. Taking a deep breath, she hurried inside. Neither the sudden warmth from fires on four large hearths nor the good smells of cooking from the kitchens eased her tight shoulders.

The common room was large, and every table beneath the bright red ceiling beams was taken. By plainly-dressed merchants for the most part, and a sprinkling of well-to-do craftsfolk with rich embroidery covering colourful shirts or dresses. She hardly noticed them. No fewer than five sisters were staying at The Gates of Heaven, and all sat in the common room when she walked in. Master Helvin, the innkeeper, would always make room for an Aes Sedai even when he had to force other patrons to double up. The sisters kept to themselves, barely acknowledging one another, and people who might not have recognized an Aes Sedai on sight knew them now, knew enough not to intrude. Every other table was jammed, yet where any man sat with an Aes Sedai, it was her Warder, a hard-eyed man with a dangerous look about him however ordinary he might seem otherwise. One of the sisters sitting alone was a Red; Reds took no Warder.

Tucking her gloves behind her belt and folding her cloak over her arm, Moiraine started towards the stone stairs at the back of the room. Not too quickly, but not dawdling, either. Looking straight ahead. She did not need to see an ageless face or glimpse the golden serpent biting its own tail encircling a finger to know when she passed close to another sister. Each time, she felt the other woman's ability to channel, felt her strength. No one here matched her. She could sense their ability, and they could sense hers. Their eyes following her seemed the touch of fingers. Not quite grasping. None spoke to her.

Then, just as she reached the staircase, a woman did speak behind her. 'Well, now. This is a surprise.'

Turning quickly, Moiraine kept her face smooth with an effort as she made a brief curtsy suitable for a minor noblewoman to an Aes Sedai. To two Aes Sedai. She did not think she could have encountered two worse than this pair in sober silks.

The white wings in Larelle Tarsi's long hair emphasized her serene, copper-skinned elegance. She had taught Moiraine in several classes, as both novice and Accepted, and she had a way of asking the last question you wanted to hear. Worse was Merean Redhill, plump and so motherly that hair more grey than not, and gathered at the nape of her neck, almost submerged the agelessness of her features. She had been Mistress of Novices under Tamra, and she made Larelle seem blind when it came to discovering just what you most wanted to hide. Both wore their vine-embroidered shawls, Merean's fringed blue. Blue was Moiraine's Ajah, too. That might count for something. Or not. It was a surprise to see them together; she had not thought they particularly liked one another.

Both were stronger in the Power than she, unfortunately, though she would stand above them eventually, but the gap was only wide enough that she had to defer, not obey. In any case, they had no right to interfere in anything she might be doing. Custom held very strongly on that. Unless they were part of Tamra's search and had been told about her. An Amyrlin's commands superseded the strongest custom, or at least altered it. But if either said the wrong thing here, word that Moiraine Damodred was wandering about in disguise would spread with the sisters in the room, and it would reach the wrong ears as surely as peaches were poison. That was the way of the world. A summons back to Tar Valon would find her soon after. She opened her mouth hoping to forestall the chance, but someone else spoke first.

'No need trying that one,' a sister alone at a table nearby said, twisting around on her bench. Felaana Bevaine, a slim yellow-haired Brown with a raspy voice, had been the first to corner Moiraine when she arrived. 'Says she has no interest in going to the Tower. Stubborn as stone about it. Secretive, too. You would think we'd have heard about a wilder popping up in even a lesser Cairhienin House, but this child likes to keep to herself.'

Larelle and Merean looked at Moiraine, Larelle arching a thin eyebrow, Merean apparently trying to suppress a smile. Most sisters disliked wilders, women who managed to survive teaching themselves to channel without going to the White Tower.

'It is quite true, Aes Sedai,' Moiraine said carefully, relieved that someone else had laid a foundation. 'I have no desire to enrol as a novice, and I will not.'

Felaana fixed her with considering eyes, but she still spoke to the others. 'Says she's twenty-two, but that rule has been bent a time or two. A woman says she's eighteen, and that's how she's enrolled. Unless it's too obvious a lie, anyway, and this girl –'

'Our rules were not made to be broken,' Larelle said sharply, and Merean added in a wry voice, 'I don't believe this young woman will lie about her age. She doesn't want to be a novice, Felaana. Let her go her way.' Moiraine almost let out a relieved sigh.

Enough weaker than they to accept being cut off, Felaana still began to rise, plainly meaning to continue the argument. Halfway to her feet she glanced up the stairs behind Moiraine, her eyes widened, and abruptly she sat down again, focusing on her plate of black peas and onions as if nothing else in the world existed. Merean and Larelle gathered their shawls, grey fringe and blue swaying. They looked eager to be elsewhere. They looked as though their feet had been nailed to the floor.

'So this girl does not want to be a novice,' said a woman's voice from the stairs. A voice Moiraine had heard only once, two years ago, and would never forget. A number of women were stronger than she, but only one could be as much stronger as this one. Unwillingly, she looked over her shoulder.

Nearly black eyes studied her from beneath a bun of iron-grey hair decorated with golden ornaments, stars and birds, crescent moons and fish. Cadsuane, too, wore her shawl, fringed in green. 'In my opinion, girl,' she said drily, 'you could profit from ten years in white.'

Everyone had believed Cadsuane Melaidhrin dead somewhere in retirement until she reappeared at the start of the Aiel War, and a good many sisters probably wished her truly in her grave. Cadsuane was a legend, a most uncomfortable thing to have alive and staring at you. Half the tales about her came close to impossibility, while the rest were beyond it, even among those that had proof. A long-ago King of Tarabon winkled out of his palace when it was learned he could channel, carried to Tar Valon to be gentled while an army that did not believe chased after to attempt rescue. A King of Arad Doman and a Queen of Saldaea *both* kidnapped, spirited away in secrecy, and when Cadsuane finally released them, a war that had seemed certain simply faded away. It was said she bent Tower law where it suited her, flouted custom, went her own way and often dragged others with her.

'I thank the Aes Sedai for her concern,' Moiraine began, then trailed off under that stare. Not a hard stare. Simply implacable. Supposedly even Amyrlins had stepped warily around Cadsuane over the years. It was whispered that she had actually *assaulted* an Amyrlin, once. Impossible, of course; she would have been executed! Moiraine swallowed and tried to start over, only to find she wanted to swallow again.

Descending the stair, Cadsuane told Merean and Larelle, 'Bring the girl.' Without a second glance, she glided across the common room. Merchants and craftsfolk looked at her, some openly, some from the corner of an eye, and Warders too, but every sister kept her gaze on her table.

Merean's face tightened, and Larelle sighed extravagantly, yet they prodded Moiraine after the bobbing golden ornaments. She had no choice but to go. At least Cadsuane could not be one of the women Tamra had called in; she had not returned to Tar Valon since that visit at the beginning of the war.

Cadsuane led them to one of the inn's private sitting rooms, where a fire blazed on the black stone hearth and silver lamps hung along the red wall panels. A tall pitcher stood near the fire to keep warm, and a lacquered tray on a small carved table held silver cups. Merean and Larelle took two of the brightly-cushioned chairs, but when Moiraine put her cloak on a chair and started to sit, Cadsuane pointed to a spot in front of the other sisters. 'Stand there, child,' she said.

Making an effort not to clutch her skirt in her fists, Moiraine stood as directed. Obedience had always been difficult for her. Until she went to the Tower at sixteen, there had been few people she had to obey. Most obeyed her.

Cadsuane circled the three of them slowly, once, twice. Merean and Larelle exchanged wondering frowns, and Larelle opened her mouth, but after one look at Cadsuane, closed it again. They assumed smooth-faced serenity; any watcher would have thought they knew exactly what was going on. Sometimes Cadsuane glanced at them, but the greater part of her attention stayed on Moiraine.

'Most new sisters,' the legendary Green said abruptly, 'hardly remove their shawls to sleep or bathe, but here you are without shawl or ring, in one of the most dangerous spots you could choose short of the Blight itself. Why?'

Moiraine blinked. A direct question. The woman really did ignore custom when it suited her. She made her voice light. 'New sisters also seek a Warder.' Why was the woman singling her out in this manner? 'I have not bonded mine, yet. I am told Bordermen make fine Warders.' The Green sent her a stabbing look that made her wish she had been just a little less light.

Stopping behind Larelle, Cadsuane laid a hand on her shoulder. 'What do you know of this child?'

Every girl in Larelle's classes had thought her the perfect sister and been intimidated by that cool consideration. They all had been afraid of her, and wanted to be her. 'Moiraine was studious and a quick learner,' she said thoughtfully. 'She and Siuan Sanche were two of the quickest the Tower has ever seen. But you must know that. Let me see. She was rather too free with her opinions, and her temper, until we settled her down. As much as we did settle her. She and the Sanche girl had a continuing fondness for pranks. But they both passed for Accepted on the first try, and for the shawl. She needs seasoning, of course, yet she may make something of herself.'

Cadsuane moved behind Merean, asking the same question, adding, 'A fondness for . . . pranks, Larelle said. A troublesome child?'

Merean shook her head with a smile. None of the girls had wanted to be Merean, but everyone knew where to go for a shoulder to cry on or advice when you could not ask your closest friend. Many more girls visited her on their own than had been sent for chastisement. 'Not troublesome, really,' she said. 'High-spirited. None of the tricks Moiraine played were mean, but they were plentiful. Novice and Accepted, she was sent to my study more often than any three other girls. Except for her pillow-friend Siuan. Of course, pillow-friends frequently get into tangles together, but with those two, one was never sent to me without the other. The last time the very night after passing for the shawl.' Her smile faded into a frown very much like the one she had worn that night. Not angry, but rather disbelieving of the mischief young women could get up to. And a touch amused by it. 'Instead of spending the night in contemplation, they tried to sneak mice into a sister's bed – Elaida a'Roihan – and were caught. I doubt any other women have been raised Aes Sedai while still too tender to sit from their last visit to the Mistress of Novices. Once the Three Oaths tightened on them, they needed cushions a week.'

Moiraine kept her face smooth, kept her hands from knotting into fists, but she could do nothing about burning cheeks. That ruefully amused frown, as if she were still Accepted. She needed seasoning, did she? Well, perhaps she did, some, but still. And spreading out all these intimacies!

'I think you know all of me that you need to know,' she told Cadsuane stiffly. How close she and Siuan had been was no one's business but theirs. And their punishments, *details* of their punishments. Elaida had been hateful, always pressing, demanding perfection whenever she visited the Tower. 'If you are quite satisfied, I must pack my things. I am departing for Chachin.'

She swallowed a groan before it could form. She still let her tongue go too free when her temper was up. If Merean or Larelle was part of the search, they must have at least part of the list in her little book. Including Jurine Najima here, the Lady Ines Demain in Chachin, and Avene Sahera, who lived in 'a village on the high road between Chachin and Canluum'. To strengthen suspicion, all she need do now was say she intended to spend time in Arafel and Shienar next.

Cadsuane smiled, not at all pleasantly. 'You'll leave when I say, child. Be silent till you're spoken to. That pitcher should hold spiced wine. Pour for us.'

Moiraine quivered. Child! She was no longer a novice. The woman could not order her coming and going. Or her tongue. But she did not protest. She walked to the hearth – stalked, really – and picked up the long-necked silver pitcher.

'You seem very interested in this young woman, Cadsuane,' Merean said, turning slightly to watch Moiraine pour. 'Is there something about her we should know?'

Larelle's smile held a touch of mockery. Only a touch, with Cadsuane. 'Has someone Foretold she'll be Amyrlin one day? I can't say that I see it in her, but then, I don't have the Foretelling.'

'I might live another thirty years,' Cadsuane said, putting

out a hand for the cup Moiraine offered, 'or only three. Who can say?'

Moiraine's eyes went wide, and she slopped hot wine over her own wrist. Merean gasped, and Larelle looked as though she had been struck in the forehead with a stone. Any Aes Sedai would spit on the table before referring to another sister's age or her own. Except that Cadsuane was not any Aes Sedai.

'A little more care with the other cups,' she said, unperturbed by all the gaping. 'Child?' Moiraine returned to the hearth still staring, and Cadsuane went on, 'Meilyn is considerably older. When she and I are gone, that leaves Kerene the strongest.' Larelle flinched. 'Am I disturbing you?' Cadsuane's solicitous tone could not have been more false, and she did not wait for an answer. 'Holding our silence about age doesn't keep people from knowing we live longer than they. Phaaw! From Kerene, it's a sharp drop to the next five. Five once this child and the Sanche girl reach their potential. And one of those is as old as I am and in retirement to boot.'

'Is there some point to this?' Merean asked, sounding a little sick. Larelle pressed her hands against her middle, her face grey. They barely glanced at the wine Moiraine offered before gesturing it away, and she kept the cup, though she did not think she could swallow a mouthful.

Cadsuane scowled, a fearsome sight. 'No one has come to the Tower in a thousand years who could match me. No one to match Meilyn or Kerene in almost six hundred. A thousand years ago, there would have been fifty sisters or more who stood higher than this child. In another hundred years, though, she'll stand in the first rank. Oh, someone stronger may be found in that time, but there won't be fifty, and there may be none. We dwindle.'

'I don't understand,' Larelle said sharply. She seemed to have gathered herself, and to be angry for her previous weakness. 'We are all aware of the problem, but what does Moiraine have to do with it? Do you think she can somehow make more girls come to the Tower, girls with stronger potential?' Her snort said what she thought of that.

'I would regret her being wasted before she knows up from down. The Tower can't afford to lose her out of her own ignorance. Look at her. A pretty little doll of a Cairhien noble.' Cadsuane put a finger under Moiraine's chin, tilting it up. 'Before you find a Warder like that, child, a brigand who wants to see what's in your purse will put an arrow through your heart. A footpad who'd faint at the sight of a sister in her sleep will crack your head, and you'll wake at the back of an alley minus your gold and maybe more. I suspect you'll want to take as much care choosing your first man as you do your first Warder.'

Moiraine jerked back, spluttered with indignation. First her and Siuan, now this. There were things one talked about, and things one did not!

Cadsuane ignored her outrage. Calmly sipping her wine, she turned back to the others. 'Until she does find a Warder to guard her back, it might be best to protect her from her own enthusiasm. You two are going to Chachin, I believe. She'll travel with you, then. I expect you not to let her out of your sight.'

Moiraine found her tongue, but her protests did as much good as her indignation had. Merean and Larelle objected, too, just as vociferously. Aes Sedai did not need 'looking after', no matter how new. They had interests of their own to look after. They did not make clear what those were – few sisters would have – but they plainly wanted no company. Cadsuane paid no attention to anything she did not want to hear, assumed they would do as she wished, pressed wherever they offered an opening. Soon the pair were twisting on their chairs and reduced to saying that they had only encountered each other the day before and were not sure they would be travelling on together. In any event, both meant to spend two or three days in Canluum, while Moiraine wanted to leave today.

'The child will stay until you leave,' Cadsuane said briskly. 'Good; that's done, then. I'm sure you two want to see to whatever brought you to Canluum. I won't keep you.'

Larelle shifted her shawl irritably at the abrupt dismissal, then stalked out muttering that Moiraine would regret it if she got underfoot or slowed her reaching Chachin. Merean took it better, even saying she would look after Moiraine like a daughter, though her smile hardly looked pleased.

When they were gone, Moiraine stared at Cadsuane incredulously. She had never seen anything like it. Except an avalanche, once. The thing to do now was keep silent until she had a chance to leave without Cadsuane or the others seeing. Much the wisest thing. 'I agreed to nothing,' she said coolly. Very coolly. 'What if I have affairs in Chachin that will not wait? What if I do not choose to wait here two or three days?' Perhaps she did need to learn to school her tongue a little more.

Cadsuane had been looking thoughtfully at the door that had closed behind Merean and Larelle, but she turned a piercing gaze on Moiraine. 'You've worn the shawl five months, and you have affairs that cannot wait? Phaaw! You still haven't learned the first real lesson, that the shawl means you are ready to truly begin learning. The second lesson is caution. I know very well how hard that is to find when you're young and have *saidar* at your fingertips and the world at your feet. As you think.' Moiraine tried to fit a word in, but she might as well have stood in front of that avalanche. 'You will take great risks in your life, if you live long enough. You already take more than you know. Heed carefully what I say. And do as I say. I will check your bed tonight, and if you are not in it, I will find you and make you weep as you did for those mice. You can dry your tears afterwards on that shawl you believe makes you invincible. It does not.'

Staring as the door closed behind Cadsuane, Moiraine suddenly realized she still held the cup of wine and gulped it dry. The woman was . . . formidable. Custom forbade physical violence against another sister, but Cadsuane had not sidestepped a hair in her threat. She had said it right out, so by the Three Oaths she meant it exactly. Incredible. Was it happenstance that she had mentioned Meilyn Arganya and Kerene Nagashi? They were two of Tamra's searchers. *Could* Cadsuane be another? Either way, she had very neatly cut Moiraine out of the hunt for the next week or more. If she actually went with Merean and Larelle, at least. But why only a week? If the woman was part of the search . . . If Cadsuane knew about her and Siuan . . . If

. . . Standing there fiddling with an empty wine-cup was getting her nowhere. She snatched up her cloak.

A number of people looked around at her when she came out into the common room, some with sympathy in their eyes. Doubtless they were imagining what it must be like to be the focus of attention for three Aes Sedai, and they could not imagine any good in it. There was no commiseration on any sister's face. Felaana wore a pleased smile; she probably thought the Lady Alys's name as good as written in the novice book. Cadsuane was nowhere in sight, nor the other two.

Picking her way through the tables, Moiraine felt shaken. There were too many questions, and not an answer to be found. She wished Siuan was there; Siuan was very good at puzzles, and nothing shook her.

A young woman looked in at the door from the street, then jerked out of sight, and Moiraine missed a step. Wish for something hard enough, and you could think you saw it. The woman peeked in again, the hood of her cloak fallen atop the bundle on her back, and it really was Siuan, sturdy and handsome, in a plain blue dress that showed signs of hard travel. This time she saw Moiraine, but instead of rushing to greet her, Siuan nodded up the street and vanished again.

Heart climbing into her throat, Moiraine swept her cloak around her and went out. Down the street, Siuan was slipping through the traffic, glancing back at every third step. Moiraine followed quickly, worry growing.

Siuan was supposed to be six hundred miles away in Tar Valon, working for Cetalia Delarme, who ran the Blue Ajah's network of eyes-and-ears. She had let that secret slip while bemoaning her fate. The whole time they were novice and Accepted together Siuan had talked of getting out into the world, seeing the world, but Cetalia had taken her aside the day they received the shawl, and by that evening Siuan was sorting reports from men and women scattered through the nations. She had a mind that saw patterns others missed. Cetalia equalled Merean in the Power, and it would be another three or four years before Siuan gained enough strength to tell Cetalia she was leaving the job. There would be snow at Sunday before Cetalia let her go short of that. And the only other possibility for her being in Canluum . . . Moiraine groaned, and when a big-eared fellow selling pins from a tray gave her a concerned look, she glared so hard that he started back.

It would be just like Sierin to send Siuan to bring her back, so their worry could feed on each other during the long ride. Sierin was a hard woman, without an ounce of mercy. An Amyrlin was supposed to grant indulgences and relief from penances on the day she was raised; Sierin had ordered two sisters birched and exiled three from the Tower for a year. She might well have told Siuan the penance she intended to impose. Moiraine shivered. Likely, Sierin would manage to combine Labour, Deprivation, Mortification of the Flesh, *and* Mortification of the Spirit.

A hundred paces from the inn, Siuan looked back once more, paused till she was sure that Moiraine saw her, then darted into an alley. Moiraine quickened her stride and followed.

Her friend was pacing beneath the still-unlit oil-lamps that lined even this narrow, dusty passage. Nothing frightened Siuan Sanche, a fisherman's daughter from the toughest quarter in Tear, but fear glittered in those sharp blue eyes now. Moiraine opened her mouth to confirm her own fears about Sierin, but the taller woman spoke first.

'Tell me you've found him, Moiraine. Tell me the Najima boy's the one, and we can hand him to the Tower with a hundred sisters watching, and it's done.'

A hundred sisters? 'No, Siuan.' This did not sound like Sierin. 'What is the matter?'

Siuan began to weep. Siuan, who had a lion's heart and had never let a tear fall until after they left Merean's study. Throwing her arms around Moiraine, she squeezed hard. She was trembling. 'They're all dead,' she mumbled. 'Aisha and Kerene, Valera and Ludice and Meilyn. They say Aisha and her Warder were killed by bandits in Murandy. Kerene supposedly fell off a ship in the Alguenya during a storm and drowned. And Meilyn . . . Meilyn . . .'

Moiraine hugged her, making soothing sounds. And staring

past Siuan's shoulder in consternation. They had learned five of the women Tamra had selected, and all five were dead. 'Meilyn was . . . hardly young,' she said slowly. She was not sure she could have said it at all if Cadsuane had not spoken so openly. Siuan gave a startled jerk, and she made herself go on. 'Neither were any of the others, even Kerene.' Close to two hundred was not young even for Aes Sedai. 'And accidents do happen. Bandits. Storms.' She was having a hard time making herself believe. *All* of them?

Siuan pushed herself away. 'You don't understand. Meilyn!' Grimacing, she scrubbed at her eyes. 'Fish guts! I'm not making this clear. Get hold of yourself, you bloody fool!' That last was growled to herself. Merean and others had gone to a great deal of trouble to clean up Siuan's language, but she had reverted the moment the shawl was on her shoulders. Guiding Moiraine to an upended cask with no bung, she sat her down. 'You won't want to be standing when you hear what I have to say. For that matter, I bloody well don't want to be standing myself.'

Dragging a crate with broken slats from further up the alley, she settled on it, fussing with her skirts, peering towards the street, muttering about people looking in as they passed. Her reluctance did little to soothe Moiraine's stomach. It seemed to do little for Siuan's, either. When she started up again, she kept pausing to swallow, like a woman who wanted to sick up.

'Meilyn returned to the Tower almost a month ago. I don't know why. She didn't say where she had been, or where she was going, but she only meant to stay a few nights. I . . . I'd heard about Kerene the morning Meilyn came, and the others before that. So I decided to speak to her. Don't look at me that way! I know how to be cautious!' Cautious was a word Moiraine had never thought to apply to Siuan. 'Anyway, I sneaked into her rooms and hid under the bed. So the servants wouldn't see me when they turned down her sheets.' Siuan grunted sourly. 'I fell asleep under there. Sunrise woke me, and her bed hadn't been slept in. So I sneaked out and went down to the second sitting of breakfast. And while I was spooning my porridge, Chesmal Emry came in to . . . She . . . She announced that Meilyn had been found in her bed, that she'd died during the night.' She finished in a rush and sagged, staring at Moiraine.

Moiraine was very glad to be sitting. Her knees would not have supported a feather. She had grown up amid *Daes Dae'mar*, the scheming and plotting that dominated Cairhienin life, the shades of meaning in every word, every action. There was too much here for shadings. Murder had been done. 'The Red Ajah?' she suggested finally. A Red might kill a sister she thought intended to protect a man who could channel.

Siuan snorted. 'Meilyn didn't have a mark on her, and Chesmal would have detected poison, or smothering, or . . . That means the Power, Moiraine. Could even a Red do that?' Her voice was fierce, but she pulled the bundle around from her back, clutching it on her lap. She seemed to be hiding behind it. Still, there was less fear on her face than anger, now. 'Think, Moiraine. Tamra supposedly died in her sleep, too. Only we know Meilyn didn't, no matter where she was found. First Tamra, then the others started dying. The only thing that makes sense is that someone noticed her calling sisters in and wanted to know why badly enough that they bloody risked putting the Amyrlin Seat herself to the question. They had to have something to hide to do that, something they'd risk anything to keep hidden. They killed her to hide it, to hide what they'd done, and then they set out to kill the rest. Which means they don't want the boy found, not alive. They don't want the Dragon Reborn at the Last Battle. Any other way to look at it is tossing the slop bucket into the wind and hoping for the best.'

Unconsciously, Moiraine peered towards the mouth of the alley. A few people walking by glanced in, but none more than once. No one paused at seeing them seated there. Some things were easier to speak of when you were not too specific. 'The Amyrlin' had been put to the question; 'she' had been killed. Not Tamra, not a name that brought up the familiar, determined face. 'Someone' had murdered her. 'They' did not want the Dragon Reborn found. Murder with the Power certainly violated the Three Oaths, even for . . . for those Moiraine did not want to name any more than Siuan did.

Forcing her face to smoothness, forcing her voice to calm, she forced the words out. 'The Black Ajah.' Siuan flinched, then nodded, glowering.

Any sister grew angry at the suggestion there was a secret Ajah hidden inside the others, dedicated to the Dark One. Most sisters refused to listen. The White Tower had stood for the Light for over three thousand years. But some sisters did not deny the Black straight out. Some believed. Very few would admit it even to another sister, though. Moiraine did not want to admit it to herself.

Siuan plucked at the ties on her bundle, but she went on in a brisk voice. 'I don't think they have our names – Tamra never really thought us part of it – else I'd have had an "accident", too. Just before I left, I slipped a note with my suspicions under Sierin's door. Only, I didn't know how much to trust her. The Amyrlin Seat! I wrote with my left hand, but I was shaking so hard, no one could recognize my writing if I'd used my right. Burn my liver! Even if we knew who to trust, we have bilge water for proof.'

'Enough for me. If they know everything, all the women Tamra chose, there may be none left except us. We will have to move fast if we have a hope of finding the boy first.' Moiraine tried for a vigorous tone, too. It was gratifying that Siuan only nodded. She would not give up for all her talk of shaking, and she never considered that Moiraine might. Most gratifying. 'Perhaps they know us, and perhaps not. Perhaps they think they can leave two new sisters for last. In any case, we cannot trust anyone but ourselves.' Blood drained from her face. 'Oh, Light! I just had an encounter at the inn, Siuan.'

She tried to recall every word, every nuance, from the moment Merean first spoke. Siuan listened with a distant look, filing and sorting. 'Cadsuane could be one of Tamra's chosen,' she agreed when Moiraine finished. 'Or she could be Black Ajah.' She barely hesitated over the words. 'Maybe she's just trying to get you out of the way until she can dispose of you without rousing suspicion. The trouble is, any of them could be either.' Leaning across her bundle, she touched Moiraine's knee. 'Can you bring your horse from the stable without being seen? I have a good mount, but I don't know if she can carry both of us. We should be hours from here before they know we're gone.'

Moiraine smiled in spite of herself. She very much doubted the good mount. Her friend's eye for horseflesh was no better than her seat in the saddle, and sometimes Siuan fell off nearly before the animal moved. The ride north must have been agony. And full of fear. 'No one knows you are here at all, Siuan,' she said. 'Best if it stays so. You have your book? Good. If I remain until morning, I will have a day's start on them instead of hours. You go on to Chachin now. Take some of my coin.' By the state of Siuan's dress, she had spent the last part of that trip sleeping under bushes. A fisherman's daughter had no estates to provide gold. 'Start looking for the Lady Ines, and I will catch you up there.'

It was not that easy, of course. Siuan had a stubborn streak as wide as the Erinin. Quite aside from that, as novice and Accepted it had been the fisherman's daughter who led, not the king's niece, something that had startled Moiraine at first, until she realized that it felt natural somehow. Siuan had been born to lead.

'I have enough for my needs,' she grumbled, but Moiraine insisted on handing her half the coins in her purse, and when Moiraine reminded her of their pledge during their first months in the Tower, that what one owned belonged to the other as well, she muttered, 'We swore we'd find beautiful young princes to bond, too, and marry them besides. Girls say all sort of silly things. You watch after yourself, now. You leave me alone in this, and I'll wring your neck.'

Embracing to say goodbye, Moiraine found it hard to let go. An hour ago, her worries had been whether she might be stuck away on a farm, or at worse birched. Now . . . The Black Ajah. She wanted to empty her stomach. If only she had Siuan's courage. Watching Siuan slip down the alley adjusting that bundle on her back again, Moiraine wished she was Green. Only Greens bonded more than one Warder, and she would have liked at least three or four to guard her back right then.

Walking back up the street, she could not help looking at everyone she passed, man or woman. If the Black Ajah – her stomach twisted every time she thought that name – if they were involved, then ordinary Darkfriends were, too. No one denied that some misguided people believed the Dark One would give them immortality, people who would kill and do every sort of evil to gain that hoped-for reward. And if any sister could be Black Ajah, anyone she met could be a Darkfriend. She hoped Siuan remembered that.

As she approached The Gates of Heaven, a sister appeared in the inn's doorway. Part of a sister, at least; all she could see was an arm with a fringed shawl over it. A tall man who had just come out, his hair in two belled braids, turned back to speak for a moment, but the shawl-draped arm gestured peremptorily, and he strode past Moiraine wearing a scowl. She would not have thought twice of it if not for thinking about the Black Ajah and Darkfriends. The Light knew, Aes Sedai did speak to men, and some did more than speak. She had been thinking of Darkfriends, though. And Black sisters. If only she could have made out the colour of that fringe. She hurried the last thirty-odd paces frowning.

Merean and Larelle were seated together by themselves near the door, both still wearing their shawls. Few sisters did that except for ceremony, or for show. Both women were watching Cadsuane go into that private sitting room, followed by a pair of grey-haired men who looked as hard as last year's oak. She still wore her shawl, too, with the white Flame of Tar Valon bright on her back. It could have been any of them. Cadsuane might be looking for another Warder; Greens always seemed to be looking. Moiraine did not know whether Merean and Larelle had Warders. The fellow's scowl might have been for hearing he did not measure up. There were a hundred possible explanations, and she put the man out of her head. The sure dangers were real enough without inventing more.

Before she was three steps into the common room, Master Helvin bustled up in a green-striped apron, a bald man nearly as wide as he was tall, and handed her a new irritation. With three more Aes Sedai stopping at his inn, he need to shuffle the beds, as he put it. The Lady Alys would not mind sharing hers, certainly, under the circumstances. Mistress Palan was a most pleasant woman.

Haesel Palan was a rug-merchant from Murandy with the lilt of Lugard in her voice. Moiraine heard more of it than she wanted from the moment she stepped into the small room that had been hers alone. Her clothes had been moved from the wardrobe to pegs on the wall, her comb and brush displaced from the washstand for Mistress Palan's. The plump woman might have been diffident with 'Lady Alys', but not with a wilder who everybody said was off in the morning to become a novice in the White Tower. She lectured Moiraine on the duties of a novice, all of it wrong. She followed Moiraine down to dinner and gathered other traders of her acquaintance at the table, every woman of them eager to share what she knew of the White Tower. Which was nothing at all. They shared it in great detail, though. Moiraine thought to escape by retiring early, but Mistress Palan appeared almost as soon as she had her dress off and talked until she dropped off to sleep.

It was not an easy night. The bed was narrow, the woman's elbows sharp and her feet icy despite thick blankets that trapped the warmth of the small stove under the bed. The rainstorm that had threatened all day broke, wind and thunder rattling the shutters for hours. Moiraine doubted she could have slept in any event. Darkfriends and the Black Ajah danced in her head. She saw Tamra being dragged from her sleep, dragged away to somewhere secret and tortured by women wielding the Power. Sometimes the women wore Merean's face, and Larelle's, and Cadsuane's, and every sister's she had ever seen. Sometimes Tamra's face became her own.

When the door creaked slowly open in the dark hours of morning, Moiraine embraced the Source in a flash. *Saidar* filled her to the point where the sweetness and joy came close to pain. Not as much of the Power as she would be able to handle in another year, much less five, yet a hair more would burn the ability out of her now, or kill her. One was as bad as the other, but she wanted to draw more, and not just because the Power always made you want more.

Cadsuane put her head in. Moiraine had forgotten her promise, her threat. Cadsuane saw the glow, of course, could feel how much she held. 'Fool girl,' was all the woman said before leaving.

Moiraine counted to one hundred slowly, then swung her feet out from under the covers. Now was as good a time as any. Mistress Palan heaved on to her side and began to snore. Channelling Fire, Moiraine lit one of the lamps and dressed hurriedly. A riding dress, this time. Reluctantly she decided to abandon her saddlebags along with everything else she had to leave behind. Anyone who saw her moving about might not think too much of it even at this time of the morning, but not if she had saddlebags over her shoulder. All she took was what she could fit into the pockets sewn inside her cloak, little more than some spare stockings and a clean shift. Mistress Palan was still snoring as she closed the door behind her.

The skinny groom on night duty was startled to see her with the sky just beginning to turn grey, but a silver penny had him knuckling his forehead and saddling her bay mare. She regretted leaving her packhorse behind, but not even a fool noble – she heard the fellow mutter that – would take a pack animal for a morning jaunt. Climbing into Arrow's high-cantled saddle, she gave the man a cool smile instead of the second penny he would have received without the comment, and rode slowly out into damp, empty streets. Just out for a ride, however early. It looked to be a good day. The sky looked rained out, for one thing, and there was little wind.

The lamps were still lit all along the streets and alleys, leaving no more than the palest shadow anywhere, yet the only people to be seen were the Night Watch's patrols and the Lamplighters, heavily armed as they made their rounds to make sure no lamp went out. A wonder that people could live so close to the Blight that a Myrddraal could step out of any dark shadow. No one went out in the night, though. Not in the Borderlands.

Which was why she was surprised to see she was not the first to reach the western gates. Slowing Arrow, she stayed well back from the three very large men waiting with a packhorse behind their mounts. Their attention was all on the barred gates, with now and again a word shared with the gate guards. They barely glanced at her. The lamps here showed their faces clearly. A grizzled old man and a hard-faced young one wearing braided leather cords tied around their heads. Malkieri? She thought that was what that meant. The third was an Arafellin with belled braids. The same fellow she had seen leaving The Gates of Heaven.

By the time the bright sliver of sunrise allowed the gates to be swung open, several merchants' trains had lined up to depart. The three men were first through, but Moiraine let a train of a dozen wagons behind eight-horse teams rumble ahead of her before she followed across the bridge and on to the road through the hills. She kept the three in sight, though. They were heading in the same direction so far, after all.

They moved quickly, good riders who barely shifted a rein, but a trot suited her. The more distance she put between herself and Cadsuane, the better. The merchants' wagons fell back out of sight long before they reached the first village near midday, a small cluster of tile-roofed stone houses around a tiny inn on a forested hill slope. Moiraine paused long enough to ask whether anyone knew a woman named Avene Sahera. The answer was no, and she galloped on, not slowing until the three men appeared on the hard-packed road ahead, their horses still in that ground-eating pace. Maybe they knew nothing more than the name of the sister the Arafellin had spoken to, but anything at all she learned about Cadsuane or the other two would be to the good.

She formulated several plans for approaching them, and discarded each. Three men on a deserted forest road could well decide a young woman alone was a good opportunity, especially if they were what she feared. Handling them presented no problem, if it came to it, but she wanted to avoid that. Woods gave way to scattered farms, and farms faded to more woods. A red-crested eagle soared overhead and became a shape against the descending sun.

As her shadow stretched out behind her, she decided to forget the men and find a place to sleep. With luck she might see more farms soon, and if a little silver did not bring a bed, a hayloft would have to do.

Ahead, the three men stopped, conferring for a moment, then one took the packhorse and turned aside into the forest. The others dug in their heels and galloped on.

Moiraine stared after them. The Arafellin was one of the pair rushing off, but if they were travelling together, maybe he had mentioned meeting an Aes Sedai to his companion. And one man would certainly be less trouble than three, if she was careful. Riding to where rider and packhorse had vanished, she dismounted.

Tracking was a thing most ladies left to their huntsmen, but she had taken an interest in the years when climbing trees and getting dirty had seemed equal fun. Broken twigs and kicked winter-fall leaves left a trail a child could have followed. A hundred paces or so into the forest, she spotted a pond in a hollow through the trees. The fellow had already unsaddled and hobbled his bay – a fine-looking animal – and was setting the packsaddle on the ground. It was the younger of the Malkieri. He looked even larger, this close. Unbuckling his swordbelt, he sat down facing the pond, laid sword and belt beside him, and put his hands on his knees. He seemed to be staring off across the water, still glittering through the late afternoon shadows. He did not move a muscle.

Moiraine considered. Plainly he had been left to make camp. The others would come back. A question or two would not take long, though. And if he was unnerved a little – say at finding a woman suddenly standing right behind him – he might answer before he thought. Tying Arrow's reins to a low branch, she gathered her cloak and skirts and moved forward as silently as possible. A low hummock stood humped up behind him, and she stepped up on to that. Added height could help. He was a very tall man. And it might help if he found her with her beltknife in one hand and his sword in the other. Channelling, she whisked the scabbarded blade from his side. Every little bit of shock she could manage for him –

He moved faster than thought. Her grasp closed on the scabbard, and he uncoiled, whirling, one hand clutching the scabbard between hers, the other seizing the front of her dress. Before she could think to channel, she was flying through the air. She had just time to see the pond coming up at her, just time to shout something, she did not know what, and then she struck the surface flat, driving all the wind out of her, struck with a great splash and sank. The water was *freezing*! *Saidar* fled in her shock.

Floundering to her feet, she stood up to her waist in the icy water, coughing, wet hair clinging to her face, sodden cloak dragging at her shoulders. Furiously she twisted around to confront her attacker, furiously embraced the Source once more. The test for the shawl required channelling with absolute calm under great stress, and far worse than this had been done to her then. She turned, prepared to knock him down and drub him till he squealed!

He stood shaking his head and frowning at the spot where she had stood, a long stride from where he had sat. When he deigned to notice her, he came to the edge of the pond and bent to stretch out a hand. 'Unwise to try separating a man from his sword,' he said, and after a glance at the coloured slashes on her dress, added, 'My Lady.' Hardly an apology. His startlingly blue eyes did not quite meet hers. If he was hiding mirth . . . !

Muttering under her breath, she splashed awkwardly to where she could take his outstretched hand in both of hers . . . and heaved with all of her might. Ignoring icy water tickling down your ribs was not easy, and if she was wet, so would he be, and without any need to use the –

He straightened, raised his arm, and she came out of the water dangling from his hand. In consternation she stared at him until her feet touched the ground and he backed away.

'I'll start a fire and hang up blankets so you can dry yourself,' he murmured, still not meeting her gaze.

He was as good as his word, and by the time the other men

appeared, she was standing beside a small fire surrounded by blankets dug from his packsaddles and hung from branches. She had no need of the fire for drying, of course, or the privacy. The proper weave of Water had taken every drop from her hair and clothes while she stayed in them. As well he did not see that, though. And she did appreciate the flames' warmth. Anyway, she had to stay inside the blankets long enough for the man to think she had used the fire as he intended. She very definitely held on to *saidar*.

The other men arrived, full of questions about whether 'she' had followed into the woods. They had known? Men watched for bandits in these times, but they had noticed a lone woman and decided she was following them? It seemed suspicious.

'A Cairhienin, Lan? I suppose you've seen a Cairhienin in her skin, but I never have.' That certainly caught her ear, and with the Power filling her, so did another sound. Steel whispering on leather. A sword leaving its sheath. Preparing several weaves that would stop the lot of them in their tracks, she made a crack in the blankets to peek out.

To her surprise, the man who had dunked her – Lan? – stood with his back to her blankets. He was the one with sword in hand. The Arafellin, facing him, looked surprised. 'You remember the sight of the Thousand Lakes, Ryne,' Lan said coldly. 'Does a woman need protection from your eyes?'

For a moment, she thought Ryne was going to draw despite the blade already in Lan's hand, but the older man, a much battered, greying fellow though as tall as the others, calmed matters, took the other two a little distance away with talk of some game called 'sevens'. A strange game it seemed to be. Lan and Ryne sat crosslegged facing one another, their swords sheathed, then without warning drew, each blade flashing towards the other man's throat, stopping just short of flesh. The older man pointed to Ryne, they sheathed swords, and then did it again. For as long as she watched, that was how it went. Perhaps Ryne had not been as over-confident as he seemed.

Waiting inside the blankets, she tried to recall what she had been taught of Malkier. Not a great deal, except as history. Ryne remembered the Thousand Lakes, so he must be Malkieri, too. There had been something about distressed women. Now that she was with them, she might as well stay until she learned what she could.

When she came out from behind the blankets, she was ready. 'I claim the right of a woman alone,' she told them formally. 'I travel to Chachin, and I ask the shelter of your swords.' She also pressed a fat silver coin into each man's hand. She was not really sure about this ridiculous 'woman alone' business, but silver caught most men's attention. 'And two more each, paid in Chachin.'

The reactions were not what she expected. Ryne glared at the coin as he turned it over in his fingers. Lan looked at his without expression and tucked it into his coat pocket with a grunt. She had given them some of her last Tar Valon marks, she realized, but Tar Valon coins could be found anywhere, along with those of every other land.

Bukama, the grizzled man, bowed with his left hand on his knee. 'Honour to serve, my Lady,' he said. 'To Chachin, my life above yours.' His eyes were also blue, and they, too, would not quite meet hers. She hoped he did not turn out to be a Darkfriend.

Learning anything proved to be difficult. Impossible. First the men were busy setting up camp, tending the horses, making a larger fire. They did not seem eager to face a new spring night without that. Bukama and Lan barely said a word over a dinner of flatbread and dried meat that she tried not to wolf down. Her stomach remembered all too well that she had not eaten that day. Ryne talked and was quite charming, really, with a dimple in his cheek when he smiled, and a sparkle in his blue eyes, but he gave no opening for her to mention The Gates of Heaven or Aes Sedai. When she finally enquired why he was going to Chachin, his face turned sad.

'Every man has to die somewhere,' he said softly, and went off to make up his blankets.

Lan took the first watch, sitting crosslegged not far from Ryne, and when Bukama doused the fire and rolled himself up in his blankets near Lan, she wove a ward of Spirit around each man. Flows of Spirit she could hold on to sleeping, and if any of them moved in the night, the ward would wake her without alerting them. It meant waking every time they changed guard, but there was nothing for it. Her own blankets lay well away from the men, and as she was lying down, Bukama murmured something she could not catch. She heard Lan's reply plainly enough.

'I'd sooner trust an Aes Sedai, Bukama. Go to sleep.'

All the anger she had tamped down flared up. The man threw her into an icy pond, he did not apologize, he . . . ! She channelled, Air and Water weaving with a touch of Earth. A thick cylinder of water rose from the surface of the pond, stretching up and up in the moonlight, arching over. Crashing down on the fool who was so free with his tongue!

Bukama and Ryne bounded to their feet with oaths, but she continued the torrent for a count of ten before letting it end. Freed water splashed down across the campsite. She expected to see a sodden, half-frozen man ready to learn proper respect. He *was* dripping wet, a few small fish flopping around his feet. He was standing on his feet. With his sword out.

'Shadowspawn?' Ryne said in a disbelieving tone, and atop him, Lan said, 'Maybe! Guard the woman, Ryne! Bukama, take west; I'll take east!'

'Not Shadowspawn!' Moiraine snapped, stopping them in their tracks. They stared at her. She wished she could see their expressions better in the moonshadows, but those cloud-shifting shadows aided her, too, cloaking her in mystery. With an effort she gave her voice every bit of cool Aes Sedai serenity she could muster. 'It is unwise to show anything except respect to an Aes Sedai, Master Lan.'

'Aes Sedai?' Ryne whispered. Despite the dim light, the awe on his face was clear. Or maybe it was fear.

No one else made a sound, except for Bukama's grumbles as he shifted his bed away from the mud. Ryne spent a long time moving his blankets in silence, giving her small bows whenever she glanced his way. Lan made no attempt to dry off. He started to choose a new spot for his watch, then stopped and sat back where he had been, in the mud and water. She might have thought it a gesture of humility, only he glanced at her, very nearly meeting her eyes this time. If that was humility, kings were the most humble men on earth.

She wove her wards around them again, of course. If anything, revealing herself only made it more necessary. She did not go to sleep for quite a while, though. She had a great deal to think about. For one thing, none of the men had asked *why* she was following them. The man had been on his *feet*! When she drifted off, she was thinking of Ryne, strangely. A pity if he was afraid of her, now. He was charming, and she did not mind a man wanting to see her unclothed, only his telling others about it.

Lan knew the ride to Chachin would be one he would rather forget, and it met his expectations. It stormed twice, freezing rain mixed with ice, and that was the least. Bukama was angry that he refused to make proper pledge to the diminutive woman who claimed to be Aes Sedai, but Bukama knew the reasons and did not press. He only grumbled whenever he thought Lan could hear; Aes Sedai or not, a decent man followed certain forms. As if he did not share Lan's reasons. Ryne twitched and peered wide-eyed at her, fetched and trotted and offered up compliments on 'skin of snowy silk' and the 'deep, dark pools of her eyes' like a courtier on a leash. He seemed unable to decide between besotted and terrified, and he let her see both. That would have been bad enough, but Ryne was right; Lan had seen a Cairhienin in her skin, more than one, and they had all tried to mesh him in a scheme, or two, or three. Over one particularly memorable ten days in the south of Cairhien, he had almost been killed six times and nearly married twice. A Cairhienin *and* an Aes Sedai? There could be no worse combination.

This Alys – she told them to call her Alys, which he doubted as much as the Great Serpent ring she produced, especially after she tucked it back into her beltpouch and said no one must know she was Aes Sedai – this 'Alys' had a temper. Normally, he did not mind that, cold or hot, in man or woman. Hers was ice. That first night he had sat in the wet to let her know he would accept what she had done. If they were to travel together, better to end it with honours even, as she must see it. Except that she did not.

They rode hard, never stopping long in a village and sleeping under the stars most nights, since no one had the coin for inns, not for four people with horses. He slept when he could. The second night she remained awake till dawn and made sure he did as well, with sharp flicks of an invisible switch whenever he nodded off. The third night, sand somehow got inside his clothes and boots, a thick coating of it. He had shaken out what he could and ridden covered in grit the next day. The fourth night . . . He could not understand how she managed to make ants crawl into his smallclothes, or make them all bite at once. It had been her doing for sure. She was standing over him when his eyes shot open, and she seemed surprised that he did not cry out. Clearly, she wanted some response, some reaction, but he could not see what. Surely not the pledge of protection. Bukama's sufficed, and besides, she had given them money. The woman did not know insult when she offered it.

When they had first seen her behind them, outpacing the merchant trains and the shield of their guards, Bukama had offered a reason for a woman alone to follow three men. If six swordsmen could not kill a man in daylight, perhaps one woman could in darkness. Bukama had not mentioned Edeyn, of course. In truth, it plainly could not be that, or he would be dead instead of uncomfortable, yet Alys herself never made any explanation, however much Bukama waited for one. Edeyn might set a woman to watch him, thinking he would be less on his guard. So Lan watched her. But the only suspicious thing he saw, if it could be called that, was that she asked questions whenever they came to a village, always away from him and the others, and she went silent if they came too near. Two days from Canluum, she stopped asking, though. Perhaps she had found an answer in the market village called Ravinda, but if so, she did not seem happy about it. That night she discovered a patch of blisterleaf near their campsite, and to his shame, he almost lost his temper.

If Canluum was a city of hills, Chachin was a city of mountains. The three highest rose almost a mile even with their peaks sheared off short, and all glittered in the sun with colourful glazed tile roofs and tile-covered palaces. Atop the tallest of those the Aesdaishar Palace shone brighter than any other in red and green, the prancing Red Horse flying above its largest dome. Three towered ringwalls surrounded the city, as did a deep dry moat a hundred paces wide spanned by two dozen bridges, each with a fortress hulking at its mouth. The traffic was too great here, and the Blight too far away, for the guards with the Red Horse on their chests to be so diligent as in Canluum, but crossing the Bridge of Sunrise amid tides of wagons and people flowing both ways still took some little while. Once inside, Lan wasted no time drawing rein.

'We are within the walls of Chachin,' he told the woman. 'The pledge has been kept. Keep your coin,' he added coldly when she reached for her purse.

Ryne immediately started going on about giving offence to Aes Sedai and offering her smiling apologies, while Bukama rumbled about men with the manners of pigs. The woman herself gazed at Lan with so little expression, she might even have been what she claimed. A dangerous claim if untrue. And if true . . .

Whirling Cat Dancer, he galloped up the street scattering people afoot and some mounted. Bukama and Ryne caught him up before he was halfway up the mountain to the Aesdaishar. If Edeyn was in Chachin, she would be there. Wisely, Bukama and Ryne held their silence.

The palace filled the flattened mountaintop completely, an immense, shining structure of domes and high balconies covering fifty hides, a small city to itself. The great bronze gates, worked with the Red Horse, stood open beneath a red-tiled arch, and once Lan identified himself – as Lan Mandragoran, not al'Lan – the guards' stiffness turned to smiling bows. Servants in red-and-green came running to take the horses and show each man to rooms befitting his station. Bukama and Ryne each received a small room above one of the barracks. Lan was given three rooms draped in silk tapestries, with a bedchamber that overlooked one of the palace gardens, two square-faced serving women to tend him, and a lanky young fellow to run errands.

A little careful questioning of the servants brought answers. Queen Ethenielle was making a progress through the heartland, but Brys, the Prince Consort, was in residence. As was the Lady Edeyn Arrel. The women smiled when they said that; they had known what he wanted from the first.

He washed himself, but let the women dress him. Just because they were servants was no reason to insult them. He had one white silk shirt that did not show too much wear, and a good black silk coat embroidered along the sleeves with golden bloodroses among their hooked thorns. Bloodroses for loss and remembrance. Then he set the women outside to guard his door and sat to wait. His meetings with Edeyn must be public, with as many people around as possible.

A summons came from her, to her chambers, which he ignored. Courtesy demanded he be given time to rest from his journey, yet it seemed a very long time before the invitation to join Brys came, brought by the *shatayan*. A stately, greying woman with a presence to match any queen, she had charge of all the palace servants, and it was an honour to be conducted by her personally. Outsiders needed a guide to find their way anywhere in the palace. His sword remained on the lacquered rack by the door. It would do him no good here, and would insult Brys besides, indicating he thought he needed to protect himself.

He expected a private meeting first, but the *shatayan* took him to a columned hall full of people. Soft-footed servants moved through the crowd offering spiced wine to Kandori lords and ladies in silks embroidered with House sigils, and folk in fine woollens worked with the sigils of the more important guilds. And to others, too. Lan saw men wearing the *hadori* he knew had not worn it these ten years or more. Women with hair still cut at the shoulders and higher wore the small dot of the *ki'sain* painted on their foreheads. They bowed at his appearance, and made deep curtsies, those men and women who had decided to remember Malkier.

Prince Brys was a stocky, rough-hewn man in his middle years who looked more suited to armour than his green silks, though in truth he was accustomed to either. Brys was Ethenielle's Swordbearer, the general of her armies, as well as her consort. He caught Lan's shoulders, refusing to allow him to bow.

'None of that from the man who twice saved my life in the Blight, Lan.' Brys laughed. 'Besides, your coming seems to have rubbed some of your luck off on Diryk. He fell from a balcony this morning, a good fifty feet, without breaking a bone.' He motioned his second son, a handsome dark-eyed boy of eight in a coat like his, to come forward. A large bruise marred the side of the boy's head, and he moved with the stiffness of other bruises, but he made a formal bow spoiled only somewhat by a wide grin. 'He should be at his lessons,' Brys confided, 'but he was so eager to meet you, he'd have forgotten his letters and cut himself on a sword.' Frowning, the boy protested that he would never cut himself.

Lan returned the lad's bow with equal formality, then had to put up with a deluge of questions. Yes, he had fought Aiel, in the south and on the Shienaran marches, but they were just men, if dangerous, not ten feet tall; they did veil their faces before killing, but they did not eat their dead. No, the White Tower was not as high as a mountain, though it was taller than anything made by men that Lan had ever seen, even the Stone of Tear. Given a chance, the boy would have drained him dry about the Aiel, and the wonders of the great cities in the south like Tar Valon and Far Madding. Likely, he would not have believed Chachin was as big as either of those.

'Lord Mandragoran will fill your head to your heart's content later,' Brys told the boy. 'There is someone else he must meet now. Off with you to Mistress Tuval and your books.'

Edeyn was exactly as Lan remembered. Oh, ten years older, with touches of white streaking her temples and a few fine lines at the corners of her eyes, but those large dark eyes gripped him. Her *ki'sain* was still the white of a widow, and her hair still hung in black waves below her waist. She wore a red silk gown in the Domani style, clinging and little short of sheer. She was beautiful, but even she could do nothing here.

For a moment she merely looked at him, cool and considering, when he made his bow. 'It would have been . . . easier had you come to me,' she murmured, seeming not to care whether Brys heard. And then, shockingly, she knelt gracefully and took his hands in hers. 'Beneath the Light,' she announced in a strong, clear voice, 'I, Edeyn ti Gemallen Arrel, pledge fealty to al'Lan Mandragoran, Lord of the Seven Towers, Lord of the Lakes, the true Blade of Malkier. May he sever the Shadow!' Even Brys looked startled. A moment of silence held while she kissed Lan's fingers, then cheers erupted on every side. Cries of 'The Golden Crane!' and even 'Kandor rides with Malkier!'

The sound freed him to pull his hands loose, to lift her to her feet. 'My Lady,' he began in a tight voice.

'What must be, will be,' she said, putting a hand over his lips. And then she faded back into the crowd of those who wanted to cluster around him, congratulate him, pledge fealty on the spot had he let them.

Brys rescued him, drawing him off to a long, stone-railed walk above a two-hundred-foot drop to the roofs below. It was known as a place Brys went to be private, and no one followed. Only one door let on to it, no window overlooked, and no sound from the palace intruded. 'What will you do?' the older man asked simply as they walked.

'I do not know,' Lan replied. She had won only a skirmish, but he felt stunned at the ease of it. A formidable opponent, the woman who wore part of his soul in her hair.

For the rest they spoke quietly of hunting and bandits and whether this past year's flare-up in the Blight might die down soon. Brys regretted withdrawing his army from the war against the Aiel, but there had been no alternative. They talked of the rumours about a man who could channel – every tale had him in a different place; Brys thought it another jak o'the mists and Lan agreed – and of the Aes Sedai who seemed to be everywhere, for what reason no one knew. Ethenielle had written him that two sisters had caught a woman pretending to be Aes Sedai in a village along her progression. The woman could channel, but that did her no good. The two real Aes Sedai flogged her squealing through the village, making her confess her crime to every last man and woman who lived there. Then one of the sisters carried her off to Tar Valon for her true punishment, whatever that might be. Lan found himself hoping that Alys had not lied about being Aes Sedai.

He hoped to avoid Edeyn the rest of the day, too, but when he was guided back to his rooms, she was there, waiting languorously in one of the gilded chairs. The servants were nowhere to be seen.

'You are no longer beautiful, I fear, sweetling,' she said when he came in. 'I think you may even be ugly when you are older. But I always enjoyed your eyes more than your face. And your hands.'

He stopped still gripping the doorhandle. 'My Lady, not two hours gone you swore –' She cut him off.

'And I will obey my king. But a king is not a king, alone with his *carneira*. I brought your *daori*. Bring it to me.'

Unwillingly, his eyes followed her gesture to a flat lacquered box on a small table beside the door. Lifting the hinged lid took as much effort as lifting a boulder. Coiled inside lay a long cord woven of hair. He could recall every moment of the morning after their first night, when she took him to the women's quarters of the Royal Palace in Fal Moran and let ladies and servants watch as she cut his hair at his shoulders. She even told them what it signified. The women had all been amused, making jokes as he sat at Edeyn's feet to weave the *daori* for her. Edeyn kept custom, but in her own way. The hair felt soft and supple; she must have had it rubbed with lotions every day.

Crossing the floor slowly, he knelt before her and held out his *daori* stretched between his hands. 'In token of what I owe to you, Edeyn, always and for ever.' If his voice did not hold the fervour of that first morning, surely she understood.

She did not take the cord. Instead, she studied him. 'I knew you had not been gone so long as to forget our ways,' she said finally. 'Come.'

Rising, she grasped his wrist and drew him to the windows overlooking the garden ten paces below. Two servants were spreading water from buckets, and a young woman was strolling along a slate path in a blue dress as bright as any of the early flowers that grew beneath the trees.

'My daughter, Iselle.' For a moment, pride and affection warmed Edeyn's voice. 'Do you remember her? She is seventeen, now. She hasn't chosen her *carneira*, yet,' young men were chosen by their *carneira*; young women chose theirs, 'but I think it time she married anyway.'

He vaguely recalled a child who always had servants running, the blossom of her mother's heart, but his head had been full of Edeyn, then. 'She is as beautiful as her mother, I am sure,' he said politely. He twisted the *daori* in his hands. She had too much advantage as long as he held it, all advantage, but she had to take it from him. 'Edeyn, we must talk.' She ignored that.

'Time you were married, too, sweetling. Since none of your female relatives is alive, it is up to me to arrange.'

He gasped at what she seemed to be suggesting. At first he could not believe. '*Iselle?*' he said hoarsely. '*Your* daughter?' She might keep custom in her own way, but this was scandalous. 'I'll not be reined into something so shameful, Edeyn. Not by you, or by this.' He shook the *daori* at her, but she only looked at it and smiled.

'Of course you won't be reined, sweetling. You are a man, not a boy. Yet you do keep custom,' she mused, running a finger along the cord of hair quivering between his hands. 'Perhaps we do need to talk.'

But it was to the bed that she led him.

Moiraine spent most of the day asking discreet questions at inns in the rougher parts of Chachin, where her silk dress and divided skirts drew stares from patrons and innkeepers alike. One leathery fellow wearing a permanent leer told her that his establishment was not for her and tried to escort her to a better, while a round-faced, squinting woman cackled that the evening trade would have a tender pretty like her for dinner if she did not scurry away quick, and a fatherly old man with pink cheeks and a joyous smile was all too eager for her to drink the spiced wine he prepared out of her sight. There was nothing for it but to grit her teeth and move on. That was the sort of place Siuan had liked to visit when they were allowed a rare trip into Tar Valon as Accepted, cheap and unlikely to be frequented by sisters, but none had a blue-eyed Tairen staying under any name. Cold daylight began to settle towards yet another icy night.

She was walking Arrow through lengthening shadows, eyeing darknesses that moved suspiciously in an alley and thinking that she would have to give up for today, when Siuan came bustling up from behind.

'I thought you might look down here when you came,' Siuan said, taking her elbow to hurry her along. 'Let's get inside before we freeze.' She eyed those shadows in the alley, too, and absently fingered her beltknife as if using the Power could not deal with any ten of them. Well, not without revealing themselves. Perhaps it was best to move quickly. 'Not the quarter for you, Moiraine. There are fellows around here would bloody well have you for dinner before you knew you were in the pot. Are you laughing or choking?'

Siuan, it turned out, was at a most respectable inn called The Evening Star, which catered to merchants of middling rank, especially women unwilling to be bothered by noise or rough sorts in the common room. A pair of bull-shouldered fellows made sure there was none of that. Siuan's room was tidy and warm, if not large, and the innkeeper, a lean woman with an air of brooking little nonsense, made no objections to Moiraine joining Siuan. So long as the extra for two was paid.

While Moiraine was hanging her cloak on a peg, Siuan settled crosslegged on the not-very-wide bed. She seemed invigorated since Canluum. A goal always made Siuan bubble with enthusiasm. 'I've had a time, Moiraine, I tell you. That fool horse nearly beat me to death getting here. The Creator made people to walk or go by boat, not be bounced around. I suppose the Sahera woman wasn't the one, or you'd be jumping like a spawning redtail. I found Ines Demain almost right off, but not where *I* can reach her. She's a new widow, but she did have a son, for sure. Named him Rahien because she saw the dawn come up over Dragonmount. Talk of the streets. Everybody thinks it a fool reason to name a child.'

'Avene Sahera's son was born a week too early and thirty miles from Dragonmount,' Moiraine said when Siuan paused for breath. She pushed down a momentary thrill. Seeing dawn over the mountain did not mean the child had been born on it. There was no chair or stool, nor room for one, so she sat on the end of the bed. 'If you have found Ines and her son, Siuan, why is she out of reach?' The Lady Ines, it turned it out, was in the Aesdaishar Palace, where Siuan could have gained entry easily as Aes Sedai and otherwise only if the Palace was hiring servants.

The Aesdaishar Palace. 'We will take care of that in the morning,' Moiraine sighed. It meant risk, yet the Lady Ines had to be questioned. No woman Moiraine had found yet had been able to *see* Dragonmount when her child was born. 'Have you seen any sign of . . . of the Black Ajah?' She had to get used to saying that name.

Instead of answering immediately, Siuan frowned at her lap and fingered her skirt. 'This is a strange city, Moiraine,' she said finally. 'Lamps in the streets, and women who fight duels, even if they do deny it, and more gossip than ten men full of ale could spew. Some of it interesting.' She leaned forward to put a hand on Moiraine's knee. 'Everybody's talking about a young blacksmith who died of a broken back a couple of nights ago. Nobody expected much of him, but this last month or so he turned into quite a speaker. Convinced his guild to take up money for the poor who've come into the city, afraid of the bandits, folks not connected to a guild or House.'

'Siuan, what under the Light –?'

'Just listen, Moiraine. He collected a lot of silver himself, and it seems he was on his way to the guild house to turn in six or eight bags of it when he was killed. Fool was carrying it all by himself. The point is, there wasn't a bloody coin of it taken, Moiraine. And he didn't have a mark on him, aside from his broken back.'

They shared a long look, then Moiraine shook her head. 'I cannot see how to tie that to Meilyn or Tamra. A blacksmith? Siuan, we can go mad thinking we see Black sisters everywhere.'

'We can die from thinking they aren't there,' Siuan replied. 'Well. Maybe we can be silverpike in the nets instead of grunters. Just remember silverpike go to the fishmarket, too. What do you have in mind about this Lady Ines?'

Moiraine told her. Siuan did not like it, and this time it took most of the night to make her see sense. In truth, Moiraine almost wished Siuan would talk her into trying something else. But Lady Ines had seen dawn over Dragonmount. At least Ethenielle's Aes Sedai advisor was with her in the south.

Morning was a whirlwind of activity, little of it satisfying. Moiraine got what she wanted, but not without having to bite her tongue. And Siuan started up again. Arguments Moiraine had dealt with the night before cropped up anew. Siuan did not like being argued out of what she thought was right. She did not like Moiraine taking all the risks. A bear with a sore tooth would have been better company. Even that fellow Lan!

A near-dawn visit to a banker's counting house produced gold. After the stern-eyed woman used an enlarging glass to study the Cairhienin banker's seal at the bottom of the letter-of-rights Moiraine presented. An enlarging glass! At least the letter itself was only a little blurred from its immersion in that pond. Mistress Noallin did not bother to hide her surprise when the pair of them began distributing purses of gold beneath their cloaks.

'Is Chachin so lawless two women are not safe by daylight?' Moiraine asked her civilly. 'I think our business is done. You may have your man show us out.' She and Siuan clinked when they moved.

Outside, Siuan muttered that even that blacksmith must have staggered, loaded down like a mule. And who could have broken his back that way? Whatever the reason, it must be the Black Ajah. An imposing woman with ivory combs in her hair heard enough of that to give a start, then hike her skirts to her knees and run, leaving her two gaping servants to scramble after her through the crowd. Siuan flushed but remained defiantly unrepentant.

A slim seamstress with a haughty air informed Moiraine that

what she wanted was easily done. At end of the month, perhaps. A great many ladies had ordered new gowns. A king was visiting in the Aesdaishar Palace. The King of Malkier!

'The last King of Malkier died twenty-five years ago, Mistress Dorelmin,' Moiraine said, spilling thirty gold crowns on the receiving table. Silene Dorelmin eyed the fat coins greedily, and her eyes positively shone when she was told there would be as much again when the dresses were done. 'But I will keep six coins from the second thirty for each day it takes.' Suddenly it seemed that the dresses could be finished sooner than a month after all. Much sooner.

'Did you see what that skinny trull was wearing?' Siuan said as they left. 'You should have your dresses made like that, ready to fall off. You might as well enjoy men looking at you if you're going to lay your fool head on the chopping block.'

Moiraine performed a novice exercise, imaging herself a rosebud in stillness, opening to the sun. As always, it brought calm. She would crack a tooth if she kept grinding them. 'There is no other way, Siuan. Do you think the innkeeper will hire out one of her strongarms?' The King of *Malkier*? Light! The woman must have thought her a complete fool!

At mid-morning two days after Moiraine arrived in Chachin, a yellow-lacquered carriage driven by a fellow with shoulders like a bull arrived at the Aesdaishar Palace, with two mares tied behind, a fine-necked bay and a lanky grey. The Lady Moiraine Damodred, coloured slashes marching from the high neck of her dark blue gown to below her knees, was received with all due honour. The name of House Damodred was known, if not hers, and with King Laman dead, any Damodred might ascend to the Sun Throne. If another House did not seize it. She was given suitable apartments, three rooms looking north across the city towards higher, snow-capped peaks, and assigned servants who rushed about unpacking the lady's brass-bound chests and pouring hot scented water for the lady to wash. No one but the servants so much as glanced at Suki, the Lady Moiraine's maid.

'All right,' Siuan muttered when the servants finally left them alone in the sitting room, 'I admit I'm invisible in this.' Her dark grey dress was fine wool, but entirely plain except for collar and cuffs banded in Damodred colours. 'You, though, stand out like a High Lord pulling oar. Light, I nearly swallowed my tongue when you asked if there were any sisters in the palace. I'm so nervous I'm starting to get light-headed. It feels hard to breathe.'

'It is the altitude,' Moiraine told her. 'You will get used to it. Any visitor would ask about Aes Sedai; you could see, the servants never blinked.' She had held her breath, however, until she heard the answer. One sister would have changed everything. 'I do not know why I must keep telling you. A royal palace is not an inn; "You may call me Lady Alys" would satisfy no one, here. That is fact, not opinion. I must be myself.' The Three Oaths allowed you to say whatever you believed was true even if you could not prove it, as well as to dodge around truth; only words you knew to be a lie would not come off your tongue. 'Suppose you make use of that invisibility and see what you can learn about the Lady Ines. I would be pleased if we leave as soon as possible.'

Tomorrow, that would be, without causing insult and talk. Siuan was right. Every eye in the palace would be on the outland noblewoman from the House that had started the Aiel War. Any Aes Sedai who came to the Aesdaishar would hear of her immediately, and any Aes Sedai who passed through Chachin might well come. Siuan was right; she was standing on a pedestal like a target, and without a clue as to who might be an archer. Tomorrow, early.

Siuan slipped out, but returned quickly with bad news. The Lady Ines was in seclusion, mourning her husband. 'He fell over dead in his breakfast porridge ten days ago,' Siuan reported, dropping on to a sitting room chair and hanging an arm over the back. Lessons in deportment were something else forgotten once the shawl was hers. 'A much older man, but it seems she loved him. She's been given ten rooms and a garden on the south side of the palace; her husband was a close friend to Prince Brys.' Ines would remain to herself a full month, seeing no one but close family. Her servants only came out when absolutely necessary.

'She will see an Aes Sedai,' Moiraine sighed. Not even a woman in mourning would refuse to see a sister.

Siuan bolted to her feet. 'Are you mad? The Lady Moiraine Damodred attracts enough attention. Moiraine Damodred Aes Sedai might as well send out riders! I thought the idea was to be gone before anyone outside the palace knows we were here!'

One of the serving women came in just then, to announce that the *shatayan* had arrived to escort Moiraine to Prince Brys, and was startled to find Suki standing over her mistress and stabbing a finger at her.

'Tell the *shatayan* I will come to her,' Moiraine said calmly, and as soon as the wide-eyed woman curtsied and backed out, she rose to put herself on a more equal footing, hard enough with Siuan even when one had all the advantage. 'What else do you suggest? Remaining almost two weeks till she comes out will be as bad, and you cannot befriend her servants if they are secluded with her.'

'They may only come out for errands, Moiraine, but I think I can get myself invited inside.'

Moiraine started to say that might take as long as the other, but Siuan took her firmly by the shoulders and turned her around, eyeing her up and down critically. 'A lady's maid is supposed to make sure her mistress is properly dressed,' she said, and gave Moiraine a push towards the door. 'Go. The *shatayan* is waiting for you. And with any luck, a young footman named Cal is waiting for Suki.'

The *shatayan* indeed was waiting, a tall handsome woman, wrapped in dignity and frosty at being made to wait. Her hazel eyes could have chilled wine. Any queen who got on the wrong side of a *shatayan* was a fool, so Moiraine made herself pleasant as the woman escorted her through the halls. She thought she made some progress in melting that frost, but it was difficult to concentrate. A young footman? She did not know whether Siuan had ever been with a man, but surely she would not just to reach Ines' servants! Not a *footman*!

Statues and tapestries lined the hallways, most surprising for what she knew of the Borderlands. Marble carvings of women with flowers or children playing, silk weavings of fields of flowers and nobles in gardens and only a few hunting scenes, without a single battle shown anywhere. At intervals along the halls arched windows looked down into many more gardens than she expected, too, and flagged courtyards, sometimes with a splashing marble fountain. In one of those, she saw something that pushed questions about Siuan and a footman to the back of her mind.

It was a simple courtyard, without fountain or columned walk, and men stood in rows along the walls watching two others, stripped to the waist and fighting with wooden practice swords. Ryne and Bukama. It was fighting, if in practice; blows landed on flesh hard enough for her to hear the thuds. All landed by Ryne. She would have to avoid them, and Lan, if he was there too. He had not bothered to hide his doubts, and he might raise questions she did not dare have asked. Was she Moiraine or Alys? Worse, was she Aes Sedai or a wilder pretending? Questions that would be discussed in the streets by the next night, for any sister to hear, and that last was one any sister would investigate. Fortunately, three wandering soldiers would hardly be present anywhere she was.

Prince Brys, a solid, green-eyed man, greeted her intimately in a large room panelled red and gold. Two of the Prince's married sisters were present with their husbands, and one of Ethenielle's with hers, the men in muted silks, the women in bright colours belted high beneath their breasts. Liveried servants offered sweetmeats and nuts. Moiraine thought she might get a sore neck from looking up; the shortest of the women was taller than Siuan, and they all stood very straight. Their necks would have bent a little for a sister, men's and women's alike, but they knew themselves the equals of the Lady Moiraine.

The talk ranged from music and the best musicians among the nobles at court to the rigours of travel, from whether rumours of a man who could channel might be true to why so many Aes Sedai seemed to be about, and Moiraine found it difficult to maintain the expected light wittiness. She cared little for music and less for whoever played the instruments; in Cairhien, musicians were hired and forgotten. Everyone knew that travel was arduous, with no assurance of beds or decent food at the end of the day's twenty or thirty miles, and that was when the weather was good. Obviously some of the sisters were about because of rumours about the man, and others to tighten ties that might have loosened during the Aiel War, to make sure thrones and Houses understood they were still expected to meet their obligations to the Tower, both public and private. If an Aes Sedai had not come to the Aesdaishar yet, one soon would, reason enough for her to make heavy going of idle chat. That and thinking about other reasons for sisters to be wandering. The men put a good face on it, but she thought the women found her particularly dull.

When Brys's children were brought in, Moiraine felt a great relief. Having his children introduced to her was a sign of acceptance to his household, but more, it signalled the end of the audience. The eldest son, Antol, was in the south with Ethenielle as heir, leaving a lovely green-eyed girl of twelve named Jarene to lead in her sister and four brothers, formally aligned by age, though in truth the two youngest boys were still in skirts and carried by nursemaids. Stifling her impatience to find out what Siuan had learned, Moiraine complimented the children on their behaviour, encouraged them at their lessons. They must think her as dull as their elders did. Something a little less flat.

'And how did you earn your bruises, my Lord Diryk?' she asked, hardly listening to the boy's soberly delivered story of a fall. Until . . .

'My father says it was Lan's luck I wasn't killed, my Lady,' Diryk said, brightening out of his formality. 'Lan is the King of Malkier, and the luckiest man in the world, and the best swordsman. Except for my father, of course.'

'The King of Malkier?' Moiraine said, blinking. Diryk nodded vigorously and began explaining in a rush of words about Lan's exploits in the Blight and the Malkieri who had come to the Aesdaishar to follow him, until his father motioned him to silence.

'Lan is a king if he wishes it, my Lady,' Brys said. A very odd thing to say, and his doubtful tone made it odder. 'He keeps much to his rooms,' Brys sounded troubled about that, too, 'but you will meet him before you – my Lady, are you well?'

'Not very,' she told him. She had hoped for another meeting with Lan Mandragoran, planned for it, but not here! Her stomach was trying to twist into knots. 'I myself may keep to my rooms for a few days, if you will forgive me.'

He would, of course, and everyone was full of regret at missing her company and sympathy for the strain travelling must have put on her. Though she did hear one of the women murmur that southlanders must be very delicate.

A pale-haired young woman in green-and-red was waiting to show Moiraine back to her rooms. Elis bobbed a curtsy every time she spoke, which meant she bobbed quite often in the beginning. She had been told of Moiraine's 'faintness', and she asked every twenty paces whether Moiraine wished to sit and catch her breath, or have cool damp cloths brought to her rooms, or hot bricks for her feet, or smelling salts, or a dozen more sure cures for 'a light head', until Moiraine curtly told her to be quiet. The fool girl led on in silence, face blank.

Moiraine cared not a whit whether the woman was offended. All she wanted right then was to find Siuan with good news. With the boy in her arms, born on Dragonmount, and his mother packed to travel would be best of all. Most of all, though, she wanted herself out of the halls before she ran into Lan Mandragoran.

Worrying about him, she rounded a corner behind the serving girl and came face to face with Merean, blue-fringed shawl looped over her arms. The *shatayan* herself was guiding Merean, and behind the motherly-looking sister came a train of servants, one woman carrying her red riding gloves, another her fur-trimmed cloak, a third her dark velvet hat. Pairs of men bore wicker pack-hampers that could have been carried by one, and others had arms full of flowers. An Aes Sedai received more honour than a mere lady, however high her House.

Merean's eyes narrowed at the sight of Moiraine. 'A surprise to see you here,' she said slowly. 'By your dress, I take it you've given over your disguise? But no. Still no ring, I see.'

Moiraine was so startled at the woman's sudden appearance that she hardly heard what Merean said. 'Are you alone?' she blurted.

For a moment Merean's eyes became slits. 'Larelle decided to go her own way. South, I believe. More, I don't know.'

'It was Cadsuane I was thinking of,' Moiraine said, blinking in surprise. The more she had thought about Cadsuane, the more she had become convinced the woman must be Black Ajah. What surprised her was Larelle. Larelle had seemed bent on reaching Chachin, and without delay. Of course, plans could change, but suddenly Moiraine realized something that should have been obvious. Black sisters could lie. It was impossible – the Oaths *could* not be broken! – yet it had to be.

Merean moved close to Moiraine, and when Moiraine took a step back, she followed. Moiraine held herself erect, but she still came no higher than the other woman's chin. 'Are you so eager to see Cadsuane?' Merean said, looking down at her. Her voice was pleasant, her smooth face comforting, but her eyes were cold iron. Abruptly glancing at the servants, she seemed to realize they were not alone. The iron faded, but it did not disappear. 'Cadsuane was right, you know. A young woman who thinks she knows more than she does can land herself in very deep trouble. I suggest you be very still and very quiet until we can talk.' Her gesture for the *shatayan* to lead on was peremptory, and the dignified woman leaped to obey. A king or queen might find themselves in a *shatayan*'s bad graces, but never an Aes Sedai.

Moiraine stared after Merean until she vanished around a corner far down the corridor. Everything Merean had just said could have come from one of Tamra's chosen. Black sisters could lie. Had Larelle changed her mind about Chachin? Or was she dead somewhere, like Tamra and the others? Suddenly Moiraine realized she was smoothing her skirts. Stilling her hands was easy, but she could not stop herself trembling faintly.

Elis was staring at her with her mouth open. 'You're Aes Sedai, too!' the woman squeaked, then gave a jump, taking Moiraine's wince for a grimace. 'I won't say a word to anyone, Aes Sedai,' she said breathlessly. 'I swear, by the Light and my father's grave!' As if every person behind Merean had not heard everything she had. They would not hold their tongues.

'Take me to Lan Mandragoran's apartments,' Moiraine told her. What was true at sunrise could change by noon, and so could what was necessary. She took the Great Serpent ring from her pouch and put it on her right hand. Sometimes, you had to gamble.

After a long walk, mercifully in silence, Elis rapped at a red door and announced to the grey-haired woman who opened it that the Lady Moiraine Damodred Aes Sedai wished to speak with King al'Lan Mandragoran. The woman had added her own touches to what Moiraine told her. King, indeed! Shockingly, the reply came back that Lord Mandragoran had no wish to speak with any Aes Sedai. The grey-haired woman looked scandalized, but closed the door firmly.

Elis stared at Moiraine wide-eyed. 'I can show my Lady Aes Sedai to her own rooms now,' she said uncertainly, 'if –' She squeaked when Moiraine pushed open the door and went in.

The grey-haired serving woman and another a little younger leaped up from where they had been sitting, apparently darning shirts. A bony young man scrambled awkwardly to his feet beside the fireplace, looking to the women for instruction. They simply stared at Moiraine until she raised a questioning eyebrow. Then the grey-haired woman pointed to one of the two doors leading deeper into the apartments.

The door she pointed to led to a sitting room much like Moiraine's own, but all of the gilded chairs had been moved back against the walls and the flowered carpets rolled up. Shirtless, Lan was practising the sword in the cleared area. A small golden locket swung at his neck as he moved, his blade a blur. Sweat covered him, and more scars than she expected on a man so young. Not to mention a number of half-healed wounds crossed by dark stitches. He spun gracefully out of the forms to face her, the point of his sword grounding on the floor-tiles. He still did not quite meet her gaze, in that strange way he and Bukama had. His hair hung damply, clinging to his face despite the leather cord, but he was not breathing hard.

'You,' he growled. 'So you are Aes Sedai *and* a Damodred today. I've no time for your games, Cairhienin. I am waiting for someone.' Cold blue eyes flickered to the door behind her. Oddly, what appeared to be a cord woven of hair was tied around the inner handle in an elaborate knot. 'She will not be pleased to find another woman here.'

'Your lady love need have no fear of me,' Moiraine told him drily. 'For one thing, you are much too tall, and for another, I prefer men with at least a modicum of charm. And manners. I came for your help. There was a pledge made, and held since the War of the Hundred Years, that Malkier would ride when the White Tower called. I *am* Aes Sedai, and I call you!'

'You know the hills are high, but not how they lie,' he muttered as if quoting some Malkieri saying. Stalking across the room away from her, he snatched up his scabbard and sheathed the sword forcefully. 'I'll give you your help, if you can answer a question. I've asked Aes Sedai over the years, but they wriggled away from answering like vipers. If you are Aes Sedai, answer it.'

'If I know the answer, I will.' She would not tell him again that she was what she was, but she embraced *saidar*, and moved one of the gilded chairs out into the middle of the floor. She could not have lifted the thing with her hands, yet it floated easily on flows of Air, and would have had it been twice as heavy. Sitting, she rested her hands on crossed knees where the golden serpent on her finger was plain. The taller person had an advantage when both stood, but someone standing must feel they were being judged by someone sitting, especially an Aes Sedai.

He did not seem to feel anything of the kind. For the first time since she had met him, he met her eyes directly, and his stare was blue ice. 'When Malkier died,' he said in tones of quiet steel, 'Shienar and Arafel sent men. They could not stop the flood of Trollocs and Myrddraal, yet they came. Men rode from Kandor, and even Saldaea. They came too late, but they came.' Blue ice became blue fire. His voice did not change, but his knuckles grew white gripping his sword. 'For nine hundred years we rode when the White Tower called, but where was the Tower when Malkier died? If you are Aes Sedai, answer me that!'

Moiraine hesitated. The answer he wanted was Sealed to the Tower, taught to Accepted in history lessons yet forbidden to any except initiates of the Tower. But what was a penance alongside what she faced? 'Over a hundred sisters were ordered to Malkier,' she said more calmly than she felt. By everything she had been taught, she should *ask* a penance for what she had told him already. 'Even Aes Sedai cannot fly, however. They were too late.' By the time the first had arrived, the armies of Malkier were already broken by endless hordes of Shadowspawn, the people fleeing or dead. The death of Malkier had been hard and blood-soaked, and fast. 'That was before I was born, but I regret it deeply. And I regret that the Tower decided to keep their effort secret.' Better that the Tower be thought to have done nothing than to have it known Aes Sedai had tried and failed. Failure was a blow to stature, and mystery an armour the Tower needed. Aes Sedai had reasons of their own for what they did, and for what they did not do, and those reasons were known only to Aes Sedai. 'That is as much answer as I can give. More than I should have, more than any other sister ever will, I think. Will it suffice?'

For a time he simply looked at her, fire slowly fading to ice once more. His eyes fell away. 'Almost, I can believe,' he muttered finally, without saying what he almost believed. He gave a bitter laugh. 'What help can I give you?'

Moiraine frowned. She very much wanted time alone with this man, to bring him to heel, but that had to wait. 'There is another sister in the palace. Merean Redhill. I need to know where she goes, what she does, who she meets.' He blinked, but did not ask the obvious questions. Perhaps he knew he would get no answers, but his silence was still pleasing.

'I have been keeping to my rooms the past few days,' he said, looking at the door again. 'I do not know how much watching I can do.'

In spite of herself, she sniffed. The man promised help, then looked anxiously for his lady. Perhaps he was not what she had thought. But he was who she had. 'Not you,' she told him. Her visit here would be known throughout the Aesdaishar soon, if it was not already, and if he was noticed spying on Merean . . . That could be disaster even if the woman was as innocent as a babe. 'I thought you might ask one of the Malkieri I understand have gathered here to follow you. Someone with a sharp eye and a close tongue. This must be done in utter secrecy.'

'No one follows me,' he said sharply. Glancing at the door once more, he suddenly seemed weary. He did not slump, but he moved to the fireplace and propped his sword beside it with the care of a tired man. Standing with his back to her, he said, 'I will ask Bukama and Ryne to watch her, but I cannot promise for them. That is all I can do for you.'

She stifled a vexed sound. Whether it was all he could do or all he would, she had no leverage to force him. 'Bukama,' she said. 'Only him.' Going by how he had behaved around her, Ryne would be too busy staring at Merean to see or hear anything. That was if he did not confess what he was doing the moment Merean looked at him. 'And do not tell him why.'

His head whipped around, but after a moment he nodded. And again he did not ask the questions most people would have. Telling him how to get word to her, by notes passed to her maid Suki, she hoped she was not making a grave mistake.

Back in her own rooms, she discovered just how quickly news had spread. In the sitting room, Siuan was offering a tray of sweetmeats to a tall, full-mouthed young woman in pale green silk, little older than a girl, with black hair that fell well below her hips and a small blue dot painted on her forehead about where the stone of Moiraine's kesiera hung. Siuan's face was smooth, but her voice was tight as she made introductions. The Lady Iselle quickly showed why.

'Everyone in the palace is saying you are Aes Sedai,' she said, eyeing Moiraine doubtfully. She did not rise, much less curtsy, or even incline her head. 'If that is so, I need your assistance. I wish to go to the White Tower. My mother wants me to marry. I would not mind Lan as my *carneira* if mother were not already his, but when I marry, I think it will be one of my Warders. I will be Green Ajah.' She frowned faintly at Siuan. 'Don't hover, girl. Stand over there until you are needed.' Siuan took up a stance by the fireplace, back stiff and arms folded beneath her breasts. No real servant would have stood so – or frowned so – but Iselle no longer noticed her. 'Do sit down, Moiraine,' she went on with a smile, 'and I will tell you what I need of you. If you *are* Aes Sedai, of course.'

Moiraine stared. Invited to take a chair in her own sitting room. This silly child was certainly a suitable match for Lan when it came to arrogance. Her *carneira*? That meant 'first' in the Old Tongue, and plainly something else here. Not what it seemed to, of course; even these Malkieri could not be that peculiar! Sitting, she said drily, 'Choosing your Ajah should at least wait until I test you to see whether there is any point in sending you to the Tower. A few minutes will determine whether you can learn to channel, and your potential strength if you –'

The girl blithely broke in. 'Oh, I was tested years ago. The Aes Sedai said I would be very strong. I told her I was fifteen, but she learned the truth. I don't see why I could not go to the Tower at twelve if I wanted. Mother was furious. She has always said I was to be Queen of Malkier one day, but that means marrying Lan, which I would not want even if mother weren't his *carneira*. When you tell her you are taking me to the Tower, she will have to listen. Everyone knows that Aes Sedai take any woman they want for training, and no one can stop them.' That full mouth pursed. 'You *are* Aes Sedai, aren't you?'

Moiraine performed the rosebud exercise. 'If you want to go to Tar Valon, then go. I certainly do not have time to escort you. You will find sisters there about whom you can have no doubts. Suki, will you show the Lady Iselle out? No doubt she does not wish to delay in setting off before her mother catches her.'

The chit was all indignation, of course, but Moiraine wanted only to see the back of her, and Siuan very nearly pushed her out into the corridor.

'That one,' Siuan said as she came back dusting her hands, 'won't last a month if she can equal Cadsuane.' The Tower clung like iron bands to any woman who had the smallest chance of earning the shawl, but those who could not or would not learn did find themselves put out, and channelling was only part of what had to be learned.

'Sierin herself can toss her from the top of the Tower for all I care,' Moiraine snapped. 'Did you learn anything?'

It seemed that Siuan had learned that the young footman knew how to kiss, a revelation that did not even pinken her cheeks, and aside from that, nothing whatsoever. Surprisingly, learning that Moiraine had approached Lan upset her more than Merean's appearance.

'Skin me and salt me if you don't take idiot risks, Moiraine. A man who claims the throne of a dead country is nine kinds of fool. He could be flapping his tongue about you right this minute to anybody who'll bloody listen! If Merean learns you're having her watched . . . Burn me!'

'He is many kinds of fool, Siuan, but I do not think he ever "flaps his tongue". Besides, "you cannot win if you will not risk a copper", as you always tell me your father used to say. We have no choice but to take risks. With Merean here, time may be running out. You must reach the Lady Ines as quickly as you can.'

'I'll do what I can,' Siuan muttered, and stalked out squaring her shoulders as if for a struggle. But she was smoothing her skirt over her hips, too.

Night had long since fallen and Moiraine was trying to read by lamplight when Siuan returned. Moiraine set her book aside;

she had been staring at the same page for the past hour. This time, Siuan did have news, delivered while digging through the dresses and shifts Mistress Dorelmin had made.

For one thing, she had been approached on her way back to Moiraine's rooms by 'a gristly old stork' who asked if she was Suki, then told her Merean had spent almost the entire day with Prince Brys before retiring to her apartments for the night. No clue there to anything. More importantly, Siuan had been able to bring up Rahien in casual conversation with Cal. The footman had not been with the Lady Ines when the boy was born, but he did know the day, one day after the Aiel began their retreat from Tar Valon. Moiraine and Siuan shared a long look over that. One day after Gitara Moroso had made her Foretelling of the Dragon's Rebirth and dropped dead from the shock of it. Dawn over the mountain, and born during the ten days before a sudden thaw melted the snow. Gitara had specifically mentioned the snow.

'Anyway,' Siuan went on, beginning to make a bundle of clothes and stockings, 'I led Cal to believe I'd been dismissed from your service for spilling wine on your dress, and he's offered me a bed with the Lady Ines's servants. He thinks he might be able to get me a place with his Lady.' She snorted with amusement, then caught Moiraine's eyes and snorted again, more roughly. 'It isn't *his* bloody bed, Moiraine. And if it was, well, he has a gentle manner and the prettiest brown eyes you've ever seen. One of these days, you're going to find yourself ready to do more than dream about some man, and I hope I'm there to see it!'

'Do not talk nonsense,' Moiraine told her. The task in front of them was too important to spare thoughts for men. In the way Siuan meant, at least. Merean had spent all day with Brys? Without going near Lady Ines? One of Tamra's chosen or Black Ajah, that made no sense, and it went beyond credibility to believe Merean was not one or the other. She was missing something, and that worried her. What she did not know could kill her. Worse, it could kill the Dragon Reborn in his cradle.

* * *

Lan slipped through the corridors of the Aesdaishar alone, using every bit of the skill he had learned in the Blight, avoiding the eyes of passersby. His own serving women took Edeyn's commands ahead of his, now, as though they believed that some part of Malkieri ways. She might have told them it was. He expected that anyone in the Aesdaishar wearing livery would tell Edeyn where to find him. He thought he knew where he was, now. Despite previous visits, he had got lost twice, without a guide. He felt a fool for wearing his sword. Steel was no use in this battle.

A flicker of movement made him flatten himself against the wall behind a statue of a woman clad in clouds, her arms full of flowers. Just in time. Two women came out of the crossing corridor ahead, pausing in close conversation. Iselle and the Aes Sedai, Merean. He was as still as the stone he hid behind.

He did not like skulking, but while Edeyn was untying the knot in his *daori* that had kept him penned for two days she had made it clear that she intended to announce his marriage to Iselle soon. Bukama had been right. Edeyn used his *daori* like reins, and he did not believe she would stop just because he married her daughter. The only thing to do when faced by an opponent you could not defeat was run, and he wanted to.

At a sharp motion from Merean, Iselle nodded eagerly and went back the way they had come. For a moment Merean watched her go, face unreadable in Aes Sedai serenity. Then, surprisingly, she followed, gliding in a way that made Iselle look awkward.

Lan did not waste time wondering what Merean was up to, any more than he had in wondering why Moiraine wanted her watched. A man could go mad trying to puzzle out Aes Sedai. Which Moiraine really must be, or Merean would have her howling up and down the corridors. Waiting long enough for the pair to be out of sight again, he moved quietly to the corner and peeked. They were both gone, so he hurried on. Aes Sedai were no concern of his today. He had to talk to Bukama.

Running would end Edeyn's schemes of marriage. If he avoided her long enough, she would find another husband for Iselle.

Running would end Edeyn's dream of reclaiming Malkier; her support would fade like mist under a noon sun once people learned he was gone. Running would end many dreams. The man who had carried an infant tied to his back had a right to dreams, though. Duty was a mountain, but it had to be carried.

Ahead lay a long flight of broad, stone-railed stairs. He turned to start down, and suddenly he was falling. He just had time to go limp, and then he was bounding from step to step, tumbling head over heels, landing on the tiled floor at the bottom with a crash that drove the last remaining air from his lungs. Spots shimmered in front of his eyes. He struggled to breathe, to push himself up.

Servants appeared from nowhere, helping him dizzily to his feet, all exclaiming over his luck in not killing himself in such a fall, asking whether he wanted to see one of the Aes Sedai for Healing. Frowning up the stairway, he murmured replies, anything in hope of making them go away. He thought he might be as bruised as he had ever been in his life, but bruises went away, and the last thing he wanted at that moment was a sister. Most men would have fought that fall and been lucky to end with half their bones broken. Something had jerked his ankles up there. Something had hit him between the shoulders. There was only one thing it could have been, however little sense it made. An Aes Sedai had tried to kill him.

'Lord Mandragoran!' A stocky man in the striped coat of a palace guard skidded to a halt and nearly fell over trying to bow while still moving. 'We've been looking for you everywhere, my Lord!' he panted. 'It's your man, Bukama! Come quickly, my Lord! He may still be alive!'

Cursing, Lan ran behind the guard, shouting for the man to go faster, but he was too late. Too late for the man who had carried an infant. Too late for dreams.

Guards crowding a narrow passage just off one of the practice yards squeezed back to let Lan through. Bukama lay face down, blood pooled around his mouth, the plain wooden hilt of a dagger rising from the dark stain on the back of his coat. His staring eyes looked surprised. Kneeling, Lan closed those eyes and murmured a prayer for the last embrace of the mother to welcome Bukama home.

'Who found him?' he asked, but he barely heard the jumbled replies about who and where and what. He hoped Bukama was reborn in a world where the Golden Crane flew on the wind, and the Seven Towers stood unbroken, and the Thousand Lakes shone like a necklace beneath the sun. How could he have let anyone get close enough to do this? Bukama could *feel* steel being unsheathed near him. Only one thing was sure. Bukama was dead because Lan had tangled him in an Aes Sedai's schemes.

Rising, Lan began to run. Not away from, though. Towards. And he did not care who saw him.

The muffled crash of the door in the anteroom and outraged shouts from the serving women lifted Moiraine from the chair where she had been waiting. For anything but this. Embracing *saidar*, she started from the sitting room, but before she reached the door, it swung open. Lan shook off the liveried women clinging to his arms, shut the door in their faces, and put his back to it, meeting Moiraine's startled gaze. Purpling bruises marred his face, and he moved as if he had been beaten. From outside came silence. Whatever he intended, they would be sure she could handle it.

Absurdly, she found herself fingering her beltknife. With the Power she could wrap him up like a child, however large he was, and yet . . . He did not glare. There certainly was no fire in those eyes. She wanted to step back. No fire, but death seared cold. That black coat suited him with its cruel thorns and stark gold blossoms.

'Bukama is dead with a knife in his heart,' he said calmly, 'and not an hour gone, someone tried to kill me with the One Power. At first I thought it must be Merean, but the last I saw of her, she was trailing after Iselle, and unless she saw me and wanted to lull me, she had no time. Few see me when I do not want to be seen, and I don't think she did. That leaves you.'

Moiraine winced, and only in part for the certainty in his

tone. She should have known the fool girl would go straight to Merean. 'You would be surprised how little escapes a sister,' she told him. Especially if the sister was filled with *saidar*. 'Perhaps I should not have asked Bukama to watch Merean. She is very dangerous.' She *was* Black Ajah; Moiraine was certain of that, now. Sisters might make painful examples of people caught snooping, but they did not kill them. But what to do about her? Certainty was not proof, surely not that would stand up before the Amyrlin Seat. And if Sierin herself was Black . . . Not a worry she could do anything about now. What was the woman doing wasting any time at all with Iselle? 'If you care for the girl, I suggest you find her as quickly as possible and keep her away from Merean.'

Lan grunted. 'All Aes Sedai are dangerous. Iselle is safe enough for the moment; I saw her on my way here, hurrying somewhere with Brys and Diryk. Why did Bukama die, Aes Sedai? What did I snare him in for you?'

Moiraine flung up a hand for silence, and a tiny part of her was surprised when he obeyed. The rest of her thought furiously. Merean with Iselle. Iselle with Brys and Diryk. Merean had tried to kill Lan. Suddenly she saw a pattern, perfect in every line; it made no sense, but she did not doubt it was real. 'Diryk told me you are the luckiest man in the world,' she said, leaning towards Lan intently, 'and for his sake, I hope he was right. Where would Brys go for absolute privacy? Somewhere he would not be seen or heard.' It would have to be a place he felt comfortable, yet isolated.

'There is a walk on the west side of the palace,' Lan said slowly, then his voice quickened. 'If there is danger to Brys, I must rouse the guards.' He was already turning, hand on the doorhandle.

'No!' she said. She still held the Power, and she prepared a weave of Air to seize him if necessary. 'Prince Brys will not appreciate having his guards burst in if Merean is simply talking to him.'

'And if she is not talking?' he demanded.

'We have no proof of anything against her, Lan. Suspicions against the word of an Aes Sedai.' His head jerked angrily, and he growled something about Aes Sedai that she deliberately did not hear. 'Take me to this walk, Lan. Let Aes Sedai deal with Aes Sedai. And let us hurry.' If Merean did any talking, Moiraine did not expect her to talk for long.

Hurry Lan surely did, long legs flashing as he ran. All Moiraine could do was gather her skirts high and run after him, ignoring the stares and murmurs of servants and others in the corridors, thanking the Light that the man did not outpace her. She let the Power fill her as she ran, till sweetness and joy bordered pain, and tried to plan what she would do, what she could do, against a woman considerably stronger than she, a woman who had been Aes Sedai more than a hundred years before her own great-grandmother was born. She wished she was not so afraid. She wished Siuan was with her.

The mad dash led through glittering state chambers, along statuary-lined hallways, and suddenly they were into the open, the sounds of the palace left behind, on a long stone-railed walk twenty paces wide with a vista across the city roofs far below. A cold wind blew like a storm. Merean was there, surrounded by the glow of *saidar*, and Brys and Diryk, standing by the rail, twisting futilely against bonds and gags of Air. Iselle was frowning at the Prince and his son, and surprisingly, further down the walk stood a glowering Ryne.

'. . . and I could hardly bring Lord Diryk to you without his father,' Iselle was saying petulantly. 'I *did* make sure no one knows, but why –?'

Weaving a shield of Spirit, Moiraine hurled it at Merean with every shred of the Power in her, hoping against hope to cut the woman off from the Source. The shield struck and splintered. Merean was too strong, drawing too near her capacity.

The Blue sister – the Black sister – did not even blink. 'You did well enough killing the spy, Ryne,' she said calmly as she wove a gag of Air to stop up Iselle's mouth and bonds that held the girl stiff and wide-eyed. 'See if you can make certain of the younger one this time. You did say you are a better swordsman.'

Everything seemed to happen at once. Ryne rushed forward, scowling, the bells in braids chiming. Lan barely got his own sword out in time to meet him. And before the first clash of steel on steel, Merean struck at Moiraine with the same weave she herself had used, but stronger. In horror Moiraine realized that Merean might have sufficient strength remaining to shield her even while she was embracing as much of *saidar* as she could. Frantically she struck out with Air and Fire, and Merean grunted as severed flows snapped back into her. In the brief interval, Moiraine tried to slice the flows holding Diryk and the others, but before her weave touched Merean's, Merean sliced hers instead, and this time Merean's attempted shield actually touched her before she could cut it. Moiraine's stomach tried to tie itself in a knot.

'You appear too often, Moiraine,' Merean said as though they were simply chatting. She looked as if there were no more to it, serene and motherly, not in the slightest perturbed. 'I fear I must ask you how, and why.' Moiraine just managed to sever a weave of Fire that would have burned off her clothes and perhaps most of her skin, and Merean smiled, a mother amused at the mischief young women get up to. 'Don't worry, child. I'll Heal you to answer my questions.'

If Moiraine had had any lingering doubts that Merean was Black Ajah, that weave of Fire would have ended them. In the next moments she had more proof, weavings that made sparks dance on her dress and her hair rise, weavings that left her gasping for air that was no longer there, weavings she could not recognize yet was sure would leave her broken and bleeding if they settled around her, if she failed to cut them . . .

When she could, she tried again and again to cut the bonds holding Diryk and the others, to shield Merean, even to knock her unconscious. She knew she fought for her life – she would die if the other woman won, now or after Merean's questioning – but she never considered that loophole in the Oaths that held her. She had questions of her own for the woman, and the fate of the world might rest on the answers. Unfortunately, most of what she could do was defend herself, and that always on the brink. Her stomach *was* in a knot, and trying to make another. Holding three people bound, Merean was still a match for her, and maybe more. If only Lan could distract the woman.

A hasty glance showed how unlikely that was. Lan and Ryne danced the forms, their blades like whirlwinds, but if there was a hair between their abilities, it rested with Ryne. Blood fanned down the side of Lan's face.

Grimly, Moiraine bore down, not even sparing the bit of concentration necessary to ignore the cold. Shivering, she struck at Merean, defended herself and struck again, defended and struck. If she could manage to wear the woman down, or . . .

'This is taking too long, don't you think, child?' Merean said. Diryk floated into the air, struggling against the bonds he could not see as he drifted over the railing. Brys's head twisted, following his son, and his mouth worked around his unseen gag.

'No!' Moiraine screamed. Desperately, she flung out flows of Air to drag the boy back to safety. Merean slashed them even as she released her own hold on him. Wailing, Diryk fell, and white light exploded in Moiraine's head.

Groggily she opened her eyes, the boy's fading shriek still echoing in her mind. She was on her back on the stone walk, her head spinning. Until that cleared, she had as much chance of embracing *saidar* as a cat did of singing. Not that it made any difference, now. She could see the shield Merean was holding on her, and even a weaker woman could maintain a shield once in place. She tried to rise, fell back, managed to push up on an elbow.

Only moments had passed. Lan and Ryne still danced their deadly dance to the clash of steel. Brys was rigid for more than his bonds, staring at Merean with such implacable hate it seemed he might break free on the strength of his rage. Iselle was trembling visibly, snuffling and weeping and staring wide-eyed at where the boy had fallen. Where Diryk had fallen. Moiraine made herself think the boy's name, flinched to recall his grinning enthusiasm. Only moments.

'You will hold a moment for me, I think,' Merean said, turning from Moiraine. Brys rose from the walk. The stocky man's face never changed, never stopped staring hatred at Merean.

Moiraine struggled to her knees. She could not channel. She had no courage left, no strength. Only determination. Brys floated over the railing. Moiraine tottered to her feet. Determination. That look of pure hate etched on his face, Brys fell, never making a sound. This had to end. Iselle lifted into the air, writhing frantically, throat working in a effort to scream past her gag. It had to end now! Stumbling, Moiraine drove her beltknife into Merean's back, blood spurting over her hands.

They fell to the paving stones together, the glow around Merean vanishing as she died, the shield on Moiraine vanishing. Iselle screamed, swaying where Merean's bonds had let her drop, atop the stone railing. Pushing herself to move, Moiraine scrambled across Merean's corpse, seized one of Iselle's flailing hands in hers just as the girl's slippers slid off into open air.

The jolt pulled Moiraine belly-down across the railing, staring down at the girl held by her blood-slick grip above a drop that seemed to go on for ever. It was all Moiraine could do to hold them where they were, teetering. If she tried to pull the girl up, they would both go over. Iselle's face was contorted, her mouth a rictus. Her hand slipped in Moiraine's grasp. Forcing herself to calm, Moiraine reach for the Source and failed. Staring down at those distant rooftops did not help her whirling head. Again she tried, but it was like trying to scoop up water with spread fingers. She would save one of the three, though, if the most useless of them. Fighting dizziness, she strove for *saidar*. And Iselle's hand slid out of her bloody fingers. All Moiraine could do was watch her fall, hand still stretched up as if she believed someone might still save her.

An arm pulled Moiraine away from the railing.

'Never watch a death you don't have to,' Lan said, setting her on her feet. His right arm hung at his side, a long slash laying open the blood-soaked sleeve and the flesh beneath, and he had other injuries besides the gash on his scalp that still trickled red down his face. Ryne lay on his back ten paces away, staring at the sky in sightless surprise. 'A black day,' Lan muttered. 'As black as ever I've seen.'

'A moment,' she told him, her voice unsteady. 'I am too dizzy to walk far, yet.' Her knees wavered as she walked to Merean's body. There would be no answers. The Black Ajah would remain hidden. Bending, she withdrew her beltknife and cleaned it on the traitor's skirts.

'You are a cool one, Aes Sedai,' Lan said flatly.

'As cool as I must be,' she told him. Diryk's scream rang in her ears. Iselle's face dwindled below her. 'It seems Ryne was wrong as well as a Darkfriend. You were better than he.'

Lan shook his head slightly. 'He was better. But he thought I was finished, with only one arm. He never understood. You surrender after you're dead.'

Moiraine nodded. Surrender after you are dead. Yes.

It took a little while for her head to clear enough that she could embrace the Source again, and she had to put up with Lan's anxiety to let the *shatayan* know that Brys and Diryk were dead before word came that their bodies had been found on the rooftops. Understandably, he seemed less eager to inform the Lady Edeyn of her daughter's death. Moiraine was anxious about time, too, if not for the same reasons. She Healed him as soon as she was able. He gasped in shock as the complex weaves of Spirit, Air, and Water knit up his wounds, flesh writhing together into unscarred wholeness. Like anyone who had been Healed, he was weak afterwards, weak enough to catch his breath leaning on the stone rail. He would run nowhere for a while.

Carefully Moiraine floated Merean's body over that rail and down a little, close to the stone of the mountain. Flows of Fire, and flame enveloped the Black sister, flame so hot there was no smoke, only a shimmering in the air, and the occasional crack of a splitting rock.

'What are you –?' Lan began, then changed it to, 'Why?'

Moiraine let herself feel the rising heat, currents of air fit for a furnace. 'There is no proof she was Black Ajah, only that she was Aes Sedai.' The White Tower needed its armour of secrecy again, more than it had when Malkier died, but she could not tell him that. Not yet. 'I cannot lie about what happened here, but I can be silent. Will you be silent, or will you do the Shadow's work?'

'You are a very hard woman,' he said finally. That was the only answer he gave, but it was enough.

'I am as hard as I must be,' she told him. Diryk's scream. Iselle's face. There was still Ryne's body to dispose of, and the blood. As hard as she must be.

Next dawn found the Aesdaishar in mourning, white banners flying from every prominence, the servants with long white cloths tied to their arms. Rumours in the city already talked of portents foretelling the deaths, comets in the night, fires in the sky. People had a way of folding what they saw into what they knew and what they wanted to believe. The disappearance of a simple soldier, and even of an Aes Sedai, escaped notice alongside grief.

Returning from destroying Merean's belongings – after searching in vain for any clue to other Black sisters – Moiraine stepped aside for Edeyn Arrel, who glided down the corridor in a white gown, her hair cut raggedly short. Whispers said she intended to retire from the world. Moiraine thought she already had. The woman's staring eyes looked haggard and old. In a way, they looked much as her daughter's did, in Moiraine's mind.

When Moiraine entered her apartments, Siuan leaped up from a chair. It seemed weeks since Moiraine had seen her. 'You look like you reached into the bait well and found a fangfish,' she growled. 'Well, it's no surprise. I always hated mourning when I knew the people. Anyway, we can go whenever you're ready. Rahien was born in a farmhouse almost two miles from Dragonmount. Merean hasn't been near him, as of this morning. I don't suppose she'll harm him on suspicion even if she is Black.'

Not the one. Somehow, Moiraine had almost expected that. 'Merean will not harm anyone, Siuan. Put that mind of yours to a puzzle for me.' Settling in a chair, she began with the end, and hurried through despite Siuan's gasps and demands for more detail. It was almost like living it again. Getting to what had led her to that confrontation was a relief. 'She wanted Diryk dead most of all, Siuan; she killed him first. And she tried to kill

Lan. The only thing those two had in common was luck. Diryk survived a fall that should have killed him, and everyone says Lan is the luckiest man alive or the Blight would have killed him years ago. It makes a pattern, but the pattern looks crazy to me. Maybe your blacksmith is even part of it. And Josef Najima, back in Canluum, for all I know. He was lucky, too. Puzzle it out for me if you can. I think it is important, but I cannot see how.'

Siuan strode back and forth across the room, kicking her skirt and rubbing her chin, muttering about 'men with luck' and 'the blacksmith rose suddenly' and other things Moiraine could not make out. Suddenly she stopped dead and said, 'She never went near Rahien, Moiraine. The Black Ajah knows the Dragon was Reborn, but they don't bloody know *when*! Maybe Tamra managed to keep it back, or maybe they were too rough and she died before they could pry it out of her. That has to be it!' Her eagerness turned to horror. 'Light! They're killing any man or boy who *might* be able to channel! Oh, burn me, thousands could die, Moiraine. Tens of thousands.'

It did make a terrible sense. Men who could channel seldom knew what they were doing, at least in the beginning. At first, they often just seemed to be lucky. Events favoured them, and frequently, like the blacksmith, they rose to prominence with unexpected suddenness. Siuan was right. The Black Ajah had begun a slaughter.

'But they do not know to look for a boychild,' Moiraine said. As hard as she had to be. 'An infant will show no signs.' Not until he was sixteen at the earliest. No man on record had begun channelling before that, and some not for ten years or more later. 'We have more time than we thought. Not enough to be careless, though. Any sister can be Black. I think Cadsuane is. They know others are looking. If one of Tamra's searchers locates the boy and they find her with him, or if they decide to question one of them instead of killing her as soon as it is convenient . . .' Siuan was staring at her. 'We still have the task,' Moiraine told her.

'I know,' Siuan said slowly. 'I just never thought. Well, when there's work to do, you haul nets or gut fish.' That lacked her usual force, though. 'We can be on our way to Arafel before noon.'

'You go back to the Tower,' Moiraine said. Together, they could search no faster than one could alone, and if they had to be apart, what better place for Siuan than working for Cetalia Delarme, seeing the reports of all the Blue Ajah eyes-and-ears? The Blue was a small Ajah, but every sister said it had a larger network than any other. While Moiraine hunted for the boy, Siuan could learn what was happening in every land, and knowing what she was looking for, she could spot any sign of the Black Ajah or the Dragon Reborn. Siuan truly could see sense when it was pointed out to her, though it took some effort this time, and when she agreed, she did it with a poor grace.

'Cetalia will use me to caulk draughts for running off without leave,' she grumbled. 'Burn me! Hung out on a drying rack in the Tower! Moiraine, the politics are enough to make you sweat buckets in midwinter! I hate it!' But she was already pawing through the trunks to see what she could take with her for the ride back to Tar Valon. 'I suppose you warned that fellow Lan. Seems to me, he deserves it, much good it'll do him. I heard he rode out an hour ago, heading for the Blight, and if that doesn't kill him – where are you going?'

'I have unfinished business with the man,' Moiraine said over her shoulder. She had made a decision about him the first day she knew him, and she intended to keep it.

In the stable where Arrow was kept, silver marks tossed like pennies got the mare saddled and bridled almost while the coins were still in the air, and she scrambled on to the animal's back without a care that her skirts pushed up to bare her legs above the knee. Digging her heels in, she galloped out of the Aesdaishar and north through the city, making people leap aside and once setting Arrow to leap cleanly over an empty wagon with a driver too slow to move out of her way. She left a tumult of shouts and shaken fists behind.

On the road north from the city, she slowed enough to ask wagon-drivers heading the other way whether they had seen a Malkieri on a bay stallion, and was more than a little relieved the first time she got a yes. The man could have gone in fifty directions after crossing the moat bridge. And with an hour's lead . . . She would catch him if she had to follow him into the Blight!

'A Malkieri?' The skinny merchant in a dark blue cloak looked startled. 'Well, my guards told me there's one up there.' Twisting on his wagon-seat, he pointed to a grassy hill a hundred paces off the road. Two horses stood in plain sight at the crest, one a packhorse, and the thin smoke of a fire curled into the breeze.

Lan barely looked up when she dismounted. Kneeling beside the remains of a small fire, he was stirring the ashes with a long twig. Strangely, the smell of burned hair hung in the air. 'I had hoped you were done with me,' he said.

'Not quite yet,' she told him. 'Burning your future? It will sorrow a great many, I think, when you die in the Blight.'

'Burning my past,' he said, rising. 'Burning memories. A nation. The Golden Crane will fly no more.' He started to kick dirt over the ashes, then hesitated and bent to scoop up damp soil and pour it out of his hands almost formally. 'No one will sorrow for me when I die, because those who would are dead already. Besides, all men die.'

'Only fools choose to die before they must. I want you to be my Warder, Lan Mandragoran.'

He stared at her unblinking, then shook his head. 'I should have known it would be that. I have a war to fight, Aes Sedai, and no desire to help you weave White Tower webs. Find another.'

'I fight the same war as you against the Shadow. Merean was Black Ajah.' She told him all of it, from Gitara's Foretelling in the presence of the Amyrlin Seat and two Accepted to what she and Siuan had reasoned out. For another man, she would have left most unsaid, but there were few secrets between Warder and Aes Sedai. For another man, she might have softened it, but she did not believe hidden enemies frightened him, not even when they were Aes Sedai. 'You said you burned your past. Let the past have its ashes. This is the same war, Lan. The most important battle yet in that war. And this one, you can win.'

For a long time he stood staring north, towards the Blight. She did not know what she would do if he refused. She had told him more than she would have anyone but her Warder.

Suddenly he turned, sword flashing out, and for an instant she thought he meant to attack her. Instead he sank to his knees, the sword lying bare across his hands. 'By my mother's name, I will draw as you say "draw" and sheathe as you say "sheathe". By my mother's name, I will come as you say "come" and go as you say "go".' He kissed the blade and looked up at her expectantly. On his knees, he made any king on a throne look meek. She would have to teach him some humility for his own sake. And for a pond's sake.

'There is a little more,' she said, laying hands on his head.

The weave of Spirit was one of the most intricate known to Aes Sedai. It wove around him, settled into him, vanished. Suddenly she was aware of him, in the way that Aes Sedai were of their Warders. His emotions were a small knot in the back of her head, all steely hard determination, sharp as his blade's edge. She knew the muted pain of old injuries, tamped down and ignored. She would be able to draw on his strength at need, to find him however far away he was. They were bonded.

He rose smoothly, sheathing his sword, studying her. 'Men who weren't there call it the Battle of the Shining Walls,' he said abruptly. 'Men who were, call it the Blood Snow. No more. They know it was a battle. On the morning of the first day, I led nearly five hundred men. Kandori, Saldaeans, Domani. By evening on the third day, half were dead or wounded. Had I made different choices, some of those dead would be alive. And others would be dead in their places. In war, you say a prayer for your dead and ride on, because there is always another fight over the next horizon. Say a prayer for the dead, Moiraine Sedai, and ride on.'

Startled, she came close to gaping. She had forgotten that the bond's flow worked both ways. He knew her emotions, too, and apparently could reason out hers far better than she could his. After a moment, she nodded, though she did not know how many prayers it would take to clear her mind.

Handing her Arrow's reins, he said, 'Where do we ride first?'

'Back to Chachin,' she admitted. 'And then Arafel, and . . .' So few names remained that were easy to find. 'The world, if need be. We win this battle, or the world dies.'

Side by side they rode down the hill and turned south. Behind them the sky rumbled and turned black, another late storm rolling down from the Blight.